**"I've seen th... eyes ever sin... show up at th... I didn't quit on you before. And that's why I'm not quitting on you now. I am not leaving."**

Drew's eyes narrowed. His hands tightened around Deanna's shoulders, drawing her closer to him, until there was not an inch of breath to be had between her body and his. "And what if I kissed you again now?"

He was trying to make her run.

She knew it as surely as she knew her own name.

And even though she felt weak in the knees and shivers were slipping down her spine, she lifted her chin.

Her gaze met his. "What if you did?"

Dear Reader,

I've always believed that *family* is the most important thing one can have in their life. Personally, I have been deeply blessed to know that strong foundation in my life, with parents and extended family who have always shown their love and support, and I hope that this is the same foundation that I've passed on to my children as they find and make their places in the world.

Not everyone is so lucky to be raised with unswerving support. Not every family is so lucky to be able to pull together in a time of crisis—whether great or small. For anyone who is in that situation, my wish for you is to create a family that does just that for you. Find it with your friends. Find it with your community. But, like Deanna Gurney, keep your heart open to it. Because, in the end, family is what we make of it, no matter who those members turn out to be or from where we find them.

Family.

It's what Deanna finds with Drew and the remarkable Fortune clan, and it's with deep pleasure that I get to welcome *you* to their family fold, too.

*Allison*

# FORTUNE'S PROPOSAL

BY
ALLISON LEIGH

MILLS & BOON®

First published in Great Britain 2012
by Mills & Boon, an imprint of Harlequin (UK) Limited,
Eton House, 18-24 Paradise Road, Richmond, Surrey TW9 1SR

Special thanks and acknowledgement to Állison Leigh for her contribution to the *Fortunes of Texas: Lost…and Found* miniseries.

© Harlequin Books S.A. 2011

2in1 ISBN: 978 0 263 89424 0

23-0412

Harlequin (UK) policy is to use papers that are natural, renewable and recyclable products and made from wood grown in sustainable forests. The logging and manufacturing processes conform to the legal environmental regulations of the country of origin.

Printed and bound in Spain
by Blackprint CPI, Barcelona

There is a saying that you can never be too rich or too thin. **Allison Leigh** doesn't believe that, but she does believe that you can *never* have enough books! When her stories find a way into the hearts—and bookshelves—of others, Allison says she feels she's done something right. Making her home in Arizona with her husband, she enjoys hearing from her readers at Allison@allisonleigh.com or PO Box 40772, Mesa, AZ 85274-0772, USA.

In loving memory of Larry

## Chapter One

"Happy New Year, Deanna. Hope you have fun tonight."

The farewell was echoed three times over as Deanna Gurney watched the last of her coworkers at Fortune Forecasting head out the office door.

She sighed faintly and looked at the round watch on her wrist.

It was nearly eight. Four more hours, and she could put the close on another year.

She sighed again and slowly tapped the end of her red pen on the surface of her desk as she stared blindly at the article she was supposed to be proofreading.

The tapping might as well have been a clock ticking.

A new year was supposed to be the start of new things, wasn't it?

Unfortunately, she couldn't help but think that the "new" was likely to turn out worse than the "old."

Depressed by her own thoughts, she shook her head and focused again on the article that her boss had decided just had to be completed before the office took their brief New Year break.

Trust Andrew Fortune not to realize that his latest burst of creative, financial genius was inconveniently timed when it came to the rest of his staff.

She corrected a spelling error and felt her gaze drifting upward to the opened doorway of her boss's office.

Drew wasn't sitting at his desk. If he had been, she would have had a straight-on view of him. Instead, she only caught the occasional glimpse of him as he paced around his spacious office, passing behind his desk occasionally to stop and look out the windows that offered a near-panoramic view of San Diego. During the day, she knew he'd be able to see all the way to the coastline.

Now the only thing he'd see out those windows was the night sky and city lights.

Even as she watched, he paced past the doorway, completely oblivious—as he had been for most of the day, since he'd spread the word that he wanted this last project done before they shut down for the long weekend—to anything that was transpiring beyond his office doorway.

He wore a Padres ball cap on his brown head, the bill pulled down low over his brow. A sure sign that his mood was just as dark as the grim set of his angular jaw suggested. When he was feeling particularly good-natured, that hat would have been turned backward with the bill scooting down his neck and there would have been a cocky half twist to his lips, a faint dimple in his right cheek and a wicked glint in his dark brown eyes. He'd have been holding a golf club in his hand, practicing his putting across the smooth, thick, beige carpet that lined his office instead of clenching the end of a baseball bat in his hand.

The faint buzzing of her cell phone drew her attention and she picked it up off the desk, looking at the display.

Gigi.

She sighed again and set the phone down, unanswered.

Her mother had already called her a half dozen times that day. Deanna had no desire to talk to her, yet again. Hard as it had been, she had already said what she'd had to say.

But the vibrating phone reminded her that she did have work to do that didn't involve lollygagging around, worrying about her boss's state of mind.

She had plenty of reason not to feel particularly celebratory. But Drew Fortune had the world by the tail. He was thirty-four years old—eight years older than she—and handsome as sin, plus he was poised to take the helm of the hugely successful trend analysis firm his father had founded decades earlier. And if not for the fact that she knew what his plans for that day were supposed to have been—flying to Texas—she was certain that he would have been heading out with one of his leggy, buxom blondes on his arm who'd have undoubtedly ensured that she rang in his new year in a major way.

Deanna made a face and scratched her red pen through a redundant phrase.

"Hell, Dee. That page looks like it's bleeding."

She didn't look up at her boss. "It's one of the things you pay me for, remember?" She corrected another misspelling.

Brilliant, he was. But a good speller?

Not exactly.

"Seems to me I'm also paying some other folks who ought to still be around." Drew sat on the corner of her desk and picked up her cell phone as if he had every right to do so. He tapped the end of his baseball bat against the toe of his leather shoe.

"We didn't need the rest of the staff here to finish up the article." Everyone had pulled together the data that he'd needed. The only thing left now was for her to finish proofing it, send it via email to their bazillion clients and then to the newspaper that was printing it in Saturday's New Year's Day edition.

He made a low sound that seemed distinctly displeased. "So you decided who stayed and who went?"

"Everyone stayed as long as they did because you asked them to," she said evenly. "But once their tasks were complete, did you really expect them to sit around and twiddle their thumbs until I finish my end of it?"

He grimaced.

"Besides, it's New Year's Eve," she reminded. "People had plans that didn't necessarily include hanging around here." Including him, because he was supposed to have been on the company jet hours ago.

He lost interest in the phone and picked up her stapler instead. "Did you have plans?"

She sighed, set down her red pen and folded her hands on top of the draft. "Yes, as a matter of fact."

"A date, I suppose." His dark, level brows were barely visible beneath his pulled-low cap. "What was his name? Mike?"

She kept her expression calm. It was easy enough. She'd had plenty of practice staying calm in the four years she'd worked for him. And before that, a lifetime of being Gigi's daughter. "It was Mark, actually." Which Drew knew very well because he'd met the man several times during the nine months she'd dated him. "And we broke up."

His brows pulled together. "Since when?"

*Since my mother.* The caustic answer leaped into her brain, but she held it back. The problems that she had with Gigi had nothing to do with her work. "A few months ago."

Drew's lips twisted. "Nothing like true love," he muttered. He set down her stapler and pushed off the desk. "So who is the date, then?"

She couldn't imagine what was spurring his sudden interest in her love life, but then she couldn't imagine what had put that hard, grim look on his face either, or this sudden, unusual...hovering...while she worked.

"Dates. Plural." She smiled slightly, wryly enjoying the novelty of the speculative look from him that she earned. "Three of my girlfriends," she added. "So stop looking so impressed. We're planning a spa weekend, as it happens."

Her phone vibrated again and she pressed a button, silencing it. "No men at all," she concluded. And no frantic calls from Gigi, she vowed silently.

Her mother had made it very clear that she'd expected her little Deedee to drop everything and come sit by her side in her latest hour of need, even if it was New Year's Eve. And she'd made it abundantly plain how she considered Deanna's refusal to do so an utter betrayal.

But then, Gigi was nothing if not melodramatic.

It didn't matter to her mother that Deanna had spent

most of her life rearranging her life to accommodate Gigi's needs.

"Where at?"

"Up in La Jolla." She named the resort. "I was supposed to meet them two hours ago so we could all drive up together. Instead, I'll have to meet them there." She knew better than to expect Drew to apologize, though. That wasn't exactly his method. And it wasn't as if La Jolla was far. A handful of miles only.

It just was not what they'd planned.

And all because Drew was in a clearly bad temper.

He was pressing the end of the bat into the thick carpet, his expression still black, and she chewed the inside of her lip as she tried not to watch him.

But it was hard.

He was a man made to be watched. Thick brown hair that was usually just this side of rumpled—unless he had an important meeting and then he'd slick it back and look even more devastating. Wide shoulders and a lean build that looked just as good beneath his custom-made suits as they did when he was shirtless and entertaining clients on the beach.

Yes, Drew Fortune was certainly watchable.

But not touchable, her mind whispered.

She knew better than to mix business with pleasure. She'd learned that well simply by watching the messes that her mother made. That her mother was continuing to make.

Not that Deanna had to worry that Drew might think of her in that way anyway. She did her job and she did it well, and that was the only thing he cared about.

Which was exactly how she wanted it. Give her professional respect over a romantic dalliance every day of the week and twice on Sundays.

She enjoyed her work with Fortune Forecasting, and ordinarily, she liked working for Drew Fortune. And right now, given Gigi's latest exit from reality, Deanna needed the distraction of her work more than ever.

She picked up her pen and forced her attention back to the page. "I'll be done with this in ten minutes," she promised. "Then you can get out of here, too." So could she. She'd join her girlfriends and try to forget for a few days that her mother—still jobless since her last one ended in its usual emotional meltdown—was on the verge of financial ruin and blamed Deanna for not wanting to save her.

She couldn't understand at all that Deanna simply couldn't save her.

"Hallelujah," Drew was saying, his tone flat, almost as if he were answering her own silent thoughts. "Just get the article done."

Her jaw tightened a little with annoyance. What did he think she was doing?

Once again, her cell phone softly buzzed against the surface of the desk and she opened the top drawer of her desk, tossed it inside and closed the drawer again.

She still imagined she could hear it silently vibrating against the collection of pens and paper clips inside.

"Why don't you just turn the damn thing off if you're not going to answer it?"

Good question. "She'd just start calling the office line, then."

He lifted the baseball bat and rested it over his shoulder. "She?"

"Gigi."

"Your mom must be pretty anxious to talk to you. Six calls from her at least."

Which he knew because he'd looked at her cell phone.

"She's annoyed that I didn't include her in my little New Year's vacation." At the mammoth understatement, her pen nearly went right through the paper as she struck out another phrase. "Did you know that you repeated yourself twice here about the Decker rebound?"

He sat again on the edge of her desk and slid the paper out from beneath her pen. He glanced at it, then handed it back. "That's what I've got you for."

Misspellings were usual for him. Repetitive phrasing was not.

She quickly continued reading, but for some reason it was harder than it usually was ignoring the bulge of his very well-shaped thigh beneath his charcoal-gray trousers.

And there was at least a yard of space between them.

"I, um, I hope you're already packed for your trip to Texas." She realized she was skimming the last paragraph and made herself slow down. The last thing she wanted to do was disseminate something with an error that she should have caught just because she was feeling particularly distracted by her boss. "Because you're supposed to meet the jet at the airfield in two hours." She'd arranged, then rearranged the corporate jet for him, when it became clear earlier that day that he was not going to make the first flight as she'd scheduled it, nor the second.

He was supposed to be in Red Rock by morning where his father, William, was to be married. And even though Drew had a jet at his disposal, the earliest he'd be arriving now would be the middle of the night.

"What's the weather supposed to be like there at this time of year anyway?" She knew Red Rock was about twenty miles outside of San Antonio, but only because she'd looked for it on the map.

"Breezy with a scent of hell," he muttered.

She lifted her eyebrows a little, giving him a quick glance. "I know you're no fan of marriage—" he made that abundantly clear to every woman who passed through his revolving door "—but this is your father's wedding. Aren't you happy for him?" William Fortune had lost his wife—Drew's mother—four years earlier.

She remembered that time distinctly and not simply because she'd just begun working for Drew. It was the only time she'd ever seen him completely devastated.

It was also the only time she'd ever come close to making the mistake of forgetting that he was her boss.

Perilously close.

She blew out a silent puff of air, feeling ridiculously warm.

Four years had passed since that time, but it might as well have been yesterday for how clear it was in her mind.

He'd kissed her.

One time.

One...very...memorable time.

And she'd been a head case for much too long afterward.

Which was all over now, thank goodness. No way would she let herself fall into the same behavior as her mother.

"No, I'm not happy." His voice was short. "And why are you nodding?"

She blinked, focusing in on the present and the look Drew was giving her. "I, um, I was just glad to be finished with the proof." She raced through the last few sentences and was relieved that it was perfect as drafted and set down her pen.

She turned to her side desk where her computer sat and moved the papers next to her. "Don't you like the woman your father is marrying?"

"Lily? She's his cousin's widow." He leaned across the desk and slid open her drawer, pulling out the cell phone. It was buzzing, yet again.

Afraid he was going to answer it, she snatched it out of his hand and slid it into the side pocket of her jacket. She definitely didn't want chancing her mother getting her boss's ear. "So?"

"So I don't see why they have to rush into anything. Wouldn't it just be easier to talk to your mother?"

She let out a faint laugh. Her fingers worked quickly over the keyboard as she made her corrections to his document. "You're obviously dreading the trip to your father's wedding. Maybe you shouldn't be giving me advice on dealing with my parent."

He exhaled roughly and shoved off the desk again. "It's not the wedding," he muttered. "Not entirely."

Her fingers slowed fractionally and realizing it, she hastened her pace again. Letting Drew get under her sympathetic nerve was not a wise course of action.

His father was getting married. Effectively replacing his mother. And Deanna had seen for herself, up close and personally, how deeply affected he'd been when she'd died.

"Your brothers will be there," she offered, trying to be helpful. He'd told her once that he had four of them, but only he and one other brother, Jeremy, didn't live in Texas. "How long's it been since you've seen them?"

"We were all in Red Rock together a few years ago."

She didn't have any siblings and so often had wished she had. She wouldn't have felt so alone in the world. "Well, then, aren't you looking forward to that?"

He swung his bat like a golf club, but he looked anything but leisurely. "What the hell does it matter?"

Irritation skittered along her nerves. "I guess it doesn't," she snapped back, "except that this whole project—" she waved her hand over the stacks of papers littering her desk "—that you insisted had to be done now, is obviously just a way for you to put off going to Texas. Were you hoping that we wouldn't actually get it finished, so you could claim that you couldn't get away at all?"

Drew nearly did a double take at his assistant's tart words. Her hazel eyes were practically snapping up at him and a blaze of color was burning in her lightly tanned cheeks.

Usually, she was the soul of calm.

And for some reason, the fact that she suddenly wasn't was just one more thorn under his saddle.

"Guess I didn't realize how important your spa weekend with the girls was," he countered.

Her lips tightened. "You know, Drew, sometimes you are such a—" She broke off and shook her head so hard that her brownish-red hair bounced around her shoulders. She turned her softly pointed chin back to her computer monitor and began typing, her fingers pounding furiously over the keys.

"A what?"

"Nothing." She was typing even faster, the keys clicking madly.

"Just say it, Dee." He blamed the urge to goad her even more on his father. William wasn't satisfied with ruining his own life with his damn marriage plans, but now he wanted to ruin Drew's, too. "Why hold back now?"

She gave him a stern look that reminded him, strangely enough, of his mother. Probably because his mother was on Drew's mind, because she clearly was not on William's mind, he reasoned.

"Why don't you just go back into your office and let me finish without distraction?" she countered. She lifted her left hand to wave it in dismissal, and her right hand never stopped moving over the computer keyboard. "Decide what you want your new business cards to say when you replace your dad as the CEO now that he's retiring. Maybe that will improve your mood."

"Maybe the fact that I'm not likely to be the new CEO will improve yours."

The clacking keys went abruptly silent.

She stared up at him and the fiery green glint faded in her eyes, leaving confusion in their depths. "What?"

He tightened his grip around the baseball bat.

He wanted to throw the damn thing through one of the windows.

"I'm not taking over as CEO." The words tasted like acid-coated boulders.

She looked bewildered. "But everyone knows you're taking over for him."

"Yeah, well, I guess Dad didn't read the memo." His voice was short.

"Drew—"

He exhaled. "As far as I know, he's not planning to close down this office. He just wants to close me down."

The high color faded from her cheeks and she looked pale. "But you do a remarkable job here."

"Not remarkable enough for him."

She shook her head a little, making her hair swing again. "Your father's never seemed anything but proud of the work you've done here. For heaven's sake, he even told me once when he was visiting the office how he thinks you're a chip off the old block."

"And there's the problem," he said flatly. "Since he thinks he didn't really get his act together and start up this place until he married my mother and settled down, he's gone and decided that I have to do the same damn thing!"

He swung the bat hard and it connected with the soft cushion of one of the upholstered chairs sitting outside the door to his office.

The cushion dented, and Deanna let out a startled squeak.

Neither was as satisfying as a broken window, and cursing his father, he tossed the bat onto the chair and stomped back into his office.

Deanna followed him, her hands clenched around the lapels of her drab brown jacket that matched her knee-length drab brown skirt. "Your father thinks you should get married?"

His head was pounding. He wanted a drink. He wanted a cigarette and he'd finally managed to quit the damn things six months earlier. He wanted to forget that the past year had ever happened and he particularly wanted to forget his father's ultimatum.

If only he could.

He threw himself down onto the chair behind his desk and yanked off his hat. "He doesn't just think it," he said wearily. "He expects it. Or no CEO for Drew."

She slowly sank down onto one of the chairs facing his desk. She looked dazed, which was probably the only reason she wasn't smoothing her skirt circumspectly around her pretty knees the way she usually did. "Are you sure you're not—" she swallowed and moistened her lips "—well, overreacting? Maybe you misunderstood what he meant. Maybe you heard the word *marriage* and a wire in your brain went poof."

He gave a bark of laughter that was completely devoid of humor. "Oh, he was perfectly clear. My life lacks balance, he said." He hunched forward, clenching his fists on top of his desk. "I'm too committed to the company, he said."

His fist hit the desk, sending a pen rolling off the side. "What the hell else should I be but committed? This company is everything to me and he damn well knows it. But now, dear old Dad has decided that unless my neck ends up in a marriage noose again, I'm suddenly not fit to run it after all."

Deanna's eyes were wide. "Um…again?"

He could practically feel the steam wanting to pour out of his pounding head. "And he'll go find someone who isn't even a Fortune to head things up instead." Even more than the marriage nonsense that William had been threatening for much of the past year—ever since he'd gotten involved with Lily—telling Drew just that morning that he'd bring in someone else to run the company if Drew didn't heed his words had been an even worse slam.

Their telephone conversation—if the argument that had ensued could be called that—had disintegrated from there.

Drew was still stinging from it.

"I'll be damned if I'll work for somebody else at what should be my own freaking company."

Her brows drew together, creating a little vertical line between them. "You'd just give it up, then?" She lifted her hand and tucked her hair behind her ear. "Walk away from everything you've worked for?"

"It's not like I have any women around I'd remotely consider marrying. Dad decided to marry Lily and look what happened. He's lost his marbles."

"I—I'm stunned," she said after a moment. "I don't know what to say."

He scrubbed his hands down his face and leaned back in his chair again, watching his assistant through his narrowed eyes.

But his mind was still replaying the argument with his father.

Despite his wedding to Lily scheduled for the following day—a new year and a new life with his new wife—William had had the cojones to bring up Drew's mother, Molly. To use her memory as a tool in his arsenal against Drew's footloose lifestyle.

That had been the ultimate slam.

And he'd responded in kind. If William were so concerned about Molly, then what the hell was he doing getting married again?

Drew pinched his nose and closed his eyes again. The angry words still circled in his head. "As if a marriage certificate has anything to do with success," he muttered. "It's insane." He looked at Deanna.

She was sitting straight as a poker in her chair. Instead of twisting the life out of her jacket, her hands were now twisted together in her lap. She still had that frown etched on her face and her eyes were dark with concern. "I, um, imagine for you, marriage certainly is a deal breaker."

And Drew had never failed to close a deal.

He'd always had the singular ability to put the right

pieces together, even when people—including his father—said it would be impossible.

His brain suddenly shifted. Boulders rolled and he saw a glimmer of light. "This is a deal," he murmured, wondering why he hadn't seen it before.

Maybe Deanna was right. He'd heard *marriage,* and the wiring in his brain had short-circuited.

Her eyebrows had climbed up her smooth forehead. "Excuse me?"

"A deal." He sat forward. For the first time that day he felt a grin hit him. "And all I need is a signed marriage license to seal it."

The corners of her lips curved in response to his, but she was still watching him warily. "Usually that involves a marriage," she pointed out. "Which you've already said you're not interested in."

"I'm not," he assured. "But a marriage license just comes with wedding. All I need for that is a wife."

She lifted her hands. "Exactly."

"I can hire a wife."

She blinked for a moment. "You can't possibly be serious."

"Sometimes you need specialized people at the table to close a deal. I just need the right woman to agree to the terms."

"Which are what?"

"Sign the paper, say 'I do' and then act like my wife for a short while—long enough for Dad to calm down, retire like he's planned to do all along and name me as his replacement—then go on her way."

She snorted softly and shook her head. Her hair gleamed under the overhead light. "Do I need to remind you that the women you usually date—before they reach the three-month expiration, that is—will be looking for a whole lot more out of your deal than going on her way?"

Because he usually marked his way out of his brief romantic entanglements with gifts of jewelry that Deanna arranged for him, she had a point.

"I'd need someone convincing," he mused. He drummed his fingers on the desk as his thoughts coalesced into the perfect solution.

He looked his assistant square in the eyes.

"Someone like you."

## *Chapter Two*

Like her?

Alarm had Deanna shooting out of her chair. "Now I think you've lost your marbles."

But Drew was sitting there in his chair as calm now as he'd been agitated earlier, and she felt her stomach sink even lower when he picked up the hat he'd discarded earlier and put it on.

Backward.

The small scar near his hairline that showed because of it gave him a particularly rakish look.

"It's the perfect solution," he reasoned. The faint dimple in his cheek appeared.

She gaped. "You are mad."

He spread his hands, his palms upward. "Think it through, Dee. If a new CEO is named—someone from outside—what's the likelihood that you and everyone else who's worked here will get to stay? Bring in a new person at the top and changes are bound to trickle down. It's the nature of the beast."

A fresh wave of panic began forming at the edges of her sanity. "You already said that a new CEO wouldn't mean closing this office."

"Closing is one thing. Clearing the decks to bring in his—" he shrugged "—or her, I suppose—own people is not unusual, though. If I were going into a new place, I'd want some of my own people around me. Dad will officially be retired by then. Living permanently in Texas. He's the one ready to bring in new blood. You think he hasn't realized the ramifications to the people who've worked for him all along?"

"I can't believe that your father wouldn't have some plan for that. I've met him. He's a very caring person!"

"He's a man who has made it plain that he is starting his new life, no matter how it affects everyone else, including his own family," Drew said flatly, and his dimple was nowhere in evidence.

Her knees suddenly felt wobbly and she closed her hands over the back of the chair where she'd been sitting.

She needed her job. Now, more than ever.

And while she felt certain that she'd be able to find alternate work if she had to, she knew that she'd never be able to start out at the pay level that she'd risen to at Fortune Forecasting.

She wasn't getting rich by any means, but she made enough to keep her head above water…and until Gigi's latest spending jag…hers, too.

"Nobody would believe that you and I… That we… well, that we—"

"—were in love?"

She could practically see the calculating wheels turning in his mind when he picked up a pen and began drumming the end of it on his desk.

"Why not?" he asked. "I think it'll make perfect sense to anyone who bothers to think about it. My whole family knows that you're the only female who has been in my life for longer than a twelve-week stretch."

"Sure. Because you pay me well and usually leave me alone to do my job!" She shook her head. "I'm not even your type."

He looked amused and the dimple was definitely back. "And what type would that be?"

"Six feet tall, blonde and big-chested."

"Sounds like you're describing the guy who runs the magazine stand down in the lobby."

She grimaced. "Hilarious. You know exactly the kind of woman I mean. The only kind you ever date more than twice." She could count on one hand the number of women he'd seen who'd had more interest in him than the size of his bank account or what they could get out of being on Drew Fortune's arm for a while.

None of those women had ever made it past a second date with him; he'd made certain of that.

His pen was still tapping. "I do know what you mean. And you're right. You are not a gold digger," he said smoothly. "Nobody could ever make the mistake of thinking that. You've worked by my side for four years now. You're the soul of discretion, you're calm and sensible. Hell, if we're honest here, my father will probably think you're too good for me."

He made her sound like a lap dog.

She shook off the unwanted shard of pique as she shook her head. "I can't believe I'm even standing here discussing this with you. It's insane. And I have friends still waiting for me. So am I supposed to distribute your article or was that whole episode just an exercise on your part to exert your power one last time before you take to the road?"

He ignored that. "One year of your time, Deanna, for a simple business deal. A marriage of convenience. Hands-strictly-off, right? So what's that worth to you? A raise? A promotion? A new title?"

"No! I don't want any of those things! Not when it's a simple business deal that involves getting married to you—however you want to describe it—and lying to your own father about the real reason for it!"

"And you think what he's demanding is all that reasonable?" he shot back.

She pressed her lips together. Because, if everything that Drew said was true, then of course she didn't think it was reasonable at all.

Yes, Drew played hard.

But he worked even harder.

And she'd worked for him long enough to know that there was nothing he valued more than the company that his father had founded.

She raked her hands through her hair and turned away from the chair to pace across the office. Her knees were still shaking, but that was nothing compared to the quivering going on inside her belly.

Marry Drew Fortune?

Her?

Nerves skittered through her.

She paced back. "How do I even know that you're not exaggerating the situation?"

He gave her a look. "For what purpose? To get myself a wife? Come on, Dee."

She flushed. All right. So that was pretty unlikely,

given Drew's opinion about marriage. And if he weren't practically allergic to the very idea of it, he'd have had ample opportunity to find a wife among the scores of women he'd dated. Just because she'd considered the majority of them to be shallow twits didn't mean that he had to think of them the same way.

He got up and rounded his desk and her nerves reached a screaming pitch when he dropped his arm over her shoulder.

The warmth of him seared her right through the lightweight wool of her suit and she felt like she might scream right out loud to match those nerves, note for note.

"You always play fair, Deanna," he coaxed smoothly. "Think about all the people who're going to be affected by this."

"Don't try to schmooze me, Drew Fortune. I'm immune, remember?"

If only.

She shrugged out from beneath his easy, buddy-to-buddy arm, putting some much-needed space between them. "I've seen you in action too many times before."

"Fair enough." He exhaled and sat on the edge of his desk. "I need you, Deanna. Trust me. We can make this work."

His words sounded so sincere that he could have been trying to persuade her to marry him for real. Forever.

Her throat felt infuriatingly tight. "For a year," she reminded.

He gave a brief nod in acknowledgment. "Don't make it sound so horrible. Since the dawn of time, people have been making marriages of convenience."

She almost laughed. "Somehow I never thought that term would ever pass your lips."

He grimaced. "True enough. But my point is that plenty of people have married for reasons that had nothing to do with love."

"Well, pardon me, but I never figured that I would be one of them!"

"I never figured I'd be forced to barter for the company that I've earned the right to run with a marriage license, either. S...tuff happens."

How well she knew that.

She had only to think about her mother if she wanted proof.

He flipped off his hat and tossed it unerringly onto the iron-armed coat stand that he'd once told her had been a gift from his mother and watched her. "I don't expect you to get nothing out of this, either," he said seriously.

Which made her all the more nervous.

She had defenses against Drew the Schmoozer and Drew the Charmer. She could trade insincere banter with him until the cows came home.

But when he dropped the tactics? When he was just Drew Fortune, straight talking and perfectly sincere?

That's when she knew she was wading in waters much too deep for her peace of mind.

"I told you. There's nothing I want," she insisted.

He stood again and closed the distance between them. It took all of her willpower not to nervously back away. And when he reached out an arm toward her, she positively froze.

But all he did was reach into her pocket and withdraw her cell phone that had been buzzing almost constantly since she'd stuck it there. He held it up so that she could see the display.

Gigi, it read.

"Not even to send your mother on a vacation of her own?"

She grabbed the phone, and this time, she did power it off. Her mother could call the office line all she wanted. At the moment, Deanna considered that a lesser problem than Drew. "It would take more than a vacation to solve the matter of Gigi."

"What would it take?"

She huffed and threw out her hands. "About fifty grand." Which might as well be fifty million because it was just as unattainable. And the admission was just proof that his so-called proposal had sent her sense of discretion right into orbit and no matter what it looked like to him, she took a step backward. Then another. "So, I still need an answer about your article," she reminded, feeling almost desperate to get them back on track. Work track.

His eyes narrowed slightly. "If it's ready to send, then send it," he said after a moment.

Surprise had her feeling uneasy.

She nodded anyway, taking him at face value and returned to her desk. Within minutes she'd sent the article off into the magical cosmos of electronic mail as well as to the newspaper editor who was printing it.

Her work done, she shut down the computer, pulled her purse out of the bottom drawer of her filing cabinet and locked up her desk.

Drew hadn't come out of his office. She could see him sitting in his chair again, but he'd swiveled it around so that he was facing the windows.

She told herself that she didn't want to be a part of

his charade, but she also couldn't just walk out of the office as if nothing at all had happened. He'd been a good and fair—if sometimes challenging—boss to her. To everyone who worked in the San Diego office, for that matter.

Which was exactly the reason why they'd all been willing to give up even a portion of their holiday evening when he'd asked.

She sighed and dropped her purse next to the baseball bat on the chair he'd beat before going back into his office. She could see him reflected in the dark windows. "What are you going to do?"

He looked at the window as if it were a mirror, meeting her gaze there. "What are you going to do?" He turned in his chair until he was facing her again, and he set his own cell phone down on the center of his leather desk blotter. "Your mother lost her job again."

She looked from his phone to his face. Horror warred with anger. "What'd you do? Call her?"

"I called Joe Winston. Remember, he's the HR head over at Blake & Philips?"

Her mouth went dry. Blake & Philips was the law firm her mother had worked for...until a few months ago when she'd been fired. And the only reason that Drew knew that Gigi had worked there was because he was the one who'd told Deanna a year ago that his college buddy, Joe, was looking for legal secretaries and he knew that her mother—between jobs, again—had been worried about losing her house if she didn't find work soon.

More like Deanna was worried about her mother losing her house, because she'd been the one trying to pay Gigi's mortgage as well as her own rent.

"That was none of your business," she said stiffly.

"We're supposed to be golfing next week," he went on. "He thinks I called to tell him our tee time."

Embarrassment burned inside her. "And you just happened to mention my mother's name?"

"I didn't bring her up at all."

"Right. How else would you know?"

His gaze was steady. "You've worked for me for a while, Dee. Just because you don't go around airing your personal business as much as most of the people do around here, doesn't mean I haven't picked up some things. And your mother goes through jobs like I go through—"

"—women?" she inserted caustically.

"I was going to say shirts." He sat back in his chair, his hand slowly turning his cell phone end over end. "Joe didn't have to mention your mother. All I had to do was make an educated guess and watch your face."

Which she could feel burning now. "Fine. Yes, my mother lost her job. Again. Story of our lives." But only part of the story. "She'll find another one." She always did.

Another job. Another unattainable man to make a play for that always ended in a dramatic parting of employment when it didn't work out. Another reason to go off the financial deep end and expect Deanna to "save" her.

"Your article is sent." She pulled back her sleeve and looked at her watch. "And you're supposed to be at the airport soon. Try not to grimace all through your father's wedding tomorrow." She turned on her heel. "It'll ruin the family pictures."

"I'll give you the fifty grand." His low voice followed her.

Her feet dragged in the carpet, coming to a stop. She didn't look at him. "I shouldn't have told you that."

He was silent, but her nape prickled and she knew he'd left his desk and was walking up behind her. "You wouldn't have if you weren't upset about it."

She closed her eyes for a moment. On one hand, it was unnerving to think that he knew her that well. On the other hand, was she really surprised? There was a reason why they worked well together and she was realistic enough to know that that wasn't only because of her understanding of him. "I don't want your money."

"But do you need it?" He touched her arm, moving around until he was in front of her. "Hey." He nudged her chin until she couldn't avoid looking at him. His faint smile was crooked. And sympathetic. "I don't want to get married. But I need to."

She could feel a burning deep behind her eyes and because she couldn't will it away, hoped to heaven that it would just stay where it was because she'd be darned if she'd cry in front of her boss. "Even if I…agreed…the money would just be a quick-fix for Gigi's problem."

"Which is what?"

She looked up at him and found her gaze trapped in his. "She has a shopping addiction."

His brows twitched together. "What?"

At least he hadn't laughed.

She sighed and moved the bat and her purse from the chair, sinking down onto it.

"A shopping addiction. And not the kind of thing people are often teasing women about, either. She doesn't just like to go out shopping for shoes or…whatever." She waved her hand. "When Gigi's…between jobs—" which in Gigi-speak really meant between the men with whom she inevitably got unwisely involved "—she gets depressed. And when she gets depressed, she shops. On-line or on the home shopping networks. It doesn't matter which and it doesn't matter what. She orders stuff that she neither needs nor can afford. And it doesn't matter what I say or what I do, she won't stop and she won't get help."

She pressed her palms together, staring at her bare fingers. "She's behind on her mortgage again, she's man-aged to open new credit cards that I didn't even know she had and she figures that I ought to be able to solve it all for her."

"Why you?"

"Because I've been paying things off for her since I got my first job when I was fifteen." The year her father had left. The year that Gigi started blaming Deanna for her very existence. "As long as I continue bailing her out, she's never going to get the help she needs." Deanna had finally faced that truth because she had sought the counseling that her mother refused to believe she needed.

"At least you realize that."

"Realizing it and being able to stick to it are two different things." She swallowed the knot in her throat. "It's not easy to say no to your own mother."

"It's not all that easy to say no to your father, either." He crouched down in front of her, taking her hands in his. "We can help each other here, you know."

His hands were warm and steady and nearly dwarfed hers. "It's not a, uh, a good idea. Getting involved at the workplace never is." She felt that threatening burn get even hotter. "That's what my mother does, and it never leads to anything but disaster." Certainly not the fairy-tale wedding Gigi kept hoping for.

"People have been marrying the boss for centuries. There doesn't have to be anything wrong with that."

"Right. When the two people are actually in love." She realized her fingers had slid through his until they were twined together. She pulled her hands free and wrapped them over the arms of the chair. "And, like I said, throwing money on the situation doesn't solve the ultimate problem."

"Then we'll get your mother into counseling. For as long as it takes. Even after our arrangement is ended."

She pressed her fingers harder into the upholstery to keep them from trembling. "She'll refuse. She always does."

"We'll make sure she doesn't. We'll find a way."

"We?"

He covered her hands with his. "Yeah, we."

Her heart was climbing in her chest. She felt light-headed. She hadn't had any support where her mother was concerned since her father walked out the door and never came back.

It had been just her.

Drew was watching her with that steady gaze and his voice, so quietly assured, was ringing in her head.

*We.*

The lure of that word alone seemed impossible to resist. "Okay," she whispered and felt a shudder work down her spine.

His gaze sharpened. "You'll marry me?"

She swallowed hard and had to clear her throat. "Yes."

His smile was sudden and nearly blinding. "I've always said you are the perfect assistant!" He straightened and leaned over her, pressing a fast kiss to her forehead before turning away. "This is going to work out perfectly," he was saying as he strode back into his office. "You'll come with me to Red Rock. We'll announce it there."

Deanna could hear his raised voice. Could understand his words even.

But she couldn't do much of anything but stare at her tidy desk across from her and feel the imprint of his lips as if they were still grazing her skin.

"Dee, how fast can you pack?"

She scrubbed her hands down her cheeks, attempting to drag her utterly rattled self back together. "C-couldn't you just tell your dad about us? I'd feel like I'm intruding if I go with you to Texas."

He reappeared in his doorway. The ball cap was back on his head—backward—and the dimple was back in his cheek.

He was also holding up a bottle of champagne that had been delivered that afternoon from one of his clients.

"I'm pretty sure my fiancée would be welcome at a family event," he said drily. "More than that, she'll be expected." He waved the end of the bottle in front of her. "Call the pilot again. Tell him we'll be an hour later than I planned."

Deanna felt a ridiculous surge of laughter. Or maybe it was simply that she was on the verge of hysteria.

Had she really agreed to marry him?

"I already built in an hour cushion when I rescheduled your flight the last time I talked to him," she admitted.

His eyebrows shot up. "Sounds like you were handling me." Then he grinned again. "Well done."

She managed a weak smile.

"Come on. We'll pop open this baby and celebrate.

Get a few glasses, would you?" He went back into his office. "And you should let your girlfriends know you won't be making it to the spa after all."

She very nearly slapped her hand against her forehead. She'd completely forgotten about her friends. She pulled out her cell phone and turned it on again. Ignoring the little indicator that told her she had messages waiting, she quickly called Susan, the one who'd arranged the weekend, and left her own message when her friend didn't answer.

And then, holding the phone, she debated whether to call Gigi. Her mother already expected her to be gone for the long weekend. That hadn't changed, even if Deanna's destination had.

And what would she tell her mother when she did call?

That she was marrying the boss?

Gigi would probably think she'd died and gone to heaven. If she couldn't achieve that status, then at least her daughter had.

Deanna heard the distinctive sound of the champagne cork popping, and ignoring the sense of guilt she felt, she turned off her cell phone again. The only harmful thing that Gigi would do over the weekend would be to order more needless items. Items that Deanna would ensure were returned, along with all the other things she'd expected to have to deal with.

No, she'd call her mother after the holiday when she was back in town.

Maybe by then, Deanna would have figured out a way to couch her news so that Gigi wouldn't start flying over the moon.

She hurried into the small employee break room,

pulled out two plastic cups from the cupboard and returned to Drew's office.

He was pulling off his linen, button-down shirt.

She nearly dropped the cups. "What are you doing?"

The shirt came off his shoulders and he balled it up, pitching it aside. The white T-shirt he was wearing beneath it clung to every centimeter of his wide chest.

"Champagne bubbled over." He picked up the bottle and she could see a ring of shimmering liquid on his desk where the bottle had been sitting. "Here." He grabbed her hand with one of the cups in it and filled it more than halfway.

"That's too much." She had to force herself not to stare at his chest. It wasn't as if she had never seen it before, and even completely, gloriously bare. When he was playing beach volleyball at their branch picnic every year, for one. But she'd never been his convenient fiancée and been faced with him less than fully dressed...

She could feel hysteria rising and ruthlessly tramped it down.

"Live a little." He was grinning as he took the second cup from her. "It's New Year's Eve."

She was glad to surrender the cup, because that meant that she could wrap both hands around her own, and maybe stop shaking like she was some schoolgirl faced with her first crush.

He filled his own cup, then held it out. "Here's to marriage."

Her stomach dipped and swayed, but she managed to give him a stern glare. "You shouldn't joke about it."

"Who's joking?" He nudged the side of his cup against hers in the toast. "At least we both know exactly what we'll be getting out of the deal. No illusions. No surprises."

"Right." She dipped her nose toward the cup. The first taste of champagne was as bitter as the nerves tightening her stomach. She swallowed it anyway.

"A ring," he said suddenly.

She looked up at him. "Excuse me?"

"We need an engagement ring." He snatched his phone off his desk again and scrolled through the phone numbers stored in it.

"You're not going to find a jeweler open on New Year's Eve," she warned. "Not even Zondervan's."

He grinned as he punched a number and held the phone to his ear. "As much business as I've given Bob Zondervan over the years? Want to bet?"

"Um…no, thanks," she managed with at least a little wisdom considering the number of orders she'd made on his behalf.

"Smart girl."

Feeling strangely weak, she sat down and shook her head.

Her mother had always told Deanna that a smart girl could catch herself the boss. Deanna had always said that would never, ever be her way.

And yet…here she was.

Her mother's daughter after all.

## Chapter Three

"Come on, Sleeping Beauty. Up and at 'em." Drew nudged Deanna's shoulder.

But she just sighed and shifted, and instead of her sleeping head resting against the backseat of the limousine that had been waiting for them when they'd landed in San Antonio, it slid sideways until it was resting on his shoulder.

Her hair smelled like green apples.

He closed his eyes for a minute, reminding himself that this was Deanna. His young assistant who was, once again, smoothing out the kinks in his life.

Yeah, okay, so she was going to get something out of it. Namely, getting some help with her crazy mother.

But as far as Drew was concerned, that was a drop in the bucket compared to what he was going to get out of it.

rtune Forecasting once and for al.

"De            ach for her hand where it was rest         itated.

The dia        'd chosen from the two-dozen rings        by the office less than an hour aft       im was on her ring finger. Even        ck of the limo, the ring gleamed.

How many ti        edding ring was just a noose in dis

Yet now, he had      par of the damned things—platinum to    ne band on the engagement ring—in his pocket. All ready to go for the big day.

Whenever they decided that would be.

Given the way his father was harping on the subject, it wouldn't be soon enough for William.

Drew ignored her slender fingers and jiggled her narrow wrist with the oversize watch on it instead. "Rise and shine, Dee," he said more loudly.

Her head shifted again and her eyes slowly opened. She stared at him drowsily. "Hmm?"

She'd have that expression in bed, he thought, and abruptly went hard.

An oath zipped around inside his head and he stared over her head out the window, focusing on the lines of the fencing that marked off his brother's property.

Deanna was his assistant. His fiancée for convenience's sake. Not a woman he needed to be envisioning—way too easily envisioning, at that—in his bed. Or pressed back against the deep limo seat…

"We're almost at Molly's Pride." He cleared his throat. "My brother's ranch."

She blinked a little, then seemed to realize that she

was all but sprawled over the side of him, and straightened like she'd been stung by a bee.

Her hand went to her hair, smoothing it back from her face. "I fell asleep." She grimaced. "How embarrassing. I hope I wasn't drooling."

She hadn't been, but knew he was damnably on the verge of it. "Snoring, maybe," he said blandly.

She gave him a narrow look, then rolled her eyes. "I was not."

No, she hadn't been. She'd been soft and warm and the desire had hit him nearly out of the blue. He'd thought he'd conquered it a long time ago when she first started working for him. And he'd made a monumental ass out of himself by kissing her at one of the lowest points in his life.

Good assistants were hard to find.

Sexual partners weren't.

Fortunately, she'd turned her attention out the windows and he ran his hand around the back of his neck, feeling like he was ready to boil over.

"Oh, my. Is that your brother's ranch?" She was practically pressing her nose against the window like a little girl.

Only thanks to the way she'd slept for the past hour with her body snuggled up against his, he knew that beneath the shapeless green sweater she'd changed into at her apartment before they'd gone to the airport, the little girl was all woman.

"It's so beautiful." Fortunately, she was oblivious to his failure to comment. "It looks like it should be in an old movie. A Western." She looked at him over her shoulder, her smile flashing. "With John Wayne striding over to the old hacienda. I can't wait to see it when the sun is up."

Deanna was an excellent assistant and extremely good with marketing. Was it any wonder her imagination had gone into overdrive at the sight of his brother's place? "Clearly, you need more sleep."

She turned up her nose and looked out the window again. The limousine halted in front of the house with its stone entrance and Moorish-style arch and without waiting for the driver, he pushed open the door and climbed out of the car. The drive from San Antonio hadn't taken all that long, but he still felt stiff and cramped from being on the plane in the first place.

Drew liked space.

It was one of the reasons he liked living in San Diego so well. Whenever he wanted space around him, he just headed for the beach. How much more space could a man need when he was staring out at the rolling waves of the Pacific Ocean?

Still, his gaze ran over the house that his oldest brother had bought, pretty much out of the clear blue sky a few years ago, when he'd transplanted himself lock, stock and barrel from Los Angeles to Texas. J.R. had given up his position at the headquarters of Fortune Forecasting, as well as his designer suits and cars and coffee, in favor of jeans and cattle and pickups. He'd also quickly turned around and married Isabella Mendoza, who'd helped him decorate the place.

It had been a year since Drew had last seen Molly's Pride and even though it was well past midnight, he could see the property and the two-hundred-year-old hacienda gleamed with care.

He pulled open Deanna's door and she climbed out, her somewhat-awed gaze still focused on the house rather than Drew. Which was a good thing because he still felt like he was about ready to bust out of his jeans.

Maybe it would've helped if she hadn't changed. If she'd just stayed in that boxy, matronly looking suit that she'd worn to the office.

All her suits were the same. They all disguised the fact that her rear was pretty much made for filling out a snug pair of soft blue denims.

Annoyed with his thoughts, he left her to gather her tote and jacket and grabbed their few bags from the trunk when the driver opened it. "I've got 'em. Thanks." He gave the guy a generous tip that earned him an enthusiastic smile.

"Thank you, Mr. Fortune. Happy New Year. You, too, ma'am." The driver slammed the trunk shut and quickly climbed back behind the wheel, no doubt anxious to get on with his own celebrating. A moment later, the long vehicle was driving off, leaving him and Deanna standing there alone in the moonlight.

It felt intensely…intimate. And despite the chill in the air, he felt hotter than ever.

At any other time, he would have probably found the situation ironically humorous.

Right now, he just felt like he was ready to put his head in a noose, and was almost—almost—glad to do it.

She was watching him, her eyes looking dark and mysterious, though the way she moistened her lips warned him that she was more likely just nervous as hell. "Are you sure we're doing the right thing?"

The only thing he was sure of right then was that he was having a heck of a time remembering why he should not be wanting her the way he was.

He freshened his grip on her suitcase—one of those

hard-sided kind of things invented long before rollers
had come along—and turned toward the arched entrance, gesturing with his chin. "Yeah. Let's go."

She moistened her lips again, leaving them even more
softly shiny, and walked ahead of him through the arch
that led to a massive wood door.

"Better knock," he advised. It was hours past the time
he'd warned J.R. that he'd be arriving, and he figured
walking in might not be such a good idea. God only
knew if J.R. had taken to keeping loaded weapons at
the ready along with his other Texas rancher ways…

She reached out and knocked tentatively on the
door.

"Come on, Dee. They're never gonna hear that."

She gave him a look, then curled her fist and knocked
harder. "Satisfied?"

Since he heard the slide of a lock a moment later, he
just smiled at her. Then the door was swinging open and
his brother appeared.

"About damn time," J.R. greeted, but there was still
a faint smile on his face.

"Good to see you, too," Drew returned and then, because he wasn't much one for putting off the inevitable,
he slid his free hand around Deanna's shoulder and felt
the little start she gave. They'd have to work on that.
"You remember my assistant, Deanna," he began. J.R.
nodded. "We're late because just tonight, she agreed to
marry me."

A full heartbeat of silence followed his abrupt an-
nouncement.

Then J.R.'s smile became a little more broad, though
Drew recognized the disbelief in his brother's hazel
eyes, as he turned his focus on Deanna. "Well, then,"
J.R. said smoothly, "that sure does make up for the pip-

squeak's tardiness." He reached out and took the tote bag that was slung over Deanna's shoulder and wrapped his hand around her elbow, drawing her inside.

"Pip-squeak?" Deanna laughed a little and looked over her shoulder at Drew.

"Better than runt," he muttered. "That's what he used to call Darr." Two years younger than Drew, Darr was the baby of the family. He was also a firefighter and could probably take them all down without breaking a sweat.

"You're all still on the easy side of forty," J.R. was saying, as he chuckled and wrapped an arm around Drew's neck, hugging him hard. "So I'll call you whatever the heck I want. Damn, it's good to see you." Just as abruptly, he was pushing Drew away and taking Deanna's cumbersome suitcase. "Even if I was beginning to wonder if you were going to get here before dawn or not."

He turned and headed barefoot along the distressed wood floor through the silent house. "Isabella stayed up for a while but finally bit the dust a few hours ago." He looked over his shoulder at Deanna. "My wife."

Deanna nodded. "Drew's told me about her. I hope I'm not putting you out too badly. I warned Drew that he should have called ahead to let you know I was coming with him."

"Don't you worry any about that," J.R. assured. "We're glad to have you." He grinned. "Particularly when you're brave enough to take on our Andrew, there. And what's better to have around for a wedding than more family?"

Drew could see the color come into her cheeks.

"You're very gracious."

"My wife would kick me otherwise," J.R. assured.

He turned down a hall. "Jeremy's out for the count, too." He jerked his chin. "He's in that room there at the end of the hall. Got in yesterday."

Deanna's wide gaze was taking in the white plaster walls around them, which Drew knew were relatively fresh even if they did look authentic to the old house. "Is that one of your wife's tapestries?" She pointed to a colorful weaving on one wall as they passed it. "Drew's told me what a talented artist she is."

J.R. nodded and the look of pride on his face was plain to see. "There's not a corner of this place where she hasn't made her mark," he said before pushing open a door. "You'll be in here." He stepped aside and hopefully missed the panicked glance that Deanna threw in Drew's direction as she entered the bedroom.

The most notable feature was the wide bed that took up a good portion of the space.

His damnable body stirred again and he felt heat start to climb up his neck when his gaze ran into J.R.'s. "Looks comfortable," he said, ignoring the heat both in his neck and in his gut, and went into the room behind her.

He dropped his duffel and suit bag on the white comforter covering the bed and watched Deanna's fingertips gently graze the petals of one of the roses clustered in a vase on the chest of drawers next to one of the windows. Her reflection jumped back at him from the big, heavily framed mirror that sat on the floor against the wall across from the bed. Next to that was a fireplace where logs were already placed, just waiting for a match.

Her auburn hair was tousled around her shoulders and her expression was almost unbearably soft as she touched the flowers.

He felt a bead of sweat angling down his spine. He

shrugged out of the leather bomber jacket and pitched it across a chair in the corner that sat next to a small table with a reading lamp.

His brother had a faint smile on his lips as he ambled into the room after them. He set Deanna's suitcase on the floor at the foot of the bed. "Bathroom's attached through there," he gestured. "Extra blankets and pillows are in the closet, there. If you need anything else, just yell."

Drew figured that what Deanna needed was a separate bedroom, and was grateful as all get-out when she only smiled and quietly told his brother that everything was lovely and she was certain they'd be just fine.

"Right, then. See you at breakfast." J.R. stepped out of the room. He grinned. "Or not." He reached for the door and pulled it closed.

Alone, Deanna turned away from the pink roses and looked at Drew.

"I can't help it," he said in a low voice. "What do you want me to do? Tell him we don't sleep together?"

She made a face. "He'd never believe you weren't sleeping with any woman you brought with you, much less your own fiancée."

He almost felt himself flush, which was stupid. He was no kid. Of course he had sex with the women he saw.

That was pretty much all he had with the women he saw. It wasn't as if he was looking for a partner in life after all.

"Then I'll sleep on the floor if it makes you feel better."

"Not exactly comfy." She tapped her soft-soled boot on the hardwood floor and let out a huge breath. "We'll just have to make do with the bed." She shook her head and looked away. "At least it's huge," she added. "You could sleep a family of five in that thing."

It was definitely an exaggeration, but he let it pass. Because whatever she wanted to think, there would still only be the two of them on that soft-looking mattress.

And his imagination was becoming increasingly fertile.

Her hair would look like burning embers against that white, white comforter…

He cleared his throat a lot more easily than he did the images from his head. "It's been a long night. You go ahead and—" he waved toward the bed "—you know, go to sleep. I'm still too keyed up anyway. I'm going to go find J.R.'s whiskey."

The relief that filled her eyes would have been comical if it weren't so deflating. Just because—at the moment—he was having a hard time remembering the purpose of their engagement didn't mean that she was having the same problem.

"If you're sure…" She left the words hanging and he made himself nod.

He needed to be remembering how she'd acted the last time he'd been uncontrolled enough to kiss her and not how she'd felt, pressed against him in the limo.

Then she'd been clearly appalled, and he knew to this day that the only reason she hadn't quit on the spot was that she'd felt sorry for him because his mother had just died. That, and the fact that he'd sworn to her it would never happen again.

"Yeah," he lied. "I'm sure. Get some sleep. Tomorrow will be a busy day."

She looked at her watch. "Today will be a busy day, actually."

"Right. Today." He reached for the doorknob and quietly turned it. "Happy New Year, Dee."

Deanna's smile felt almost as shaky as her knees.

She knew it was best if he left for a little while, but a strong part of her wanted to ask him not to.

And that fact alone was reason enough to need some distance from her boss-slash-fiancé, even if it were only for a few minutes. So she kept the words to herself. "Happy New Year, Drew."

And then he was stepping out of the room, closing the door silently behind him.

Once he was gone, Deanna's smile died and she drew in a deep breath.

Without his intoxicating presence, the room felt as spacious as her common sense told her it actually was. It was only when she was closed in with him that it seemed as if the walls were only two inches from that big…wide…bed.

She caught her reflection in the oversize mirror. "This is what you get for making rash decisions," she whispered to herself.

The only response she got was her own glazed-looking expression staring back at her.

The silence of the house seemed to tick like the hands of a clock, and she grabbed her suitcase, hefting it onto the foot of the bed. Drew had given her a reprieve of sorts and she knew she'd better darn well use it wisely. The last thing she wanted was for him to come back and find her still standing around like some ninny who was afraid to climb into bed for what was left of a night's sleep.

She unfastened the stiff latches and flipped open the case, taking out the dress that she'd added on top of her other clothing. When they'd stopped at her apartment on the way to the airport, she'd done her level best to discourage Drew from accompanying her inside. But the man simply hadn't taken the hint and she hadn't exactly known how to tell him flat-out to stay in the car when she couldn't even come up with a plausible excuse.

So he'd walked up the iron-and-cement flight of stairs to her door and had braced herself for his comments when she'd let them in.

But all he'd done was silently glance over the stacks of shipping boxes that were crammed into her dining room, covering the floor and the small table and even the end of the couch. Boxes containing every item imaginable from small travel-size baby-food mills to closet organizers and exercise equipment that she'd taken from her mother's home to send back to the companies from which Gigi had ordered them.

He hadn't gaped. He hadn't even raised his eyebrows.

She'd been so grateful for that that she hadn't even thought to protest when he'd followed her down the short hallway to stand in the doorway of her bedroom while she'd opened her ancient suitcase that had already been packed for her spa weekend.

He'd told her that they would be in Texas for four days—through the weekend, and returning to San Diego on Wednesday. That didn't necessitate a lot of clothing, fortunately, because she didn't have much in her wardrobe that wasn't either kick-around-the house casual, or wear-to-work professional. She had sweats that she wore to the gym where she coached girls' volleyball in exchange for her membership fee, and she had jeans and shorts and suits.

But there wasn't much call for her to own dresses suitable for an afternoon wedding, and when she'd scooted through her assortment of hangers for the second time without finding anything she could imagine wearing, she'd looked over her shoulder at him and told him that he would be better off going to Texas alone. He could announce their engagement without her being there, couldn't he?

But he'd just given her that Drew look, the one that saw right through her excuses, and told her to pack one of her suits and to stop worrying about it.

"I'm not wearing something like this to a wedding." She'd shrugged out of her blazer and shook it at him. "This is for work."

"Well, even that might be debatable," he'd drawled, and had joined her in front of her tight closet. He'd reached in and pulled out a frothy thing shoved far to the side. "Wear this, then."

"What's that supposed to mean?"

"It means," he'd held the hanger up against her shoulders. "It doesn't look like something you'd wear to work. So? Good for a wedding or not?"

She hadn't been thinking about the dress. She'd been thinking about his comment about her suits. They fit and they were professional-looking and the complete opposite of the short skirts and clingy blouses that her fashionista mother preferred.

But knowing that the jet was waiting for them and not wanting to be the cause of their being any later than they already were, she hadn't pursued the matter.

And now, she held the dress up to her shoulders in much the same way that Drew had, and turned to look at herself in the mirror.

It was a vivid, bright pink for one thing, and with her hair, that wasn't a color she ever wore.

For another, it was ruffled.

Well, not exactly ruffled. The skirt was just made of dozens of pieces of fabric that all seemed to float independently of each other, making it look like it rippled even when she was holding it still. And the narrow, halter-style bodice was snug. And low.

She'd never worn it before.

For that matter, she hadn't bought it.

Gigi had. She'd given it to Deanna for her last birthday, and when Deanna had protested that it was too expensive—a more tolerable excuse than that the dress simply wasn't to Deanna's taste—her mother had produced the receipt to prove that the clearance-priced dress wasn't returnable. She'd lamented how her little Deedee just thrived on thwarting her and in the end, rather than go to battle over what was supposed to be a birthday gift, Deanna had taken the dress and put it in the back of her closet.

Where it had stayed. Lurking, as if it had been biding its time, waiting for Drew Fortune to find there.

Even as tired as she was, Deanna recognized the ridiculousness of the notion and she rubbed her eyes. At least the dress had come with a matching wrap. It was thin and almost translucent, but it would cover up her bare shoulders.

And as much as she didn't want to wear a dress chosen by her mother, she did have to admit that it was more suitable for the occasion than anything else her closet had contained. So she hung up the dress and its wrap behind the door that J.R. had indicated, and she made quick work of unpacking the rest of her items, most of which she left folded and tucked in one of the empty chest drawers. When the suitcase was empty, she wedged it out of the way in one corner of the closet on the floor, hung Drew's garment bag on the rack as far from her dress as was physically possible, and then turned to ponder his well-used duffel bag that was still sitting on the bed.

As his assistant, she really shouldn't have had any issue with simply unpacking his things for him. And as his fiancée, if she were one of the true variety, she wouldn't have had any issue, either.

Instead, she stared at the thing as if it would singe her fingers raw if she dared to unzip it.

In the end, she chickened out of dealing with it entirely, and transferred it from the foot of the bed to the chair in the corner.

Then she carried her small tote bag into the attached bathroom where she quickly washed her face and cleaned her teeth, changed into her cotton tank top and flannel pajama pants, and padded barefoot back to the bed.

Which side of the bed did Drew like?

She felt her skin flush just from having the question enter her mind and chewing on her lip, she jerked back the downy-light comforter to reveal crisp white sheets with a lovely embroidered edge.

She would have sighed with purely feminine appreciation for the beautiful, luxurious bedding if her heart hadn't felt like it had climbed up into her throat. As it was, she climbed into bed, keeping so close to the edge of the mattress that she was in danger of rolling off, only to realize that she'd forgotten to turn off the light.

She got out of bed again, turned on the light in the bathroom and pulled the door nearly closed so there was only a sliver of light showing, then turned off the bedroom lamp and returned to bed.

Her head sank into the fluffy pillows and she determinedly closed her eyes.

The image of Drew's face seemed burned into the back of her eyelids and she opened them again.

She was tired right down to her bones for a whole host of reasons, not the least of which was her boss.

Who was, sooner or later, going to be sharing this very bed with her.

She dragged the comforter up to her chin, but it still didn't block out the reality of it all and she trembled so hard suddenly that it was a wonder the bed didn't vibrate from it.

At this rate, it was going to be a very long four days.

## *Chapter Four*

"Guess you found what you were looking for." J.R.'s voice was quiet behind Drew where he was sitting in an alcove that overlooked the outdoor courtyard at the center of the house.

"You always do have the good stuff." Drew picked up the decanter of amber liquid and poured another finger into his squat, crystal glass. "Texas hasn't changed that, at least."

"Don't know what you have against Texas." J.R. folded his long body into a leather side chair. "You used to enjoy coming to Red Rock when you were a kid, too."

There'd been a lot of summer visits to the Double Crown Ranch where their father's cousin Ryan, and his wife, Lily, lived.

"Riding horses and fishing and playing at cowboy was all right when I was ten." Warmth slid down his throat as he sipped his brother's fine whiskey. "I still can't believe you gave up everything in L.A. to come and live here." If his brother hadn't resigned from Fortune Forecasting, he would have been in line to run the place.

Drew couldn't help wondering if William would have demanded that his eldest son toe up to the marriage line before handing the company over, or not.

But J.R. had resigned. He'd walked away from it all, so the question was now moot.

"I gained everything that matters to me when I came to Red Rock," J.R. said quietly.

"You mean Isabella, I suppose. But you barely knew her before you moved here."

His brother shrugged. "Isabella. The ranch. California was fine for its time, but this is home now. I can't imagine life anywhere else."

"You sound like you're channeling Dad," Drew muttered. He swirled the glass, watching the liquid glisten in the light from the small lamp he'd turned on next to his chair. "He acts as if life didn't begin for him until he left California, too."

He heard J.R. sigh. "That's not it at all."

"Isn't it?" Drew looked over at his brother. J.R. was forty-two, married to a woman ten years younger. Their father was seventy-five, still fit and still hardy—and planning to marry a woman ten years younger. "He had a life in California. Now he acts as if none of it matters."

"He acts as if he's ready to move on and live the rest of his life," J.R. countered. "Face it, Drew. He's happy. And just because he's marrying Lily doesn't mean he's forgotten Mom."

Drew stiffened. He didn't want to discuss their

mother. He particularly didn't want to think about the way William had thrown her memory in his face that morning when they'd argued about the company.

Strike that.

Yesterday morning.

It was past midnight. Officially New Year's Day.

And their father's wedding day.

He scrubbed his hand down his face and tossed back the rest of his drink.

"So for a guy who's been allergic to marriage ever since you told us things didn't work out the first time, how'd you come to be engaged to your assistant?"

Drew should have known better than to expect his brother to accept his engagement at face value and he supposed it was just as well to get some practice in early, before he faced the rest of the family—and their father—later that day at the wedding. "When you meet the right one, it doesn't matter what you thought you believed." It was true enough in a sense.

It was also something that his mother had told him more than once since his first—and until now, only—attempt at wedded bliss had quickly and miserably failed.

He could feel the weight of J.R.'s gaze.

"How soon did you know that Isabella was the right woman for you?"

"Almost immediately," J.R. said easily.

"So I'm not as quick on the uptake as you are."

"Hmm."

His brother's speculative tone made Drew warier than ever and he hunched forward and pushed out of the deep chair. "Guess I'd better let you catch some z's before breakfast." He lifted his empty glass. "Thanks for the hot milk."

He caught the wry tilt of J.R.'s smile from the corner of his eye as he headed back to the bedroom, stopping off at the kitchen only long enough to set his glass in the sink.

Unfortunately, the anesthetizing effects of his brother's expensive booze evaporated when Drew made it to the bedroom and silently pushed open the door.

The faint light from the bathroom cast a glow over the bed, but the bump of Deanna beneath the fluffy comforter on the side closest to the bathroom was barely visible, except for the cascade of her dark hair across the pillow. The sight did a bang-up job of refreshing the images that had sent him running out of the damn room in the first place.

He stood in the doorway for a while, waiting for her head to lift or for her to make some noise to indicate whether she was awake and knew he was hovering there.

But there wasn't the faintest whisper of movement from the bed and he figured that he'd better get inside the room before the breakfast bacon started sizzling. So he quietly stepped into the room and shut the door.

He'd never gone to such trouble before to keep a woman from waking. He'd never brought a woman to his own place in San Diego. It was always easier to go to hers, simply because it was always easier to leave.

He could make out the shape of his duffel bag sitting on the chair in the corner and it was only then that he realized he hadn't bothered packing any sort of pajamas or robe. He generally didn't bother with either, and when he'd shoved his clothes into his bag in the morning before going to the office, he certainly hadn't expected to be bringing a fiancée along.

He shoved his hands through his hair and wanted to

curse all over again at the situation his father had created. He unbuttoned his shirt and tossed it on the chair and winced at the thud of his shoes on the floor and jangling of his belt buckle when his pants followed the shirt.

He looked over at the bed.

Still no movement, thank God.

He wasn't sure how his ordinarily unflappable assistant would react if she woke up and saw him standing like a fool next to the bed, wearing nothing but his boxers and an erection, particularly after he'd assured her more times than he could count that their union would be entirely hands-off.

He let out a long breath and carefully lifted back the comforter and sheet and sat on the side of the bed. She still didn't move.

He rolled his eyes heavenward. If anyone who knew him could see him now, he'd never live it down.

Still moving at the speed of a sloth, he managed to stretch out on the mattress. More importantly, he managed not to groan in appreciation of the comfortable bed after the long, trying day.

He drew the covers over him and stared up into the dark shadows of the beamed ceiling.

He'd thought that once he got to Red Rock, the only thing he'd be able to think about was the looming specter of his dad getting married. But the warm presence of the woman lying within arm's reach of him had taken front and center. And as comfortable as the bed was, he figured it'd be highly unlikely for him to get any sleep that day.

He sighed and stretched out a little more, throwing his arm over his head and his knuckles accidentally rapped against the antique headboard.

The bedding rustled next to him and he clenched his teeth so tightly he'd probably need dental work.

"Drew?"

A fresh litany of curses went through his brain. "Sorry. Didn't mean to wake you up."

She turned on her side to face him and bunched her pillow under her cheek. He could feel her gaze as acutely as if she were pressing her cheek against him. "Are you all right?"

He was going to hell, sure as the sun was going to rise in a few hours, that's how he was. "I'm fine." His voice was short. "Go back to sleep."

Of course, she didn't. And the shadowed weight of her gaze simply continued boring into him.

He could stop that, simply enough. Just roll over and pull her into his arms. That would send her scurrying back to her own corner of the bed for certain.

"People get up early around here," he finally warned.

"I get up early at home." Her voice was even. "And much as I'd like to sleep, somehow it's difficult when you're two feet away, simmering like a pot on the stove."

There wasn't two feet between them. Not even close.

Drew would be better off if there were.

He even found himself strongly considering the wisdom of sleeping on the floor, but was damned if he'd move now. Who knew what she'd end up making of that.

"I'm not simmering," he muttered. A patent lie that she had the nerve to actually snort softly over.

Then she was shifting again, turning onto her back. She smoothed the comforter under her arms and he realized they were bare. He could see the creamy sheen of her skin from her fingertips right up her arms and over the curve of her shoulders until her hair blocked the view.

He closed his eyes.

Yup. Open the doors to Hades. He was moving in.

"Your brother has a really nice home."

"Yeah."

Merciful silence ticked for a few seconds.

"How much older is he than you?"

"Eight years."

"And your other brothers?"

He sighed. "You're not going to go to sleep, are you."

"Are you?"

He doubted the reasons for their wakefulness were even in the same library much less on the same page. "Nick's thirty-nine. He and Charlene have a baby. Matthew." The pictures that Nick emailed him of the little guy were cute as hell, even though Drew still had a hard time envisioning his brother as a family man. Drew had his reasons for being wary of marriage, but Nick had been a diehard bachelor from the womb. "He's a financial analyst at the Fortune Foundation."

Deanna shifted again. Now she was looking at him once more, her head propped on her hand.

The comforter fell away enough for him to realize she was wearing some skinny-strapped thing that was almost as pale as her skin.

And it didn't hide a damn thing the way her boxy suits did. The swell of her breasts was apparent.

He figured he ought to be grateful that the light from the bathroom was as faint as it was. But a strong part of him was wishing it weren't.

Which just proved what a hell-bound dog he was.

"That's a philanthropic organization, right?"

Who knew she'd be such a chatty Cathy in the wee hours of the morning when she was generally pretty quiet in the office?

Feeling way too warm, he shoved back the comforter, but kept the sheet in place. The light was dim, but he wasn't going to take any chances.

And every time he thought the simmering want inside of him was going to settle and cool down, something— like that clinging shirt of hers—just fueled the fire all over again.

"The foundation was begun in memory of Ryan Fortune. My dad's cousin." And his dad's fiancée's deceased husband.

He felt his jaw tighten again. Maybe his father should be worrying about how that would have sat with his wife instead of tossing her memory into Drew's face.

"Did you know him well?"

He dragged his thoughts together. "Well enough, I guess. Ryan was a good guy. Believed in good things. He was always trying to help others. Sharing what he considered his own good fortune. Maybe he's up there somewhere watching what the foundation does now." He didn't want to think what Ryan might be thinking about his own cousin marrying his wife. "The agency has grown a helluva lot more than anyone ever expected. It started out as a small storefront and now they've got a big building on the highway just outside of Red Rock."

"What about your other brothers?"

Fortunately, they were easier subjects. "Jeremy's three years older than me. You'll meet him at breakfast, no doubt. I'll be surprised if he stays past tonight after the wedding, though. Hardly anything keeps him away from his practice in Sacramento. He's an orthopedic surgeon." And no happier about William's impending marriage than Drew was.

"He's not married either, right?"

"Nope." Not for lack of trying from plenty of women, though, who seemed to find his workaholic brother's blue eyes as irresistible as his status as a surgeon.

"Then there's you," she quickly dipped her chin, nodding toward him.

The faint scent of green apple taunted him. "And Darr brings up the rear," he added abruptly.

"The firefighter."

"Yeah. He and Bethany have a little girl named Randi." Another cutie who looked just like her mother with wavy blond hair and big blue eyes.

He could appreciate cute kids as long as they weren't his own. Being an uncle suited him just fine.

"And who else should I know when we go to the wedding?"

"Does it matter?"

"It does if you want anyone to believe we're really… involved." She said the word as if it were something that should only be voiced if you were wearing hazmat gear.

He could relate.

"What about Lily?" she continued. "The bride? She was married to Ryan Fortune and you've said that he was a good guy. What's she like?"

Drew had liked her just fine until his dad had lost all sense over her. "I always thought she was devastated when Ryan died."

"How long ago was that?"

He didn't even have to calculate. "Six years ago." Just two years before his mother had died.

And not long after that, neither Lily's nor William's supposed devastation over the losses of their spouses had seemed to matter quite so much.

They'd gotten involved and according to his father, William would have married Lily a year ago if it weren't for Lily's insistence that they give Drew and his brothers some time to adjust to the situation.

As if that was likely to happen.

"Will it be a large wedding?"

"There's likely to be a lot of guests, I suppose."

"You don't know?"

"It's not like I'm supposed to stand up there with them. J.R.'s acting as his best man."

"That's nice." She lowered her head finally, resting it on her arm on top of the pillow. "You, um, seem to get along well with J.R."

"Yeah."

"And your other brothers?"

"Yeah." He wondered where she was heading.

But all she did was make a soft little sound that had a ripple working down his spine. "I always thought it would be nice to have a large family."

"Growing up, it had its moments," he allowed. And even though they'd all kind of gone along their own paths when they'd become adults, Drew supposed he was still pretty close to his brothers. They might not see each other all that often—not with J.R. and Nick and Darr all living in Red Rock, while he and Jeremy were still in California—but they managed to keep up with each other's lives all the same.

"There are a boatload of cousins, too," he added. "My dad's brother Patrick and his wife and all of them will probably be around. You won't get a chance to meet my aunt Cindy, though." He hadn't asked for details about the wedding, but William had offered up that information. "She's only a few years younger than dad, but she's probably still out there sowing wild oats somewhere. Total character." It was easy enough to appreciate when she was his aunt. As a mother to her four kids, though, Drew knew she'd seriously left something to be desired. Nurturing, she wasn't.

Which made him think about Deanna's mother. "What are you going to tell your mother?"

She rolled onto her back again and pulled the comforter up to her chin. "Nothing until I have to." She evidently didn't feel like she was in danger of overheating just because they were in the same bed. "And then nothing more than I have to."

He very nearly asked her then about her father, but she yawned widely and rolled again, until her back was toward him and he swallowed his curiosity. As far as he could recall, he'd never heard Deanna mention the man.

He didn't know if her father was alive or dead or even if he'd ever been a part of her life at all.

When it came down to it, his assistant knew a lot more about his life than he did about hers.

It wasn't a point that had ever bothered him much before, but now, it niggled at him.

But he said no more about it. He and Deanna might not be involved "that" way, but he was smart enough to know that when a woman—any woman—turned her back like that, it was definitely the end of the conversation as far as she was concerned.

So he just stared into the shadows until he heard

the cadence of her breathing finally change. Slow. Lengthen.

Only then did he finally manage to close his eyes and get some peace from his troubled thoughts. But a short while later, when he felt the soft shape of his sleeping companion brush against him, he was wide-awake again.

And his troublesome body seemed doomed to keep him there.

She was roasting.

Deanna kicked at her blankets, only realizing when her bare feet encountered the silky smooth texture of expensive cotton sheets that she wasn't in her own bed in her own apartment.

She went stock still, staring at the window across from her.

Shutters were closed across it, but sunlight was sneaking around the dark, wood slats.

It wasn't the sunlight that had her attention, though.

It was the warm, hair-roughened, sinewy arm that was lying heavily over her waist. And it was the long-fingered hand that belonged to that arm that was cupping her breast.

She sank her teeth into her bottom lip. She would have held her breath, if she could. But her heart was suddenly pounding so fast that she didn't seem able to even accomplish that.

But when she realized that her nipples were tightening and Drew's thumb was lazily brushing across it, she gingerly wrapped her hand around his wrist and started to push his hand away from her.

He mumbled something and simply tightened his arm around her waist and she found herself sliding against the smooth sheet until the entire back side of her was pressed against him.

She might have taken comfort in the fact that his hand had strayed away from her breast to press flat against her belly, except that it had snuck beneath the edge of her camisole and was pressing flat against her bare skin.

And all of him was pressing hard against the back of her.

She swallowed a squeak and scrabbled at his arm again. "Let go."

He mumbled something again, then his arm mercifully lightened up around her as he rolled back. "Geez, Dee. Can't you let a guy sleep?"

She scrambled out of the bed, dragging down the hem of her camisole with one hand and shoving back her tumbled hair with her other. The diamond ring on her finger felt heavy and wholly unfamiliar as it tangled in her hair.

"Don't geez me," she countered, yanking her hand free. "What is wrong with you?"

His hair was falling over his forehead and his angular jaw was heavily shadowed. Against the backdrop of the pristine, white bedding, he looked dark and dangerous and utterly, totally seductive. Particularly when he focused a heavy-lidded gaze on her face. The corner of his lips kicked up, adding to his devilish appeal. "Evidently, nothing."

Her cheeks felt as if they were on fire. She wasn't naive enough to think that she, personally, had anything to do with that...well...what she'd felt pressing insistently against her backside. "Obviously, we'll have to do something about, um, about this."

He lifted an eyebrow. "Oh, yeah?"

She flushed even harder. "Not that."

"This. That." His grin widened. "You've always been so good with descriptions, Dee, but right now you're outdoing yourself."

She crossed her arms tightly, even though it was too late to hope that he hadn't already taken in the rigid points of her nipples that she knew had to be plainly visible through the snug cotton knit of her cami. For heaven's sake, he'd had his hand there! "I'm glad that you're so amused by me. You know good and well I meant our sleeping arrangements."

He smiled outright, and annoyed as much with him as she was with her damnable weakness where he was concerned, she huffed and strode into the bathroom, slamming the door shut behind her.

When she heard his laugh through the door, she would have locked it, too, if the thing had possessed one.

Instead, she caught her reflection in the mirror over the sink.

"You are in trouble here," she accused softly.

"Did you say something?"

She nearly jumped out of her skin. Drew's voice was so clear she suspected he was standing right on the other side of the door. "No!"

"Sounded like you did."

She felt around the entire door handle and still found no lock. He wouldn't walk in on her, would he?

It seemed unfathomable.

But then she never could have imagined that she'd wake up with his arms wrapped around her body, either.

Well, no. That wasn't strictly true, either. She could imagine it.

But she just hadn't really expected it to ever happen.

"Deanna?"

She swallowed and raked her hair back from her face. "I, um—" She cleared her throat and spoke a little more loudly. "I was just promising myself coffee soon." She winced at the poor excuse. She didn't even drink coffee.

"O-kay." He plainly didn't believe her, but at least he didn't make more of the matter than he already had. "I'm gonna go see if we slept right through breakfast."

"All right." She turned on the tap and water rushed into the sink, but she crept back to the door and listened against it. She felt like an idiot, but she didn't relax the least bit until she heard the sound of the bedroom door creaking open and then closing again.

She very nearly slid down the wall into a pile of mush.

Only the fear that he could be back sooner rather than later kept her moving and she practically tore open her tote bag, pulling out her shampoo and cosmetics. She raced through the shower, barely allowing herself enough time to appreciate the luxurious spray of water— twice as hot and twice as full as her miserly shower back home—before she was stepping out again onto the thick, woven bath mat. She wrapped a fluffy white towel around herself and tucked in the end as tightly as the plush thickness would allow.

She raked the tangles out of her hair with her comb and managed to put on her makeup using the only corner of the mirror that hadn't steamed up. Not that she wore much in the way of makeup. She rarely did. But there was to be a wedding that day, so she added a touch more eye shadow and blush than she normally used, and hoped it was good enough to cover the fact that there were shadowy circles under her eyes from too little sleep.

Fortunately, there was still no sound of Drew's return and she plugged in her blow-dryer and made just as fast work out of getting her thick hair dry and lying smooth and flat against her shoulders. It was actually a little long. She was long overdue for a trim, but she'd been saving up for her New Year's weekend with her friends.

So much for that.

She tucked everything back into her small tote and stowed it on the empty shelf below the one that held the towels and walked back into the bedroom, tightening the towel again. She was just pulling fresh panties out of the drawer where she'd stowed them when the bedroom door creaked softly and she whirled around.

Drew, wearing jeans and nothing else, gave her a look that seemed just as shocked.

"Coffee," he muttered and extended his arm and the sturdy, brilliant red mug he was holding.

She'd worked for the man for four years. She'd personally fixed and served him countless pots of coffee during that time. Knew that he liked it stronger than most people preferred, and that only when he was nursing a hangover did he want any sugar added.

Clearly, he'd never noticed that not once had she ever had any coffee herself.

But that's what she got for lying.

If the worst thing that happened that weekend was having to choke down a cup of the vile stuff, she supposed it was a small price to pay, particularly when a part of her was ogling the hard, cut lines of his abdomen.

So she managed a smile and reached out to take

the mug, only realizing then that her panties were still clutched in her fist. She flushed and pitched them back into the drawer then reached for the coffee mug again. "Thanks."

Unfortunately, when she reached, the tucked towel gave way.

And all she could do was stand there, frozen, as the thick, thick towel fell right to the hardwood floor beneath her bare feet.

## Chapter Five

Hell and damnation.

The oath exploded inside Drew's head just as quickly as it passed his lips when that white towel seemed to hit the ground almost in slow motion where it mounded around Deanna's bare feet and slender ankles.

He knew only a second had passed before they were both reaching down for the thing, but what he'd seen in that second was blistered into his brain.

No. Not even blistered. Because a blister would heal and disappear.

More like tattooed.

Because the image of her sleek figure was not likely to leave his mind. Ever.

His hand reached the towel, only to collide with hers. Realizing his gaze was straying back to the expanse of creamy, tanned skin that covered her from shoulders to toes—save a few intriguingly tiny, pale triangles—he let her take the towel as they straightened, and instead concentrated on the depths of the rich coffee that Isabella had prepared. He never would have figured his assistant for a bikini type, but he damn sure could recognize the source of those tan lines.

"Sorry." His voice came out like chunks of gravel, and he coughed. "I didn't mean to startle you."

Deanna was looking anywhere but at him. She was holding the towel so tightly around herself that her fingers were nearly white. "No. It's my fault. I, um, I—" she broke off and shook her head. Her hair bounced against her bare shoulders. "This is what I get for lying," she mumbled.

"It was a simple accident." He reached past her, aware of the way she jumped when he did so, and set the coffee mug on top of the chest. "Once we're married and living together—"

"Living together!"

He frowned, looking through the half-closed door out into the hallway. Fortunately, the only sounds he could hear were the laughter and voices coming from the other side of the house where everyone else was still gathered in the kitchen.

He closed the door.

"Yeah, living together." Only by some pity from God was he able to keep his eyes focused on her face. "That's what generally happens when couples marry." He kept his voice low. The adobe-looking walls were probably thick here, but he didn't want to take any chances.

"We—" her free hand waved between them "—are not a couple," she reminded.

He caught that waving hand and held it up between them. The diamond on her finger sent prisms of light dancing around the walls. "For all intents and purposes, we became one when I put this rock on your finger. What the hell kind of marriage do you think it would look like we have if we don't live together after the I dos? For that matter, it's already striking some of them as odd that we're not already doing so."

She yanked her hand out of his. "Tell them I'm old-fashioned." Her voice was shaky and she looked away from him again only to suddenly shove the chest drawer closed.

But that was a little like trying to undo the whole towel-drop thing.

He'd already seen the hanks of ribbon and sheer lace lying neatly inside.

And because he'd seen, up close and personally, the stunningly perfect body they'd be covering, he had a double dose of fresh torment for his overactive mind.

"That's exactly what I told Jeremy," he said. "That you're old-fashioned." And for some reason, his brother had found that statement riotously funny.

Isabella had simply smiled serenely as she'd set a platter of bacon and sausage on the table between them that she and Evie—the housekeeper and cook that his brother had brought with him from L.A.—had reheated for him because he'd overslept everyone else by a good three hours, and said she thought "old-fashioned" was still a good trait to possess.

"Great." Deanna made a face. "Now they'll wonder even more what on earth you're doing, supposedly marrying me."

"What do you want me to say, Deanna?" He was frustrated on so many levels that he couldn't keep it out of his voice.

"I don't know!" She turned away, still clutching the towel around her like a drowning person clutched a life vest. She sat down on the edge of the bed, only to bounce back up and move away from it, too.

Irritation joined frustration. "I'm not likely to attack you, for God's sake. Just because we woke up the way we did doesn't mean I don't have some self-control."

"I didn't say you didn't."

"You were the one cozying up to me in your sleep, you know," he added. "Now you're acting like a virginal nun who's afraid to be alone with a man."

She went red. The color spread from the tips of her ears behind which she'd tucked her shining hair to the hollow at the base of her throat, over her smooth, toned shoulders and right down beyond the edge of the towel cinched above her breasts.

He actually found himself watching her shapely calves below the towel to see if she blushed there, as well.

And then horror dawned on him, and he barely kept himself from swearing all over again. "You're not, are you?" Just because she'd covered up all that glory of a body with her ugly suits at the office didn't mean she had kept the wonders from her boyfriend.

What had she said his name was?

Mike? Mark?

He realized he was pretty much hating the other guy right about now, which was ludicrous.

Drew didn't do jealousy.

He hadn't when the woman he'd vowed to love until death did them part cheated on him with his best friend, so why the hell was he feeling that way now when he thought about a guy who Deanna had already admitted she was no longer even seeing?

Her lips had pinched together. "No, I'm not a virgin," she said witheringly. "Not that it's any of your business."

"Why the hell not? You know all about my love life."

"That's because you bring it into the office," she exclaimed, her arms flying out to her sides. "And expect me to help you get rid of them when they no longer amuse you."

"I don't do that," he dismissed.

She gave him an "Oh, really?" look that was just as effective as any similar ones he'd gotten from his mother growing up whenever he'd tried to claim innocence over some infraction. He would have run his finger around his too-tight collar if he'd been wearing a shirt. Instead, all he could do was grimace and try not to shift his feet like some damn guilty kid.

"Okay, so I've had you order some pieces of jewelry for me," he allowed.

"Humph. You order so much from Zondervan's that when you asked for this—" she held up her hand and wiggled the ring on her finger "—they jumped to help you out!"

"So?" His voice tightened defensively. "At least I don't have my assistant break up with the girls I date! I'm not that big a crumb."

She exhaled noisily, the fight seeming to go out of her in one big rush. "You're not a crumb." She sat back down again on the bed. She gave him a sidelong look, and actually managed to stay sitting there, though she did rearrange the edges of the towel to cover her knees.

He considered telling her that it was too late for her to bother covering much of anything now that he'd seen it all.

In glorious, God-given, high-definition detail.

Maybe he should be running Hades instead of just moving in. It might suit him better even than running Fortune Forecasting.

Drew Fortune, vice president of hellfire and damnation.

"It's just the situation," she said, drawing him back to terra firma. "It's making me a little—or a lot—crazy."

He would have sat down beside her, but common sense warned him it would be better all around if he didn't.

And because his common sense felt in dangerously short supply, he figured he'd better pay attention when it did rear its head.

"It's only for a few days," he assured, speaking to himself as much as to her. "Then we'll go back home and things can get back to normal."

"Until we have to come up with a wedding and move in together," she countered in a low voice. "What if people ask if we've set a wedding date? What are we supposed to tell them, then?"

"We'll tell them we're still deciding on a date. Hell, we'll tell them we're planning a quick trip to Vegas. I don't know, all right? We'll think of something."

She gave him a quick, narrow look. "You're not breaking out into a rash or anything are you? I mean, we are tossing around the terms marriage and wedding quite a bit here."

"Smart aleck." But at least she'd recovered her equanimity enough to razz him about it.

That at least was something they were both comfortable with. He teased her about being completely anal when it came to details around the office and she gave him heck about everything else.

It was the constant in their relationship.

And now, now he'd had to go and remember what he'd spent nearly four years trying to forget.

That Deanna Gurney wasn't just a stellar assistant.

She was a desirable woman.

And as far as everyone else in Red Rock was concerned, she was ostensibly his woman.

It was ironic as anything in life could be that she was even more off-limits than she'd ever been, thanks to the agreement they'd struck.

Not only could he still remember how it had felt to kiss her four years ago, but now he had the Technicolor image of her body indelibly etched in his head, and his skin still felt singed from the heat of her body in his arms.

"We'll work things out," he finally said.

She was looking down at her hands, spread flat on her lap. "Promise?"

"I do. Promise, that is." He smiled crookedly when she looked at him and was glad to see the small one she gave him in return. "Drink your coffee if it's not gone cold," he urged. "I don't know what Isabella puts in it, but it's pretty good."

She pressed her lips together for a moment. "Okay."

"And I'll go find something to do for thirty minutes. Is that enough time for you to finish dressing?"

At that, her smile did widen. Wryly. "Five minutes would do."

In his experience, he hadn't met a woman who could dress that quickly.

Undress, sure.

His gaze kept straying to the hollow at the base of

her throat. He'd never realized before just how sexy that spot was...

"Drew?"

He shook off the haze that encroached on him way too easily and reached behind him for the door. "Fifteen minutes, then. After I shower and change, we'll probably have to head off for the church, but you can still grab some food from the kitchen while I'm getting ready. There was stuff left after I ate, and I know Isabella is looking forward to meeting you."

Which just had her looking worried all over again.

"Don't worry. There're all gonna love you," he assured. And before he could say anything else that would either worry her more or set them back on the sex track where they had no business running, he let himself out of the room and closed the door.

The sooner they got through his father's wedding and the next few days and they could get back to San Diego and some normalcy, the better.


"So there's the newly engaged!"

The loud greeting was called across the expanse of lawn between the crowded parking lot and the church when they arrived nearly two hours later.

Deanna felt Drew's hand tighten around hers as they crossed the grass leading up to a lovely, old-fashioned-looking church. It was white with a tall steeple, and outside, the building was surrounded by an expanse of emerald-green lawn and lush greenery dotted with pink and red flowers. There were garlands of green and white wound around the railings of shallow steps leading up to the wooden double doors, which were bedecked with wreaths of even more flowers.

And for the first time since the debacles of the

morning, she was able to forget everything but that moment.

Mostly.

The feel of Drew's hand wrapped around hers wouldn't let her completely forget.

Still, the sight of the church was like something out of a magazine. Or a fantasy. "It's beautiful," she breathed.

"Too bad it'll be the sight of Dad's worst mistake," Drew said in a low tone.

"Judging by the happy looks I'm seeing on people's faces, they don't share your view," Deanna pointed out, just as low. "Just promise me you won't stand up and shoot off a flare gun when the minister asks if there's anyone present who objects."

They'd driven into town by themselves, using one of the trucks from Molly's Pride and judging by the scarcity of available parking spots and the number of people milling around on the grass outside the church, they weren't exactly beating any early arrival records.

Not surprising, given Drew's continuing displeasure with the entire affair.

"That's Nick," he told her as he lifted his free hand in a wave toward the guy who'd called out the greeting.

She would have guessed that, from the description that Drew had given her of his brothers. Nick was about the same height as Drew, although a little more leanly built. But he had the same brown hair and as they got closer, she realized, the same brown eyes. More specifically, though, it was the pretty redhead who stood beside him with a baby on the hip of her narrow blue sheath dress that helped identify him.

"And Darr, presumably, is standing beside him?"

"Yeah."

The youngest Fortune brother was not quite as tall as Nick, but he was stocky and muscular. He was also wearing a string tie with his blinding-white shirt and dark suit, while his brothers wore traditional ones with theirs, and he had a cowboy hat on his head.

Drew had told her that Darr was the most "Texan" of the Fortune transplants to Red Rock, and the seriously good-looking man was definitely living up to that. Particularly when he doffed his hat once she and Drew stopped in front of him and greeted her with a "ma'am," an up-and-down look that told her he was taking her measure and a grin that she hoped meant he wasn't entirely disappointed with the results.

She shouldn't care so much whether Drew's family liked her, but she did, and hoped her smile was not as shaky as it felt when they reached the group. All eyes seemed to turn toward her as Drew began naming off the players before lifting her hand that he was holding. "And this is Deanna Gurney."

"Your fiancée. That news made it around the family by the time the sun came up this morning." Bethany, the petite blue-eyed blonde holding Darr's hand, gave her a dimpled smile.

"Thank God we had time to get over the shock," Nick drawled, giving Deanna a quick, charming wink, and everyone laughed.

"Oh, you." Bethany shushed him with a wiggle of her fingers as she turned to Deanna and caught her unaware in a quick hug. "We're all just so happy for you." She stepped back and her eyes twinkled. She could have been made from spun sugar, she had such a sweet face. "You look radiant. I love that shade of pink on you. I can never get away with anything darker than this." She dashed her hand over her soft pink dress. "I just look all washed out."

Deanna managed to get out a "Thank you." She thought that "neon" might be more appropriate than "radiant" given the vivid color of her dress, but it was the only compliment she'd received since she'd put it on. Drew had only given her a sort of stunned look when he'd joined her in the great room after he was finished getting ready himself.

Because she'd been a little busy trying not to swallow her tongue at the sight of him in his perfectly tailored black suit, white shirt and pale gray tie with his hair ruthlessly combed back from his handsome face, she had just quickly set aside the hot tea that she'd made for herself and pointed out the keys that J.R. had left behind for them, and they were off.

Bethany had turned to Drew, pulling his head down to plant a kiss on his cheek. "But you're a rascal, Andrew. You had me convinced that you were positively allergic to marriage!"

Deanna's gaze collided with his over his sister-in-law's softly waving hair and she hoped that she was the only one who saw the irony in his eyes. "What can I say?" He patted Bethany's shoulder as she stepped back to make room for Charlene—Nick's red-haired wife—and her similar greeting.

Drew gently chucked the baby Charlene was holding under the chin, earning a chortling giggle, and Deanna barely managed not to stare.

For some reason, she'd never thought what Drew would be like around little ones, but to watch him now, he seemed much more natural than she'd have expected.

He looked at Bethany. "And where's your munchkin?"

"She's off with Josh. You get Randi anywhere within ten feet of Brandon and Maribel and she wants nothing more to do with her own mama and daddy."

Bethany turned to Deanna again. "Randi is actually Miranda. Our two-year-old. But she moves so fast these days, we started shortening up her name." She grinned. "And Brandon is Josh's little boy. He's—Josh, that is—is Frannie's oldest and Maribel is Frannie's youngest."

Even though Deanna had tried to get a primer on the family names from Drew, she still felt lost.

"Frannie's one of my cousins," Drew provided, evidently recognizing her failure to keep up. "Josh is her son. Frannie and her husband, Roberto Mendoza, have been helping Josh raise Brandon."

"Ah." She nodded, managing to follow the branches of the family tree her mind was drawing. "Mendoza? Isn't that Isabella's—"

"Yeah. They're distant cousins. And those are the rest of the Fortune cousins over there. Frannie's brothers." He pointed toward a trio of men and a woman standing near the steps leading up to the church doors. "The guy leaning against the railing is Ross. He's Aunt Cindy's oldest. He's the P.I. I told you about, and the brunette with him is his wife, Julie. They got married a year ago. Cooper's next. Brown hair, no hat. He's worked on ranches all around the U.S. pretty much, but doesn't spend a helluva lot of time here. So I understand anyway. And then there's Flint. Black hat. Has a spread in upstate New York. And, I don't see Frannie anywhere around." He slid his arm so casually around Deanna's shoulder that she almost didn't startle. "She's the youngest of them and the only girl," he added.

"You talking about Frannie? I just saw her inside with Lily," Jeremy provided, walking up to them.

Deanna had already met him at J.R.'s while Drew had been getting ready and had immediately liked the somewhat soft-spoken surgeon. She had the feeling he didn't say anything until he knew exactly what he was talking about.

It was something Deanna practiced herself, and usually succeeded at, except when she was dealing with Drew.

Only then did that particular trait seem to completely desert her.

"Has Dad arrived yet?" Jeremy asked. He shot his cuffs and glanced around, his blond hair gleaming in the sunlight.

"Haven't seen him," Nick provided.

"Maybe he's come to his senses," Drew said.

"Thought you'd have given up on that by now," Darr said, giving Drew and Deanna a pointed look. "Dad's in love with Lily. And she's in love with him. Maybe if you spent more than two days a year around here you'd see that for yourself." He looked down at Bethany when she put a hand on his arm.

"Dad's driving himself over from the hotel," Nick said, his tone calm. "He probably went in the church through the back. J.R.'s in there already. There's a room they quarantine the groom in so he doesn't see his bride before it's time."

Charlene swatted him with her hand. "Quarantine," she chided with a smile. "I love it that William and Lily chose New Year's Day for their wedding. I think it's a perfect way to start their life together. And who could ask for a more beautiful day?" She started to shift little

Matthew in her arms, but Nick lifted the tot and held him up to his shoulder.

"You think any day is a perfect day for a wedding," he teased.

Deanna had to bite back a little sigh of envy. The fact that he adored his wife was as plain as the nose on his face. And holding that little baby just added to the appeal. "It is lovely out," she said. "It's warmer than I expected it to be." She'd thought she might be chilly with only the sheer length of fabric that matched her dress wrapped around her shoulders, but the sun was bright in the mildly cloudy sky and there was barely even enough breeze to tickle the floating fabric of her skirt.

"Well, well, cuz." A deep voice came from behind them and Drew and Deanna turned to see Cooper Fortune ambling toward them, a grin on his ruggedly handsome, weathered face. "Ross just told me the news. Guess your claim that once was more than enough didn't stick after all." He swept up Deanna's hand and pressed a kiss to the back of it. "You sure you know what you're getting yourself into with this guy, little lady?"

Her nerves prickled and she quickly glanced at Drew. She still hadn't forgotten his comment about putting his head in a marriage nose "again" and felt shocked all over again at the evidence that he'd obviously been married at one point.

But all he said was, "Don't try charming my girl." He was grinning at his cousin, either oblivious to or choosing to ignore Deanna's questioning gaze. "Damn, Coop. You get uglier every year."

"Older, too," Coop allowed wryly. He also had what Deanna was coming to think of as the Fortune brown eyes.

"Honey, why don't we go check on the groom?"

Bethany looked at Drew. "It's about time for things to be getting started, isn't it?"

"Actually—" Charlene was looking at the delicately jeweled watch on her wrist "—it's a little late." She looked around at the guests milling about. "Honestly, I don't even recognize half the people here. Can you believe the turnout?" She tucked her hand around Nick's arm. "Maybe we should start moving inside. Give people a start."

Thinking that Charlene had the right idea, Deanna took a step after them along with the rest, but Drew slid his hand down her arm from her shoulder—an act that made her shiver beneath her thin wrap—and caught her hand, staying her.

"No hurry," he said.

No hurry for him, he meant, but considering the others who were still easily within earshot, she kept the thought to herself.

But as soon as the others were far enough away, having reached the stone walkway circling the church, she pinned him with a look.

"Once was more than enough?" she repeated. "You have been married before, haven't you. When?"

"Does it matter?"

"Uh…yeah." She wanted to pinch him. "If I had a former spouse around somewhere don't you think it'd be odd if I hadn't mentioned him to you, particularly now?" She held up her hand and nudged the diamond ring with her thumb. "What was her name? What happened?"

He grimaced. "Paula. It was right after college. And it lasted for the sum total of three months."

Even though she'd been prepared, she still felt stunned hearing him confirm that he had been married before. Her mouth suddenly felt like she was sucking on a lemon. "Three months. The usual expiration date. Have you ever been with a woman longer than that before tiring of her?"

"Other way around." His voice went flat. "She tired of me."

"Who on earth would get tired of you?" she exclaimed and promptly felt her face go hot.

"The woman I married, obviously, which was made very plain to me when I found her getting busy in our bed with my best friend."

She was floored. "You're serious."

His jaw canted to one side for a moment before centering again. "Unfortunately."

A wave of sympathy plowed over her for the young man he'd been. "And you were just out of college. How awful for you."

He just grimaced and looked as if he wished she'd drop the matter altogether.

"And your family obviously knows what happened. I can't believe your cousin was insensitive enough to bring it up like that."

"All they know is that it didn't work out."

She stared. "You...didn't tell them why?"

"And prove what a miserable judge of women I was?"

"Drew..."

"It's ancient history." His voice was short. "I was briefly married. It didn't work out. End of story."

"But it's not." She moved into his path when he took a step toward the church. "You know, ever since we arrived in Red Rock, I've been trying to figure out what instilled such a vehement dislike of marriage in you. I'd always just assumed it had something to do with your growing up—trouble between your mom and dad or something—but then I met J.R. and it's obvious that there's no tension between any of you. And aside from Jeremy—who hasn't said much of anything about the wedding—you're the only one here who isn't openly happy for your father. But now it all makes sense. She broke your heart."

He smoothed down his tie. "Don't start painting a sentimental glaze over it."

Her stomach tensed. "Do you still love her?"

"Hell, no." His voice rose and he glanced around, but nobody was paying them any heed. Everyone was still focused on filing through the opened double doors of the church.

But then his eyes narrowed and Deanna turned to see what had garnered his attention. All she could see was the crowd of people.

But then she realized that one woman in particular was making her way out of the church. She was dressed in a silvery-blue dress that even from several yards away, Deanna could see suited the breathtakingly beautiful woman.

"What's Frannie doing?" Drew mused.

So that was the other cousin. Deanna realized she shouldn't be surprised at the woman's magazine-perfect looks. To a one, all the Fortune men that she'd met had received ample blessings from the genetic pool of good looks.

"I'd say she's looking for someone," Deanna guessed and quickly fell into step when Drew headed toward Frannie.

When they neared, she realized that the cheerful noise of the guests as they'd collected had muted into hushed whispers and furtive glances.

Drew's hand caught hers in a tight grip. He, too, had noticed the mood shift.

They made their way through the people and joined Nick and Darr and their wives who'd joined Frannie.

"What's wrong?" Drew asked.

Frannie looked at him. Her eyes were plainly worried. "We can't find William."

## Chapter Six

Three hours later, the groom was still missing.

All the guests had departed, but the family members were still inside the church, either pacing between the pews that were bedecked with clusters of hydrangeas and white roses that matched the enormous sprays decorating the chancel, or sitting in them.

In the rear of the church where the double doors had been closed against the afternoon as well as the departed guests, Bethany was sitting on the floor, her lovely dress spread around her crossed legs as she held Charlene and Nick's baby in her lap and rolled a ball back and forth to her little Randi, keeping the active toddler more or less content.

At the front of the church where she ought to have stood with Drew's father exchanging their marriage vows, Lily was pacing, her long hands twisting together around the cell phone she was clutching.

Every few minutes for the past few hours, she'd held up the small phone and peered at it or dialed it, and every few minutes later, she'd clutch it at her waist again, and pace some more.

She wore high, caramel-tinted ivory pumps that added even more height to her long-limbed figure, and with her dark, sultry features she looked much younger than the sixty-five that Deanna knew her to be. Her dark hair was pinned into a twist with tiny roses at the back of her head that were matched in style with the rose-patterned embroidered lace that covered her bodice and worked its way down into points over the full, wide tea-length skirt. It would have looked like a party dress right out of the '50s except for the color—cream with a hint of coffee added to it—that seemed to add a thoroughly modern edge.

Despite the woman's obvious strain, Deanna could hardly tear her gaze from Lily. She looked elegant and stylish and so lovely that it was heartbreaking to know her groom had seemingly disappeared from the face of the planet.

And then a side door opened and Lily whirled.

Her expression fell, though, when it was Darr and Drew who entered the sanctuary.

"I've checked with the police," Darr said without preamble. "There's been no report of accidents in the vicinity of Red Rock. Closest thing was a single car accident a good seventy miles out, on the highway heading toward Haggarty."

Lily paled but Darr lifted his hand. "There was only one person involved, a woman." He looked solemn. "She didn't make it, but that has nothing to do with Dad, Lily. There've been no emergency calls out of Red Rock, and no incidents between here and San

Antonio. I've got some friends at the firehouse who've promised to recheck all the hospitals in a few hours." He shook his head. "Drew checked the hotel where Dad was staying."

Drew sat on the edge of front pew next to Deanna. "His suitcase was packed and sitting on his bed like he was ready to put it in his car," he told them. "But nobody who works there remembers seeing him leave this morning and he definitely didn't check out."

"Lily, why don't you sit down," Isabella suggested softly, stepping into Lily's path to stop her pacing for at least a moment. Like Lily, Isabella had a river of dark brown hair, though hers was a straight sheet down the back of her vibrant, red dress. Deanna was glad to see that Isabella gently maneuvered the cell phone out of Lily's hand.

She might have surrendered the fruitless device, but the older woman just shook her head and continued pacing. "Something has happened," she fretted. "I know William. He was looking forward to this day as much as I was. He could be sick somewhere or…" She shook her head again, her voice trailing off.

Deanna slid a glance toward Drew beside her, but he didn't comment. His thoughts looked far away.

"Of course he was looking forward to being your husband," Isabella soothed. "It's practically all he's talked about for the past few years. We'll figure everything out soon." Her head lifted when J.R. came through the same door that Drew had used. J.R. had driven out to the Double Crown where the wedding reception was to have been held to see personally if there'd been any news there. William had already moved in with Lily, though he'd evidently checked into a hotel to observe the propriety of not seeing his bride on the day before the ceremony.

But J.R. just shook his head. "I told the caterer they could go ahead and pack up." He eyed Lily. "I didn't think you needed to have to deal with that, too."

"Thank you, dear." Lily turned to face the simple wooden cross that hung above the chancel area. Her shoulders slowly lifted and fell. "Ever since I lost Ryan I've felt that he's been there, still watching out for us all." Lily's voice was husky. "I have to still believe that."

Deanna blinked hard and looked away.

But a moment later, the bride had turned around to face them. Her expression was drawn, but her chin was lifted. "I do still believe that. But there's no purpose to hanging around here." She stepped down the three shallow steps leading up to the chancel and her beautiful gown swayed slightly around her shapely ankles. "The caterer won't take away the food. So if anyone is hungry, they should come out to the Double Crown. Nothing will be solved by any of us collapsing from hunger." She looked toward Isabella. "Would you be so kind and let the reverend know we're finally getting out of the way so the custodian and groundskeeper can clean up around here? I know they still need to prepare for regular services tomorrow." She cradled her hand around the spray of flowers decorating the end of the pew were Deanna and Drew were sitting. "If any of you want some flowers, take them. They're too lovely to waste."

Not surprisingly, nobody seemed inclined to enjoy the flowers now, beautiful or not.

Drew pushed to his feet beside her. "Has anyone considered the notion that something else might have happened to Dad?"

Deanna sucked in a breath. "Drew—" He surely wouldn't offer the suggestion that William had changed his mind, would he?

He shook his head sharply, though, and she fell silent. She hadn't seen such an expression on his face since the morning she'd gotten to the office early and found him sitting at his desk with an empty bottle of whiskey beside him, looking at a photograph of his mother.

"He's a Fortune," Drew continued. "We can't allow ourselves to forget that fact."

J.R. folded his arms across his wide chest. Like his brothers, he too had discarded his suit coat and rolled the sleeves of his dress shirt up his forearms. "What are you thinking?"

"I don't know. But we all know it wouldn't be the first time someone's deliberately brought harm to this family."

Deanna gasped. "No." But she saw the way Lily's hand jerked, then moved away from the hydrangea blossom and the petals that rained down onto the carpet after. She quickly slid her arm around the woman's slender waist and nudged her toward the pew. "Sit. Please."

Lily sat. She pressed her fist against her chest. "Nobody would want to harm William," she said, but there was a fresh shimmer of fear in her voice.

"Maybe not," Darr allowed and Deanna saw the look he and Drew exchanged. "But this family *has* had more than a few incidences."

"What about kidnapping?" Drew looked toward Nick and J.R. He hated being the one to voice the possibility, but he already knew that he and Darr were on the same page.

"Dear Lord," Isabella whispered. She, too, sat, then

suddenly leaned her head forward until it touched her knees.

"Honey?" J.R. started.

But she just lifted a hand, waving at him. "I'm fine. I just got dizzy for a minute."

Frowning, J.R. sat next to her, his hand resting on her back.

"We're all getting ahead of ourselves." The voice of reason came, surprisingly, from the cotton candy-soft-looking Bethany who walked up the aisle with her miniature version toddling after her.

Charlene brought up the rear, holding her sleeping baby. "She's right. Imagining outlandish scenarios isn't helping the situation."

"It's not outlandish, though," Lily countered shakily.

Isabella had sat up again. Her face was pale. "The fires a few years ago. First at Jose and Maria's restaurant and then the one at your barn."

Lily was nodding.

"But Lloyd Fredericks is dead, Lyndsey Pollack is locked safely away in a psychiatric facility and her mother's still rotting in jail," Nick pointed out. His tone was reasonable, but Deanna—feeling more lost than ever—could see that his expression, too, had taken on a new worry.

"Well, if it is a kidnapping," Bethany said, "then someone ought to be at the Double Crown in case they try contacting Lily, right?" She grimaced. "One thing I've learned from having a father who owns the largest private oil company in Texas is what to expect in situations like his. My father was always fearful that my brother and sister and I would end up being targets for people like that."

"Bethany is right." Lily pushed to her feet. She was still pale, but at least she looked steadier. And resolved. "I want to go back to the ranch no matter what."

"We'll drive you," J.R. immediately offered.

"Thank you, dear."

Isabella stood, too, and smoothed down her dress. "I'll speak with the reverend first and meet you out front."

Lily nodded and took J.R.'s arm when he offered it and they all began recessing out of the church. But it was as far as it could get from the recessional they'd all expected when they'd started out that day.

The air had taken on a strong chill when they left through the front doors, gray clouds gathering where only hours ago there had been pretty white puffs of clouds and sunshine.

It was horribly fitting and Deanna shivered.

"Here." Drew slid his suit coat over the thin wrap around her shoulders.

"Thanks." She clutched it around herself. The scent of him that clung to the fabric was even more comforting than the warmth. Then Isabella joined them and everyone silently aimed across the grass for the parking lot.

It looked desolate, compared to how crowded it had been earlier that day.

No one noticed the person standing in the lengthening shadow cast by the church, a large push broom in hand, watching them climb into their trucks and cars and slowly drive away from the church.

When they were gone, the groundskeeper turned and eyed the pile of flower petals and other bits of debris that the broom had collected from the back of the church. Only one of the Fortunes would have thought to decorate the rear door of the church that was only ever used by staff.

But it really wasn't the pile of trash that had the groundskeeper's full attention.

It was the tiny infant swaddled in a car seat.

The groundskeeper had found the baby sitting next to the rear door more than two hours ago, but even when the guests started streaming out of the church after the wedding that wasn't, nobody came back to claim the kid, even though it had been crying its head off. Eventually, the baby had stopped its thin wails and gone to sleep.

And still no one came to get the baby.

Everyone inside the church was too concerned about the old Fortune guy to bother looking around for a baby who evidently shouldn't have been there in the first place.

Now, the worker crouched down and touched the gold medallion that hung from a thin chain around the baby and blanket. It wasn't a large medallion but against the baby it sure looked that way. It also looked valuable.

"Who do you belong to?"

But the baby just continued sleeping, its little mouth sucking its own lip.

The groundskeeper straightened and finished sweeping up, moving faster because fat raindrops had begun to fall, making the task even more of a pain.

Cleaning up after other people had never really been part of the plan…

Then, after putting the cleaning gear away, the worker returned to pick up the car seat and the baby.

Nobody noticed…or cared…when they disappeared into the evening.

\* \* \*

Drew and Deanna drove back to Molly's Pride in silence.

Everyone else had gone to the Double Crown to be with Lily.

Drew couldn't bring himself to be among them.

Not because of his feelings where Lily was concerned. He'd seen for himself just how devastated she'd been when his father hadn't made it to the church.

But because Drew couldn't get the last, angry words he'd had with William out of his head.

He'd told his father he could go to hell and take his new wife with him, if William really expected Drew to find a freaking wife.

What if his father didn't come back?

What if he couldn't?

"Who are Lloyd Fredericks and Lyndsey Pollack?" Deanna's soft voice finally broke the silence when they went inside his brother's hacienda.

"It's an old story."

"It didn't sound that way back at the church."

His hands tightened at his sides, remembering the turmoil the duo had wrought on the family. He turned toward the center of the house, his shoes echoing hollowly against the distressed floor as his thoughts kept whirling inside his head.

"Lloyd was Frannie's first husband," he finally answered. "Lyndsey was Josh's girlfriend. She was pregnant with Brandon, but her real interest wasn't in making a family with Josh—it was the huge inheritance from Frannie's father that he came into when he turned eighteen."

"Frannie's father being your aunt Cindy's husband," Deanna clarified.

"One of four husbands." He reached the alcove that overlooked the center courtyard and stared out at the open space. Scrolled iron sconces cast pools of light around the courtyard and the sprinkles of rain were increasing, making the tile on the fountain gleam.

He looked at Deanna.

She was still clutching his jacket around herself and her eyes looked huge for her face. Her mother might have some emotional problems to deal with, but he seriously doubted that Deanna had the kind of traumatic events in her family tree that the Fortunes did.

And now, he felt like the worst kind of selfish idiot for not having forewarned her. God only knew what was going on in Red Rock with his father disappearing.

"You should go back to San Diego," he said abruptly.

"What? Now? No way."

"What if things get dangerous?"

Her brows pulled together, a mutinous set to her slightly pointed chin that he'd seen often enough in the past to know she meant business. "What if they do?" she challenged. "Your family believes we're engaged." She waved her hand with the ring, as if he needed reminding. "What kind of a person would I seem like if I cut and ran now?"

"They'd think maybe I was trying to keep you safe!"

She looked bewildered. "From what?"

"Murder. Arson. Take your pick." His voice turned flat. He looked back out at the rain. It was easier than looking at her. Because when he did, all he wanted to do was pull her in his arms and just hang on. "We've had all of that touch our family at one time or another," he finished.

"Good Lord." Her dress rustled as she sat on the edge of one of the deep leather chairs positioned to look out on the courtyard. "Just fill me in, all right? Because my imagination will come up with things probably much worse than what actually has happened."

"Don't count on it." He exhaled.

"What happened with Josh's father?"

"Lloyd, you mean?" He grimaced. "Turned out he wasn't Josh's father at all, but everyone—including Frannie, thanks to her mother's machinations—thought he was." He sat down on the coffee table, still looking out on the courtyard. "In any case, the inheritance that Lyndsey had her eyes on was the same money that Lloyd wanted to get his hands on—one of the reasons why he married Frannie in the first place."

"Sounds like a prince."

"Yeah. I don't think anyone in the family ever much cared for him, except maybe Cindy. She thought he was a great catch for her daughter, whether Frannie agreed or not. Anyway, Lyndsey and her lunatic mother weren't interested in having to compete for Josh's inheritance when it did come through, and they caused all sorts of trouble. They tampered with Cindy's brakes on her car when she was in town trying to make nice with Frannie after all the crap she'd pulled on her, they practically burned down Red—it's a great Mexican place owned by the Mendozas." He glanced at her. "The Fortunes and the Mendozas go way back. Isabella's half brother manages the place now. Anyway, they also tried to torch Lily's barn when she had an event going on there with hundreds of kids. Darr got hurt, actually, trying to save the horses in the barn. Lily still lost one, but nobody but Darr was hurt."

"And he obviously recovered," Deanna observed.

Drew nodded once. The fact that Darr's injuries had healed didn't make up for the fact that the crime had occurred in the first place. "Lloyd eventually ended up dead and Frannie was initially arrested for it. Then Roberto—Josh's real dad and the guy that Frannie's married to now—confessed to the murder. They were both just trying to protect Josh, who they feared might have done it. But ultimately, it turned out that Lyndsey and her mother had been behind all of the violence all along."

"How horrible for them all. And that poor little baby." She moved from the chair to the coffee table beside him, slipping his jacket off her shoulders to rest across her lap.

The useless strip of thin fabric she'd had wrapped around her shoulders at the church had slid down, exposing the silky-looking expanse of her shoulders.

He focused on the hardwood floor. It was old. It was scuffed and nicked.

And it gleamed with an unexpected, shining warmth.

So did Deanna's sun-kissed, bare shoulders.

He closed his eyes for a moment.

What the hell was wrong with him?

His father had gone missing, for Christ's sake.

He cleared his throat, too aware of the silent house breathing around them. "Wouldn't worry about Brandon much. He's in good hands now. Frannie and Roberto are helping Josh with him. But they've all had to come to terms with some pretty serious lies from Cindy and Lloyd that opened the door for what ended up happening in the first place. Toss in psychotic Lyndsey and it was a recipe for disaster."

Deanna let out a long breath and shook her head

slightly. She put her hand on his arm, squeezing a little before moving it back to her lap. But the zinging
warmth of her touch remained. He curled his fist and
was damned if he knew if he was trying to hold on to
the warmth or get rid of it.

"I thought I had a crazy mother," she was saying. "But
the worst thing that Gigi's ever done was get fired for
engaging in inappropriate behavior in the workplace."

He gave her a look. "What's that supposed to
mean?"

She looked away. "Use your imagination."

He could think of only a few things. Stealing. Doing
drugs. Or having sex.

Somehow—maybe it was the way Deanna always was
the soul of propriety in the office—he was betting on
the last. And he also figured that her mother had done
a few other things that weren't so great.

Like spending herself into the poorhouse and expecting her daughter to bail her out.

There was something seriously upside down there.

Not that he was in any position to judge family
relationships.

He'd accused his father of forgetting his own family
in favor of Lily.

And dammit all to hell, he couldn't stop smelling the
green apple scent of his assistant's glossy red hair.

He pushed to his feet again, moving to the window.
The glass felt chilly against his palm when he pressed
his hand against it. "I'd feel better if you went back."

"Because you don't want me in the way?"

He shot her a look. "Did I say that?"

"No, but that doesn't mean it wasn't what you meant.
It's one thing to need a fiancée for appearances' sake
at a wedding. It's another thing to have her hanging

around where you don't want her when the situation has changed."

He turned toward her, staring. "God help a woman's mind. All I was thinking about is your freaking safety!"

"Well, you don't have to yell at me!"

"I'm not." But his voice was raised. And so was hers.

He turned again and looked out at the courtyard and wished he were standing on the beach. But not even having an ocean spread out in front of him was going to be enough to swallow up the roiling turmoil inside of him.

"Drew." Her voice was soft. She set aside his jacket and stood up, moving beside him. Her fingertips grazed his arm. "Your father is going to be all right."

His jaw tightened until it ached. "None of us know that."

Deanna swallowed past the lump in her throat. She covered his clenched fist with hers. Maybe their engagement wasn't rooted in the normal things, but that didn't mean she didn't genuinely care about him. "I'm not leaving until we do."

He turned and closed his hands around her shoulders. "What if something happens to you?"

She swallowed the shiver that had absolutely nothing to do with some imagined fear on his part and everything to do with him. "Nothing is going to happen. And I am not leaving."

"I could fire you."

She met his gaze head-on. "You won't."

"I could tell everyone that we broke up."

Her jaw tightened. "You could."

"They'd figure it was my fault, that I was just acting

true to form. Blowing through women. Nobody would think less of you for deserting me during a crisis."

"I think you're underestimating your family's opinion of you."

"You've been here less than twenty-four hours and you've come to that conclusion, have you?"

Deanna almost could have smiled if the situation weren't so serious. "It doesn't take a genius to recognize how much you all care for each other." The fact that she didn't have those family relationships made it particularly obvious to her. "And we could debate this for the rest of the evening, or you can just accept the fact that I am not leaving you."

His brows pulled together. She could see the argument he still wanted to make in his stance. Could feel it in the fingers he was pressing into her shoulders.

"Why?"

There it was again. Just Drew. Plain and simple and wholly devastating and he made her mouth run dry.

But he was waiting for an answer and just then, she didn't have the strength—or even the desire—to prevaricate. So she swallowed past the dryness and told the truth. "Two weeks after I started working for you, I came into the office early one morning. To prep for an important meeting. Nobody should have been there yet. But the light was on in your office." She watched his jaw tighten. Shift slightly to one side before centering again. "You were—"

"—passed out," he said flatly.

"—asleep at your desk," she softened the truth, because his all-night bender wasn't really her point. "You'd been there all night." His mother's funeral had been only days before.

"You dragged me up and pulled me together for the biggest meeting of my career."

"I fixed you coffee and found a clean shirt and tie for you."

"And I paid you back by trying to jump your bones."

Her cheeks felt like they were on fire. "You kissed me," she corrected moderately.

"But you didn't walk, didn't sue. You could have done both."

"I believed you when you said it wouldn't happen again." He'd made that point abundantly clear. And in the years since, she'd recognized why. She simply was not the type of woman he was attracted to, which also wasn't her point.

Although even thinking about that long-ago morning was as much a double-edged sword as it ever was.

"But what made me stay," she finished quietly, "was the look in your eyes that morning."

"Hungover?" His voice turned caustic.

"No. The look that told me you were a man who knew what it meant to honestly, really care—deeply—about someone. I knew then that you were going to be a good man to work with."

"So says the woman who sent my staff home early yesterday because she thought I was being unreasonably demanding."

She drew in a breath. That was the layer of Drew that made him more of a challenge.

"A good man, period," she said. "And I've seen that same look in your eyes ever since your father didn't show up at the church. That's why I didn't quit on you before. And that's why I'm not quitting on you now. I am not leaving."

His eyes narrowed. His hands tightened around her shoulders, drawing her closer to him, until there was not an inch of breath to be had between her body and his. "And what if I kissed you again now?"

He was trying to make her run.

She knew it as surely as she knew her own name.

And even though she felt weak in the knees and shivers were slipping down her spine, she lifted her chin.

Her gaze met his. "What if you did?"

## *Chapter Seven*

Drew's lashes narrowed until all Deanna could see was the thin glimmer of golden-brown. Her breath stalled in her throat when his hands slowly slid over her shoulders, to her neck.

He lowered his head. "What if I did?" His thumbs rested at the base of her throat and she became acutely aware of her pulse throbbing there.

His thumbs slowly climbed her throat until they reached the underside of her chin. They nudged it upward.

His lips hovered above hers, so close that if either one of them moved an inch…less than an inch…they'd meet.

A door suddenly slammed somewhere in the house.

It might as well have been cymbals crashing behind them.

Drew's head lifted.

Deanna jumped back.

"Christ," he muttered, shoveling his hands through his hair.

Deanna scrabbled with her wrap that had fallen to the floor without her even noticing. The thin fabric slithered through her shaking fingers as she picked it up and tried to pull it around her shoulders. It just kept tangling and in the end, she bunched it between her hands.

She couldn't look at Drew.

After the way she'd behaved when she'd wakened that morning, for her to turn around and practically throw herself at him now?

Her entire body felt flushed.

Sadly, she knew it wasn't exactly embarrassment, either.

If he really would have kissed her...

"Oh, there you are." Isabella appeared in the doorway. "I knew you had to be around somewhere because the truck was out front." She brushed aside a long lock of dark hair from her pale cheek. "I don't suppose you've heard any—no. Of course you haven't, or you would have let us know." Thankfully, as Isabella settled on the arm of the same chair that Deanna had used what seemed only moments ago, Isabella didn't seem to notice the air that—to Deanna—felt as thick as molasses. "Seems fitting that this rain came out of nowhere, doesn't it?" She shook her dark head and sighed. "J.R. is staying out with Lily for a while. Jeremy came back with me, though. He said he had some calls to return." Her lips stretched into a humorless smile. "I guess when you're in medicine you're not allowed to get completely away from emergencies even when you're having one of your own."

Deanna made a faint sound of agreement. She could

see Drew in her periphery, standing like a stone mono-lith in front of the windows. "How...how was Lily?"

"Out of her mind. And holding herself together with as much dignity as she always does." Isabella ran her hands down her red dress. "I don't know how she does it, if it's just practice after having lost Ryan as suddenly as she did or what. Not that William is lost," she added rapidly. "We don't know that at all."

"Yet." Drew's voice was dark.

Deanna bit her lip. Their hostess looked nearly as upset as Drew sounded with a pallor under her smooth complexion that clearly showed her strain. "Isabella, why don't you and Drew try to relax a little. I could fix you something to eat. Jeremy may need something, too." Deanna didn't have any idea if either Isabella or Jeremy had eaten something out at the Double Crown, but if they hadn't, then it had been hours since they'd had breakfast before they'd gone to the church.

"Eat." Isabella shook her head and pushed herself off the arm of the chair. "My brain is just not tracking today. That's why I came back. Evie left after breakfast for a few weeks of vacation and I knew you all would be hungry by now. Lily was right about her caterers leaving a ton of food, but all we did was pack it up and store it in the freezer. Nobody was in the mood to have wedding reception food, you know?"

"I can imagine. You look exhausted, though. You shouldn't be worrying about feeding us," Deanna assured quickly. She'd forgotten all about Isabella and J.R.'s housekeeper, Evie. She'd only met her in passing when she'd made herself tea while waiting for Drew to get dressed for the wedding. "If you don't mind me intruding in your kitchen, I'm happy to put something together." She'd seen for herself that the large kitchen was amply stocked.

And truthfully, Deanna wanted something—any-thing—that she could turn her attention to.

The other woman tucked her hair behind her ear. "You're practically family, Deanna. There's no intrud-ing at all. We'll both do it. It won't be hard. Evie's left us with a ton of food. I think she's afraid J.R. and I might starve in her absence." She glanced at Drew. "Is there anything I can get you right now, Drew? Coffee? Beer?"

He shook his head and finally moved away from the windows. "I need to talk to Jeremy," he said and brushed past Deanna as he strode out of the room.

Deanna's hands strangled the balled-up fabric as her gaze followed him.

"Poor man," Isabella murmured after a moment. "This has to be making him as crazy as it is J.R. and the others." She tucked her hand through Deanna's arm as they left the alcove. "We're all so glad that you're here with him. That he's not alone."

Deanna managed a weak smile. "I'm glad I'm here, too." That, at least, was the absolute truth. "Do you and J.R. get to see a lot of Mr. Fortune?"

"William," Isabella corrected with a gentle smile. "He's going to be your father-in-law, remember? I refuse to think otherwise."

Deanna knew what Isabella meant, but she still felt her face flushing all over again.

Fortunately, they'd reached the spacious kitchen and Isabella let go of Deanna's arm and headed toward the wide refrigerator. "And to answer your question, yes, we see William and Lily quite a bit. For one thing, Lily is a natural hostess. She always has something going on out at the Double Crown." She turned with a large chunk of cheese in her hand and set it on the center island. "Jeremy's probably going to tell Drew. We had the radio on during the drive here from Lily's. The news outlets have already gotten hold of the story."

"Mr. Fortune—William—is a prominent business-man." Deanna set her crumpled scarf on a bar stool. "I can't say that I'm really surprised at that." She bit her lip. If she hadn't been so concerned with Drew, she would have foreseen the matter herself. "Drew should issue an official statement on behalf of Fortune Forecasting." And how awful it was going to be to carefully craft that statement when they knew so little.

"That's what Jeremy said." Isabella set two enormous, red tomatoes next to the cheese. "What was unexpected though, was they speculated that William wanted to disappear. Not just skip out on his wedding, but skip out on his life. They were even referring to things in his life that happened more than forty years ago. Business failures, that sort of thing."

Deanna stared. "But that's ridiculous."

"You know that. I know that. Everyone in the fam-ily—" Isabella waved her hand around "—everyone who knows William knows that. But there are people who don't, and people who love to gossip and make up things out of the clear blue sky." She pulled a knife out of a drawer. "And we're the ones who have to hear such nonsense." She shook her head, her lips twisting. "As if this isn't hard enough to deal with."

"I don't know what to say. Try not to think about it?" Deanna smiled weakly.

But the other woman tilted her head and nodded. "You're right, actually. Focus on the positive." Her eyes focused again on Deanna. "So that's what we'll do. I meant to tell you earlier. That dress is beautiful on you."

"That wasn't exactly what I meant," Deanna managed wryly. But if talking about clothes helped keep the worry out of Isabella's eyes, she was game. "But I really never thought this dress suited me at all. I kind of packed in a hurry."

"The color's spectacular with your hair. And if my shoulders and arms were as toned as yours, I'd wear halters, too. You should either change or put on an apron, though."

Deanna lifted her eyebrows. "You're as dressed up as I am, Isabella," she reminded gently.

"Right." The other woman shook her head again, as if she were clearing it of cobwebs. "My brain today. We'll both change. Meet you back here." She set her knife down with a clatter.

Deanna nodded and they headed to their respective bedrooms and her feet slowed as she passed the closed door to Jeremy's room. She could hear the murmur of voices behind the door and took an easier breath. Drew was obviously still talking with his brother.

She let out a long breath and made herself move on. When she reached the bedroom they were sharing, she quickly pulled out her jeans and a sweater before reaching back to unfasten the tiny dress hook behind her neck. But when she caught her reflection in the oversize mirror leaning against the wall, she paused.

Maybe the fact that Gigi had given her the dress had colored her opinion about it.

Her gaze strayed to the chest of drawers where her purse was sitting. Her phone was inside it, still turned off. Heaven only knew how many messages from Gigi were waiting.

What was wrong with Deanna that even now, considering the way all of the Fortunes were frantic with concern over their parent, she still couldn't bring herself to turn on that phone and speak with her own very alive-and-well mother?

She wasn't even sure if her reluctance made her feel guilty or not.

"You're a horrible daughter," she whispered to her reflection. It was a frequent refrain, although before that week when Deanna had finally taken a stand with her mother, it was a refrain that had always been sung strictly by Gigi.

She sighed and removed the dress, hanging it on one of the hangers in the closet. Then she changed into the comfort zone provided by her well-worn jeans and the faded green sweater that she'd knitted for herself during high school Home Ec and went back out to the kitchen.

Isabella was already there. She, too, had changed into soft-looking jeans and a sweater.

But what sent Deanna's heart plunging through her stomach was the sight of the other woman sitting on the bar stool, her head bent forward over her knees.

"Isabella?" She rushed into the kitchen. "Is there news?"

Isabella lifted her hand, but not her head. "It's okay." Her voice was muffled. "It's not William. Just give me a second."

Deanna leaned against the island, letting her panic subside until she could breath. She frowned at the woman's downturned head, then went to the cupboards near the sink, opening and closing doors until she found a glass. She filled it with water and took it over to Isabella.

She crouched down on her heels so she could see Isabella's face beneath her thick curtain of hair. "You got dizzy again, didn't you?" she guessed. "Like you did at the church."

Isabella opened her eyes, sliding a guilty look her way before slowly sitting up. Her curtain of dark hair slid down behind her back as she nodded.

"Drink some water." Deanna fit the glass into Isabella's hand, prepared to catch it if she wasn't able to hold on to it. "Are you feeling sick?"

Isabella lifted the glass and drank down half the contents. Then she let out a long breath. "I think I might be pregnant," she said in a low voice.

Deanna's lips parted. "That sounds...wonderful... doesn't it?"

Isabella's lips turned up at the corners. "Absolutely. It just seems like now isn't exactly the time to add that to everyone's plate." Her glance slipped past Deanna toward the empty doorway as she set the glass on the counter. "J.R. and I didn't tell anyone at the time, but I had a miscarriage about six months ago."

"Oh, Isabella..."

The other woman raised her hand. "It's all right. And we weren't really trying to keep it a secret or anything. It was a blow, of course, once we realized, but I was so early along, I didn't even know I'd been pregnant until the doctor told me. I just don't want J.R. worrying about this right now."

"Not that I have even twenty-four hours to base this on," Deanna offered, "but I'm pretty sure he would want to be worrying about you. He's clearly devoted to you."

Isabella smiled. The color was coming back into her cheeks, much to Deanna's relief. "And I am to him," she assured. She slid off the bar stool and went around the island again to pick up the knife she'd left there. "We've wanted to start a family ever since we got married two years ago. I know J.R. will be thrilled. And I know he'll be worried whether he admits it or not. I'm already thirty-two. Like it or not, this sort of thing just seems to get more complicated with every year past thirty. And I don't know for certain, yet. I haven't done a test. It's just a hunch. Not only do I not want him worrying more just now, but I also don't want to raise his hopes if I'm wrong." She deftly sliced a tomato in half. "You can understand that, right?"

Deanna nodded. "Yes." She lifted her hands. "But what can I do to help?" She meant more than just the dinner preparation, and the other woman knew it.

"You're the only one I've told," Isabella said. She let out a deep breath. "Just being able to tell someone is a lot, believe me." She reached below the island and pulled out a cheese grater and a plastic bowl and set them on the counter. "And you can grate."

Deanna knew that the other woman would never have shared her suspicion if she didn't believe Deanna and Drew were heading toward the altar, and her conscience weighed heavily.

But she nodded and moved around the island to stand beside the other woman, and began unwrapping the cheese. "You'll let me know if you do need something, all right? Even if it's just to sneak a pregnancy test into the house for you."

Isabella laughed softly. "I knew I liked you, Dee."

And Deanna liked Isabella.

She liked every member of Drew's family that she'd met since arriving in Red Rock.

And she hated the deception that she and Drew had created.

But she hated the thought of letting him down more.

They ate their late supper of salad and spicy enchiladas and chased it down with the most delicious caramel cake that Deanna had ever tasted in her life. But she strongly suspected that the only reason Jeremy and Drew did any justice to the meal was because they didn't want to disappoint Isabella.

Then, while they were eating the decadent dessert that Evie had left for them, J.R. returned. Lily had finally gone to bed, he reported, primarily because William's brother Patrick and his wife, Lacey, had come to the Double Crown and Lacey had been able to convince her cousin-in-law that she simply had to get some rest.

"Would she take a sedative?" Jeremy asked.

"I doubt it," Isabella cautioned.

"Given the state she was in, let's hope that doesn't become necessary," J.R. told him.

"Is anyone staying with her?" Deanna asked.

"Lacey," J.R. said. "For tonight at least. She and Patrick have a brief trip they're leaving on tomorrow that they can't postpone." J.R. leaned back in his seat at the head of the table. Isabella sat adjacent to him and their hands were linked on top of the table. "I don't think any of us want her to be alone right now. Fortunately, there are enough family members around town that we can keep that duty covered without too much effort."

"I could go tomorrow," Isabella offered immediately.

J.R. eyed her. "You look more tired than I feel," he

said. "Frannie's already said she'll go over tomorrow. You can all work out details then."

Deanna quickly focused on the bright yellow-and-orange linen napkin on her lap, folding it in fourths. If Isabella was right, she had a good reason to look tired right now.

"Lily doesn't look like the type to appreciate being babysat."

They all turned to look at Drew. He hadn't said a word at the table to anyone other than Deanna sitting beside him, when he'd told her they'd craft a media release before morning.

"She's not," Isabella agreed after a moment. "She'd hate feeling coddled. But right now, I know she's more focused on William than she is on herself." She stood and began reaching for plates.

Deanna rose to help. She was more than a little surprised when the others did, too. Even Drew.

Since the man didn't even order his own lunch at the office if he could avoid it, she wasn't exactly used to seeing him carrying dirty dishes anywhere, much less to the kitchen sink, where he began rinsing them, as well as the others that were quickly stacked beside him before J.R. disappeared to take care of some ranch matters and Jeremy went off to return yet another call from his service.

"I'll finish up in here," Deanna offered to Isabella, who looked ready to shoo Drew out of the way, and was relieved when the other woman accepted, even subsiding to her husband's none-too-subtle efforts before he'd left that she retire for the night.

"Tomorrow is going to be a better day," she said before she left the kitchen.

Which left Deanna alone in the room with Drew.

And the last time they'd been alone—

She cut off the treacherous thoughts.

It was harder than it should have been, though, and only by mentally pulling on one of her ugly suits as a paltry armor against the feelings inside her did she find the strength to move naturally next to him as if she hadn't thrown herself at him the way she had.

But her gaze still kept straying to his sinewy forearms below the rolled-up sleeves of his white shirt. "I can do that," she told him a little more abruptly than her "act natural" act called for.

"So can I." He stuck a plate under the running water and rinsed it. Water sluiced over his bronzed wrist. "I did have a mother, you know." He set the plate aside. "You can load the dishwasher."

Too bemused to form an argument, Deanna figured out the latch on the fancy dishwasher and opened the door. Bending over, she began loading the rinsed items inside. But not even that action was familiar, since her modest apartment didn't possess even a nonfancy variety.

"Did you have regular chores as a kid, then?" Her gaze had automatically started to rise when she spoke, but it went dead still when she found her eyes nearly on a level with his rear.

One of the plates clattered as it slid into its slot too quickly and she carefully redirected her gaze from the painfully excellent cut of his custom-tailored trousers over those glutes and was grateful that he couldn't see her.

"We all had chores." His hand moved and a water glass appeared almost in front of her nose. Mindful that it probably wouldn't tolerate the same carelessness as the plate, she carefully lifted it out of his hand as he continued. "Inside the house and out," he was saying. "Until he got old enough that he realized the payment wasn't worth the chore, I used to bribe Darr into taking most of mine."

She straightened. "That sounds more like the man I know," she said wryly and caught a wisp of a smile around his lips. The first in hours.

And no matter what sort of mess she was in, she still felt as if she'd won some great prize at the sight.

"I didn't mind the yard work so much," he admitted. "It was outside at least." He looked at the window above the sink, but all that was visible were their own reflections against the darkness outside.

It was strange enough to be standing alongside him working on the dishes, much less to see their images in that windowpane.

It was far too…domestic.

Particularly when she couldn't stop thinking that, sooner or later, they were going to be sleeping in the same bedroom again.

Same bedroom.

Same bed.

She bent over the dishwasher rack again, fitting another plate into place, only this time she was careful to keep her eyes focused where they belonged. "If, uh, if you want me to, I could draft the media release for you. Maybe a few versions for you to look at." She'd done so dozens of times before for him; just not ones that dealt with such a serious, personal matter.

"Did you have to do chores?"

She straightened again. "What? Oh. Yeah." All of them, pretty much, since Gigi had usually been incapable of it. "Most kids do." She took the last dish from him and placed it in the rack, then closed the door and went out of the kitchen, back to the dining-room table where she took her time gathering up the colorful woven place mats and napkins before carrying them into the kitchen in hope that he would lose his sudden curiosity about her childhood.

He was standing where she'd left him, only he'd turned his back to the sink and his arms were crossed over his chest. His brooding gaze tracked her movements as if he were trying to calculate something while she brushed off the place mats and left them stacked on the island. She carried the cloth napkins into the laundry room next to the kitchen that she'd noticed earlier, but eventually, she couldn't pretend there was any more busywork.

He was still studying her when she stopped next to the granite-topped island again. She felt like a bug on the end of a pin, and didn't care for it at all. She lifted her hands. "What?"

"When you were a kid, what did you want to be when you grew up?"

She hadn't known what was ticking around in his mind, but she certainly hadn't expected that. He couldn't have chosen a question that would have surprised her more.

She blinked and shrugged a little. "I don't know. A ballerina for a while. Isn't that what all little girls want to be?"

"After you were older than five," he drawled.

"What did you want to be when you were five?" she returned tartly.

"A fireman, but I grew out of that. Obviously, Darr didn't." His lips twisted. "He always did have a hero complex."

She wrapped her fingers around the wrought-iron

back of one of the bar stools. "You admire him." Despite his dark humor, she'd seen that already for herself.

"Not everybody has what it takes to run into a burning building when everyone else is trying to get out of it."

"I guess that's true. I've never really thought about it before," she admitted. And as nice as she considered his younger brother to have been, she was much more fascinated with what made Drew tick. It didn't seem to matter that part of her knew it wasn't wise to indulge such a fascination at all. "So after the fireman, what'd you want to be?"

"I was asking you that question, remember?"

She exhaled. "Fine. I wanted to be a pilot. You?"

"President of Fortune Forecasting."

"Even when you were a kid?" She was surprised. She'd always suspected he'd gone into the family business because it had been expected, not because it was something at which he'd turned out to be exceptionally good.

"Even then." His gaze was steady. "What stopped you from being a pilot?"

Her hands twisted around the wrought iron and the band of the engagement ring dug into her finger.

She didn't know what was spurring Drew's sudden interest, but the sooner it ended, the more comfortable she'd feel. "Money. More specifically, the lack of it. So, about that press release?"

"If you had the money now, would you still want to become one?"

"No."

"Why not?"

"Why all the questions, Drew?"

"Just trying to get to know my fiancée better."

She squelched her response just in time. For all they knew, given his father's disappearance, her position as his fiancée could well turn out to be unnecessary after all.

And in comparison to what he was going through, the reason behind her desire to be a pilot seemed utterly unimportant. She unwound her fingers from the wrought iron and rubbed her reddened palms down the sides of her jeans. "Because I realized even if I could fly off to be like my father, it still wouldn't have brought him back home to me."

His gaze stayed steady on her face and she mentally braced herself for yet another intrusion into her life.

But after a moment, all he did was unfold his arms and push away from the edge of the farmhouse-style sink. "Draft up whatever you think the release should say. I'll look at it when I get back. You can send it first thing in the morning."

Her wits felt scattered trying to keep up with him. "Where are you going?"

"Out."

He scooped a set of keys off the rack of them by the kitchen door before quietly letting himself out into the night.

Feeling abruptly spent, Deanna could only stand there and watch him go.

# Chapter Eight

Deanna was talking on the phone in J.R.'s office. He'd kindly offered it for her and Drew's use after their stay in Red Rock quickly lengthened from four days to ten when she heard the slam of a door elsewhere in the house.

Drew and Jeremy must be back from town where they'd gone to see Darr at his fire station, because Isabella didn't make that much noise and J.R. was out at Lily's.

Ten days had passed since William's disappearance.

Ten torturously slow days.

And ten even more torturously…slow…nights.

She couldn't marshal her pulse that sped up just from knowing that Drew was in the house, but she could still pretend. So she focused on the task at hand—namely her telephone conversation with Fortune Forecasting's L.A.-based Human Resources director.

"Send a hard copy of the proof overnight," she finished telling Chelsea. "I'll let you know if there are any changes by the end of tomorrow, and if not, you can sign off on the brochure and get it into production." Fortune Forecasting had long been scheduled to be part of a three-day job fair in Los Angeles later that week, and the brochure was part of the printed collateral that was to be made available there. Drew had been scheduled to give a speech at the event, but she'd already arranged a replacement—a professional baseball player that Drew was friends with who was a popular figure on the motivational circuit.

She heard another door slam and a raised voice. J.R.'s. She could easily distinguish now the differences in his voice compared with Drew's and Jeremy's.

She glanced at her watch. It was the middle of the day. She still had at least a dozen calls to return on Drew's behalf, and more than twice that many emails to attend to. But the sound of J.R.'s voice when she'd thought he was going to be gone all afternoon was unusual enough that when she hung up with Chelsea, she left the office and went to investigate.

She found them all in the great room, including Drew. Even Isabella had come out of her workroom where she had a loom on which she wove her amazing tapestries and blankets.

What surprised Deanna most, though, was the sight of Lily Fortune.

She hadn't seen the woman since the day of her non-wedding, although Deanna knew that in addition to J.R., Isabella and Jeremy had been regular visitors out to her ranch. She couldn't hazard a guess whether Drew had been. Aside from knowing that he—along with his brothers—had visited every police station, hospital and morgue in half the state, he never said where he was going when he disappeared from the hacienda every evening or what he was doing when he went.

All Deanna knew was that for the past ten days, every evening after supper—which Deanna had continued helping Isabella to prepare since that first night—he left the house and didn't return until after Deanna was in bed and asleep. Or at least pretending to be asleep.

And when morning dawned and she did wake, he'd be gone again, leaving only the impression of his head on the pillow as proof that he'd ever been there at all.

He couldn't have made it more plain that he wasn't interested in chancing any more close encounters of the intimate kind upon waking.

She looked from him to Lily, who was pacing back and forth in front of Jeremy near the windows. She was wearing jeans and a button-down plaid shirt with her hair braided down her back and couldn't have looked more different than the bride she'd been, yet she still possessed the same indefinable, elegant strength that Deanna couldn't help but admire.

"Ross has news," Isabella told Deanna quietly. "He was on the road when he called and Molly's Pride was closer than Lily's place, so he's coming here to meet with us all at once."

Deanna felt queasy. Ross was Drew's investigator cousin. And if he felt compelled to deliver his news to Lily in person...

She looked back at Drew. He'd sprawled in one of the oversize chairs that filled the space, his long, jean-clad legs crossed at the ankles. But she knew the lazy-looking position was deceptive. She could feel the tension emanating from him from across the room. Could see it in the lines bracketing his lips and the long fingers that were silently drumming against the leather arm of the chair.

Even though she'd spent plenty of time with Drew's family, she nevertheless still felt like an intruder. But she also knew that only she and Drew would know the reason why, so she made herself cross the room and perch on the ottoman that was near his chair. "Are you all right?"

His gaze slanted toward her. "Peachy."

Her lips tightened. Just sitting near him made her feel shaky inside, but that didn't mean she enjoyed his sarcasm. "I was only asking," she said under her breath.

"I know." He drummed his fingertips again. "Sorry."

She chewed the inside of her lip and managed not to close her hand over his restless one. He was wearing a brown shirt that was the same color as his eyes. She assumed he must have borrowed it from his brother because it wasn't one that had been hanging in their closet.

They'd already stayed nearly a week longer than they'd originally planned. Isabella had offered the use of their washer and dryer, which Deanna had by necessity taken up. She should have laundered Drew's things as well, but something had stopped her.

Washing his clothes, strangely enough, seemed even more personal than sleeping on opposite sides of the same bed.

She looked down at her folded hands. She'd grown accustomed to the feel of the diamond ring on her finger, but she still hadn't grown used to the sight of it there. It had been jarring from the first moment he'd slipped it on her finger. It was still jarring now.

And frightening considering the pang of...longing... that was only increasing by the day.

"Everything set for the job fair?"

She nodded, glad of the distraction, even though she was vaguely surprised that he remembered it. As large an event as it was, she'd been handling all of the arrangements for it all along. His only involvement was to have been his scheduled "motivational" rah-rah session. "Chelsea said they're expecting over five thousand people," she told him. It would be a well-orchestrated zoo.

"It's the first year you'll miss it."

She lifted her shoulder, again surprised that he'd realized that. "Chelsea and her department have things well in hand. They won't miss me." And the organizers handling the half dozen companies being represented at the fair wouldn't, either. They cared about missing Drew, but had been slightly mollified by the celebrity athlete she'd been able to produce.

"Hmm." His fingers continued drumming.

"Do you need this back?" She pulled his BlackBerry out of the pocket of her sweater and held it out. She'd been using his phone to handle all of the business calls rather than J.R. and Isabella's house line.

"Any emergencies at the office that I don't know about and need to?"

"No." Aside from the employees' anxiety caused by William's disappearance and the media's attention that had been deflected for the most part by the press release they'd issued, everything at Fortune Forecasting was at least running smoothly.

"Then, no, I don't need it." He shook his head, and because she knew she still had plenty of use for it, she slid it back into her pocket.

Her own cell phone was still turned off and shoved inside her purse. She'd listened to her mother's numerous voice mails. And she'd sent her an email that she was in Texas with her boss…on business. Not that Gigi had bought that story, which she'd told Deanna in a long voice message immediately after. Gigi didn't live under a rock, after all. She, too, had heard the news that William Fortune was missing. And she'd archly suggested that Deanna make "good use" of her time with her boss during his hour of need.

Deanna had been furious enough to return that call, but the results had been typical—Gigi accusing Deanna of abandoning her when she needed her most, and Deanna feeling guilty. So she'd told her mother to find a counselor and not to call her again until she had.

Since then, her voice mailbox had been unusually empty. Deanna still couldn't decide if that was progress or not.

A doorbell chimed and everyone jumped.

Isabella quickly hurried out of the room and just as quickly returned with Ross Fortune on her heels.

His brown gaze traveled the room, landing on Lily, who'd gone stock-still at the sight of him, holding her arms around her waist.

Everyone else rose to their feet, waiting…

"His car's been found," he said bluntly.

Jeremy moved next to Lily, as if he were afraid she might collapse. But all she did was pale. "And?" Lily's chin was lifted, but she looked braced for anything.

Ross looked only marginally better than his cousins

did. His brown hair was rumpled and he had the same weary lines creasing his face. "And there's no sign of William." His voice was careful and Deanna caught the look that passed between him and the other men.

Her stomach sank and she looked toward Isabella and was grateful that the other woman had sat down again. Deanna was certain that Isabella hadn't yet confided her suspicion to her husband. And because Isabella hadn't shared with Deanna that it had been a false alarm, she assumed that her hostess's suspicion was probably even closer to certainty now.

"Where was the car?" Lily asked. She was still standing upright, but her voice had gone thin.

"Outside of Haggarty."

Deanna started at the name of the town. She remembered Darr mentioning it the day of the wedding. He'd said an accident had occurred near there.

A fatal accident.

Lily made a sound then and covered her mouth with her hand. A moment later, she seemed to crumple.

Jeremy leaped forward, catching her in his arms before she collapsed right to the floor.

Isabella cried out, jumping out of her chair and rushing to them.

"She fainted. She needs to lie down," Jeremy said tersely. "I have smelling salts in my medical bag."

"Take her to our bedroom. It's the closest. I'll bring your bag." Isabella practically ran out of the room, leading the way for Jeremy to carry the tall woman out of the room.

Deanna watched them go. Her heart was thudding so hard she could feel it inside her head. She didn't even realize that she'd reached out for Drew's hand until she felt his fingers curl around hers in response.

"The police aren't tying that other accident together with William's." When they were gone, Ross answered the question that nobody had asked but everybody had thought. "Yet." His voice was grim as he looked from J.R. to Drew. "The other car had no signs of collision with another vehicle. They found no debris that didn't come from the car where it ran off a curve and collided with several trees before going down the embankment, so the authorities over there still maintain that it was a single-car accident. William's Mercedes, on the other hand, is at the bottom of an embankment some distance away. It's heavily shaded by trees and brush. The only reason it was found at all was because of a couple who were hiking back in there over the weekend. It's not a popular spot at all."

"I want to see the car," Drew said abruptly. J.R. nodded.

"So do I," Ross agreed. "I also want to talk to the police in Haggarty and interview the couple who found the car. And I want to do it as soon as possible while everything is fresh in their mind."

"Then let's go," Drew said immediately.

"J.R.?"

J.R. turned to see Isabella walking back into the room. "How's Lily?"

"She's coming around already. Jeremy wants her to lie down for a while, though. Her blood pressure is up and he's threatening her with a sedative if she doesn't behave." Her liquid-brown gaze flickered over Deanna and Drew, then back to her husband. "Can I talk to you for a second?"

J.R. gave a quick frown, but went to her immediately and followed her out of the room.

"Do you know how badly damaged Dad's car is?" Drew asked Ross.

His cousin shook his head. "The investigators were heading out to the site when I got the call from my contact at the Haggarty P.D., so there's no official information yet. I want to get there soon while there's still enough daylight left to see things for myself. We've already had rain since the accident, so who knows what evidence will be left to find after so many days."

J.R. returned in time to hear the tail end of Ross's comment. "You and Drew can go. I've got something else I need to take care of."

"More important than finding out where the hell Dad's gone?" Drew demanded. He gave Deanna an impatient look when she made a faint sound and squeezed his hand.

"Right now, yes," J.R. returned evenly. "I'm taking my wife into town to see her doctor."

Drew swore under his breath. "Sorry, man. Is she all right?"

"She thinks she's pregnant."

Deanna exhaled. Thank goodness.

"If she is, I'm not taking any chances with her."

Drew was nodding. "Of course." He clapped a hand on his brother's shoulder. A faint smile had mercifully replaced the drawn lines on his face. "A baby, huh? That would be some good news around here about now."

J.R. looked a little pale beneath his bemused expression, but he nodded. "That's for sure."

Ross was smiling, too. "Going to have to get used to the idea of you changing diapers," he drawled.

"Well, first, we need to make sure nothing happens this time," J.R. said. He headed out of the room again.

"Call me with whatever you find, though," he added before he left.

"This time?" Ross looked at Drew, who shook his head.

"Isabella had a miscarriage several months ago," Deanna provided quietly. Because J.R. had opened the door, and Isabella herself had said that it wasn't really a secret, she didn't feel too much like she was divulging a confidence.

"How do you know that?"

Drew's incredulousness stung. Just because all she was to him was his assistant and fiancée-for-appearances'-sake didn't mean everyone else saw her that way. "I have gotten to know Isabella a little since we've been here," she reminded.

"Women talk," Ross summed up, fortunately not seeming to share Drew's surprise at all. "We'd better take separate vehicles to Haggarty. I might be there longer than you'll want to stay. It's rough terrain. Make sure you take one of the four-wheel drives." His gaze ran over Deanna. "And wear boots if you've got 'em."

She started, watching the man leave the room. He assumed she'd be accompanying them.

Drew's brooding gaze trapped hers. "Do you want to go?" He sounded doubtful.

It would be a simple matter to tell him that she didn't. She had enough Fortune Forecasting matters to take care of for him to easily fill the rest of the afternoon.

But she didn't for the simple reason that—no matter what they found or didn't find—she wanted to be there for him.

And that desire had nothing to do with being a good assistant.

She lifted her chin. "Do you want me to go?"

His eyes narrowed. "What are you mad about?"

"I'm not mad." Irritated, maybe, that he so easily thought of her only as his assistant. Which was an irritation in itself—but with herself—for being foolish enough to think otherwise. "Yes or no? Your cousin is waiting."

His lips thinned. "Yes," he snapped.

"All right, then," she snapped back.

"Go find some boots."

"I have tennis shoes and I have the high heels I brought to go with that dress for the wedding." She wiggled her feet. "These will have to do because I am not raiding Isabella's closet."

"Why not?"

"Because she hasn't offered and it wouldn't feel right," she hissed under her breath. "So are we going to go or not?"

He gave her a strange look, as if she'd grown a third eye, but nodded. "We're going."


Deanna could say she wasn't mad about something, but everything Drew knew about women told him otherwise as she sat beside him in the truck they'd borrowed from Molly's Pride.

Aside from the telephone calls that Deanna fielded while they followed Ross's truck out of town, and the messages that she tapped out on Drew's BlackBerry, she didn't say more than a half dozen words directly to him.

If that wasn't a woman pissed off about something, what was it?

And as they drove, Drew found it easier to puzzle over the workings of his assistant's mind than it was to think about what they might find once they reached their destination.

"No, Maggie, you'll have to tell Horning that Drew's unavailable for an interview right now." She was on the phone again, this time with one of the secretaries. "He knows exactly why Drew's out of town, which is why he's calling. And I know what he can be like, but don't let him bully you. Yes, I know I could call him for you, but you can handle it. Just apologize for the inconvenience, but be firm. We'll reschedule an interview when we can. Don't worry. You'll be fine. Yes. Call me back if you need me."

Drew glanced at her when she hung up. "John Horning is a pain in the neck." And right now, he had even less desire to talk to the man than usual.

"I know that and you know that. But he's also one of the most popular investigative reporters in San Diego. He's not going to be that easy to avoid if he's intent on getting a statement from you beyond the press release we issued. He's obviously following the story—he'll learn soon enough that your dad's car has been found." His BlackBerry rang again and she answered it.

Her gaze slid toward him a moment later. She pressed a button, then held the phone toward him. "It's on mute. You can handle this call yourself. It's Stephanie Hughes."

He waved off the phone. "Get rid of her."

Deanna made a face. She pressed a button and put the phone back to her ear. "I'm sorry, Ms. Hughes. Unfortunately, Drew is unavailable right now. Can I give him a message?" She suddenly winced and held the phone out from her ear.

Drew could hear the strident, feminine tones spewing out of the phone, every third word an expletive and every fourth, Deanna's name.

He exhaled roughly and grabbed the phone out of her hand. "Steph? It's Drew. I told you things were over a month ago. It had nothing to do with Deanna then, but considering the way you're talking about her, it does now." He hung up while the woman was still swearing at him, and tossed the phone onto the console. "Sorry about that. She heard about the engagement from a clerk at Zondervan's." Where she'd probably gone to find out the value of the bracelet Deanna had procured as an exit gift from Drew. In the month that Drew had seen Stephanie, he'd been hard-pressed to decide if she was more interested in his connections or his money. Either way, he'd gotten tired of the woman even more quickly than usual.

"I gathered that." Denim rustled as Deanna crossed her jean-clad legs and looked out the window beside her.

Ross was slowing ahead of him, and Drew did the same.

"Has she been calling a lot?"

The ends of Deanna's hair slid over her shoulder. "Only this once. You've had calls from Erin, Sonya, Mindy and Alexa, though. Several, each, actually. Oh, and Belinda, too." She gave him a bland look. "She left you quite an...inventive...message on your voice mail. I saved it for you."

He actually felt his neck get hot. "I met her a few weeks ago. She's a model."

"A lingerie model." She'd looked back out the window, sounding bored. "Yes. I heard that part, too. Unintentionally."

He could only imagine what else she might have

heard. Belinda Reeves was nothing if not verbal about what she wanted. Namely, him, in some definitely adventurous ways, which she'd made more than plain when he'd met her at a friend's beach house. "I haven't slept with her." He hadn't ruled it out, but realized now that the possibility had lost its appeal.

Primarily because he couldn't get his assistant out of his head.

Deanna didn't even budge. "That's none of my business."

"If not yours, then whose? You're my fiancée."

At that, her head did turn. Her hazel eyes were cool. "So you do remember."

"Do you think it's something I'm likely to forget?" His hand tightened around the steering wheel. Every freaking time he walked into the bedroom they were sharing, it was the only thing he could think about.

She wore his ring. They were sleeping—more or less—in the same bed.

It was making him insane.

She was the only woman on the planet he'd ever wanted and not done something about it.

Which was why he'd been spending as little time around her as was humanly possible.

"Look," he began carefully, "I know this hasn't been easy on you. I've dumped everything from back at the office on you and—"

"I don't care about that."

"And you've obviously had to field more personal calls than I expected. I'm sorry about that, too."

"It's nothing I don't deal with in San Diego."

His patience was thinning and he exhaled roughly. "Then what's the burr you've got under your blanket all about?"

"Nothing that I'm not smart enough to get over," she said coolly.

Which was no answer at all.

He tried another tack. "Have you talked to your mother?"

She gave him a suspicious look. "Not in the past few days. Why?"

He shrugged. Given the temper on her face, he figured now wouldn't be the best time to admit that he'd called Gigi Gurney himself several days earlier. She'd been positively simpering when she'd realized who he was, and had girlishly giggled and promised that, of course, she was willing to go to counseling if that would make her little Deedee happy. He'd felt in need of a strong bolt of coffee afterward just to get the woman's overblown, cloying sweetness out of his head.

Deanna really was nothing at all like her mother.

Thank God.

He realized Ross was slowing to a crawl, pulling off the side of the empty road onto a very narrow shoulder, and Drew pulled in behind him to park. "Wait here."

He waited until Deanna nodded, her expression as abruptly solemn as he felt inside, and got out of the truck.

He met Ross halfway. "Is this the spot?"

Ross shook his head. He unfolded a map and spread it out against the side of his truck. "From what the boys in Haggarty told me, William's car probably went off about a mile up." He stabbed a sharply curving line on the map. "They warned me that there's no spot to stop there, though."

Drew didn't know if he was relieved or not that he wasn't standing in the exact spot his father's vehicle had left the highway. He looked from the map to the road ahead and realized then that leading from the shoulder ahead of Ross's truck was a road of sorts.

Dirt and steep as hell, the glorified path cut through the tall brush from the main road and disappeared into the trees. "That how we get down there?"

His cousin nodded. "The road goes about two miles before it dead-ends at a dry creek. We'll have to go on foot the rest of the way." He folded the map until only one square section showed. He traced his finger in a circle around a small area. "That'll give you an idea of the lay." He handed the map to Drew. "How long's it been since you've gone four-wheeling?"

Drew grimaced. "Not long, but that was for enter-tainment."

Ross grunted. "Sure you're up to this? It's not going to be a picnic to see."

"Yeah."

"What about Deanna?"

Drew looked over his shoulder at the truck. Despite the distance, he could see the little frown lines on her forehead. Could see the worry in her wide eyes. "She'll be all right."

"Yeah, well, she looks like she's about ready to vomit."

Drew frowned. Deanna did look almost as sick as he felt. "She wouldn't have come with me if she didn't want to be here."

"You sure?"

He nodded.

There were more than a few things he was realizing he hadn't known about Deanna Gurney.

She jogged every morning for an hour before she showered with that green apple–scented shampoo of hers and headed into the hacienda's kitchen for a cup of hot tea.

Tea. Not coffee. Turns out she didn't even drink the stuff.

He'd always appreciated her incredibly bright mind and used it to his advantage. But now he knew she had a body that was made to be worshipped to go along it. And he knew that her mossy-green eyes turned to emerald when her emotions were high, which was far more often than he would ever have suspected of his pragmatic, all-about-business assistant.

He'd learned all of that in the ten days that had passed since he'd woken up in bed with her, her seductive body unintentionally all but glued to his.

And there were an infinite number of things more to learn that taunted him.

Tempted him.

But the one thing he did know about Deanna?

"I'm sure. She's stronger than you think," he told Ross.

Then he pushed the map in his pocket and walked back to the truck.

# Chapter Nine

"Oh my God." Deanna's hushed voice seemed to echo around the small clearing where William Fortune's luxury sedan had finally come to a crashing stop.

Luxury was no more.

The hood of the car was caved in thanks to the gigantic boulder, which was undoubtedly what had stopped the car from heading even farther along the wooded ravine where they'd found it. All but one of the windows were shattered out, and the roof of the car was dented in as if it had rolled.

Probably more than once.

And who knew what was responsible for the mangled rear of the car and the passenger door that hung off its frame in a gaping tilt as if it, too, wanted to scream.

She turned her eyes away from the sight.

"You okay?" Drew was standing next to her. Unlike her, he didn't seem out of breath at all. Not from the strenuous walk they'd had once they'd left the trucks behind, nor from the grim sight of his father's demolished vehicle.

"I should be asking you that." She pulled in a deep breath, scented strongly of scrub brush and dirt and biting cold air. She hadn't realized how tiring it would be to walk on the shifting gravel and rock of a not entirely dry creek bed. But that had been easier than trying to navigate the unfriendly land beside it.

Her jeans were caked with mud up to her knees. It even squished between her toes where it had worked into her shoes and through her socks. And neither Drew nor Ross looked any better.

"I'd rather see it than not know," Drew told her. Like her, he was carrying one of the bottles of water that Ross had come prepared with and he handed it to her. "Finish it if you need more," he offered.

She took the bottle, though she had no intention of drinking his share in addition to her own, and watched him work his way over and around the tumble of rocks and boulders where his father's car was lodged.

Ross was already crawling around in the front seat of it. Or as much of the front seat as was left.

She didn't know how either one of them could bear it and even though she was glad to have accompanied Drew, glad in some deep part of her that he'd wanted her with him, she finally had to simply look away from the wreckage.

She propped the two water bottles on the sandy, graveled ground next to a weathered, rotting log, and carefully picked her way around the area, seeing nothing but more mud.

More rocks.

More scraping, poking shrubs and scarred trees.

How could William have walked away from that devastatingly mangled vehicle, much less through such inhospitable terrain?

"Watch out." Ross spoke beside her and she stopped cold, startled nearly out of her wits. He pointed. "That's a footprint." His heavy boots—much more suited to hiking than her tennis shoes—circled a small area.

All she saw was a drying patch of mud.

He pulled out a slender digital camera and crouched down, taking several shots of the patch at differing angles. Then he rose, and slowly followed some path that Deanna couldn't detect, stopping every now and then to crouch down again and take more pictures. Before long, he'd disappeared into a tangle of bushes that were so tall that she could barely see the top of his head.

She looked back at the car, and even knowing what to expect, still felt the sight of it in some deep, uneasy portion of her stomach.

Drew was still inside the front of the car, his wide shoulders wedged into the driver's seat now. His legs were braced outside of the car against the pitched ground.

She blew out a long breath, hoped she wouldn't be sick and moved over to the side of the car.

Inside, she could see the limp remains of spent safety airbags. Dirt and stones littered the seats and the floor where it had come in through the windows. The windshield was a mass of spidery cracks.

"There really is no blood," Drew murmured. "Not even the smallest spatter."

Deanna focused on his face instead of the wreckage. Ross had told them that the police who'd investigated the scene had reported that there wasn't any evidence of human injury, but it still seemed hard to believe. "I don't know how anyone can even tell, considering how much debris and dirt there is." There was even a small tree branch caught in the seat beside him.

Drew looked at her. "I rolled a car when I was a senior in college." He grimaced and looked away. His hand brushed over the passenger seat. Dust puffed up and glimmered in the fractured sunlight slanting through the windshield. "Three of us were in the car. We all ended up with plenty of cuts and bruises and that was nothing as bad as this. But there was still blood smeared on a few windows and the seats and doors."

Deanna hastily shut off the images that brought to her mind. "Were you hurt badly?"

"That's where I got this." He touched the small scar near his hairline. "But none of us were really hurt. Thank God."

"How'd it happen?"

"Being stupid. As usual." He grimaced. "We'd driven down to Rocky Point in Mexico to party and were on our way back to the States. I swerved to avoid a guy pushing a cart who came out of nowhere. Missed him. Rolled the car. The only good thing was that I wasn't drinking or it would have been a helluva mess."

He let out a breath and shook his head again. "The search dogs the police brought through here would have scented Dad's blood if there'd been any to find. Inside or outside the car."

"Then maybe the airbags did what they were supposed to do," Deanna posed.

"Maybe." He leaned over and swept his hand inside the glove compartment where the door was already hanging askew. "It's empty."

"The police could have emptied it."

"Hmm." He sat back up again. His hands circled the

steering wheel that was sitting at an unnaturally close angle to the seat and his body. "I wonder if Dad was even in the car when it went down the embankment."

"Like he'd gotten thrown from the car before it went over?" She looked upward, trying to follow the line the car seemed to have taken. But they were too deep in the ravine to see the road.

"Maybe."

"Or do you still think there's a possibility of foul play?"

"Ross doesn't. If it were a kidnapping, we'd have gotten a ransom demand by now."

"What do you think?"

"I don't know what to think." He opened the console. Pulled out a small notepad and flipped through the pages. Deanna could see that they were blank. "Not anymore." He tossed the notepad back in the console and closed it with a snap. Then he reached up and flipped down the sun visor.

A slip of paper fell from it and hit his knee, then slid onto the floor.

He reached down, his hands sweeping for it.

"I've got it." She could see where the white square had fallen, almost beneath the seat and she knelt next to him, reaching around his legs. Her muddy shoe slipped a few inches just as she felt the slick paper under her fingertip and she steadied herself with the closest object.

His thigh.

She hastily adjusted her footing and let go of him before grabbing the item as she straightened again.

"Here." She handed him what turned out to be a black-and-white photograph of a dark-haired woman.

"That's my mother." His thumb slowly flicked the

corner of the photograph as he stared thoughtfully through the crackled windshield.

"And the baby she's holding?"

He didn't even glance at the picture again. "J.R."

Deanna's teeth worried the inside of her cheek when he said nothing more. But a moment later, she heard rustling and looked over to see Ross emerging from the bushes again.

"Seen enough?" he asked as he walked closer.

She had. More than enough. But this wasn't about her and she knew that if Drew wanted to stay, then she would suck up her horror and stay with him for as long as he needed to be there.

But he was working himself out of the crushed-in car and she moved away to give him more space to maneuver.

When he was out, he looked at his cousin. "Find anything useful?"

"A boatload of partial footprints." Which didn't seem to make Ross very happy, judging by the frown on his face. "Most of them probably made by the police when they came through with the tracking dogs. Hard to tell, particularly after the rain. From what I could see, the shoe treads all looked pretty rugged, like hiking boots. Because we don't know what William was wearing—" He broke off, grimacing, and slid his small camera back in his jacket pocket. "It's going to take us a while to get back to the trucks and we'll lose the light if we don't get started soon."

"I've seen enough of the car." Drew closed his hand over Deanna's shoulder and nudged her forward.

"Wait." She turned back after several steps to grab their water bottles and hurried back to them and then, aside from the slip of gravel under their feet, they silently began their trek back to their trucks.

Just as Ross had predicted, by the time they reached the two vehicles, the sun was hanging low, reddening the sky with an impossibly beautiful sunset.

Ross pulled two fresh water bottles out of the pack in his vehicle and held them out. "I'm going to book it to Haggarty. I can still catch the guy who caught the call before his shift ends. You coming or heading back?"

Drew tossed their empty bottles into the truck bed and took the fresh supply, handing one to Deanna. "Back."

"I'll let you know if I learn anything. Drive careful up the road." And then with a wave, he climbed in his big truck and was heading off, bumping over the rocky bank of the creek bed.

Deanna headed around their truck for the passenger side, but stopped short of getting in when she realized Drew hadn't moved.

Instead, he'd balanced his water bottle on the side of the truck and remained there with his arms propped next to the water.

He was holding up the photograph.

"He used to keep this same picture on his desk at the office. A larger one, I mean." He squared the picture between his long fingers. "He had six in all. One of the two of them on their wedding day. And one each of her with all of us as babies."

"That's lovely," she said softly.

"Why'd he keep this picture in his car?"

"What do you mean?"

"Why not one of Lily?"

"Sentiment," Deanna suggested. "You just said how he kept the ones in his office."

"True," he mused softly and looked at the photo again. Then he smiled slightly. "I remember one time she was redecorating Dad's office for him and took away all those old pictures. Gave him one framed picture instead—some family portrait she'd made us all get spit-shined for when I was in junior high. But he made her bring all the other ones back."

He glanced across the truck bed at Deanna, holding up the photo between his fingers. "She wanted to know why he wanted those old photos when there was such a nice new one where she was looking the best she'd ever looked in her life, and he told her because the others were reminders of every moment in his life when his love for her had doubled."

Her heart squeezed. Not just from the story, but because Drew was actually sharing it. She almost didn't want to say a word, afraid he'd stop if she did. But she couldn't keep silent. She set her water bottle inside on her seat. "He must have loved her very much."

"We all did," he murmured. He looked back at the photograph. "She would have liked you."

She swallowed. "Why?"

"You're here. Even after I tried to get you to go, you're here."

Just that easily, she felt tears burning deep behind her eyes.

She blinked them back, hard, before he could notice and moved around the truck beside him.

She slipped the photograph out of his fingers and looked into the long-ago face of his mother. Molly Fortune was sitting up in a hospital bed wearing a pale-colored bed jacket and staring into the camera with a serene smile.

It was a small photograph. Maybe three inches square.

But the woman's contented happiness as she held her firstborn son in her arms still managed to shine out of it.

Deanna couldn't recall ever seeing photos of her mother holding her as a baby. If there had been photos from her childhood, they'd disappeared somewhere along the way.

"Your mother probably kept a baby book for each of you," she guessed. Along with the woman he described, the image in the photograph seemed to suggest that Molly had been the kind of mother who would have done so. As well as making sure they had family portraits through the years.

Something else that had been absent from Deanna's upbringing. A happy-looking family, recorded for posterity.

For the Gurneys, there had been no happiness. No family. Just a mother who basically blamed her only daughter for existing.

Deanna focused on Drew, who was looking at her with a small frown.

"Didn't your mom keep a baby book?"

"I doubt it." She shrugged, not entirely comfortable having the focus back on her. "If she did, she's never showed it to me. And Gigi's not big on that sort of thing anyway."

"What is she big on, aside from the home shopping channels?"

"Grandiose dreams of finding the perfect romance."

"Sounds like a lot of women I know."

Deanna made a face. "She just chooses to continually look in the wrong place."

"Is there a right place?"

"Don't ask me. I'm not the one with the experience. Where'd you meet your ex-wife?"

"College. But that doesn't count because it obviously wasn't real."

"Or she wouldn't have cheated on you?"

His lips twisted. "Presumably."

She chewed the inside of her lip. "Cheating has no place in true love."

"So you've been in love? With who? That Mike guy?"

"Mark." She shook her head. "And no. But you still haven't said whether or not you had a baby book."

He gave her a sideways look that told her he knew she was being evasive, then shrugged. "Yeah. Baby books for all of us. Scrapbooks. My mother did 'em all. Filled with hair from our first haircuts and birthday cards and report cards once we got into school." He grinned crookedly. "Even though some of those report cards definitely weren't worth saving, at least on my part."

"I find that hard to believe."

"Why?"

She laughed a little. "Because you're fiercely brilliant, which you very well know. Aside from the whole spelling thing, that is."

"Well, believe it. I goofed off more in school than I should have. Used to drive my father crazy."

"And your mother?"

Drew's wry smile died. "She'd shake her head and tell me that she knew I could do better." He was silent for a moment, remembering.

So he had done better. Or at least he'd tried to.

His throat suddenly felt tight. "She gave all the books to each of us when she got sick."

Deanna's hand squeezed his shoulder. "She looks like

a beautiful woman," she said softly and handed him the photograph. "Inside and out."

He took the photograph, too aware of the way his fingers brushed hers.

His memories of his mother were so clear they were just as much a physical ache inside him as the other unassuaged ache he'd developed for Deanna.

But remembering his mother was easier than thinking about that mangled car. And wondering what on God's earth had become of his father.

Was the picture that William had kept in his car significant? Or was it, like Deanna suggested, simply sentiment?

He turned his back against the side of the truck and his arm brushed against the soft fullness of her breast.

He squinted into the sunset, very aware of the fact that Deanna didn't take a step back. Didn't put a breathing space carefully between them as she usually did.

She remained right where she was, facing him, one arm propped against the side of the truck bed.

Or maybe it was just easier talking about things he usually didn't because Deanna was watching him and her eyes were soft in the rosy light. Almost as soft as the feel of her body when he brushed against her.

"She was beautiful," he said abruptly. "I grew up hearing my father tell her that, and she'd always blush and wave away his words and tell him she was never going to be winning any beauty contests. But we all knew that wasn't what he meant."

Deanna tilted her head slightly. Her cheek rested on her hand. "You were lucky."

He'd known that, but never more dearly until he'd realized they were losing her. "She never let anyone down." The laugh that hit him came out of nowhere.

"Not that she was a saint. Man, did she have a temper. And she wouldn't let anything slip by her."

"Ah." Deanna gave him a knowing look. "I suppose you tried, though."

He smiled. "Hell, yeah. And not just me. We all did. Except for maybe J.R. He was always a pretty straight arrow." He gave a short chuckle. "One time when I was fourteen, a friend of mine and I swiped his dad's car keys—it was a classic Mustang he'd restored—and we went joyriding. Tommy sideswiped a Dumpster outside a bar and ran into a brick fence. We weren't hurt, but the police hauled us down to the station and put us in a cell. Scared the holy hell out of us. Told us we were going to be there overnight. Maybe a lot of overnights."

"Good grief. You were only fourteen?" Deanna looked shocked. He wasn't sure if it was because of the stunt they'd pulled or the jail issue.

"Nearly fifteen. Figuring we were going to be driving soon enough." They'd been cocky little idiots. "So once we're in jail, we make our one phone call we're allowed. Shaking in our boots, scared out of our minds. Tommy calls his folks, who are pretty damn furious about the car, but tell him they're on their way. Then I call my father, figuring he'll use his influence to get us off the hook altogether, 'cause there was no way that one of the sons of William Fortune was going to be run in for some mostly harmless fun. But he said no way. That we deserved to spend the night in jail. Said it would be a good lesson."

"Ouch." She winced. "What'd you do?"

He shrugged. "Tommy's folks came down as promised and he was released to them, but I had to go back to the cell."

"For how long?"

At the time, it had felt like an eternity. "Most of the night. But about three o'clock in the morning, one of the officers came and got me. My mom had come to bail me out after all." He shook his head, remembering. "She was seriously pissed. Didn't want to hear any excuses. Told me to shut up and get in the car. But the worst of it was that I knew I'd disappointed her."

"So what happened?"

"Right before we got home, she told me that just because she loved me didn't mean she always had to like me. But no matter what, she would always be there." And she had been, until cancer had stolen her right out from under their noses.

His jaw tightened. According to William, Drew's footloose, bachelor lifestyle would have disappointed Molly, too.

Deanna shifted and took the photograph again. "Always being there. That seems the mark of true beauty to me," she murmured. Then she slid the small picture inside the lapel pocket of the shirt he'd borrowed from J.R., and softly patted it.

Her gaze lifted to his, a faint smile on her lips.

Always being there.

Just like Deanna.

Her palm started to move away from his chest and he caught her hand, holding it in place. "Yeah." His voice was suddenly coming from somewhere deep and gruff. "That's beauty."

The curve on her lips slowly died.

Her eyes widened for a breath of a second, giving him a glimpse into something even softer, even more inviting, than the inadvertent brush of her body, before she suddenly blinked.

He felt her hand start to slide out from beneath his.

"Don't."

She went still.

Her hair looked even more deeply red in the setting sunlight and he lifted his other hand, threading his fingers through the strands, slowly sliding it away from her sun-kissed cheek.

"Drew—"

He pressed his thumb across her lips, silencing whatever it was she was going to say.

If it was a protest, he didn't want to fight it.

If it was some logical argument, he didn't want to debate it.

And if it was a challenge?

At that moment, he was beyond trying to win it.

Instead, he skimmed his fingertips along the line of her jaw and wondered if she knew just how fine her skin felt, or how delicate her bones felt. Or how intensely fascinating he found it watching the long, lovely line of her throat work when she swallowed—nervously?—or how much he wanted to touch his tongue to the base of her throat, right where he figured her pulse was beating…

He watched her eyelids flicker, then go heavy when his fingertips found the nape of her neck beneath that wealth of thick, silky hair.

Her chin slowly lifted. But those eyes didn't close. Instead, her emerald gaze searched his.

What did she see?

Her boss? The man she claimed to believe was a good man? Or maybe the fallible guy who was not only a disappointment to the man he'd admired most in the world, but to the mother he still couldn't believe was gone?

And maybe it was none of them.

Maybe right then he was just a man.

A man who wanted her even when he tried not to.

The fingers he was still holding captured against his chest curled. She leaned closer into him. "Don't look at me like that if you're not going to kiss me," she whispered.

So he did.

He slowly brushed his lips over hers. Explored the shape of her full lower lip, tasted the faint bow of her upper and absorbed the soft, soft, feel of the faint sigh she gave.

It might as well have been the first kiss he'd ever had for the way it shook him.

And when he finally stopped to pull in a breath and pressed his forehead against hers, still holding her close, he realized it could have been the last kiss he'd ever need for the way it soothed him.

Her free arm came up, wrapping behind him, her hand cradling his head.

He felt her tremble.

Or maybe it was him who was shaking.

Either way, it scared the hell out of him in a way that a jail cell never had when he'd been a stupid, foolish kid.

He lifted his head.

The sun was even lower. The sunset dwindling.

"We should get back."

Deanna had tears in her eyes as she looked up at him and the sight of them had something that had nothing whatsoever to do with sex or grief aching inside him.

She nodded. Moistened her lips and looked down as she stepped away from him. Then she picked up his water bottle that had fallen to the ground without his notice and handed it to him before silently walk-

ing around the truck and climbing inside and quietly
shutting the door.

He took one last look along the creek bed that had led
to his father's car. But he had no more answers when it
came to his missing father than he did when it came to
the woman sitting in the truck waiting for him.

So he did the only thing he could do.

He climbed in behind the wheel beside her, and they
drove away.

## Chapter Ten

They made the trip back to Molly's Pride in silence.

It was dark out when Drew stopped in front of the house to drop her off and Deanna climbed out. Her legs felt stiff, not just from the unaccustomed trek they'd made, but also because the mud on her jeans had dried and turned hard.

"I'm going to take a shower," she told him.

"Is that a warning?"

Had she meant it as one? Or had she meant it as an invitation?

She didn't know. Particularly after everything that had happened that afternoon. After the way he'd talked.

After he'd kissed her the way he had and destroyed once and for all the notion that she had any semblance of control where her feelings for him were concerned.

She looked at him. In the interior light of the truck, his hooded gaze was steady, but gave no hint whatsoever of his thoughts. If he'd been as moved by that kiss as she'd been. Or if he was afraid she'd make something out of it that she shouldn't.

Maybe all it had meant to him was a moment of… comfort…in a difficult period.

Her fingers curled around the door handle. "Do you need it to be a warning?"

"Probably."

Her heart clutched.

And even though she was no closer to understanding what emotions were going on behind those inscrutable brown eyes, she made herself nod. "Then that's what it is," she said before closing the truck door.

Then she backed away as he put the truck in motion and drove toward the set of outbuildings next to the barn.

"So how bad was it?"

Startled, she whirled around to see Isabella standing inside the opened doorway of the house, light shining out around her like some sort of halo.

The other woman meant the accident site, of course, not the effect that Drew Fortune was having on her heart.

"Devastating," Deanna answered. Which answered both.

She brushed her hands down the sides of her filthy jeans and headed toward the door. "The car was a mess, but there was no sign of William at all. Drew wonders if he was even in the car."

Isabella was nodding. "Ross called J.R. and filled him in. I think that's something they're all wondering."

"And Lily? How's she doing?"

"Her faith is unswerving, that's how she's doing. More than once she said how strongly she feels that

Ryan is watching out for William." Isabella drew in a long breath. "Whether or not that's good, she was still steady enough to want to go home after we heard from Ross. Jeremy went with her. He's going to stay with her for a while and make sure she has no more episodes like she did here. Evidently, he arranged for a leave of absence so he could stay on in Red Rock until things are more…settled."

"That's good."

"I think so." Her gaze traveled over Deanna. "By the looks of you, it must not have been a walk in the park getting there."

"It wasn't. I'm aiming straight for the shower. But I shouldn't even walk through your house."

Isabella just waved away the words as she backed into the house and closed the door after Deanna. "You can borrow some clothes. You're taller than I am, but I'm sure I have a few things that would work."

"I don't want to impose any more than I already have."

"Oh, now that's just silly." Isabella tucked her arm through Deanna's as they headed along the hallway. "If I'd been thinking straight at all, I would have thought to offer before. You must think I'm a terrible hostess."

"I think you've had plenty on your mind," Deanna assured, "and none of us expected for us to be here this long. But—" she looked down at herself again, thinking about the meager contents of their guest closet that she'd laundered more than once already "—maybe a pair of pants would be handy while I get these jeans washed. Assuming they'll even come clean."

Isabella smiled. "They will. You're no muddier than J.R. has been on occasion." They'd reached Deanna and Drew's guest room door. "I'll bring several things in for you, not just one pair of pants. And if there's something you need that I don't think of, just say so. Please."

"Thanks." Her practical nature overrode her natural inclination not to impose any more than she already felt she was doing. "So, how did the doctor visit go?"

"Wonderfully." Isabella's smile told the story, though, and Deanna was struck by the similarity between her hostess's expression and the one that Molly Fortune had been wearing in the photograph.

She gave the other woman a hug, her true delight almost enough to drown out the tinge of envy she felt. "Congratulations. I'm so happy for you all."

"Thank you." Isabella returned the hug. "And thank you. For listening that day. You're very easy to talk to, you know. You have a very sympathetic ear." Then she stepped away and smiled again. "I'll get those clothes while you clean up. J.R. insists we plan a little celebration later this week, even if the timing is bad."

"I don't think there is bad timing when it comes to celebrating a new baby."

"Which makes you sound like J.R.," Isabella pointed out, looking amused as she turned toward her own room.

Deanna closed herself in the bedroom and went straight through to the bathroom. She flipped on the shower and peeled out of her clothes. Her jeans were so stiff they practically stood up on their own.

She started to step into the shower, but went stock-still when she heard movement in the bedroom.

"Just me," Isabella called out. "I put some things on the bed." And then Deanna heard the door close again.

Her shoulders slumped. What had she expected? That Drew would have changed his mind?

She sighed and stepped into the shower. And although it was easy enough to wash away the grime from the day, it wasn't at all easy to wash away the wish that he would have.

And impossible altogether to wash away the realization that she was irrevocably, wholeheartedly in love with her boss.

Drew sat on the bed in the bedroom, listening to the sound of the shower running.

He didn't have to work hard summoning an image in his head of Deanna standing beneath the spray, water flowing over her limbs, turning her hair to wet fire and her skin to wet silk.

He shoved his hands through his hair. Pressed the heel of his palm against his closed eyes.

The images remained.

And it was only when he realized his fist was making a crumpled mess of the stack of clothes that were sitting on the bed beside him, did he realize, too, that the water had stopped running.

He made an attempt at smoothing the stack of clothes.

He had been deliberately spending as little time as possible in this room they shared. He'd walked nearly every inch of Molly's Pride. He'd sat in the bar at Red until closing time. He'd sat on the freaking back porch until the sun was nearly ready to dawn in the sky.

But could he make himself move off the foot of the bed just then, even knowing what sort of danger he was inviting?

His nerves tightened as he heard the creak of the bathroom door. He stared down at his mud-caked boots, way too aware of the mirror across from him that would have reflected her in the doorway, if he'd allowed himself to look. "You're not alone," he announced abruptly.

"I see that," she answered after a moment.

He heard her soft footsteps on the floor and in his periphery, knew that she'd stopped at the closet door, because he could see her bare feet.

And her bare calves.

Hell.

His gaze lifted to the mirror, just long enough for him to know that she had a bath towel wrapped around her torso.

Sweat broke out on his brow and started creeping down his spine. He'd never thought of terry cloth as an instrument of seduction, until the day she'd lost hers right in front of his very eyes.

"You done in there?" His voice was rough.

"Yes." She plucked one of the garments off the stack sitting beside him and shook it out. It was a yellow dress that looked just like Isabella, and nothing like Deanna's usual severe style.

And he was damned if he didn't want to see it on her.

And off.

"Good." He shoved off the bed and brushed past her, heading into the bathroom himself.

It was filled with steam, but that would be solved quickly enough, because the only thing he needed on himself right now—because having her wasn't an option—was cold water.

And a lot of it.

He shut the door between them and nearly swallowed a groan as the smell of her seemed to hang in the steamy air. The clothes that she'd discarded were lying in a heap in one corner. The jeans were as filthy as his own and the minuscule strip of filmy white that was resting on top looked even whiter as a result.

A vibration in his jeans pocket startled the hell out of him, and he muttered an oath, looking away from Deanna's skimpy panties.

He'd forgotten he'd shoved his phone in his pocket after he'd returned J.R.'s truck to the oversize garage where the ranch vehicles were kept, and he pulled it out now, looking at the display. Stephanie Hughes.

He grimaced and silenced the vibration.

Even if he hadn't already ended things with the woman, the minimal interest he'd had in her would have been blown out of the water by the tidal wave that had become Deanna.

He pushed the phone back in his pocket and opened the bathroom door, leaning out, and knew he was a dog when disappointment snagged at him that Deanna had already pulled on the bright yellow dress and was standing in front of the mirror, working a comb through her wet hair.

Not because the dress didn't look nice. It did, particularly against her satiny-smooth, tanned skin.

But because he knew only too well that she looked even better with nothing on at all.

She was giving him a startled look through the mirror's reflection. "What?"

He barely managed to unscramble his thoughts. "Remember I mentioned Red? The restaurant?" He didn't wait for her wary nod. "We'll go there for dinner," he said abruptly.

She lowered her comb, still watching him through the mirror. "Why?"

"Because after this afternoon, we need a break from everything." God knows he did.

Of course, the logical thing would have been to take a break from the other source of his problems—her—too.

But he'd been trying to do that every night when she headed off to bed, and it had been failing him miserably.

"And I figure I owe you something. You know." He felt strangely inept and didn't particularly like it. "For handling everything at the office for me the way you have been. You've been taking care of everything for me and…and I owe you."

She looked over her shoulder directly at him then. Her brows pulled together. "I've been trying to do my job."

"And you've basically been doing mine, as well," he returned. "You've managed to keep everyone on task in San Diego and Los Angeles."

"Because everyone in both offices knows how to do their jobs," she pointed out.

"Maybe," he allowed. "But I just want you to know that everything you've done hasn't gone unnoticed."

Her eyes narrowed slightly. "Put it in my next performance review."

"Dammit, Deanna, I'm trying to show some appreciation here."

Her eyebrows shot up. "Fine," she said mildly. "We'll go out to dinner, then."

"Good." He pushed the door shut between them and shook his head. Why had he ever thought she was the least complicated, most predictable woman he'd ever met?

His gaze landed on the filmy white panties again.

The only thing predictable about her was turning

out to be his increasingly unquenchable interest in everything about her.

He muttered a low oath again, directed solely at himself, and flipped on the shower.

Cold.

"You're right." Two hours later, Deanna sat back in her chair and folded her napkin, setting it beside her dinner plate. "The food here is wonderful."

Sitting across the small round table from her, Drew smiled faintly. "There's a reason why Red's made a name for itself well beyond Red Rock. The food can't be beat."

Even as often as she warned herself otherwise, Deanna knew that ninety percent of the appeal that evening for her was Drew himself.

He'd set himself out to be charming, keeping her amused with no seeming effort at all, and not once dwelling on either his father, or the company that he was willing to marry her to get.

For a seeming gesture of appreciation for her work of late, if she hadn't known better, the evening would have had all the trappings of romance.

But her head did know better, even if the rest of her kept getting caught up in him.

Obviously, the appeal for the rest of the diners was the restaurant itself, which was housed in a converted hacienda that Drew told her dated back to Texas's early statehood.

Even on a weeknight at the relatively late hour, the main dining room—which struck Deanna as blatantly romantic with its seductive dark woods and touches of passionate color—was still packed. Marcos Mendoza, Isabella's handsome half brother who managed the restaurant, was frequently on the floor, visiting with his patrons, his flashing white smile clearly as much an attraction to the female part of the crowd as was the excellent fare. He'd met Drew and Deanna at the door when they'd arrived and even as consuming as her emotions for Drew were, she was no exception to that. Isabella was a beautiful woman and her half brother was an equally arresting man and he seemed quite at home helming the busy restaurant.

"We can't leave without having Maria's famous flan, though," Drew was saying as he poured the last measure of sangria into their glasses.

"I couldn't possibly eat another bite," Deanna protested. She hadn't even been able to finish her entrée, excellent as it was. The menu at Red wasn't like any menu she'd ever seen before in a Mexican restaurant. It wasn't abnormally extensive, but the choices were far more varied and inventive than the budget-friendly restaurants she was used to. In the end, she'd depended on Drew to choose, and the spicy grilled tuna concoction had been nothing short of amazing.

"You're going to want at least a forkful. They serve it over some sort of flavored cake with a chocolate mole sauce." His smile was lazy and full of promise. "You'll think you've died and gone to heaven."

Considering the datelike quality of the evening, Deanna wasn't sure she hadn't already done so. But she shook her head ruefully. "Fine. A forkful only, though. I still need to be able to fit into my clothes when we go back to California."

In the flickering light of the candle that burned in the center of the table, Drew's gaze seemed warmer than ever as it glided over her. "I'm pretty sure you're safe," he murmured.

If they'd been back at the office in San Diego, his ball cap would have been turned backward and his eyes would have been full of all sorts of wicked.

Her fingers curled where they rested in her lap, safely hidden by the linen tablecloth on the table.

*This is not a date. This is not a date.*

She'd been repeating the mantra ever since Drew had opened the door of the low-slung sports car of J.R.'s that he'd borrowed for the evening. But the words were having even less effect now than they had then.

"I, um, am going to excuse myself for a quick moment," she finally said and started to push back the heavy chair that only seemed to make her more aware of her femininity, while making him look even more impossibly masculine.

He smoothly rose, though, and had pulled out her chair for her before she could so much as move it an inch.

He was wearing a crew-neck black sweater and the soft knit closely covering his wide shoulder was so close to her that she could have brushed her cheek against it.

She inhaled carefully as desire clutched inside her, hard and fast. Her legs felt shaky as she rose and stepped away from the table, trying to focus on the delectable aromas of food all around them and not on the delectable scent of him. "Thank you."

His smile was faint and she quickly turned away, only to nearly collide with a pretty waitress bearing a heavy tray toward the table next to them. But Drew's hand closed around Deanna's waist, scooping her aside, and the waitress smiled and shifted around her, continuing on her way without mishap.

"Okay?" Drew's word stirred the hair at her temple.

"Fine." If fine meant one who could hardly breathe. She took a step and his arm fell away and before she could do something really stupid, like pull it back around her, she headed much more carefully between the crowded tables until she reached the sanctuary of the ladies' room.

She ran her hot wrists under cool water at the hammered metal sink and looked sternly at her reflection.

Her eyes looked too wide for her face and color seemed to burn up her skin from the wide, low scooping neckline of the impossibly girly dress.

"This is not a date," she muttered.

"'Scuse me?" A striking, gray-haired woman wearing a mint's worth of turquoise jewelry stepped up to the sink beside her and smiled. "You all right, honey? You look a mite shaky."

Deanna nodded. "I'm fine."

"Handsome man waiting out there for you, I bet." She grinned. "That's what always gets me to feeling a little flustered."

Deanna managed an embarrassed smile. If it was obvious to a complete and utter stranger, then it would surely be like a neon light flashing in Drew's face.

"Just remember what my mama always told me." The woman plucked a folded paper towel off the stack of them sitting between the sinks. "Doesn't matter how much a man makes you breathless, darlin', any man worth his salt is gonna work darn hard to prove you make him feel the same way before he expects to go walking in your flower garden, if you know what I mean."

Despite herself, Deanna couldn't help but laugh. "Okay. Thanks for the advice."

"Then when he does come to smell those flowers o' yours, you knock his socks right off." The woman winked and sailed out the door.

Deanna gave a faint laugh again and turned off the water.

She dried her hands and smoothed down the full skirt of the butter-yellow dress that Isabella had loaned her.

She couldn't imagine ever knocking Drew's socks off, but it was certainly an intriguing image...

"This is not a date," she whispered again.

Feeling a little more controlled, she went back out to the dining room, only to find an older woman standing next to Drew, her hand on his shoulder as they laughed together.

They both seemed to notice Deanna at the same moment, and the woman—slightly shorter than Deanna, and far more curvaceous in her black slacks and ruffled red blouse—stepped forward and caught Deanna's hands in hers. "So this is the one to catch our Andrew's heart." With no hesitation at all, she leaned up and kissed Deanna's cheeks. "And no wonder. Such a beautiful girl."

Deanna couldn't help but smile in the face of the woman's infectious greeting.

"Deanna, this is Maria Mendoza," Drew introduced. "She and her husband, Jose, are the ones who founded this place."

*"Sí, sí."* Maria tucked her arm around Deanna's waist and squeezed. "We have seen many romances come to fruition here at Red." Her dark eyes danced. "But I'm glad to see our Drew has beautiful company tonight, unlike the other evenings he's sat alone at the bar."

Deanna shot Drew a startled look.

He'd grabbed the woman's wrinkling hand and pulled her toward him to drop a noisy kiss on her cheek. "You were as much beautiful company as I could handle, Maria."

"Bah. Not even a devil like you can make my Jose jealous." She lightly slapped his hands and turned again to Deanna. "Andrew tells me how hard you work, *niña*, while he worries and searches for his father." She gave Drew a look. "That's a good woman to have by your side through life."

Drew's smile stayed in place, but Deanna wondered if Maria could see the shadows that entered his gaze as easily as she could.

"But enough of worrisome things." Maria clasped her hands together. "When is the wedding date?"

Deanna shot Drew a look. "We—"

"We haven't had a chance to set one," he said smoothly, and his gaze looked as clear as ever, making Deanna wonder if the shadows had been her imagination after all.

"But do you want a big wedding, or small…" Maria smiled, surprisingly impish for a woman who Deanna guessed was well into her seventies. "I never tire of weddings."

"Deanna doesn't like being the center of attention," Drew said, looking oddly serious.

"Ah." Maria nodded sagely. "A small, intimate affair, then. Or even an elopement?" She sighed happily. "So romantic." Then she waved at their seats. "Now, forgive an old woman and sit. Sit. Andrew wants me to bring out my flan for you, *niña*. You'll sit in the candlelight and feed each other and fall in love all over again." She squeezed Drew's cheeks, then Deanna's, and hurried through the tables, purpose in her steps.

Deanna blinked a little and slowly sat. "Wow."

"That's a good word to describe Maria." Drew took his own seat. "You could have told her we weren't really engaged. It's going to come out sooner or later, because my father's not coming back."

Deanna went still. Her unwise enjoyment of their not-a-date started to drain away. "You don't know that, Drew. You can't give up hope. Not yet."

"Can't I?" His gaze skewered hers. "What about any of this is giving you hope?"

He was talking about his father, but he might as well have been talking about them. She tried to clear the knot out of her throat and failed. "If that's the way you feel, then you…you could have corrected Maria yourself about—" She broke off and waved her hand. The diamond ring glittered in the candlelight. "Particularly because it seems you've been spending plenty of time here on your own."

His lips tightened. "I had to go somewhere." His voice was too low for anyone but her to hear.

"Why?" She lowered her voice, too, leaning toward him across the table. This, she knew, wasn't about his father. "Just to get away from me?"

"Yes."

Even though she'd expected exactly that answer, she still felt a hideous sting.

But at least now she had her answer.

The kiss they'd shared that afternoon that had rocked her existence had been from a man who'd simply needed comfort.

Even comfort from the likes of her.

She blinked hard, looking away from him.

*This is definitely not a date.*

"Here we are." Maria returned, bearing a white plate

with the beautifully presented custard dessert that she set between them with a beaming smile. She handed Deanna a sparkling silver spoon, and another to Drew. "Enjoy." With a sly smile, she quickly moved away from the table.

Deanna was afraid that if she put one spoon in her mouth she would be sick. But she was very aware of Maria watching from the sidelines and the delightful woman had done nothing to deserve being disappointed.

It wasn't Maria's fault that she—like everyone else—had all too easily believed the lie that she and Drew had perpetrated.

So Deanna dipped the tip of the spoon through the ruffles of whipped cream, glistening chocolate sauce and silky custard and tucked it into her mouth. Flavors exploded in her mouth and she forced a smile in Maria's direction. "Delicious."

Maria's eyebrows rose and she nodded, making her silver-streaked dark hair bounce around her shoulders. Her hands fluttered in an urging sort of way.

Deanna looked back at Drew. She scooped up another spoon of the confection and leaned across the table toward him. "Open up." Her voice was flat.

He slowly leaned closer, too, and put his lips around the spoon.

Her hand trembled violently and she quickly sat back in her chair, setting the spoon down on the linen tablecloth. "There. I had a bite. It's delicious. So can we go now?"

"I don't leave because I don't want to be around you." His voice was low, but deliberate. He slowly dipped his own spoon into the dessert. "I leave because I do. Too much."

The aching tightness at the back of her jaws went lax. Butterflies suddenly flitted around inside her chest. "Excuse me?"

He lifted the spoon and held it toward her. "Open."

She mindlessly parted her lips and leaned forward.

The cool silver spoon slipped past and just as mindlessly, she closed her lips softly over the tidbit.

He slowly withdrew the spoon. "Kind of tastes like flowers, doesn't it?"

A shiver worked down her spine. "Flowers?"

"Whatever stuff it is that Maria refuses to say is in her recipe." He scooped a spoonful into his mouth and his hooded eyes narrowed for a moment in appreciation.

Deanna swallowed, her mouth running dry. Her hands curled around the heavy, carved arms of her chair.

"Not that I know what a flower really tastes like," he continued, dipping the spoon yet again before extending it toward her. "But that's what I can't help thinking every time I put my mouth around it."

"Flowers," she murmured huskily.

His dimple flirted next to the faint smile on his lips. "A whole damn garden of 'em."

She exhaled and leaned forward, parting her lips for another bite.

## Chapter Eleven

"That's going to be one lucky baby coming into the world with you two as parents." Drew lifted his wineglass in a toast toward Isabella and J.R. who were standing arm in arm in front of the fireplace where a low fire was crackling with a comfortable warmth.

"Hear, hear," Jeremy echoed.

They, along with Lily and the rest of their brothers and their wives, had gathered in the great room at Molly's Pride later that week to celebrate the coming baby.

They could easily have included more of the family, but Isabella had persuaded J.R. to keep things small. "We'll have even more to celebrate with everyone when your father returns," she'd told him.

Now, as she watched the family mingle, Deanna fervently hoped that the Fortune and Mendoza families would have that opportunity. Unfortunately, judging from the expressions on some of the faces there, she knew that after two weeks since their father had gone missing, at least some of them—Drew particularly—were seriously doubting whether that day would come.

Not that Drew had said anything more than he had that evening at Red. Not that Drew had done anything more than what he'd done that evening at Red, either.

She was torn between wanting to comfort and encourage him to have more faith where his father was concerned—even though she had her own painful doubts after all this time—and wanting to kick herself for continuing to fall into his allure when she ought to know better. And in the end, all she seemed capable of doing was walking on eggshells around him whenever they were alone.

Which, thanks to his admittedly valid excuse of hunting down leads over his missing father, were increasingly rare.

She shook her head when Nick passed by with another wine bottle and lifted her glass, which was still nearly full. Everyone had a glass. Even Isabella, though hers was filled with fruit juice.

Bethany sank onto the couch next to where Deanna sat. "Darr told me that you went with Drew and Ross to see the car when they first learned about it." She kept her voice low, sliding a glance toward Lily, who was standing near the windows with Drew and Jeremy. "I don't think I could have stood to see it. It must have been so disturbing."

"It was." In so many more ways than Deanna could share with anyone, except Drew. And especially Drew. "The, uh, the car's in a very remote location," she added, trying to focus on the conversation at hand, and not the subject of her thoughts who was looking terribly solemn as he stood with his father's fiancée, his half-empty wineglass dangling from his long fingers.

Charlene joined them, perching on the arm of the couch. She'd obviously overheard. "The guys are all going back tomorrow. They're going to take some climbing equipment and do a more extensive search. Try to reach the areas where the search dogs couldn't go."

Deanna's gaze sought out Drew again. He was wearing an oatmeal-colored shirt that she knew wasn't his and blue jeans that she knew were and his dark hair was brushed severely back from his face. Even from across the room she could see his pensive expression that didn't quite fit what was supposed to be a celebration.

She could hardly envision another search of the accident site, much less imagine Drew wanting to return there. If they found William in an area even less accessible, they surely wouldn't be finding him alive.

And maybe Bethany and Charlene were thinking the same thing because neither one of them pursued the topic any further. Instead, they all looked over to where J.R. was still holding Isabella close against his side.

"I love the idea of another baby," Charlene said, grinning a little. She was obviously determined to find a more cheerful subject. "Particularly one that I don't have to be pregnant with just yet."

Bethany laughed softly. "I wouldn't mind it so much, though it would probably be wiser to wait until Randi's through her terrorizing twos. What about you, Deanna? Do you and Drew plan to have kids right away or wait a while?"

Startled, Deanna's gaze finally broke away from Drew, but she could only stare at the other woman. She couldn't come up with an appropriate response to save her soul.

"Knowing Drew, I'll bet he wants to hold off on that," Charlene inserted, seemingly unaware of Deanna's tied tongue.

Bethany nodded knowingly. "But then, we figured Drew was going to hold off forever on getting married. Turns out we didn't know as much as we thought we did. So...?" She turned her bright gaze back to Deanna.

"I...I would like to have children," she finally managed. She was miserably afraid that her cheeks were red, even though she hadn't technically lied.

"Just not right away," Bethany guessed helpfully. Her eyes sparkled with merriment.

"Settling into married life is pretty fun," Charlene agreed. "If you know what I mean."

Deanna smiled weakly as the other two women laughed.

"Mind if I steal my fiancée?" Drew suddenly appeared, leaning over them from behind the couch.

Deanna quickly slid off the couch and smoothed down the gauzy white skirt that was another loaner from Isabella. She didn't know what Drew wanted, but she was almost pathetically grateful for the interruption, despite the fear that she could very well be jumping from the fat into the fire.

And when he wrapped his hand around hers as they left the room, that fear deepened even more.

It wasn't fear of him. Just the knowledge that— where Drew was concerned—she was totally out of her depth.

Since he'd—intentionally or not—left her feeling practically seduced over Maria Mendoza's flan at Red, he hadn't so much as touched her. Nor had he changed his ways when it came to sharing the bed in their guest room.

He didn't say a word now either, as he drew her through the house, only stopping once as they went through the laundry room, to hook a jacket off one of the pegs near the back door.

"It's cold." He finally let go of her hand, only to push the jacket into it as he ushered her outside.

Her teeth were in danger of chattering, but it wasn't the chilly night air that was the cause. Nevertheless, she managed to tug the somewhat stiff, woven coat around the shoulders of the loose-knit blouse without fumbling with it too badly. "What's wrong?"

"Nothing. I just wanted some air." He made a low sound and grabbed the lapels of the jacket and pulled them close beneath her chin. "Judging by your expression in there, I thought you looked about like I felt." He headed down the shallow steps away from the house and the warm glow of light. "What were you all talking about anyway?"

She chewed her lip and followed. "They wanted to know if we were planning on having children right away or if we wanted to wait a while." She hoped the darkness did a better job of hiding her hot cheeks than it did the surprise in his expression as he looked back at her.

"And what did you tell them?"

"What does it matter? None of it's real anyway."

"Maybe I'm curious."

She let out a huff and lifted her hands. "Fine. I told them the truth. That, yes, *I* would like to have children someday. Obviously, I wasn't answering for you." The low heel of the tall boots she'd borrowed from Isabella caught slightly in the ground and Drew's arm shot out, catching her shoulder.

"Watch your step."

She was trying to. Literally and metaphorically. "Thanks," she mumbled and continued walking, grateful when his hand fell away. "What were you and Jeremy talking about with Lily?"

"What does it matter?"

"Maybe I'm curious," she returned pointedly.

He exhaled noisily. "I was apologizing to her, okay? For being such an ass about everything when she and my father got involved."

Her footsteps halted. "You apologized?"

He stopped, too. "You think I'm incapable of it or something?"

"No, of course not. I'm just—"

"—surprised."

"Yes. And glad." Maybe he'd stop torturing himself so much over what couldn't be changed.

He made a low sound that could have meant anything. "She said that it would mean a lot to my father that we were all here in Red Rock. Supporting her. Supporting each other." His lips twisted slightly. "She said how much he loved us all. How proud he was of us." Her heart ached when his voice went rough.

"She knew about the picture," he added after a moment. "The one of my mother. Jeremy told her I'd found it. But she already knew that Dad always kept it in his sun visor." He cleared his throat abruptly. "She said she knew how much my mother meant to him because that's how she felt about Ryan and it's one of the reasons she loves Dad as much as she does. Loves. Present tense." He shook his head. "She hasn't lost hope at all."

While Drew was losing more by the day. Deanna pushed her hands in the pockets of her jacket before they could reach for him. "I'm glad you talked with her," she said again.

"She also said that it means a lot to her that Jeremy and I have stayed in Red Rock."

"I'm sure it would."

He started walking again. "Since when have you wanted kids?"

Despite the aching wish that she could take away some of his pain, she felt herself bristle. "Why wouldn't I? Not everyone is phobic about such things like you are and it's a pretty average desire." They were nearing one of the barns and Drew's hand touched the small of her back, directing her around the side of it where the smell of mowed grass was strong, even at that hour.

"I never said I had a phobia about kids."

"Are you saying you'd like to have them?" Disbelief dripped from her voice.

"I never didn't want them. But kids are better off when they're raised by married parents. I know that's not the way a lot of families are now, but it's still what I believe."

Thoroughly nonplussed, she lifted her eyebrows, trying to hide it. "And since marriage is one of your phobias…"

"Our marriage excluded, of course," he said wryly.

How easily he could be wry while she felt wholly off balance. But she managed a shrug and a casual "of course."

At the rate things had gone since William disappeared, she couldn't envision their "engagement" ever reaching an altar-bound conclusion anyway. She felt certain that he was thinking the same thing, particularly after their dinner at Red.

"I just never heard you talk about wanting kids before," he added.

She couldn't fathom where his sudden interest had come from.

He was so much easier to deal with when he behaved exactly the way she expected.

No surprises.

But all he'd been since they'd arrived in Texas was one tall, disturbing, heart-wrenching surprise.

She clutched the jacket more closely around her, willing away a shiver, and quickened her step even more.

Maybe he just wanted to focus on something other than his father and his conversation with Lily. "It's not as if I spend my entire day at the office talking about my personal wishes and aspirations," she pointed out.

"No. Until New Year's Eve, you barely acted as if you had any desires outside of work at all."

She had one overriding desire, and considering everything, he had to know by now as well as she did that he was it. "Personal lives should have no place in the workplace."

"So says Gigi's daughter." He caught her shoulder again, halting her forward momentum. "Your mother has been all about being personal in the workplace, so you've gone to the opposite extreme."

There was no point in denying the truth. Particularly because he knew about her mother now, too. She crossed her arms over her chest. She couldn't imagine why he'd have an issue over her practice. Aside from his penchant for dating money-hungry bimbos that he enlisted her aid when it was time to send them on their way, he didn't really bring much of his truly personal life into the office, either. "I don't imagine that you'd want it otherwise. The thing you like best about me is that I'm a focused assistant."

So focused and dedicated in fact, she thought hopelessly, that he'd figured she'd happily disappear back into the woodwork where she'd always been once his need of her as his convenient wife was over.

He let out a faint sound caught somewhere between a laugh and a cough. "Don't be so certain that you know what I like best about you."

Which had her shivering all over again.

She might as well be a pendulum of emotion where he was concerned, swinging from one end of the spectrum to the other. And she couldn't seem to do one thing about it but stay here in Red Rock with him even when she figured that the only reason he hadn't sent her away by now was because he "appreciated" the work she'd been doing on his behalf for Fortune Forecasting.

His hand was still curving around her shoulder, adding fuel to her agitation. She shifted from one foot to the other, and tightened her folded arms.

His hand still didn't fall away.

And despite the moonlight, his hooded gaze was making her distinctly edgy. She wasn't sure her heart could take another episode of wondering if she was misinterpreting every move he made. Everything he said.

She sucked in her lower lip for a second. "Charlene said that all of you are going back to the accident site tomorrow with hiking equipment and searching the area more."

He nodded.

"You're really going to go with them?"

He nodded again. "Yes."

"Are you sure you want to?" Hadn't he seen enough of the devastation for one lifetime?

"The only thing I'm sure about right now is that I want to sleep with you."

The world felt as if it came to a screeching halt. Everything inside her went still. She stared at him.

His hand slowly, deliberately, slid over her shoulder until the warm tips of his fingers delved beneath the jacket collar to graze her skin. "Cat got your tongue?"

"Evidently." Her voice was faint. There was no danger of misinterpreting now, and she was hardly able to think past the blood suddenly thundering through her veins.

His thumb roved up and down the side of her bare neck. "Problem is, I don't want to complicate things."

She barely kept from arching her neck against his touch like a greedy cat seeking more. "It's already complicated." More complicated than he would ever suspect, at least where her heart was concerned. "That's what happens when you get mired in a lie."

His hand slid a little until his thumb found the pulse at the base of her throat.

"Yeah." His voice was deep as he pressed his thumb against her pulse with enough pressure to let them both know how rapidly it was beating. "But this isn't a lie."

She'd been sleeping—more or less—beside him for two weeks. But in that moment, the feel of her heartbeat throbbing beneath the warm pad of this thumb was so much more intensely intimate than anything that had gone before that she was in danger of dissolving into a puddle right there where they stood in the moonlit shadows of the barn.

"Drew—"

"What *would* be a lie would be continuing to pretend that I don't want to make love to you."

She pulled in a shaking breath and didn't even care just then that it sounded as openly desperate as she felt. "It's…it's the situation. If your father weren't missing, you—"

"—would still want this. Bringing you with me to Red Rock just brought it home to me." His thumb stroked up her throat until it reached her chin. He gently pushed upward, stilling her shaking head and the denial of his words. "Look at me."

She couldn't do anything but.

"You have to know by now that I can't get through the day without wanting you," he said, and even though her emotions quaked, she recognized that he sounded more grim than romantic. "And I damn sure can't get through another night. But I don't want to ruin a good thing either, and the last thing I want—when this is all over—is for you to run for the hills."

Of course he was already anticipating an "over."

Her stomach knotted. The fastest way any woman in Drew's life could lose his interest was to let him know they were falling for him. Deanna had seen it happen over and over again. And even though she didn't want to categorize herself with any of those women, she knew that she was no different.

If Drew learned how she felt, *really* felt, he'd forget all about the "good thing" they had going. Maybe— given their working relationship—he'd feel some compunction when he ultimately showed her the door, but she had absolutely no doubt that the door was where she would be destined.

He'd find himself another assistant.

And she'd find herself out of his life in every way.

What was worse? Staying with him while hiding

her true feelings, or being without him because she hadn't?

Whichever path she took was paved with misery.

All she had to do was tell him that they could become lovers and nothing would change, and she'd at least have some part of him.

Was that how her mother thought, when she fell for her unattainable suitors?

Maybe Gigi wasn't so hard to understand after all.

Maybe, in comparison to her mother's headlong rushing into impossible relationships, Deanna was the real coward.

She moistened her lips. Swallowed. Her fingers pressed into the sinewy strength of his forearms. "I don't want to ruin anything, either."

"So where does that leave us?"

"I don't know." Her voice was nearly soundless.

He exhaled roughly and stepped closer. "I need a better answer, Dee. Tell me no. Better yet, tell me hell, no. And I'll somehow figure out a way to get this under control."

"Oh, sure." She moved her hands to his chest and shoved against him, but he was immovable. "Make me be the bad guy."

"Not bad. Just stronger than I am." His hands slid behind her. Found the small of her back and deliberately urged her against him. "And you're definitely not a guy."

While he most definitely *was*.

Her fingers were suddenly curling into his chest, rather than trying to push. He'd made certain that she wore a jacket against the evening chill, but he was only in his shirtsleeves. Nevertheless, her fingers felt scorched by his heat, even through the nubby silk of his shirt.

"I don't know what to make of you," she whispered. "At Red you were—" She broke off, unable to describe what had transpired that night. "But since then—" Again she broke off, just as stuck.

And here she was supposed to be good with words.

"I know." His voice was even. "I'm the worst kind of bastard. But know this, there has barely been a minute in a single day since we came to Red Rock when I haven't thought about you. About us."

Her heart squeezed. His words sent shocking thrills straight through her.

"I should tell you no," she whispered. For both their sakes.

He claimed that he couldn't say no himself. And even though she was painfully aware that he wasn't making any professions of love, rather than frightening her off, knowing that he couldn't deny he wanted her any longer made her feel more than a little bold.

And she could feel the way he was suddenly holding himself stiffly.

As if he'd braced for rejection.

She fisted the silk shirt and levered onto the toes of her borrowed boots until her lips hovered close to his. "I should say no," she whispered again. "But I can't make myself do it."

No matter what that meant for her—for their—future.

He exhaled and she tasted his warm breath on her lips.

Then his arms tightened around her, practically lifting her right off her toes as he pulled her even closer. His mouth covered hers, and whatever doubts that might have lingered about the wisdom of their actions died an unobtrusive death beneath the brilliance of his kiss.

If it seemed as if the world had stopped spinning before, now it whirled.

Madly.

Her head felt as though it was spinning, and her heart felt like it would burst out of her chest. All she could do was hang on to the only thing that might keep her sane. Him.

Her mouth opened under his plundering kiss, her hands curled into his hair. And the world spun even more dizzily.

His mouth dragged over her cheek, her temple. "Push the door."

It took a moment for her brain to make sense out of his low growl. And a moment after that for her vision to see anything beyond his face.

But then she realized he'd lifted her into his arms and carried her around to the front of the barn doors.

No wonder she was spinning.

She stretched out an arm and gave the door a push. Despite the rustic look of it, the door smoothly slid open a foot and without a second's hesitation, Drew turned her sideways and carried her into the dark warmth.

"Do you know where you're going?"

"Heaven." He lowered her legs until her feet hit the ground and then he was stepping closer to her, brushing right up against her until the barn door at her back stopped them. "And no, I can't see a bloody damn thing. So unless you want to take a stroll back to the house right now—"

*"No."* She shook her head even though he couldn't possibly see. Not even the door that was still ajar let in any light. She couldn't even see him standing in front of her and he was so close she could feel the rise and fall of his chest against her cheek. If they went back to

the house, it would give her time to chicken out; to start thinking with her head again, instead of her heart.

And if she did that, she just might hate herself forever...

His hands pushed beneath the jacket until it fell off her shoulders. "Good. Because I don't want to wait, and I can feel everything I want to." Unerringly, his palms closed over her hips, then purposefully delved beneath the loosely knit top.

Desire clenched hard inside her and she bit down on her tongue to keep from gasping, but a faint, mewling sound still escaped.

"We're in a barn," he murmured, his lips touching her temple. "Don't hold back."

Her hands instinctively closed around his arms. "A-are there animals in here or something?" She couldn't hear anything but the thundering of her heartbeat in her head and the rustle of her skirt against the solid wood behind her back.

"Just me."

Her head fell back against the door as his hands slipped over her waist, climbing toward her breasts. "You're not an animal."

"You're not wearing a bra," he murmured, quickly discovering that particular fact for himself. "Makes me feel like an animal."

Her lips parted. She hauled in oxygen as his hands slowly shaped her breasts as if he were molding a sculpture. Only she could feel her flesh tightening, swelling, and no inanimate sculpture ever did that. Not even beneath the chisel of the most skilled artisan.

Then his fingers dragged over her aching nipples, taunting them to even harder peaks, and she couldn't stop the moan from rising in her throat. She stared up at him in the utter darkness, feeling his touch, feeling his heat, but not being able to see.

It was as disturbingly intense as the feel of his thumb had been on the pulse at the base of her throat.

Intense. Erotic. And emboldening.

She exhaled and the shaking sound of her breath sounded loud between them. Her hands slid over his forearms until they reached his wrists. They felt bony. Strong. And as her fingers explored them, she realized she could feel *his* pulse charging beneath her fingertips, too.

"Maybe there are two animals here," she whispered. Her fingers grazed past his wrists, over the backs of his hands that cupped her breasts and she pressed her palms against them. Her fingers slid between his. "Harder."

She felt his momentary stillness, then his hands tightened on her and the shards of light pulsing through her blood went even brighter, aiming straight to the center of her. Then she heard rustling again, felt his movement, and his hands moved beneath hers and she felt the wet heat of his mouth close over her breast.

She gasped. His other hand pushed at her sweater where it was tangling beneath her arms. "Take it off."

Shaking, she obediently dragged it over her head, not feeling the slightest worry for where it landed—or what it might be landing in.

She was a California girl. She didn't know barns from nothing. All she knew, right then, was that Drew was sending *her* straight to heaven and he wasn't stopping to ask directions.

Her head fell back against the door again when his mouth slowly dragged down the valley between her breasts, over her stomach, not even pausing when he reached the stretchy waist of the gauzy skirt. He just pulled it down as he went. "If you're as naked under this as you were the sweater, I'm going to have a heart attack," he muttered.

She gave a strangled laugh. "No." Her fingers slid through his hair. She'd never realized how silky or thick it was. "I'm not that hard-up for clothes." But she'd rinsed out her bra after her shower and it was still damp, hanging safely hidden in the guest room's closet where she'd thought Drew wouldn't be able to notice it.

"On second thought, that might be a shame," he drawled and she nearly jumped when she felt his lips graze her right hip. Then he was tugging the skirt down even more. She felt it pass her thighs, then her knees. "Lift." His hand circled her right knee.

She lifted and felt him pull the skirt over her boot. Her hand tightened against his shoulder as she lifted her left. And then the skirt was gone.

And even though the barn was perfectly warm, she felt chills dance over her skin. Aside from panties and leather boots, she was nude. She twisted her fingers in the fabric of his shirt. "You take something off, too."

"Honey, before we're through there won't be anything but skin between us." His hands circled behind her knees again and she felt his lips against the front of her thigh while those hands started to slowly climb. Higher and higher while he maddened her with a kiss on her leg here, then there, never in any path or order.

And then his hands reached her derriere, and she felt his fingers slowly explore the narrow bands of stretchy lace that masqueraded as panties. "If I'd only known—" his voice was low and deliciously rough "—that under those ugly suits you wore stuff straight out of a man's fantasy, I'd have never gotten anything done at the office."

She felt herself flush, but this time, it was a good flush. "I like pretty things."

"Yeah, I noticed that when I saw the things you'd unpacked in the drawer that first day when you lost the towel." His fingers hooked the lace, teasingly gliding back and forth against her hip.

"If you were a gentleman you wouldn't remind me."

"Baby, I'm a man, and that was a pretty spectacular moment for me. See, I like pretty things, too," he murmured meaningfully. "And I've been thinking about you wearing them…and then not wearing them…ever since." He continued tracing along the edges of the lace across her abdomen. Then lower.

She sucked in a breath. "Wh-what are you doing?"

"What do you think?" He waited a beat. "What do you *want?*"

For him to end this wondrous torture. "I want you."

His fingers delved between her thighs and his voice dropped a notch. "So I can feel." His fingers glided over the damp lace, then retraced his steps. Again. And again.

She made a strangled sound. "Drew—"

"So perfect," he murmured, his breath hot against her thigh. "So wet."

She had a strange sense that she ought to have been mortified. "I can't help it," she admitted breathlessly. "That's what you do to me."

"Since when?"

She blessed the pitch darkness because it blacked out inhibition. And cursed it for the very same reason. "Since always."

He drew in an audible breath that made her nerves knot even more. His palm slowly cupped her through the clinging lace. "Have you thought about us? Like this?"

He was killing her by degrees. All she had to do was deny it and keep some bit of herself protected.

She moistened her lips. Kneaded her fingers against his head. "Yes." Her admission whispered through the darkness.

He made a low, hissing sound and then he was dragging the lace aside and she cried out loud as his lips found her bare, wet flesh.

Her legs nearly gave way as flames engulfed her, driving her straight up a shuddering, quaking peak.

She was still shaking when he finally straightened and she heard the rustle of his clothes. And then his hands slid behind her thighs, lifting her legs, and she cried out again as he sank into her.

No artifice. No pretense.

He was just Drew. The man she loved.

And then he uttered her name in a rough voice and she closed her eyes against the darkness as he carried them both straight to heaven.

## Chapter Twelve

"Morning." J.R. looked up when Drew headed into the kitchen early the next morning. "You're up early."

Drew managed a grunt and headed straight for the coffeepot that his brother had already brewed. He had no intentions of telling J.R. why he was up a good hour earlier than they'd agreed upon.

Not when he wasn't ready to recognize the reason himself.

He'd made love to his assistant in a damn barn, thinking stupidly that it wouldn't ruin things. Wouldn't change things.

Maybe for Deanna it hadn't.

But the second he'd sunk into her and lost his mind in a way that he'd never lost it before, he'd known he was in serious trouble.

Trouble of the kind he'd vowed to stay away from

since he'd found his bride-of-weeks screwing the hell out of his best man.

So he pulled out a mug and started pouring some coffee. "Best we get an early start, isn't it? It's not every day we head out for a hike to find our father's body."

J.R. grimaced. "Hell, Drew. I'm hoping to hell that's not the case."

"And I can't stop feeling that it is." He slammed back a mouthful of java even though it singed all the way down. "Darr's meeting us over at Nick's place with all the hiking gear?"

J.R. looked as though he wanted to say something, but then he nodded. "Then we'll pick up Jeremy at the Double Crown on our way out of town." He poured the rest of the coffeepot into a thermos and capped it before grabbing the sturdy canvas backpack that sat on a bar stool. "Isabella packed us food last night. But you've got time to eat some breakfast before we meet up with them." He nodded toward the thickly sliced ham that was sitting on the counter where he'd obviously made himself a sandwich for his own breakfast.

The last thing Drew had on his mind was food. But he knew they were in for a long trek and he put together a sandwich, too, that he wrapped in a napkin while J.R. stowed the makings back in the refrigerator. "Might as well get going," he said. "Darr's always early. He'll be at Nick's already."

J.R. nodded. He looked no more anxious for the task than Drew felt, and they quietly let themselves out of the house. J.R.'s truck was parked near the back door and they headed for it. "Where'd you and Deanna disappear to last night anyway?"

Drew managed not to choke on the mouthful of homemade bread and salty ham. "Just took a walk," he mumbled around the food that he had to wash down with another blistering hot gulp of coffee from the mug he'd carried along. He ignored the sidelong look J.R. gave him and stretched his legs out in the truck as he forced himself to take another bite of the sandwich and after a moment, J.R. started up the truck.

"You know, she's the smartest thing you've ever done."

Drew inhaled a piece of bread and sat forward, coughing hard. J.R. reached across the wide cab and slapped him hard on the back.

Drew lifted his hand. "I'm fine," he muttered.

"Except you're as antsy as a damn cat," J.R. pointed out. "What the hell's wrong with you? You and Deanna have a fight or something?"

"No." His jaws clamped together.

J.R. shook his head. "You always were the most cussed, stubborn one of us."

"No. That would've been Darr or Jeremy. Otherwise they'd have gone into business with Dad, too."

J.R. gave a short laugh. "Yeah. Maybe so." He put the truck in motion and the headlights of his truck cut through the still, early morning, casting a wide arch over the hacienda as he smoothly backed away.

It was a damn thing to think that going on this hike—and finding whatever the hell they were destined to find—was preferable to thinking about facing Deanna.

Drew knew he'd left her confused.

Hell, he was confused.

After the most singularly erotic, mind-blowing sex he'd ever had in his life, they'd dressed and returned to the then-silent house and headed to their bedroom.

And in the soft light that had pooled over the inviting

bed and turned Deanna's green eyes to emerald as she'd shyly looked at him, clearly expecting something—a kiss, a word, a touch—he'd been terrified.

Terrified of getting into bed with her. Terrified of touching her. Terrified of not touching her.

So he'd made some fool excuse about getting himself a nightcap, and he'd walked out of the room. Same as he'd been keeping away from that room as much as humanly possible since they'd arrived.

Only this time, he knew his actions weren't forgivable.

Not after what had transpired in the barn solely because of him.

He'd never been able to satisfy any woman who mattered to him. Not his quickly ex-wife. According to Drew's father, not his own mother, either. And last night, he'd hurt the last person on earth who'd deserved it.

Deanna.

He realized that J.R. had stopped the truck again, this time in front of the barn.

The barn.

"Gotta grab some rope," his brother said as he got out of the truck. He strode over to the barn and shoved open the door.

Drew looked away.

He didn't need to look at the barn.

The memories of what had occurred there were indelibly engraved on his damned soul.

He was gone.

Again.

Deanna rolled onto her back on the mattress and looked at the pillow beside hers. There was a faint indentation left from Drew's head when he'd briefly slept there. But considering the distance that had started yawning between them the second they'd left the blissful sanctuary of darkness the barn had provided, he might as well have never been in the same bed with her at all.

She tossed her arm over her stinging eyes.

What had she hoped for?

That Drew would suddenly realize that he loved her?

That just because she'd let him into her body as well as her heart, he'd feel the same?

Hot tears leaked from beneath her tightly closed eyes.

It didn't matter that she knew he was going back to the accident site with his brothers. She still felt abandoned. She'd felt abandoned when he'd all but raced out of the bedroom the night before when they'd returned from the barn.

And it suddenly felt untenable to lie in the bed that they could have shared so much more meaningfully, and she slid off the mattress and numbly went into the bathroom.

Only there, instead of the reflection of a well-loved woman, the person looking back at her through the bathroom mirror just looked…broken.

She looked like her mother.

Her mother who was, for all of her faults, alive and well while Drew and his brothers couldn't be certain of any such thing where their father was concerned.

Deanna exhaled slowly and turned away from her reflection.

She went back into the bedroom, unearthed her cell phone from the depths of her purse and turned it on.

She was a little surprised that the battery was still hold-ing a charge since she'd forgotten to bring the charger with her to Red Rock. And even though it was still early in the morning in Texas—and two hours earlier in California—she dialed her mother's house.

After only a single ring, though, Gigi's sleepy voice—sharp with alarm—answered. "Deedee, what's wrong?"

"Nothing." Everything.

"You're calling me at—" she heard muffled move-ments "—four in the morning and nothing is wrong?"

Deanna sank onto the foot of the bed and eyed herself in the tall, slanted mirror across from her. "Mom, did you ever keep a baby book from when I was a baby?"

"Of course I did. It's in the attic in the trunk along with your baptism dress from when you were six months old and my mother's wedding dress that your crumb of a father never gave me a chance to wear." Alarm had morphed into impatience. "Deanna, what is *wrong?* You never call me like this."

She pinched the bridge of her nose and looked away from her reflection. Considering the piles of possessions that her mother had amassed, she was stunned that Gigi knew the whereabouts of anything. Much less the fact that she'd been so wrong about the baby book in the first place. And her baptism dress? Church hadn't been part of her childhood and she couldn't recall Gigi ever talking about it.

But then maybe her mother had had her reasons. Dif-ferent reasons than the basic lack of interest that Deanna had grown up believing.

"Nothing's wrong," she insisted. "I just wanted to know, that's all." She heard her mother's sigh. And then she went stock-still when she heard the murmur of a low, deep voice in the background. A man's voice. "Gigi, do you have someone there with you?"

"Just a minute." Deanna heard more rustling. "All right. I'm in the kitchen now." Gigi's voice was much less hushed. "You've messed things up with that honey of a boss of yours, haven't you? Is that why you're calling me in the middle of the night? If you want me to tell you how to fix things, just say so."

Was it disappointment sinking through her? Disillusionment? Or maybe it was just finally acceptance of the fact that Gigi would always be...Gigi. For good or bad.

"No, I don't need anything fixed," she said quietly. You couldn't fix a broken heart, could you? "I just wanted to hear your voice." Which was, she also realized, the absolute truth. "I'm sorry it's so early."

She heard Gigi sigh noisily. "Well, it is that. I'm not sure what Frank is going to think, considering the hour. It's not as if this is an emergency or anything, is it?"

"No. No emergency." Deanna propped her elbows on her knees, cupping the phone to her ear. That would imply something sudden, and there was nothing sudden about loving Drew and not being loved back. "Frank is presumably the voice I heard in the background?"

Gigi's voice suddenly turned girlish. "He's wonderful, Deedee. You see, I got another job. I tried to tell you this past week, but you haven't returned any of my messages."

"A job." She managed a smile. "That's great. Where at?"

"A law firm, naturally. Horne, Hollings, and Howard. Up in Escondido." The town was on the northern side of San Diego.

Deanna tried not to wince. Gigi was a legal secretary.

Deanna couldn't exactly be surprised that her mother kept going back to it even if Deanna kept hoping that Gigi would break her pattern at least once. "I guess that's where you met Frank?"

"Oh, good heavens, no. Everyone who works at Triple H are women. No. I met *Frank* at the counselor's office. Don't you listen to any of my messages?"

Deanna sat up straight. "You've been going to the counselor?"

"Well, I told your boss I would when he called because *you* wouldn't talk to me." Gigi sounded miffed again.

"What?" Deanna's voice went sharp. "Drew called you? When?"

"It was last week sometime. After you left me that completely unfeeling message. I've been to two appointments now."

Deanna swallowed. She was far more unnerved by Drew's actions than by her mother's chastisement. He'd told her they would handle her mother together. She hadn't believed it at the time, even if it had sounded wholly appealing.

Turns out, he'd handled it all. And succeeded where she'd failed.

Her hand shook and she pressed the phone harder against her ear. "That's really great, Mom." And it was. Even beyond her shock, she recognized that. "So, you met Frank there?" Was he another patient, or—heaven forbid—the counselor? She dreaded asking.

"Oh, he's wonderful, Deedee. I know you'll like him. He's so sensible. Just like you. He has his own business, you see. He's a plant expert, if you can believe that. Goes around putting in and taking care of the interior plants all around hundreds of office buildings in San Diego.

He just takes care of every little thing." Gigi giggled. "Even me. And he's even helped me return the last four orders I received from the shopping channel. Wasn't that the sweetest thing?"

"Yes. That sounds very sweet."

"All right, well, since nothing's wrong, I'm going to go back to bed now. Frank gets up early, you see." She giggled again. "He has a lot of energy, if you know what I mean."

Deanna was torn between a groan and a reluctant laugh. "Okay, Mom."

"Deedee, you know how old it makes me feel to be called Mom."

"Sorry." Deanna exhaled. "I'll talk with you in a week or so, okay?"

"Whenever you like," Gigi chirped. "At least now you know my news. And I hope to heaven that you're making good use of your time with your boss. Girls like you can't afford not to make a good catch. Remember that."

Deanna grimaced. "I'll keep that in mind."

But her mother had already ended the call.

Deanna slowly lowered the phone. The battery bar was dwindling and she turned off the power again. And then, because she still couldn't bear to linger in the bedroom a moment longer, she took a brisk shower, pulled on her running gear and quietly let herself out of the hacienda.

She hadn't been able to outrun her emotions since they'd arrived in Texas. She knew that this morning would be no different.

Moving automatically, she stretched and started out slowly. But as she neared the barn, she picked up her pace and didn't slow once. Not even when tears started burning their way down her cheeks.

She ran until she couldn't run anymore and finally walked her way back to the hacienda. It took two hours.

But at least she wasn't crying anymore.

Because she knew that running around Molly's Pride trying to get over Drew Fortune was not going to get her anywhere. She'd fallen in love with a man who refused to be loved.

And now, it was time to go home.


The bedroom door was ajar when Drew went inside the house after he and J.R. got back to Molly's Pride that evening, and he wearily pushed it open, blindly heading inside.

The sight of Deanna's hard-sided suitcase sitting open on top of the neatly made bed had him stopping short, though. And the sight of her turning away from the closet, with that sexy pink dress she'd worn the day his father disappeared made everything else inside him seem to stop working, too.

Her gaze shied away from him as she moved to the suitcase. She was wearing that shapeless green sweater and jeans that she'd worn when they'd flown to Red Rock. "I didn't realize you were back."

He slowly closed the door. "Going somewhere?"

Her head ducked and her glossy red hair swung down to cover her cheek. "It's become quite clear that it's past time." She pulled the dress off the hanger and folded it inside the suitcase. "How did the search go?"

The only thing he and his brothers had found beyond the accident site were more rocks, more trees and more nothing.

"We didn't find his body," he said bluntly.

She inhaled sharply and looked at him. Probably for the first time since he'd walked out of their bedroom after "the barn."

She looked as miserable as he felt. Her eyes were bloodshot, her nose pink. "Is *that* what you hoped to find?"

Had he? Or had he been hoping like hell that they wouldn't, because then maybe he could put a cork into his certainty that his father was never coming back?

"You've been crying."

Her lashes fell and she turned back to fuss with her suitcase. Moving the zippered case of her cosmetics from one corner to the other, then back again. "No."

"You're a rotten liar."

"And yet you chose me to lie about—" she waved her arm encompassing the bedroom and the two of them "—*us*." Her lips twisted as she flipped the suitcase closed. "Guess that was a mistake on both our parts." She pushed the old-fashioned latches and they snapped closed with a sharp sound.

"Why now?"

She didn't look at him. "I have a life to get back to."

Since his father went missing, Drew knew that he'd barely given any consideration to the difficulties in Deanna's life. Not the ones she'd left behind, nor the ones created by her presence in Texas.

And even though he'd spent the better part of the last day reminding himself of all the reasons he was better off without her, the sight of her ready to leave now sent every one of those reasons scattering just as wildly as the rocks that had scattered beneath his hiking boots while he'd climbed over one ravine after another, hunting for any sign of his father.

"What were you planning to do? Sneak out before I got back?"

She shook her head. "I wouldn't have done that."

"Looks to me like you were." He moved into the room and as he did, she moved, too, keeping several feet of space between them.

He bit back a sigh. "I'm not going to jump you, for God's sake."

Her cheeks went red. "I never assumed that you would," she assured witheringly. She continued to the opened closet and retrieved her tennis shoes. Then she sat down on the side of the bed and began to pull them on.

Her gaze followed him warily when he dragged the chair from the corner, positioned it in front of her and sat down.

He'd learned, over and over again, that the quickest way to get through Deanna's reserve was to get into her personal space. Considering everything, that had become just as much a curse as a useful tool, though. And now was no exception.

He leaned toward her. "I shouldn't have acted the way I did."

She jerked the laces of her shoe into a lopsided bow. "I don't know what you mean."

He just looked at her.

"Fine. You shouldn't have. And I should have known better than to expect otherwise." Her lips tightened and she looked away. "So, my bad."

It stung, but he knew he'd given her good reason.

He didn't need his mother to be around to be disappointed in him.

He was disappointed in him all by himself.

"Just because things have turned out the way they have doesn't mean I won't hold up my end of the bargain," he finished gruffly.

She went white. "I knew you'd get bored with me quickly, but that really *was* fast."

"Bored!" The word nearly choked him. "God in heaven, Deanna, where the hell'd you get that idea?"

Her arms crossed over her chest. Her ghostly white coloring was being rapidly replaced by a flush. "You obviously can't wait to get rid of me."

"You're the one who's packing up, sweetheart, remember?" He shoved the suitcase so hard it slid off the bed and crashed crookedly onto the floor.

The latches sprang open and her clothing spilled out.

"Now look what you've done!"

"I'm not bored with you," he said flatly. He had plenty of emotions where she was concerned. Emotions he hadn't wanted to face, but not a one of them was boredom. "If you want to leave, I've got no reason to make you stay. My father is gone. There's no sign of foul play. No sign of anything. He's gone." The words tasted bitter and he had to stop. Clear his throat. "Either he chose to go and doesn't want to come back, not for Lily or any of the rest of us, or he's dead."

And despite the tension between them—tension he knew that he alone was responsible for creating—her expression softened. "Drew. I wish you wouldn't think that way."

"There's hope, and then there's holding on to a fantasy."

She looked pained. "And fantasies can't live forever, can they?" She slid past him and crouched in front of her suitcase, flattening it out on the floor. The thin strappy shirt thing that she wore to sleep in slid out along with a pair of lacy panties, and she tossed both back inside. "It *has* been only a few weeks. If your father is injured somewhere—"

"—we would have heard by now." He hated the words even as he said them because there was still a part of him that wanted to believe otherwise. It was the same part that had wanted to believe the cancer treatments would save his mother.

"And with Dad gone, there's no need for you to go through with this marriage business. I'll still pay what we agreed," he assured doggedly. "The bank'll be open Monday. I'll have the money wired into your account as soon as I can arrange it."

She snatched up the pink dress again and balled it up. "I know I can thank you for prodding my mother into counseling because she never would have done so because of me, though you could have told me yourself that you'd talked with her behind my back. But I don't *want* your money." Her voice had turned chilly. She pitched the dress into the suitcase. "I never did."

The back she presented to him might as well have been a gauntlet tossed down in challenge and he spun her around on her knees, grabbing her hand. He pushed his thumb against the diamond ring that she still wore, despite everything. "I didn't intentionally do anything behind your back. And the money's why you agreed to all this."

She snatched her arm away. "I agreed because you asked for my help."

He winced. "And because you needed my help with your mother's debt," he insisted doggedly.

The look she gave him was almost pitying. "I'm not

going to argue with you." In one sweeping armful, she'd shoved everything haphazardly back into the suitcase and flipped it closed. "If you want to believe I'm all about the Benjamins, then go ahead. At the moment I have more important things to do." She hit the latches for a second time.

"Like what?"

She pushed to her feet. "Like getting away from you," she snapped. "Isabella's already offered to drive me to San Antonio." Her lips twisted. "And don't worry. I told her the truth about us this morning. So *you* won't have to." She stepped around him, heading for the door, but not quickly enough for him to miss the tears in her eyes.

He shot up and blocked her way. "If it wasn't the money, then *why?*"

"Because I'm in love with you!" She shoved at his chest. "And now that we've got that out of the way, get out of my way so I can get out of yours."

He felt an ache in the center of his chest that had nothing to do with the surprising strength of her shove. "I don't want you out of my way," he admitted slowly.

"Of course you do," she said impatiently. "Nobody knows better than I do that the quickest route out of your life is to make the mistake of falling in love with you." Her voice went hoarse as she tried to slip around him to reach the door. "So I'm just going to make it easy on all of us and go home where I belong."

"Dammit, Deanna." His thoughts were clamoring inside his head as he caught her around the waist, hauling her up against him. "Would you stop for just one minute and listen?"

"Don't worry. I'm sure with a little effort you can

find another assistant who'll be as foolishly agreeable as I've—"

He swore under his breath and shut off her words in the most effective way he could.

With his mouth.

She went rigid.

But he kept his mouth on hers. Until he felt the thin, tight line of her lips start to soften. Until he felt the fists pushing at his shoulders start to relax. Only then did he pull his lips from hers. "Where you belong is with me," he said quietly, and wondered why in the hell it had taken him so damn long to admit what his heart had been telling him.

"Is that so?" Her voice was still cool. But her mossy-green eyes had gone round.

"Yeah, that's so," he returned evenly. "And I know because where I belong is with you."

Her lips parted. She blinked rapidly, but her eyes grew even wetter. A diamond-bright tear clung perilously to her eyelashes before slowly falling to her cheek. "You don't mean that. You're just upset about your father."

"I am upset about my father," he agreed. "But if I let you walk out of that door, then I'm living up to every failure he's accused me of." He moved his unsteady hands to cup her face. "I've been so busy telling myself what you were to me that I missed *seeing* what you were to me." He caught the teardrop with his thumb. "But I'm not telling anymore." He drew in a hard breath. "I'm just…feeling," he finished roughly.

She stared at him. And even though more tears had joined the first, he could still see the uncertainty in her gaze.

Uncertainty that he'd caused.

And he realized even more just what real fear was.

It was losing what you loved most of all without ever having had a chance to show it.

"You said you loved me," he reminded, and his own eyes were suddenly burning.

Her throat worked. She looked away. Then looked up at him. Her eyes had gone to emerald. "I do. But that doesn't mean I have to always like you," she whispered.

His knees actually went weak. Maybe it was fear finally leaving him. Maybe it was relief.

But he knew in that moment that he would do everything in his power to never let this woman go.

She'd been his helper. His right hand. His conscience and his comfort. She was exactly what Drew's father had told Drew he'd needed to find.

His Molly.

And she'd been there in front of him all this time.

Drew's Deanna.

He pressed his lips to her forehead. Over her wet eyes. And finally, with more gentleness than he knew he was capable of, on her lips. "Tell me you'll never leave me."

Deanna sucked in a shuddering breath that tasted of hope and it was strong enough to dispel hopelessness. Her gaze searched Drew's. And all she saw was *him*. The same man he'd always been. The charmer. The loner.

He hadn't pushed people away to keep them out, she realized with startling clarity. He'd done it to protect what was within. The boy whose first love had cheated on him. The man whose beloved mother was stolen by cancer. And now the man whose father had seemingly disappeared from the face of the earth.

She slowly reached up and laid her palm along his

jaw. Her thumb slowly brushed over his cheek, smoothing away the trail of moisture that she'd never expected to see. Her heart stopped climbing up her throat and slowly, peacefully, settled back in her chest. Only this time, it was as wide-open as the heart that she could see in his eyes as he looked back at her.

"I loved you even before I knew I loved you," she whispered. She pushed up on her toes and pressed her lips to his. "And I will never leave you," she vowed.

His arms swept behind her back, nearly crushing her to him, he held her so tightly. But she didn't care. She was exactly where she wanted to be.

And she knew at last, with every fiber of her soul, that she was exactly where *he* wanted to be, too.

## *Epilogue*

"**H**ey, old timer." The police officer stepped out of his cruiser and warily approached the bedraggled man slowly shuffling along the side of the highway. He'd gotten a call from a concerned citizen about a possible vagrant hitchhiking on the edge of town. "Where you heading?"

The man slowly turned to look at him. Even when the officer shone the beam of his flashlight over the wanderer, the man's thick hair was too matted with grime to tell the color. There were only a few things that were obvious to the officer.

One, the old man looked like he'd been to hell and back. And the clothes that were in no better shape than the hair smelled like it, as well.

And two, the man's eyes were unfocused and vacant.

The officer sighed. The man reminded him of his own old man, when the Alzheimer's had been getting bad.

He stepped closer, keeping his voice easy. "You look like you could use a sandwich. Maybe a cup of coffee." He glanced back at his cruiser and wished that he hadn't turned on the beacon. He didn't want the flashing lights spooking the guy. "If you're on your way somewhere, I can give you a lift." *Straight to a hospital,* he thought.

He glanced back at the old man, surprised to see that he'd begun shuffling his way again along the highway. He looked dead set on leaving behind the last few lights of town, heading on down the dark road. "Hold on there." He caught up to the wanderer, wrapping his arm around the guy's arm. He felt sturdier than the officer expected, but this time he was prepared. When the wanderer tried to shove him off, he held fast. "We're going to get you some help. It'll be warm. And safe."

The man looked annoyed. "Leave me alone. I'm in a hurry." Despite his appearance and his dazed expression, his voice was strong. He looked up suddenly at the sky, his vacant eyes narrowing.

The officer glanced up, too, but all he saw were the blinking lights of a jet high in the sky. He looked back at the man. "I can help you get where you're going if I know where you're heading. Home?"

The man pushed at the officer's hands. "Not home. The baby. I've gotta find the baby."

The officer slowly tightened his grip. The wanderer was easily as tall as he was, but there'd still be no match between them. He began steering the guy toward the cruiser. "Sure," he soothed. The guy definitely needed medical attention. "We'll find the baby."

High above the highway, Deanna sprawled on one of the well-cushioned couches inside the private jet that

Drew had somehow managed to procure nearly out of thin air. She still felt breathless from the way he'd rushed her out to the airfield and onto the plane.

She felt even more breathless considering his arms were presently looped around her.

She slowly ran her palms down his forearms, loving the feel of the slightly rough hair against her palms. "We could have waited until morning to return to San Diego," she told him, not for the first time. Her palms reached his hands and her heart jiggled around when his hands turned so that his palms met hers.

"We're not heading to San Diego."

She sat upright, and looked over her shoulder at him. "But I thought—"

"I know what you thought." He threaded his fingers through her hair, slowly tucking it behind one ear. "But even the best assistant in the world doesn't know what the boss is thinking every minute of the day."

She made a point of looking at her watch. "It's actually the night," she pointed out drily. Midnight, in fact. And she recognized all too well the glint in his eyes. It was the glint that warned her Drew Fortune was up to something. Something probably brilliant, but still... something. "If we're not going to back to San Diego, then where?" She supposed Los Angeles wasn't out of the question. The headquarters of Fortune Forecasting *was* located there, and by default, both offices had been under his authority since his father disappeared.

"All in due time, Dee." He tugged her back against him and his lips pressed against the curve of her neck.

Heat streaked through her. They were completely alone in the cabin of the jet. The flight crew, comprised only of the pilot and copilot, were closed behind the cockpit door. Still, she wasn't entirely sure how she felt when Drew's hands began working their way beneath the hem of her sweater.

But then his hands reached her breasts and she let out a long, shaking breath as his fingers nimbly traced over the lace cups of her bra.

Who was she kidding?

When Drew touched her, she couldn't think of anything but *more*. More of him touching her. More of her touching him.

"That night in the barn was incredible," he murmured, still dropping kisses along her neck. "You were incredible."

Deanna's mouth went dry. Her fingers tightened around his forearms. "So were you." She sucked in a breath when he tugged the cups of her bra aside and his fingers closed around her bare flesh. She felt suddenly steeped in desire.

He shifted slightly and instead of sitting half reclined on the couch, she found herself lying on it with Drew leaning over her. His brown gaze looked like melted chocolate as it roved over her face. "There was just one problem."

She curved her hands over his shoulders, trying to tug him back down to her. But he didn't move. So she levered herself up until her lips reached his. "What was that?"

"No light."

Her entire body flushed. "I...didn't mind." Which had to have been obvious.

He laughed softly. "I didn't mind, either. But even while you were turning me inside out with the way you were seducing me—"

"—seducing *you!*"

"I couldn't help thinking about making love to you like that all over again, with every single light blazing."

Now her insides felt like melted chocolate.

She glanced again at the closed door to the cockpit. The cabin was by no means brightly lit, but it was also not in the least bit shadowy. And the couch *was* inviting...

His eyes darkened. "I really love the way you think," he murmured, and slowly pressed his mouth to hers, kissing her so deeply that colors began exploding inside her head. "But not here," he said huskily when he finally did lift his head.

She just looked at him, uncomprehending. "What?"

"Not here," he murmured, dropping another much more chaste kiss on her lips. "First we need this." He worked a hand between them and her adrenaline shot up a few thousand notches.

But he didn't do anything but pull his hand out from between them a moment later.

And when he lifted himself off her altogether and moved off the couch, she frowned, reaching out her arms for him again. "Where are you going?"

"Not far from you." He smiled faintly. "That's a promise." He closed his hands around hers and only then did she realize he was holding something else besides her. "This is what I realize we need." He nudged her ring finger and she stared in shock at the two platinum wedding bands that he slipped over the tip of her finger. The metal felt warm from having been in his pocket.

Hardly daring to breath, she looked from the matching rings to his face. "Drew?"

"Turns out, I find myself in need of a wife." His expression was uncommonly uncertain as he knelt beside the couch.

"You don't say." Her voice was faint. Probably because her heart had lodged itself several inches above where it belonged.

"I do." The corner of his lips kicked up, making her heart swell a little more. "But I also know that not just anyone will do."

She swallowed, incapable at that moment of a response.

His voice dropped a notch. "It takes a specialized person to make the terms of some deals come together just right." He slipped the two wedding bands off the tip of her finger, and then held the smaller, narrower of the two up between them.

His hand was shaking.

She didn't even try to stop the moisture collecting behind her eyes from spilling over. "What kind of terms?"

"Nonnegotiable, I'm afraid." He cleared his throat softly. "As long as we both shall live."

Her heart seemed to leave her chest altogether. Pure joy was suddenly the organ that pumped blood through her veins. "I think that is acceptable."

His gaze met hers. "Are you sure, Deanna?"

She lifted the larger, wider ring out of his hand and held it up between them.

Her hand was shaking.

"Nonnegotiable," she said softly. "I will laugh with you. I will cry with you. And as long as I have breath in my body, I will love you. Is that agreeable to you?"

"More than." His voice sounded raw. "Too bad my father won't be around to see what he brought about."

She leaned into him and slowly pressed a kiss to his forehead. Then his lips. "Your father will see. On this earth or not, he'll see."

He was silent for a moment. "I don't know if I believe that."

"Then I'll believe it enough for both of us," she whispered, "until you do."

His gaze met hers and she knew she was looking into the eyes of a man who knew what it was to love deeply.

To love *her*.

"Will you marry me, Deanna?"

Tears slid down her cheeks. "Yes, please."

His lips slanted. "We'll put this in place, then, until we get it done officially in a few hours." He slowly slid the wedding band onto her ring finger where it fit perfectly against her beautiful diamond.

"Okay." Her voice was faint as she pushed his ring onto the hand he held out for her, too.

She had to take a moment just to revel in the breathtaking sight of a wedding band—from her—on his bronzed finger. It was almost unbearably sexy.

Then his words belatedly sank in. "A few *hours?*"

"Flight plan is Las Vegas. I have it all planned out." He lifted her hand and kissed her finger over the rings, then pressed her palm flat against his chest where she could feel the heavy throb of his heartbeat. "Unless you really do want a wedding with all the frills." He grimaced a little, still Drew, no matter what. "I suppose for a short while, I can wait."

She started smiling and wondered if she would ever

stop. "Well, good for you," she murmured and she slipped her hand behind his neck and slowly drew him to her. "But I can't wait."

And a few hours later when their plane landed in Las Vegas, they didn't.

* * * * *

**The moment was so magical that Kirsten was afraid to breathe for fear it was all a dream and she'd wake up alone in her bed, her arms wrapped around her pillow.**

She was spellbound by his heady scent, by the warmth of his breath and the heat of his touch.

As the kiss deepened and their lips parted, his tongue brushed hers, making her knees go weak. So she reached for his waist to steady herself. As she did so, he slipped his arms around her, drawing her close, kissing her until she was tempted to drag him inside and see what happened next.

Oh, lordy. If this was the way Jeremy kissed a woman goodnight, she wondered what it would be like to welcome him into her bed, into her…life.

Dear Reader,

In this story, you'll meet Kirsten Allen, who has a lot on her plate these days, including an unemployed brother who needs a helping hand and a baby nephew who needs a mother's touch. But when she runs into Dr Jeremy Fortune, who is waiting in Red Rock until his missing father is found, sparks fly and love blossoms.

So find a cozy spot and curl up with a little Texas romance.

Happy reading!

*Judy*

# HEALING
# DR FORTUNE

BY
JUDY DUARTE

First published in Great Britain 2012
by Mills & Boon, an imprint of Harlequin (UK) Limited,
Eton House, 18-24 Paradise Road, Richmond, Surrey TW9 1SR

Special thanks and acknowledgement to Judy Duarte for her contribution to the *Fortunes of Texas: Lost...and Found* miniseries.

© Harlequin Books S.A. 2011

2in1 ISBN: 978 0 263 89424 0

23-0412

Harlequin (UK) policy is to use papers that are natural, renewable and recyclable products and made from wood grown in sustainable forests. The logging and manufacturing processes conform to the legal environmental regulations of the country of origin.

Printed and bound in Spain
by Blackprint CPI, Barcelona

**Judy Duarte** always knew there was a book inside her, but since English was her least favourite subject in school, she never considered herself a writer. An avid reader who enjoys a happy ending, Judy couldn't shake the dream of creating a book of her own.

Her dream became a reality in March of 2002, when her first book was released. Since then she has published more than twenty novels.

Her stories have touched the hearts of readers around the world. And in July of 2005 Judy won a prestigious Readers' Choice Award for *The Rich Man's Son*.

Judy makes her home near the beach in Southern California. When she's not cooped up in her writing cave, she's spending time with her somewhat enormous but delightfully close family.

In Memory of
Lydia Bustos, the sister I never had, the friend
I'll never  forget.
My loss is Heaven's gain.

## FORTUNE'S PROPOSAL

Nobody closes a deal like Drew Fortune. So the Fortune
scion is certain that his loyal assistant Deanna will agree
to a convenient marriage to protect his inheritance. But
Deanna could turn the temporary deal into a permanent
takeover...of a certain reticent playboy's heart!

## HEALING DR FORTUNE

Healing people was Jeremy Fortune's speciality – not
coming to the rescue of beautiful women with infants in
their arms! The California surgeon was in Texas to locate
his missing father. Instead, he might have found the
woman of his dreams...

£5.49
ISBN 978-0-263-89424-0

9 780263 894240

e book
also available

*Cherish*™
*Romance to melt the*
*heart every time*

a MILLS & BOON® book from
**HARLEQUIN** (UK) LTD
www.millsandboon.co.uk

f Find us on
Facebook

millsandboon.co.uk

# Get an **EXCLUSIVE 15% OFF ORDER**

## when you order online today!

Simply enter the code **15APR12** as you checkout and the discount will automatically be applied to your order. **BUT HURRY**, this offer ends on 30th April 2012.

All of the latest titles are available 1 MONTH AHEAD of the shops, **PLUS:**

- 🌹 **Titles available in paperback and eBook**
- 🌹 **Huge savings** on titles you may have missed
- 🌹 **Try before you buy** with Browse the Book

Shop now at **millsandboon.co.uk**

APR

# Chapter One

Dr. Jeremy Fortune stepped out the front door of the Red Rock Medical Center and headed for the parking lot, his mood dark as the storm clouds that gathered overhead.

It had been over a month since his father had disappeared on what would have been the older man's wedding day, and in spite of all the efforts to find him, there'd been very few leads and the trail had gone cold.

William Fortune had been involved in a car accident that took place a hundred miles from the Red Rock church in which he was to be wed. The other driver, a young woman, had died upon impact. But for days, authorities hadn't realized a second vehicle had been involved until they spotted William's silver Mercedes, which had plummeted down an embankment and into a deeply wooded area, where it had been partially hidden by brush and rocks.

There hadn't been any sign of William, though—no blood and no indication that he'd been injured or...worse. It was as if he'd vanished without a trace.

A photograph of Molly, his first wife, had been found tucked into his visor, which had led some of the tabloids to report that he'd been running away. But Jeremy knew better than that.

William Fortune had been eagerly awaiting the ceremony that would unite him in holy matrimony to Lily, the widow of his cousin Ryan. And he'd been looking forward to spending the rest of his life with the woman he'd recently come to love and respect. Besides, his family and his close friends were important to him, and he wouldn't have left without telling any of them. Not of his own accord, anyway.

At first, Jeremy had feared that his father had been kidnapped, but there were no ransom notes found, no phone calls demanding money.

So where was he?

As a driven and dedicated orthopedic surgeon, Jeremy relied on logic and reason to solve problems, which he always faced head-on. But there wasn't anything logical about his father's disappearance.

Jeremy didn't usually trust feelings or hunches, but he couldn't shake the belief that his father was still alive and out there—*somewhere*.

Maybe that was because Jeremy had lost too many

family members already and wasn't going to accept the possibility that he might have lost another.

Nevertheless, he wouldn't leave Texas and return to California until his father was found—one way or another. So he'd taken a leave of absence from his medical practice in Sacramento, which didn't seem to bother him nearly as much as he'd thought it would.

He suspected that had something to do with the fact that, even before coming to Red Rock for his father's wedding, he'd been reevaluating his life choices. And he hoped that a little distance would help him sort it all out.

Still, to keep himself busy during the day and to make himself useful, he'd been volunteering his time at the Red Rock Medical Center, which the Fortune Foundation helped fund. And today was no different.

He glanced at his wristwatch. It was just past four-thirty and a little too early to head for the restaurant. He was meeting his brother and new sister-in-law for dinner at Red tonight—his favorite local restaurant—and he didn't want to drive all the way back to the Double Crown Ranch, where he'd been staying.

Maybe he ought to use the extra time to stop by the bookstore and pick up a couple novels before meeting Drew and Deanna. He'd been battling insomnia lately, so he'd been doing a lot of reading.

As his shoes crunched along the gritty, leaf- and twig-littered sidewalk, a somber mood continued to weigh him down, which seemed to happen whenever his mind wasn't on his work and his patients.

Oddly enough, it had lifted last night—during a dream of all things. He wasn't one to give nocturnal fantasies much thought, but this one had been especially unusual—and real.

The scene had come upon him during the wee hours, but in his mind's eye, the afternoon sun had cast a golden glow upon a tree-lined street much like some of those that could be found in the nicer neighborhoods in Red Rock.

He'd pulled into the driveway of a two-story home, which had been freshly painted—white, with green and black trim. The lawn was lush and neatly mowed, the plants and shrubs well manicured. A petite woman sat in a wicker rocking chair on the front porch, near a black window box that was chock-full of brightly colored flowers.

It was, he decided, a typical Norman Rockwell scene, and his heart soared upon envisioning it.

He'd tried to get a glimpse of the woman's face, but she was looking down at a pink-flannel-wrapped bundle in her arms, her honey-brown hair hanging in a soft tumble of curls that blocked his view.

"I'm home," he'd said, as he'd climbed from the car and shut the door. Then he'd hurried up the sidewalk to greet the mother and child, his steps light. The somber mood that had been plaguing him recently had disappeared completely, leaving him happier and more contented than he'd remembered being in a long, long time.

As the woman turned to face him, so he would finally

be able to get a good glimpse of her, the dream had suddenly ended, transporting him from the springtime to winter, from day to night.

He knew that the subconscious did crazy things while the mind and body slept, yet for a brief moment, he'd felt whole and…alive. And when he awoke, he realized what he'd been missing in his outwardly successful life—a wife and a family of his own.

Too bad he couldn't put a name and a face to the woman he'd imagined in his dream. But it really didn't matter. Her image had been merely symbolic, a sign of what he'd been lacking.

As he neared the parking space where he'd left his car earlier in the day, he heard footsteps behind him and glanced over his shoulder to see a petite woman approaching. She wore a pair of slender-fit denim jeans, a snug white T-shirt and a pink jacket to ward off the chill. In her arms, she held a baby wrapped in a blue shawl. She was studying the child, so he couldn't quite see her face.

But damn… With hair the shade of golden honey, she could at least pass for the woman in his dream.

If he were the kind of guy to believe in premonitions, he just might wonder if she was a walking, talking dream come true.

He wasn't, though. But he turned around just the same, drawn to her for some other reason he'd yet to figure out.

As she looked up and spotted him, her lips parted and her steps slowed. She had the face of a magazine cover girl, delicate features and expressive blue eyes with thick, dark lashes.

"Excuse me," she said, adjusting the strap of the diaper bag that hung on her shoulder. "Are you a doctor?"

Jeremy, who was still wearing a lab coat over his street clothes, punctuated a nod by saying, "Yes, I am."

"Oh, good. I was hoping to have the baby examined, and I wondered if…if you could take a look at him."

"I'm not a pediatrician," Jeremy said. "I'm an orthopedic surgeon. The clinic is still open, though. I'm sure someone will be able to see him today."

She glanced over her shoulder, then to the right and the left. "I can't wait. And I'm worried about the baby. I just want to make sure that he's okay."

"What seems to be the problem?" he asked. Did the child have a fever or any particular symptoms?

"Nothing really, I suppose." She looked at the little guy in her arms, then back to Jeremy. "I just want to make sure he's healthy."

That was odd, he thought. But he eased closer to look at the baby, who appeared to be about two months old. On the upside, his eyes were bright and alert, his cheeks were plump and his little arms were filled out. There was no obvious reason to suspect he was sick or had been neglected.

Jeremy looked back at the mother, who seemed a little fidgety. "Like I said, I'm not a pediatrician. And without an actual exam, it's hard to say for sure. But I don't see anything that would make me think that he isn't healthy."

Her nervous expression melted into one of relief. "Oh, thank goodness."

Jeremy wasn't sure why she was so anxious, why she wouldn't go inside and join the other patients waiting to be seen.

"Just as a side note," he added, "the services of the clinic are free for those who can't—"

"Thank you, but it's not that. I was already inside. I waited for more than an hour, and there were still several people in front of me. But I really need to get home."

To a husband, he suspected. And he couldn't help feeling a bit disappointed by the realization.

Of course, he wasn't going to put much stock in a crazy dream and a chance meeting with a woman who bore a slight resemblance to the one he'd envisioned last night. But it wouldn't hurt to check the baby for bumps and bruises.

He reached out to stroke the child's cheek, and the little one grabbed his finger, latching on tight and causing his heart to flip-flop. What was *that* reaction all about?

The woman glanced at her wristwatch, and her breath caught. "I'm sorry. I really need to go."

Then she thanked him for his time and took off, walking at a brisk pace, heading for the street.

Jeremy stood in the parking lot for the longest time, watching as she turned toward the bus stop.

Was she in some kind of trouble? Was she involved in an abusive relationship?

Had she—or the baby—been hurt?

Each time a question struck his mind, it exploded into several others. Maybe he should have tried harder to get her into the clinic.

Moments later, he glanced at his own watch. He had plenty of time on his hands and wasn't in any hurry. So, what the hell?

He strode back to the building he'd just left, entered the waiting room and made his way to the registration desk. Millie Arden was on duty today, so he asked if she had a minute.

"Of course, Doctor." The matronly woman with graying hair, a ruddy complexion and a warm smile looked up from her work. "What is it?"

"Do you remember seeing a mother in her twenties leave here a few minutes ago? She had light brown hair and was wearing jeans and a pink jacket. Her baby was wrapped in a blue shawl."

"Yes. She signed in as…" Millie glanced down at the list of patients in front of her and ran her finger along the names. "Here it is. Kirsten Allen."

Was that her actual name? Or a phony moniker for her to hide behind?

Again one question triggered several more.

"Has she visited the clinic before?" he asked.

"Just a moment. I'll check." Millie turned to her computer and, after a brief search, said, "It doesn't appear that she has."

Jeremy really ought to let it go, but he couldn't seem to do that. Not when Kirsten Allen had reminded him of the woman in his dream.

Hell, she even had a baby…

Surely it had been a coincidence, a fluke of some kind.

But during the short time that he'd spent with her, his blue funk had actually lifted—and it had yet to return.

After getting off the city bus at the intersection just a few blocks from Lone Star Lane, Kirsten carried little Anthony home, hoping to get back before her brother Max learned that she'd taken his son to the clinic.

Their relationship had always been a little shaky, more so right now. He resented what he called her interference in his life. Truth be told, she knew she'd clearly overstepped her bounds by taking Anthony for a medical evaluation, but she'd been desperate to find out if he was healthy, or if he had any undiagnosed problems that needed to be treated—a condition that could be serious.

Things like well-baby checkups and immunizations could wait until Max decided it was necessary, but her maternal instincts had kicked in and she felt compelled to make sure that Anthony's mother hadn't neglected something important.

And that was definitely possible. A couple days ago, Courtney, her brother's ex-girlfriend, had dropped off the precious little baby at Kirsten's house, announcing that Max was his father, that she'd grown tired of motherhood and that it was his turn to parent.

Kirsten had never liked Courtney, although she'd always kept her opinion to herself. But it had been difficult to hold her tongue when the flighty young woman handed the baby to a surprised Max, offering him only a car seat, a small package of disposable diapers and a bottle of formula. Then she'd taken off without even looking back.

It was safe to say that Anthony would probably be better off without Courtney in his life, especially since he was young enough not to be traumatized by her desertion. In fact, Kirsten couldn't understand how Max had gotten involved with a woman like her in the first place—or what he'd ever seen in her.

Still, she had to give her brother credit for stepping up to the plate. He might have been young and footloose in the past, but he had accepted responsibility for Anthony.

And, of course, so had Kirsten, which was why she'd taken him to the clinic today. But since the wait had been longer than she'd expected it to be, she would just have to be content to know that, from a physician's perspective, the baby boy appeared to be healthy.

Of course, a more thorough exam might reveal otherwise, so she still felt a twinge of uncertainty.

She knew that Max would see reason eventually and come to the conclusion that an appointment for a well-baby checkup was necessary. But that only made Kirsten think about immunizations, a subject Courtney had never even broached.

And that was another reason she'd insisted that Max try to find Courtney and quiz her about those kinds of details. Of course, her insistence had been her first misstep.

But old habits were hard to break. They were both adults now, and she really needed to remember not to push Max too hard, not to mother him.

He'd gotten tired of answering to his big sister about every little thing in his life, which she hoped was due to maturity rather than stubbornness. So he'd refused to look for Courtney, claiming that he could take care of the baby on his own.

Kirsten had her doubts, though. And that was why she'd snuck out to see a doctor while Max was job hunting. She knew he'd be upset if he learned that she'd taken on a parental role with the child and that he would accuse her of interfering and running his life again.

Of course that shouldn't surprise her. He'd been rebelling against her advice and instructions since he'd been a teenager. But this was different. Surely he would see that, wouldn't he?

When it came to the baby's health and welfare, he needed to put the past behind him and listen for a change.

As Kirsten reached the front door of her house, she dug in her purse for her keys, then she let herself inside.

"Are you ready for a bottle?" she asked Anthony, as she left the diaper bag in the entryway. The baby had been eating every three to four hours, so she figured he would be hungry soon.

Once in the living room, she put his blue shawl on the carpeted floor, then laid him down. "I'll be back in a minute, precious."

Anthony started to fuss, so she hurried to the kitchen and fixed him a bottle out of powdered formula and purified water.

She wished she had more experience with babies, that she'd done some babysitting as a teenager, but she was completely out of her league with that sort of thing.

The first couple days were hard, with her and Max learning through trial and error, but they were both finally catching on. In fact, she was really enjoying having a baby in the house. It made her wonder what it would be like to have a family of her own someday.

After carrying the bottle back to the living room, she picked up Anthony and settled into the overstuffed chair near the window. As she placed the nipple to his lips, he eagerly latched on, sucking and gulping as though he was starving.

Actually, now that she thought about it, he *did* have a hearty appetite, and that was definitely a sign of health. But that didn't mean she wouldn't try to sneak him back to the clinic again the next time Max would be gone for a couple hours. Hopefully, her car would be out of the shop by then, and she wouldn't have to ride the city bus, which had taken up way too much time.

Thank goodness she'd returned to the house before Max did.

At least she'd gotten a physician to at least take a quick look at the baby, even if it wasn't what you'd call a real exam.

She couldn't believe that she'd actually stopped a doctor in the parking lot today and asked him to look at

Anthony. She'd been so anxious—and thinking with her heart instead of her head, which she was prone to do.

But then the handsome physician with surfer-blond hair and soulful blue eyes had looked at her as if they'd met somewhere before, and she'd been knocked off balance. There was no way they'd ever crossed paths. She would have definitely remembered a gorgeous hunk like him.

Looking back, she wished she would have asked his name, but she hadn't been thinking straight.

In fact, he'd probably thought she was crazy, which was too bad. It would have been nice to have put her best foot forward when meeting the handsome orthopedic surgeon, a man who'd been exceptionally kind to her. After all, he hadn't needed to take time to talk to her, but he had. He'd even reached out and caressed Anthony's little cheek, right there in the parking lot.

Too bad she'd had a bus to catch so she would beat her brother home.

As Anthony guzzled down his bottle, Kirsten stopped him long enough to get a burp out of him—an effort he objected to with grunts and squawks.

When he finally let out a little belch, and she put the bottle back into his mouth, she heard the key sound in the lock.

Moments later, Max opened the door and stepped inside.

"So how was the job search?" she asked.

Her brother blew out a sigh. "No luck yet. So I guess you're stuck with us for a while."

That might be true about Max staying with her, but she certainly didn't feel stuck with Anthony.

"It's not a problem." Kirsten glanced at the sweet little baby who'd come to live with them. "I'm happy to help out while I can."

"But what happens when you get a call from another firm looking for an accountant? You've got a mortgage to pay, so you can't continue watching Anthony for me."

That was true. And Max would be hard-pressed to job hunt all day and watch over his son without help.

He didn't seem to be stressed about that, though. Or worried about the fact that he might not be able to afford day care *and* rent when he did manage to find employment.

"Well," Kirsten said, "I can watch him for the time being. We'll just have to take one day at a time."

And she shouldn't have any trouble doing that. She'd been taking one day at a time ever since she'd allowed Max to move in with her. But what else could she do? He was the only family she had left, and looking after him was a responsibility she'd always had.

Of course, she'd come to realize that some of her help over the years had bordered on enabling in many ways. The more money she gave him, the more he seemed to need.

Then, about two years ago, she'd read a book on tough love. It made sense that she wasn't really helping him by bailing him out all the time. So she'd told Max that she was finished taking care of him, that he was an adult and would have to fend for himself. He was twenty-four at the time and had just started dating Courtney, so he'd moved in with her for a while.

Lo and behold, he landed a good job at the feed store and kept it for nearly two years—until the owner sold the business.

Losing his job had been really tough on him—and it had been tough on Kirsten, too. But the layoff hadn't been his fault. His boss had decided to retire and sell the business, and since the new owner had a large family and planned to hire his kids to work for him, Max was let go.

Of course, that meant he could no longer pay his rent. So she'd offered to let him live with her until he found a new job.

She'd been afraid that they would both fall back into destructive old patterns, yet she didn't want Max to end up on the street when he'd been clearly trying hard to get his life on track. If she looked at the big picture, he deserved her help and a second chance.

And then Anthony had come along, immediately changing the dynamics of their brother-sister relationship and complicating things. After all, there was no way Kirsten would ask Max to leave or refuse to help him when that meant turning her back on Anthony, too.

She smiled at the child in her arms, his little eyes closed, his lips still tugging at the nipple.

"So how did things go for *you* today?" Max asked, as he plopped down on the sofa. "Did the baby give you any trouble?"

"We had a good day." She didn't dare tell him that

she'd taken Anthony to the clinic. She had to tread carefully with Max these days, not make him feel as though
she was backing him into a corner. All she needed was
for him to resent her interference, bolt and take little
Anthony with him.

If he were to leave, where would he live? How would
he support himself and a baby?

"How's your own job search coming?" he asked. "Did
you get any nibbles from the résumés you filed with those
online applications?"

"I'm still waiting to hear something." But she wouldn't
actively seek a full-time position until Max found work
and knew what his options were for day care.

"So you don't have any interviews scheduled?"

"No, but I'm really not worried yet." She had a healthy
savings account, so she'd been able to pay the mortgage—so far.

"You know," Max said, "I've been thinking. The Red
Rock Medical Center offers low-cost checkups. Maybe
I ought to take Anthony one day next week."

Kirsten nearly jumped out of her chair, but she reeled
in her excitement, knowing it was best to let Max think
the whole idea had been his all along. Apparently, her
hints had sunk in after she'd dropped the subject and let
it go.

"You're probably right," she finally said in a ho-hum
sort of way. "I could…" She caught herself, realizing that
Max wanted to do the right thing, but for some reason, it
was important for him to make those kinds of decisions
on his own. "Well, I could look up the website on the

computer and give you a phone number—in case you want to set up an appointment or ask questions."

He seemed to think on that for a while, then he said, "Sure, that would be okay."

She slowly released the breath she'd been holding.

Max wasn't a kid anymore. And he wasn't as irresponsible as he'd once been. She needed to remember that. She also needed to respect his decisions—whatever they were. And if that meant minding her sisterly *P*s and *Q*s, then so be it.

"Do you think Courtney would have taken Anthony for his shots?" she asked.

He'd refused to call Courtney, but maybe Kirsten could nudge him just a bit.

Max seemed to ponder that for a moment. "She used to hate going to the doctor herself, so something tells me she wouldn't have worried about taking Anthony."

Well, Courtney certainly hadn't appeared to have a very strong maternal instinct, but Kirsten bit her tongue, reminding herself to keep quiet and to let Max come to his own conclusions about his child's mother.

"I guess it's good that you're going to be the one raising him," Kirsten said. "He's going to need a daddy like you."

Max shrugged, although the hint of a smile suggested that her comment had pleased him. And she was glad that it had. Their relationship had taken a real turn for the better today, even if she was the one who'd learned a valuable lesson in dealing with Max, in trusting him to do the right thing.

"Do you want to go with me when I take Anthony to the clinic?" he asked.

The question both surprised and delighted her—but not because she needed to be involved in Anthony's care. She was happy to see that her relationship with her brother was finally on the mend.

"Sure," she said. "I can go with you as long as I don't have an interview scheduled."

"Thanks. I'd like you to be there. I'm not sure I want to see someone poke him with a needle."

Kirsten wasn't excited about seeing that, either.

"You know," Max said, "since things might change for you anytime on the job front, maybe I ought to schedule that appointment tomorrow. Would that be better for you?"

She bit down on her bottom lip, as though giving her schedule some real thought. "Yes, it would. I don't have anything planned for tomorrow."

"Good, then I'll call the clinic in the morning."

"All right. Just let me know what they tell you."

But she already knew. She'd called today, and they'd told her that her best chance of being seen today—when it wasn't an emergency—was to come in and wait her turn.

The thought of returning to the Red Rock Medical Center turned her heart on end, but not just because they would finally learn whether Anthony was as healthy as he appeared to be.

She was also hoping she'd run into a certain orthopedic surgeon.

Uh-oh. If she *did* see him again, and if he mentioned to Max anything about meeting her and Anthony in the parking lot…well, that might dash the strides they'd made in healing their relationship.

If so, she would just have to come clean with Max. And if he blew up about it? Then she'd face the consequences.

He might get angry and tell her to go home, which meant she'd miss out on spending further time with the handsome doctor. And that would be a shame.

## Chapter Two

Even after a stop at the bookstore, Jeremy still arrived early at Red, one of the most popular restaurants in town.

Jose and Maria Mendoza, longtime friends of the Fortune family, had converted the old hacienda into a classy, romantic eatery with antique furnishings, woven tapestries and carefully selected pieces of Tejano art that nearly matched the original décor, much of which had been damaged two years ago in a fire which had turned out to be a case of arson. The Mendozas had been forced to close for a while. But with time and a great deal of effort, they'd restored the landmark.

As Jeremy entered, he was welcomed by Marcos Mendoza, who was temporarily managing Red for Jose and Maria. Some might think the handsome and personable young man had landed his position because of his relationship with the owners, but Jeremy knew that wasn't the case. Since taking over, Marcos had instigated some innovative and productive changes behind the scenes, and the restaurant seemed to be busier and more popular than ever.

"Welcome back to Red, Doc." Marcos reached out his arm in greeting. "How's it going?"

"Not bad." Jeremy shook the younger man's hand. "How about you?"

"Life is good. I can't complain." Marcos scanned the entry before returning his gaze to Jeremy. "Are you meeting someone?"

"My brother Drew and his wife."

"Then I'll take you back to the alcove. It'll give you a little more privacy. And when they arrive, I'll let them know where you are."

"Thanks." Jeremy usually preferred to eat in the courtyard, with the old-world style fountain that had been handcrafted with blue-and-white Mexican tile.

The Mendozas had heaters to make outdoor dining comfortable in the winter months, but it was already sprinkling, and the colorful umbrellas that provided shade from the sun weren't going to keep the rain off them.

As Marcos grabbed three menus, he asked, "When did the newlyweds get back from Vegas?"

The couple had eloped, and while it wasn't a secret, some of the details were sketchy. "They flew in last night."

"Oh, yeah? So they'll be staying in Red Rock?"

"I'm not sure what their plans are." Drew ran the San Diego office of Fortune Forecasting—although he'd been overseeing the entire operation in William's absence. And Deanna was his assistant. There was just so much that could be done via conference calls and email, so they'd both need to go back to work soon. But like Jeremy, Drew had been waiting on word about their father.

A beat of silence stretched between them, as they both considered the words Jeremy hadn't actually said.

"Still no word about your dad?" Marcos asked.

Jeremy slowly shook his head. "No, not yet."

"I'm sorry to hear that. Isabella came in earlier today to have lunch with some of her friends, but I didn't get a chance to ask her if there'd been any news."

Isabella, who'd married J. R. Fortune, Jeremy's oldest brother, was Marcos's sister. So Marcos was well aware of the details surrounding William's disappearance.

As they reached the empty table in the alcove, Marcos stopped and stepped to the side. "How's this?"

"Great."

Marcos removed one of the place settings, leaving three. "I'll have a server bring you some water and chips. Would you like to start off with a drink?"

"Sure. I'll have a Corona."

"You got it."

As Jeremy took a seat, he watched Marcos walk toward the bar. The ambitious young man had plans to open his own restaurant someday, and Jeremy had no doubt that he would do just that—and be successful.

Moments later, a young waitress with her long, dark hair pulled back in a ponytail brought the water, chips, salsa and his beer.

"Marcos said to tell you that the drink is on him," the woman said.

Jeremy thanked her, and as she went on her way, he got to his feet, stepped out of the alcove and scanned the area for Marcos.

He spotted him near the bar, where he was talking to the bartender and pointing out something on a shelf. When Jeremy caught the manager's eye, he lifted his longneck bottle and nodded in appreciation. Then he returned to his table and took a seat.

While waiting for Drew and Deanna, he reached for a warm tortilla chip and dipped it into the fresh salsa.

No one knew how to prepare Mexican food like the Mendozas, and Jeremy had made a point of stopping by Red at least once a week. Of course, each time he did, he often ran into one of the Fortunes or a Mendoza or two. The families had become good friends over the years. There also had been a few marriages along the way that bound them even closer—like that of J.R. and Isabella.

Jeremy had just reached for another chip when Drew and Deanna arrived. The two had been staying with J.R. and Isabella at Molly's Pride, where he assumed they would take up residence again until they needed to return to San Diego.

Drew's entire life had revolved around Fortune

Forecasting, the company William had started. But unlike his brothers, Jeremy had never wanted to take part in the family business. Instead, he'd gone to medical school. And up until the past year or so, he'd been perfectly content with that decision and the life he'd made for himself in Sacramento.

As Drew and Deanna reached the table, Jeremy stood and greeted the attractive redhead with a brotherly hug.

"You look especially pretty tonight," Jeremy told her.

And she did. Love and happiness radiated on her face, just as it did on Drew's.

"Thank you."

Drew pulled out a chair for her. As she took a seat, she flashed a loving smile at her new husband.

Jeremy couldn't help thinking that falling in love and getting married had made a big difference in his brother's entire demeanor, and as he made that decision, his thoughts naturally drifted to the mystery woman who'd stepped right out of his imagination and into his life just two hours earlier.

Drew reached for a chip. "We said six, didn't we?"

"Yes, but I finished early at the clinic." Jeremy motioned for their waitress, then returned his focus to his dinner companions. "So how was the wedding?"

"Absolutely beautiful." Deanna's eyes glimmered. "Your brother outdid himself with all the details, from the strawberries and champagne on the private flight to the long-stem red roses and the bridal bouquet waiting in the limousine to the beautiful little chapel where we were married at the stroke of midnight. It was very romantic."

A little surprised by it all, Jeremy studied his no-nonsense brother. "Who would have guessed that you had a romantic side?"

"You probably have one, too." His brother reached across the table and took Deanna's hand. "All you have to do is find the right woman."

Jeremy didn't know about that. He hadn't thought that he had a romantic bone in his body before, but he found his mind drifting in that direction ever since he ran into Kirsten Allen in the parking lot. Damn, that crazy dream must be making him soft.

As Drew and Deanna shared the details of the actual ceremony, Jeremy found himself drifting off, wondering if he'd prefer a big wedding or a small, intimate one. And that brought his thoughts back to the mystery woman.

He didn't believe in visions and premonitions, but for some wild reason, he couldn't quite shake the encounter he'd had with Kirsten or the feeling that he had to see her again.

"Are you listening?" Drew asked.

Jeremy glanced up, a little embarrassed that the couple had caught him gathering romantic wool, when he should have been listening. "I'm sorry. I've got a lot on my mind."

"Dad?" Drew asked.

"Him, too."

"Is it work-related? Is the medical group pressuring you to come back to Sacramento?"

"In a way, but…"

"Don't tell me." Drew leaned forward. "You've met a woman in Red Rock."

"No, not really." Jeremy glanced at his new sister-in-law, then back at the cocktail napkin he'd been shredding.

About that time, Deanna scooted her chair back and got to her feet. "If you guys will excuse me, I think I'll powder my nose."

Drew shot another loving look at his new wife, and something seemed to register between them, some form of silent, two-way communication.

Jeremy had seen his parents do that on occasion. Would he ever be able to communicate with a woman like that?

"What should I order for you?" Drew asked her. "A glass of wine?"

"That sounds good. Thanks."

As Deanna headed for the bathroom, Jeremy couldn't help thinking she'd made an excuse to leave so the brothers could talk in private, which was thoughtful but unnecessary. He really didn't want to talk to anyone about the wild direction his thoughts had been going.

After Deanna was out of hearing range, Drew said, "Okay, what's going on?"

Jeremy wasn't so sure he wanted to confide in his younger brother, but Drew wasn't a kid anymore. So he found himself revealing the dream he'd had and the woman he'd run into in the parking lot.

"Are you going to try to find her?" Drew asked.

Jeremy didn't know what to say, what to admit.

"Maybe you ought to give Ross a call. I'll bet he could make fast work of finding anyone."

Ross Fortune was their cousin and a private investigator, so the suggestion made sense. But Jeremy wouldn't go that far in trying to locate the mystery woman.

"I don't want to come off like some kind of stalker," he admitted. "Besides, Ross probably should focus his time on finding Dad, which he hasn't been able to do."

The truth of that statement echoed between them until Drew said, "I think we need to accept the fact that he's gone, Jeremy."

"You might be right, but I'm not able to do that yet."

"I know."

A pall fell over the brothers as they each tried to deal with their father's disappearance in their own way—Drew letting go and Jeremy refusing to give up.

When Deanna returned to the table, the conversation turned more upbeat, but Jeremy found himself sliding back into that blue funk that had been haunting him for months—even before he'd come to Red Rock for the wedding.

The only thing that seemed to help his mood was thinking about Kirsten Allen—if that was even her name.

Who was she?

What was her story?

And why in the world did it even seem to matter? Jeremy had never met a woman who could compete with his patients. He was a driven and dedicated physician, and as a result, he'd never married.

Maybe the dream and his interest in the mystery woman were just signs that his subconscious—and his hormones—were trying to rectify the situation.

Either way, something told him that he was going to have to find Kirsten Allen.

And if it took calling Ross and asking for help, then so be it.

The rain had moved on by morning, leaving a rainbow in the cloudy sky and puddles on the streets and sidewalks.

Over breakfast, Kirsten had admitted to Max that she'd taken the baby to the clinic yesterday. And she'd been right about his reaction; he'd bristled.

"I can't believe you'd do that without talking to me first," he'd said. "I don't want you to take over."

"I'm not trying to do that. I was just worried about his health, and…well, you're right. I shouldn't have gone over your head. I was wrong, and I'm sorry."

"When is it going to stop, Kirsten? You've been mothering me for years, and I've always resented it. Now you're trying to do it with Anthony. The way I see it, if you want a baby, maybe you should have one of your own."

She'd tensed at his harshness, but what he'd said was true. Even though she hadn't been around kids, she *had* always wanted to be a mom, to have a family. But that was *not* why she'd fought so hard to take good care of Max, to make sure he grew up happy and responsible.

It was not as though she wanted him to stay some kind of pseudo kid forever. Or that she'd needed someone to mother. "You're the only family I have left, Max. And I feel an obligation to make sure you're happy and able to support yourself."

"I'm doing fine on my own. I've just had a little set-back with the job and all." He raked a hand through his hair. "You're my big sister, and I get that. But I'm sick of you constantly trying to tell me what to do, how to feel, what to say. It's my life. And I want to make my own way—right or wrong."

Before she could respond, he added, "I've been on my own for two years—paying my rent, being a man. And you have no idea how it grates on me to have to live with my sister again, to accept your handouts. Believe me, all I want to do is land a new job and get out of here."

In her heart of hearts, she knew that when Max moved out, it would be the best for her, too. She needed to let go of him and focus on creating a place for herself in Red Rock.

"I'm sorry," she'd said, repeating the apology she'd made earlier. "I only meant to be helpful. And you're right. Anthony is your son, your responsibility. I'll do my best to back off."

The fight had seemed to fizzle out of him at her ac-quiescence, so she'd gone on to say, "I'm trying, Max. *Really,* I am. You're not a kid anymore. And I need to trust you to make the right decisions for yourself and now for your son. But you'll have to be a little patient with me. Old habits are hard to break."

"I still can't believe that you took him to the clinic without my permission. What did you tell them? That you were his mother?"

"I wouldn't have lied. But truthfully, I hadn't really thought that far."

He'd scoffed, and she realized just how impulsive she'd been.

"I can make a hundred excuses for what I did," she'd admitted, "but I'm not going to do that. You're Anthony's father. And you're right. I overstepped my bounds. From now on, I'm going to step back and let you live your own life—right, wrong or indifferent. Those decisions are yours to make—not mine."

Max kept quiet all through breakfast, and about the time she'd decided that he wasn't going to let her go to the clinic with him, he relented.

"Okay, Kirsten. I need you more than I'm comfortable admitting. Maybe that's why I'm fighting you so hard." He blew out a sigh. "I'd really like you to go with me—as a second pair of ears—but *not* as my spokesperson."

A part of her wanted to back off completely and let him handle it *all* on his own, but after Courtney had arrived with the baby a couple days ago and announced that Max was the father, they'd both been caught off guard. And together they'd scrambled to buy diapers, formula, bottles and a little bed for him to sleep in.

It had been almost overwhelming, yet at the same

time, there had been moments where she and Max had actually been a team for the first time in ages. And that had given her hope that the troubles they'd had in the past would soon be behind them. That they were on their way to becoming the family they'd been before their father had abandoned them, before their mother had died.

Through trial and error, frustration and smiles, she and Max had been learning how to take care of Anthony.

So the baby's arrival had turned out to be a good thing, forcing the two of them to work together for a change.

"All right," Kirsten had agreed. "You've got yourself a deal."

An hour later, they found themselves back at the clinic, checking in with a matronly receptionist whose badge announced that her name was Millie.

"Just take a seat," Millie said. "It shouldn't be too long. You arrived here early today, which is good. We always get backed up in the late afternoon."

Max shot Kirsten a glance, but she bit her tongue. She'd apologized for bringing Anthony yesterday, but she certainly wasn't going to grovel. What was done was done.

When they took seats in the waiting room, Max held the baby, so Kirsten picked up a magazine and thumbed through it. She feared that she was enabling Max again by being here, by babysitting Anthony and by offering them both a place to stay. But she couldn't very well throw out him and the baby.

She'd meant what she'd said about boundaries, though.

So how did she go about encouraging Max to find a job and to help out around the house, when he'd probably see that encouragement as interference?

She stole a glance at her brother, who held little Anthony with stiff arms and a tender expression. Anyone looking at him could tell he had feelings for the baby, even though he'd only known about him for a short time. It was obvious that he wanted to do right by his son. That, she decided, counted for a great deal.

As the door swung open, and a nurse called an elderly woman for her appointment, Kirsten found herself scanning the back room of the clinic, trying to spot the handsome orthopedic surgeon she'd met yesterday.

But what if she *did* see him? What then?

A man like that was probably only interested in sophisticated, stylish women with high-profile careers and social connections.

Still, each time the door to the exam rooms opened, each time someone in a lab coat walked by, Kirsten couldn't help searching for the doctor with sun-streaked hair and intensive blue eyes who had consumed her thoughts.

Jeremy was looking over an X-ray of a fractured scaphoid bone in a teenage boy's hand, a break that had actually occurred years earlier.

Last night, the kid had fallen during a basketball game and twisted his wrist. And since he was still complaining of pain this morning, his mother had brought him into the clinic, suspecting that he might have a serious sprain or a break. But the fall had only aggravated an old injury. And it was a good thing that it had brought him in today. If the original break had continued to go untreated, the teenager might have eventually lost the full use of his hand.

As it was, he would need surgery and a bone graft to correct it.

"Dr. Fortune?"

Jeremy turned to see Millie, the receptionist, standing in the doorway.

"I'm sorry to bother you, Doctor, but Kirsten Allen is here again. You know, the woman you were asking me about yesterday?"

Jeremy's pulse rate spiked at the news, but he maintained an unaffected facial expression. "Thanks, Millie. Where is she?"

"In the waiting room."

As much as Jeremy would like to go out and talk to her, he had to discuss his findings with the teenage patient and his mother who were waiting for the results of the X-ray.

"Do me a favor," Jeremy said. "Can you have Kirsten called into an exam room? And then let me know where I can find her?"

Millie's brow twitched, as if she found the request a little unusual, but she didn't ask his reason for it. Instead, she nodded. "I'll see what I can do."

"Thank you. I appreciate that." Jeremy didn't usually ask for favors, like moving people up in line. But Kirsten had left yesterday without waiting to be seen, and he didn't want that to happen again. Not before he had a chance to see her and talk to her again.

While Millie went to do as she was asked, Jeremy returned to the exam room to tell the teenager and his mother about the fracture and explain the surgery and healing process.

Ten minutes later, he made his way to room four, which had been assigned to Anthony Allen, Kirsten's infant son.

He knocked lightly, then opened the door, eager to see the attractive woman again, to get a chance to talk to her. But when he spotted a man in the room with her, his heart slammed against his chest.

Damn. She was married—or at least involved with someone.

Well, of course she was. What made him even think that she might not be?

A striking resemblance to the dream woman, that was what. And an overactive imagination for another. See what happened when a man read too much into a random dream and followed a hunch?

Trying not to stammer or to reveal his surprise, Jeremy reached out his hand to introduce himself to the baby's father. "Hello, I'm Dr. Fortune."

"Max Allen. Are you here to examine Anthony?"

"No, I..." Jeremy glanced at Kirsten, wondering if she had any idea why he was actually here.

Hell, how could she? He was still struggling to make sense of the thoughtless blunder himself.

He returned his focus on her husband and tried to

make light of it all. "Actually, I met Mrs. Allen in the parking lot yesterday. She'd spent a lot of time in the waiting room and hadn't been seen, so I wanted to make sure she got in quickly today."

Max stiffened. "Yeah, well, she shouldn't have done that."

Done *what?* Left without seeing a pediatrician? Talked to a man in the parking lot?

"Excuse me?" Jeremy pressed, picking up some negative vibes and hoping he hadn't gotten her in trouble.

"Kirsten brought Anthony here yesterday without my permission." Max tossed a frown her way.

Now it was Jeremy's turn to tense and give out some negative vibes. What kind of man controlled his wife like that?

"Maybe I'd better explain," Kirsten said. "First of all, I'm Max's sister. And I was babysitting his son yesterday." She turned to the young man beside her. "I shouldn't have taken it upon myself to bring the baby for a checkup without getting Max's okay."

Jeremy was still struggling to understand what Max's problem was, but that didn't stop him from realizing that Kirsten wasn't married to Max and being relieved at the news.

Just then, the door opened, and Jim Kragen, a pediatrician, stepped into the now crowded room. "Sorry. I was told to come to exam room four."

"You're in the right place," Jeremy told his colleague. "I just stopped in here for a minute. I'll leave you to your patient."

As Dr. Kragen stepped inside, Jeremy made his way to the door.

"Excuse me a minute," Kirsten said to her brother and to the pediatrician. "I'll be right back."

Was she following Jeremy out?

Apparently so. And he couldn't help feeling a rush of pleasure. That was, until he glanced at Max, who seemed to be annoyed at her departure.

If Jeremy didn't know better, he'd think that Max was sizing him up and finding him lacking. But maybe that was only his imagination.

When Kirsten and Jeremy left the small room and shut the door behind them, she said, "Thank you for coming to check on us."

"No problem. I knew you were worried about the baby, so I wanted to make sure you finally got to see a doctor."

"Actually, I kind of panicked yesterday, thinking Max wouldn't get around to making an appointment for the baby himself. But Anthony is really sweet, and he's eating well. So Dr. Kragen will probably say he's doing fine." She tucked a strand of hair behind her ear, revealing a small diamond stud. "You probably think I'm a worrywart, but I've never really been around small children before. And up until a few days ago, Max didn't even know he was a father. His ex-girlfriend just dumped the baby on him—well, on us, actually. Max is living with me for the time being. So we've had a crash course on child care and still have a lot to learn."

"How long will your brother have Anthony?"

"Permanently, I guess." Kirsten blew out a soft sigh. "And I'm sure that's for the best. His girlfriend isn't very maternal."

Was Kirsten maternal? Was she the kind of woman who'd make a good partner for a man like him?

It was hard to say without knowing more about her.

"If I'd done more babysitting as a teenager," she added, "I might not feel so out of my league. But I'm…well… my brother and I are both novices."

"I'm sure you're doing fine."

"Thanks for the vote of confidence." She flashed him a pretty smile. "You should have seen us shopping that first day. We had to buy just about everything other than a car seat, and we didn't have a clue what we were going to need. It must have been comical to anyone watching us."

"You're a good sister," he said.

Her smile faded some. "I try to be."

Something told him that Max didn't always make it easy for her, but that was only a hunch. And Jeremy rarely went with his gut feelings, even though that was exactly what he'd done when he had first spotted Kirsten in the parking lot.

They stood like that for a moment, studying each other in the narrow hallway.

She gave a little nod toward the closed door of the exam room. "I guess I'd better get back in there and make sure I don't miss anything important."

Jeremy didn't want to let her go without having some way of getting in touch with her, so he reached into the pocket of his lab coat and pulled out one of his cards. Then he took the pen he kept handy, jotted his cell number on the back and handed it to her. "If you need anything, give me a call. Like I told you before, I'm not a pediatrician, but I'll try to answer any questions you or your brother might have."

She took the card, then blessed him with a smile. The light in her eyes and a single dimple in her cheeks just about turned his stubborn heart on edge. "Thank you, Dr. Fortune. I really appreciate this. I'll try not to bother you, though."

"You won't. And call me Jeremy."

Her hand lifted to the silver necklace she wore, and she fingered the delicate heart charm that lay against the soft cotton fabric of her light blue T-shirt. Her head cocked slightly to the side, as if she was considering whatever might be brewing between them.

Of course, there wasn't anything going on between them. At least, not yet.

"So you're not married?" he asked.

"No, I'm not."

A grin tugged at his own lips. He realized that now wasn't the time to ask her out, but he wondered if her thoughts were drifting in that direction, too.

The attraction seemed to be mutual, although his interest in her had been heightened by that crazy dream he'd had. And while his rational nature knew there hadn't been anything prophetic about it, he didn't want to let her slip away again without at least having a deeper conversation with her.

If he had her number, he'd give her a follow-up phone call tomorrow. Then he might even ask her to dinner. But he didn't have her number and wouldn't go as far as to ask for it.

If there'd been anything to his dream, if his attraction to her was due to something bigger than either of them, then she would have to call him.

And he'd just have to wait and see if she did.

## Chapter Three

**W**hile Max ran into the pharmacy to pick up some vitamins and a special diaper rash ointment Dr. Kragen had recommended, Kirsten waited in the car with the sleeping baby secured in his seat in the back.

She'd been relieved to hear that Anthony was healthy and thriving. And now that her worries had been somewhat stilled, she couldn't help thinking about the kindness of Dr. Fortune—or rather, Jeremy. He seemed to have taken a special interest in her, although she couldn't say how or why she'd come to that conclusion.

It was in the way he looked at her, she supposed. The way their gazes seemed to connect and the hormones and pheromones that seemed to spark whenever he was near.

She reached into her purse and pulled out his business

card. She'd been a little surprised that he'd given it to her—and pleased that he had.

But how many doctors actually gave out their personal phone numbers? Not many, she suspected.

She turned the card over and looked on the back, where the numbers were written in bold strokes—clear and legible, unlike the proverbial doctor's scrawl she would have expected to see.

He'd given her permission to call him, but would she? *Should* she?

Maybe she could use the results of their visit with Dr. Kragen as an excuse to call him now. At least, he would then have a record of her number.

She hesitated only a moment before taking her cell phone from her purse and dialing the number he'd given her.

Jeremy answered on the third ring. "Hello?"

Her words jammed in her throat as she contemplated hanging up before indentifying herself. But she felt compelled to finish what she'd started. "Dr. Fortune? This is Kirsten Allen. I just wanted to let you know that Dr. Kragen told us Anthony looks good and appears to be healthy."

"I'm glad to hear that."

"I'd worried about not having any of Anthony's medical records, but Dr. Kragen ordered a blood test to check to see if he's had any of his immunizations yet. So that's one less thing for me to stress about."

"Jim's one of the top pediatricians in the county, so

you were in good hands. He has a private practice, but he works one day a month at the clinic."

Kirsten bit down on her lip as she contemplated a response. She wasn't ready to end the call, although they really had nothing else to talk about.

"Well," she said, "I just wanted to thank you again for being so nice to me…to us."

"It was my pleasure, Kirsten."

As silence stretched across the line, she suddenly wondered if she'd been wrong to think that he was interested in her in any way other than that of a kindhearted professional.

"Well…"

"Would you like to have dinner some night?" he asked, throwing her a curve.

Her heart dropped like dead weight, then rumbled back to life. "That sounds like fun."

*Fun?* She rolled her eyes. Why hadn't she given him a more sophisticated answer, one more grown-up and better suited to a doctor's dinner date?

"How about tomorrow night?" he asked.

So soon?

Goodness. Where would they go? What would she wear? Yet in spite of the questions and the fly-by-night insecurities that pelted her, she found herself saying, "Sure."

"I'm looking forward to it," he said.

So was she, even if a swarm of butterflies had settled in her stomach.

After he asked for her address and she gave it to him, he said, "I'll see you tomorrow night."

When the call ended, she sat dumbfounded for a while, the cell phone still in her hand.

Had she just imagined that conversation? Had the handsome doctor just asked her out to dinner? Would she have the right clothes to wear? Would she say the correct things?

Of course she would. She was a college graduate, for Pete's sake—an accountant. Okay, so she was unemployed at the moment. But that was only temporary. She had the skills and the résumé to land another job soon.

A knock sounded at the passenger window, and she turned to see Max waiting to get into the car. So she hit the unlock button and slid the cell phone back into her purse.

"Who were you talking to?" he asked, as he climbed in.

"Dr. Fortune. He asked me out to dinner tomorrow night, and I told him yes. Do you think you'll be okay by yourself with Anthony?"

Max chuffed. "I don't believe this."

"Believe what?"

"You brought Anthony to the clinic yesterday so you could hook up with a doctor? How long has that been going on?"

"What are you talking about?"

"Your crush on Dr. Fortune."

"You're imagining things. I don't have a crush on him."

"Then what's going on?"

She had no idea. She found Jeremy Fortune attractive and the thought of dating him exciting. And for some wild reason, he seemed to find her attractive, too.

"It's no big deal," she told her brother. "Like I said, I met him in the parking lot yesterday. We've talked briefly a couple of times, and he asked me out."

"A doctor seems to be a cut above your usual boyfriend. Don't you think a guy like that is out of your league?"

Jeremy Fortune *might* be, but that didn't keep Kirsten from smiling—or from dreaming about being with him.

It was all very Cinderella-ish, she supposed. And even if she didn't have stepsisters to tell her that she wasn't princess material, she didn't need them to. Between her own doubts and Max's, she was already having second thoughts about her date with the handsome doctor.

But she shook off a few lingering insecurities, as well as any possible shortcomings she might have, and looked forward to tomorrow night.

Jeremy pulled up along the curb of an older, two-story home in a quiet Red Rock neighborhood. It wasn't anything like the yard or porch he'd seen in his dream, but then why would it be?

The house in his dream had only been a random nocturnal image, he reminded himself. It didn't mean anything.

Sure, when he'd spotted Kirsten in the parking lot of

the clinic, he'd thought she bore a slight resemblance to the woman he'd envisioned, but that was just a coincidence. He would have found her attractive anyway. The similarity had only opened his eyes and allowed him to escape his troubles for the time being.

After parking his car, he made his way to the front door and rang the bell.

Max answered, a scowl plastered to his face. He invited Jeremy in, but he didn't crack a smile.

"How's it going?" Jeremy asked.

"Okay." Max closed the door. "My sister will be out in a minute. Have a seat."

Jeremy scanned the tidy room, noting the simple furnishings that had been carefully placed around the room: a beige sofa adorned with brightly colored decorator pillows, a wrought-iron floor lamp with a matching shade, dark wood furniture.

Red candles and a few photographs were displayed on the mantel over a brick fireplace.

The living room had a cozy, welcoming feel about it, and he could tell Kirsten took pride in her home.

Max sat in a recliner, his eyes glued to the television, watching a college basketball game. A portable travel crib rested beside him, where Anthony lay on his back, kicking his feet and watching a dinosaur mobile.

"Who's playing?" Jeremy asked, taking one last stab at being friendly.

Max was so focused on the game that it took him a moment to respond. "Oklahoma State at Texas A&M."

"What's the score?"

"The Aggies are up by five."

Silence again.

Jeremy decided to let it go. He was just about to take a seat when Kirsten entered the living room wearing a simple black dress and heels. Her hair had been swept up into a twist, revealing that small pair of diamond studs.

She wore only the slightest bit of makeup: mascara to highlight those pretty blue eyes, a pink shade of lipstick to accentuate a natural pout.

He'd known she was attractive in denim and T-shirts. But the transformation from casual tomboy to classy dinner date was jaw-dropping.

"You look great," he said.

Her cheeks flushed when she smiled. "Thank you."

Max lifted the remote toward the television and turned down the volume. Then he stood, crossed his arms and shifted his weight to one hip. "So where are you guys going?"

Jeremy hadn't suffered through a date-night interrogation since he'd been a teenager going to his last high school prom. And it prickled him to have to go through it now, especially from a man who was probably more than ten years his junior. But he shook off his irritation and played the game. "I thought we'd go to Bernardo's, the new Italian restaurant that just opened up a few blocks down the street from Red. That is, if Kirsten doesn't mind."

"Bernardo's sounds good to me." She offered him a breezy smile, then grabbed her purse from a small table near the door. "I'll see you later, Max. You can call me if you have a problem with Anthony."

"I'll be okay."

Good, because Jeremy was looking forward to putting some distance between them. What was that guy's problem?

Jeremy opened the door, then followed Kirsten out of the house. Moments later, they were in his rental car and headed into town for dinner.

"I'm afraid I need to apologize for my brother's rudeness," Kirsten said. "His life has been turned upside down, so he's been a little testy with everyone lately."

"No apology necessary."

"I know. But…" She pursed her lips. "I guess everyone has their cross to bear. And Max is mine."

Jeremy wasn't sure why she felt that way. "How old is he? Twenty-four?"

"Actually, he's twenty-six."

"Then I'd say it's probably time for him to move on and make a life of his own."

"I wish it were that easy." Kirsten glanced out her window at the passing scenery, then back to Jeremy. "He's between jobs, so I can't very well boot him out into the street. And now that he has Anthony…"

"I can see how that would complicate things." Jeremy had a strong sense of family loyalty, too, so he understood why she was supportive of Max. "How's it working out?"

"It's been tough." She gave a half shrug. "But there's

not much I can do about it until he lands another job and can move out."

"What kind of position is he looking for?"

"Anything at this point. I think he wants to move as badly as I'd like to see him go. But he doesn't have a high school diploma, which limits his options when it comes to finding something that will pay the rent, and now he has day-care expenses to cover."

"That's too bad."

"I know." She took a deep breath, then sighed softly. "I tried to talk him into getting his GED and picking up some college courses, but he refused to even consider it."

"Why?"

"I'm afraid it was probably because I suggested it." She rested her hands on top of the small black purse that sat in her lap. "And because he's never been particularly ambitious. After he dropped out of high school, he just drifted from job to job for one reason or another."

"In that case, you might not be doing him any favors by letting him stay with you."

"Actually, two years ago he was hired on at the feed store and was able to keep that one until a couple weeks ago. He really seemed to like it, but when the new management took over, they laid everyone off, and Max was back at square one."

Jeremy was glad to see that her brother had managed to hold a job, but he couldn't understand why the guy wouldn't try to take the GED exam or improve his chances of getting a better paying position.

He knew he should keep his thoughts to himself, but he said, "Maybe, if he won't take your advice, it might be time for you to back off and let him captain his own ship, even if it has leaks."

"I'm sure you're right. But my biggest fault is that I tend to think with my heart more than my head."

Learning that bit of news about Kirsten probably ought to throw up a red flag for a guy who'd always been methodical and rational, but Jeremy found it appealing that she had a soft heart. Maybe because she reminded him of his mother in that way.

Molly Fortune had been the one to encourage Jeremy to follow his dream and go to medical school. Not that anyone had given him a hard time when he chose not to work at Fortune Forecasting. His dad and brothers had been pretty supportive, too. But it had been Molly's proud smile at his graduation that had made it all worthwhile.

He shot a glance across the seat at Kirsten, wondering if she had any other qualities that would remind him of his mother.

Molly had been a dynamic woman—warm, loving and a real mama bear when it came to her husband and her five sons. So when she passed away four years ago, the entire family had taken it hard. But Jeremy had a feeling he might have grieved for her even more than the others had.

He hadn't spent that much time with her after he moved to Sacramento and started his practice with a prominent orthopedic medical group, but he'd valued her opinion and her unwavering support, even if he didn't always take her advice. And she'd always been just a phone call away.

Of course, he'd accepted her loss and moved on with his life, but her death had left a hole.

He looked across the seat at Kirsten and couldn't help wondering if a loving wife and a family of his own would make him feel whole again. He hoped so—whether that woman turned out to be Kirsten or not.

As he pulled into the parking lot at Bernardo's, he stole another glance at his lovely dinner date.

They'd only met a couple days ago, so he had no way of knowing whether she was the kind of woman he was looking for or not.

But he had every intention of finding out.

Kirsten sat across a romantic, candlelit table from Jeremy, listening to him tell her about his day at the clinic. It was clear that he enjoyed his work and cared about his patients, and she found herself smiling at just about everything he said.

But she wasn't the only one who was enjoying the evening so far. Jeremy's body language and ready smile told her that their date had gotten off to a good start.

"What do you do for a living?" he asked.

"I'm an accountant." She lifted her water goblet and took a sip.

"Where do you work?"

She'd hoped that wouldn't come up, but realized it might. "I'm between jobs at the moment, but I'll get another position quickly. I've got some great letters of recommendation and a solid résumé. It's just a matter of time."

He smiled, then took a bite of his manicotti.

She didn't want him to give too much thought about the only similarity she and Max had other than their family resemblance, so she decided to shift the focus of the conversation back to him. "The clinic is lucky to have you. Do you ever think you'll work in private practice?"

"Actually, I do have a practice—in Sacramento. I'm just volunteering my time at the clinic."

Her heart cramped at the thought of him leaving town, which seemed to be what he was saying. "What brought you to Red Rock? And how long will you be here?"

"I came for my father's wedding, which was supposed to have taken place last month. And I'll be in town as long as it takes to…" Jeremy glanced down at his plate, then back at Kirsten.

The sun-bleached streaks in his hair glistened in the candlelight, and his eyes locked on hers. She sensed the emotion in his voice before he even spoke a word.

"My dad disappeared on what should have been his wedding day, and he hasn't been seen or heard from since. There was no way I could leave town, so I took a leave of absence. That allows me to stay in Red Rock until he's found."

Her heart broke for him as he continued to give her the details about the vehicle accident, about the police investigation that went nowhere. "I don't usually rely on hunches and feelings, but I... Well, I believe he's going to turn up."

She reached across the table, placed her hand over his and felt his warmth, his strength in spite of his vulnerability. She understood the feeling all too well. Her own father had run off when she was fourteen. And she'd hung on to the belief that he would return, that he'd never abandon her and the family.

But he hadn't come back. And she'd had to face the hurt, the disappointment.

Jeremy's eyes locked onto Kirsten's, revealing that he might not be as hopeful as he'd said he was, as if he'd needed her agreement and support. It was the kind of emotional reaction she'd always hoped to get from her brother—the sense of unity and understanding, the realization that she was connecting with someone she cared about. Yet it was all that and more.

Something else simmered in his gaze, something warmed by the glow of the candlelight, by the romantic music playing softly in the background and by the hum of pheromones that permeated every breath they took.

Jeremy Fortune was a man to take seriously. And with time, he might even prove to be a man that she could promise to love, honor and cherish—given the chance to get to know him better. But time was a luxury they didn't have. He was only in Red Rock temporarily and would be going back to California soon.

So she slowly drew her hand away, her fingertips skimming over the top of his knuckles as she did so.

She shouldn't get any romantic ideas. This might be

the date of a lifetime for her, but it was just a diversion
for him. He wasn't in any position to form a relationship right now, so she'd be foolish to let her thoughts
drift in that direction. After all, he'd be leaving town
eventually.

And where would that leave her?

Jeremy's skin continued to tingle where Kirsten had
touched him—and so did his heart. Her compassion, her
understanding, did something to him. But before he could
ponder just what that might be, the waiter who'd introduced himself as Gordon when they'd first been seated,
asked, "Are you ready for me to take your plates?"

"Yes, I'm finished," Kirsten said. "Thank you."

Jeremy let the waiter pick up his dinner plate, too.

"Can I interest you in our dessert menu?" the young
man asked.

Jeremy wasn't ready for the evening to end, so he said,
"Sure. Let's see what you have."

The waiter had no more than walked away when Jeremy's cell phone vibrated.

Ever since his father's disappearance, he made sure
the phone was always handy. There was no telling when
a call might come in, saying his dad had been found. So
he checked the display and, after noting the Sacramento
area code, recognized a familiar number.

"Excuse me a moment," he told Kirsten. "This is a
colleague from Sacramento."

"No problem. I understand."

When Jeremy answered, Jack Danfield said, "How's it going? Any word on your father?"

"No, not yet. I'm in the middle of dinner. Can I give you a call back later?"

"Yes, but first let me tell you the reason for my call. I have a twelve-year-old boy in the E.R. who was involved in a car accident. He has multiple fractures in both legs. He's had some arterial damage, and I'm afraid we might need to amputate. But I wanted to talk to you first. You had that case last summer that was similar, and you were able to save the limb."

Jeremy looked at his watch. He needed more details, and the consult would not only take time, but it was also going to require all of his concentration. "I'll give you a call in about ten minutes, Jack. Will that be okay?"

"Certainly."

When the line disconnected, Jeremy glanced across the table at his dinner companion, who seemed to be growing prettier by the minute. "I'm really sorry, Kirsten. I've got a long-distance consultation that just might help save a boy's leg, and it's important that I spend some time on it. I'm afraid I'm going to have to end our dinner early."

She reached for the strap of her purse that hung on the back of her chair. "There's no need to explain, Jeremy. I understand."

He motioned for the waiter, who returned to the table with the menus in hand.

"I'm sorry," Jeremy told him. "We're going to have

to pass on dessert. And I'll need the bill as soon as you can bring it."

"Yes, sir. I'll be right back."

Five minutes later, Jeremy and Kirsten were in his car and on the road.

"I'm really sorry to end our evening like this," he said.

"Don't be. I understand. Your patients come first. I just hope everything turns out okay for that poor boy."

So did Jeremy.

He pulled along the curb in front of her house and parked. After getting out of the car, they walked to her front door. He really needed to return Jack's call as quickly as possible, but he couldn't help lingering on the porch just a moment longer.

Did he dare kiss Kirsten good-night?

How deeply did he want to get involved with her?

At this point, he could pretty much cut bait and run. But he'd enjoyed their time together so far, and there was so much more he wanted to know about her.

"Thank you for dinner," she said. "Bernardo's was a great choice."

"You're welcome. But I still owe you a dessert."

"No, you don't." She looked up at him and smiled, her blue eyes glimmering in the porch light. "The food was so good, I didn't leave room for anything more."

They stood like that for a moment—gazing at each other, hanging on to the moment. If Jeremy had all the time in the world, would she invite him inside?

Again, the question of a good-night kiss returned full force. Should he or shouldn't he?

He wasn't sure why he bothered to even ponder the question. The urge to kiss her was almost over-whelming.

Oh, what the hell. He placed a hand on her cheek, felt the silk of her skin, the curve of her jaw.

As her head tilted up slightly and her lips parted, it was all the encouragement he needed.

## Chapter Four

Kirsten didn't know what she'd expected to happen when Jeremy walked her to the front door, but certainly not *this,* not a soul-stirring good-night kiss.

Of course, she'd seen it coming when his gaze reached deep inside her, when he touched her cheek with a lover's caress. And she'd been filled with anticipation as their lips met.

The moment was so heart-stopping, so magical, that she was afraid to breathe for fear it was all a dream and she'd wake up alone in her bed, her arms wrapped around her pillow.

And while it was really happening, she was spellbound by his heady, woodland scent, by the warmth of his breath and the heat of his touch.

As the kiss deepened and their lips parted, his tongue

brushed hers, making her knees go weak. So she reached for his waist to steady herself. As she did so, he slipped his arms around her, drawing her close, kissing her until she was tempted to drag him inside and see what happened next.

Oh, lordy. If this was the way Jeremy kissed a woman good-night, she wondered what it would be like to welcome him into her bed, into her...life.

She'd have to get control of her runaway thoughts and emotions, though. She couldn't allow herself to get swept away in a romantic fantasy with the handsome doctor, no matter how enjoyable their evening together had been, no matter how arousing his good-night kiss was.

It was crazy to think this was anything more than it was—a pleasant dinner that had come to a nice end. One day in the not-so-distant future, he was going to return to his medical practice in California, and she'd probably end up being a fleeting memory on his part. But there was a chance that he would mean a lot more than that to her. So for that reason alone, she needed to end this sweet assault before she lost her head completely.

Yet her body found it hard to comply with common sense, leaving it all up to him.

As Jeremy broke the kiss and released her from his embrace, she tried to shake off the effects of the lingering magic to no avail. Her pulse was racing and her mind was scrambling to imagine something romantic developing between them.

Still, she knew better than to waste her time thinking about those kinds of possibilities. Not when there were twice as many reasons a relationship between her and Jeremy would never work out.

But as he looked deep into her eyes, she couldn't seem to wrap her mind around a single one of them.

"Thanks for a nice evening," he said softly. "I'll give you a call tomorrow."

Still stunned by the sweet but arousing kiss, she was afraid to speak for fear she'd stumble over the words, so she merely nodded.

When he turned and strode toward his car, she continued to watch him. She really ought to go inside the house, but her legs didn't seem to be working any better than her voice.

Once he reached the street and stood beside the driver's door, he paused long enough to look over the top of the sedan and smiled. "Good night, Kirsten."

She lifted her hand to wave, realizing that her fingers had been resting against her lips, which still tingled from the kiss they'd shared.

"Good night," she managed to say.

As he climbed into his car, she realized just how appropriate her parting words had been.

It had been a *good* night indeed.

After dropping off Kirsten at her house, Jeremy pulled into the nearest shopping center and parked under a fluorescent light, not wanting to wait any longer before returning Jack Danfield's call.

Even though he was still reeling over the heated kiss he'd shared with Kirsten, he had to shake the giddiness and focus. As he did so, he dialed his colleague's number.

Jack had been waiting with the results of the X-ray and CT scan, so they discussed the details of the surgery as well as all the complications that could arise. Thanks to the efforts of modern technology, Jeremy had been able to see the scans and pictures on his iPhone, although he would have felt better about his counsel if he'd been standing next to Jack, viewing the images together.

Nearly an hour later, Jeremy drove back to the Double Crown Ranch and parked near the barn, which had been rebuilt after an arsonist had set it on fire a couple years back.

There were still lights on in the expansive, eight-bedroom house, a solid adobe structure, with sand-colored walls and rough-hewn wooden beams, which meant Lily was still awake.

Good. That would give him a chance to talk to her and ask about her day. They'd both come to depend upon each other after William's disappearance.

Using the key ring remote, Jeremy locked the car, then strode along the curved adobe walkway to the steps that led up to the large, antique wooden door.

Each time Jeremy passed through the arched entryway and opened the wrought-iron gate to the inner courtyard, with its abundant garden of native perennials and flowering vines, he felt as though he'd come home.

He had a lot of memories of the ranch where he'd spent most of his summer vacations as a kid, and whenever he stepped on the property, all those sunny days of hard work and cowboy fun came back to him.

Aunt Lily and Uncle Ryan had been good to him, as well as his brothers. So he was determined to "be there" for Lily now, while she was awaiting word from or about his dad.

After letting himself into the tiled foyer, he called out, "Lily? I'm home."

The woman—who should have been his stepmother by now—said, "I'm in the great room, Jeremy."

He followed her voice, finding her seated in one of the custom-made leather chairs, a tea service set out in front of her on a glass-topped table.

She brightened when he entered the room. "How was your day?"

"It was great." Not only had he enjoyed having dinner with Kirsten, but he'd been part of the medical effort to save a young boy's leg. "How about yours?"

"It was all right."

Actually, Jeremy realized, nothing would ever be "all right" again until William Fortune returned to his family—one way or another.

"Would you like something to drink?" Lily asked. "I can pour you a cup of tea, but there are decanters of bourbon and Scotch in the bar, if you'd like something stronger."

"Thanks, but I'll just get myself some water. I'll be back in a minute."

When Jeremy returned with his glass, he took a seat on one of the chairs facing his aunt.

At sixty-five, Lily was still an attractive woman. Her Apache and Spanish heritage provided her with high cheekbones and large dark eyes, lending her an exotic beauty.

"I don't like to think of you staying home all alone," Jeremy said, although he knew why she did. She wanted to be near the phone in the event that William called or the police had news about him.

Lily poured a spot of tea into her delicate china cup. "There's always a ranch hand in the yard. And Rosita is just a phone call and a short walk away. So I'll be fine."

Ruben and Rosita Perez lived in a three-bedroom house on the property, which was the only reason Jeremy felt comfortable leaving her to drive into town and volunteer at the clinic. But it wasn't the same as having someone in the house with her, someone to keep her company and make sure she was eating.

"Why don't you invite Maria to join you and Rosita for lunch one of these days?" he suggested.

A slow smile settled across her face. "That's a nice idea. Maybe I should call them tomorrow and set something up."

The clock on the mantel tick-tocked softly, letting them know that it would be bedtime soon.

As Lily lifted her china cup and took a sip, Jeremy asked, "Chamomile?"

She nodded. "I thought it would help me sleep."

They'd both been plagued by insomnia lately, but he

supposed that was to be expected. They had a lot on their minds.

"Are you sure you wouldn't like a little tea or a night-cap to help you unwind?" she asked.

"Not tonight. But thanks."

He set the water on a ceramic, felt-lined coaster and scanned the room, with its traditional Western-style decor. The leather sofas and chairs were fairly new, but the rest of the furniture—the painted armoires, the long oak dining table with high-back chairs, the bookshelves and various pieces of pottery—were antiques that boasted a Spanish influence.

So did the plaster walls, which had been adorned with colorful paintings and hand-woven blankets that had been created by local artisans. One piece in particular had been made by Isabella, J.R.'s wife, and given to Lily as a gift.

Needless to say, J.R. and Isabella's home had been decorated in a similar style, which appealed to Jeremy.

When he first came to Red Rock to celebrate what should have been his father's wedding to Lily, he'd stayed in one of the many guest rooms at J.R.'s ranch. But several weeks after his dad went missing, he'd moved to the Double Crown, hoping to provide Lily with some comfort and support while they waited for William's return.

Six years ago, Lily lost her husband, Ryan, to a brain tumor, and two years later, William was left a widower when Molly died. The surviving spouses had always been friends and had grieved for each other's loss.

Over time, their friendship had deepened, and they gradually fell in love.

Jeremy couldn't have been more pleased to learn of their plan to marry. William and Lily deserved to be happy and to spend their golden years together.

But now, at least for the time being, Lily was alone again, and Jeremy's heart ached for her.

As he sat with her this evening, reflecting on the losses he'd had over the past six years, he wondered if it had been a mistake to pass on a nightcap.

Of course, he hadn't actually lost his dad—not until they found a body—but it was becoming more and more difficult to remain positive that the man would eventually come home, and that the wedding would be rescheduled.

"We'll find him," Lily had said on several different occasions. "I can't explain how I know, but I'm certain he's still alive."

Jeremy took comfort in her quiet faith, and he wondered if Lily might be the one providing support to him, rather than the other way around.

It was possible, he supposed.

There had always been something special about Lily, something that struck Jeremy as both strong and vulnerable at the same time. He wasn't sure what it was about her that he admired the most or what it was that drew him to her, but she provided him with some kind of maternal link that he'd been missing ever since his mom died.

Was that what his dad had come to appreciate about Lily? That she took the edge off his loss, too?

So how was it that Lily held on to hope that William was still alive when even Jeremy was beginning to fear the worst?

Had she experienced a dream or had some kind of premonition?

Under normal circumstances, he wouldn't have asked for an explanation, but his dream and his date with Kirsten were too fresh on his mind, and he found himself quizzing her anyway.

"Can I ask you a question, Lily?"

She glanced up from her teacup and smiled. "Of course."

"Do you ever have dreams that turn out to be real or that might even reveal the future?"

"Why do you ask?"

"Because I had a dream a few nights back. And in it, I saw a woman I'd never met before. I didn't exactly see her face, but I got a glimpse of her hair color and part of her profile. Then, the next day, I met her—or someone who could have been her."

Lily, who still held her teacup, cocked her head slightly to the side. The look in her eyes indicated that she suspected that there was more going on than a chance meeting.

He wouldn't have shared his thoughts about Kirsten and the dream with anyone else, but he trusted Lily with the details. "I had the feeling that I was married in that dream—and that I was happier than I'd ever been before. So when I spotted the woman the next day, it left me a little unbalanced."

"Did you get a chance to talk to her?"

He nodded.

"What's her name?"

"Kirsten."

Lily bent forward and returned her teacup to the saucer that rested on the table. "Maybe you should ask her out."

"Actually," Jeremy said, grinning, "we had dinner together this evening."

Lily blessed him with a slow, knowing smile. "And...?"

"I enjoyed our time together and would like to take her out again."

Lily's smile faded. "Why do I get the feeling that there's a problem?"

"Because I've got a practice in Sacramento and won't be in Red Rock forever."

Silence shrouded the room as they both realized what was keeping him in town. Finally, Lily said, "You've put your life on hold for your father, Jeremy. And I can appreciate that. But are you sure it's not going to affect your practice to be away from it for so long?"

"I took that leave of absence for several reasons," he admitted. "I need some time to reevaluate a few things in my life."

Lily leaned back in her seat and placed her hands in her lap. "And how is Kirsten affecting your reevaluation process?"

"I'm not sure. But if what I'm feeling for her continues

to grow, it's going to… Well, it will certainly complicate my life."

Hell, just meeting her seemed to have complicated his life already.

"This sounds serious," Lily said.

"If you're talking about love, it's way too soon for anything like that. I'm attracted to her, of course, but it's even more than that. She really intrigues me, and I'm drawn to her."

"It sounds like love at first sight to me."

Jeremy slowly shook his head. "No, it can't be that."

"I've been in love twice in my life," Lily said. "So no one knows better than I do how inexplicable that feeling can be."

"It's not *love*," Jeremy repeated, sure that he couldn't possibly have feelings like that so soon. "I don't even know her."

But if truth be told, he wanted to get to know her a whole lot better—starting tomorrow.

The next day, while Max was out pounding the pavement again and Anthony napped in the Portacrib that served as his bed, Kirsten decided to spend the quiet time unpacking some of the boxes she'd been storing in the hall closet, a chore she'd been putting off ever since she'd moved into the house.

She'd just pulled out a box filled with college textbooks that she hadn't wanted to get rid of, but as she looked through them now, she realized it was silly to keep them. They took up so much space—and they were heavy, too.

Maybe she could donate them to the library or sell them on eBay. As she considered her options for disposing of them, the doorbell rang.

She had no idea who it could be on a weekday afternoon. It was probably a salesman. She'd ignore the person at the door completely, but she was afraid that whoever it was might ring again. And a second chime could wake up the baby, who'd just gone down for a nap and should sleep for a couple hours.

So she got up from the floor, where she'd been kneeling before the box of books, and answered the door.

When she spotted Jeremy on her porch, wearing a pair of black slacks, a pale blue polo shirt and a dazzling smile, her breath caught.

"I hope you don't mind me stopping by unannounced," he said.

Her only concern about his impromptu visit was that it hadn't given her a chance to run a brush through her hair, to put on some lipstick and to change into something other than a UT San Antonio T-shirt and a comfy pair of frayed denim jeans.

But she shook off her momentary embarrassment and said, "Not at all." Then she stepped aside and let him in.

Needless to say, she was surprised to see Jeremy, but the two white bags he carried left her especially curious about why he'd stopped by—in spite of her being glad that he had.

Once she closed the door, she asked, "What's that?"

His eyes glimmered with mirth. "I owed you dessert, remember? So I hope you're hungry."

"You brought *dessert?*" She laughed. "I wasn't going to hold you to it." Again, she studied the bags, awed by the gesture. "What did you do? Buy out a bakery?"

"I didn't have to go that far. I just called Bernardo's and ordered takeout of every dessert they have on the menu, including the chocolate soufflé, which is still warm and supposed to be their specialty."

And he'd brought all of it to *her?*

His efforts were both adorable and mind-boggling. Was this what dating Jeremy Fortune was going to be like?

Not that they were dating, exactly.

*Oh, no?* a small inner voice asked. *And just what* would *you call it?*

"Come with me," she said. "I'll get some plates and forks."

He followed her into the small kitchen, where her dinner simmered in a Crock-Pot on the counter, filling the room with the aroma of chicken and vegetables.

"Where do you want me to set this up?" he asked.

Still amazed at his presence, as well as his gesture, she suggested he spread it out on the table, then asked, "Should I put on some coffee? Or would you rather have milk?"

"I'll have whatever you're having." He set the bags on one of the chairs, then proceeded to pull out take-out containers filled with tiramisu, cheesecake, cannoli, a fruit tart, biscotti, fresh berries and what had to be the soufflé he'd mentioned. "I hope you don't mind, but I decided not to bring the gelato. I was afraid it would melt before I got here."

"Believe me," she said, "I don't think we're going to miss the ice cream."

Within minutes, her table looked like a dessert buffet at a wedding. When Jeremy took a step back and smiled at his handiwork, she laughed. "You must have a real sweet tooth, Dr. Fortune."

"I do. But I was also a Boy Scout, and we were taught to be prepared."

"For what?" she asked, chuckling. "A sugar embargo?"

"I wanted to make sure I had whatever you would have ordered last night."

"I probably would have just asked for a bite of whatever you were having," she admitted. What in the world were they going to do with all these goodies?

"Why do women do that?" he asked. "Just ask for a bite when they'd like the whole thing?"

"Because it's a way to diet and have our cake, too." But if Kirsten had any ideas about counting carbs or calories today, she was going to be toast. Because she wanted to try a little of everything he brought.

While she put on a pot of coffee, she couldn't help but wonder just how far a man like Jeremy would go for a woman he cared about, and a smidgen of envy stirred in her heart.

If he didn't have ties to Sacramento, if he was settled here in Red Rock…

As the water began to gurgle and dribble into the carafe, she realized that he'd certainly gone out of his way for her today. Did that mean he cared about her in spite of the reasons a long-lasting relationship between them wasn't feasible?

Or was she just a date he was trying to impress?

No, that couldn't be it. The man was impressive enough in his own right and didn't need to play games like that. Any woman would be lucky to have caught his eye, even if it was just a temporary thing.

After Jeremy set out the plates, silverware and napkins, he wandered over to the Crock-Pot and peered through the glass lid. "Boy, this sure smells good."

"It's just a little something I threw in for dinner."

A part of her wanted to invite him to stay, but Max was so unpredictable these days. She never knew what he'd say or how he'd act. And she wasn't up for the stress. Not when she was hoping this "temporary thing" with Jeremy would last longer than a date or two. So she decided to let the whole thing ride.

When the coffee was finished, she poured two cups. "How do you like yours?" she asked. "Cream? Sugar? Both?"

"Black, thanks."

She added a bit of skim milk and artificial sweetener to hers, which was clearly a waste of time considering the sugar and calories they were about to consume, but she wasn't going to blink an eye at the indulgence. Instead, she joined him at the table.

He took his fork and cut into the tiramisu, then offered the bite to her. "Here, try this."

She opened her mouth, letting him feed her. The sweet, gooey taste was mesmerizing, but she was more awed by the fact that he was spoon-feeding her.

Could anything be sexier than that?

Yes, she realized. If they were feeding each other in bed after making love all afternoon.

"What do you think?" he asked.

About feeding each other in bed? She forced herself to focus on the taste of the tiramisu instead. "It's delicious. You're going to have to try it, too."

Then she reached for a fork, filled it with a man-size portion, and offered it to him. As he opened his mouth, something wild and exciting rushed through her—setting off a vision of the two of them sitting amid tangled sheets, romantic music on the radio, feeling both sated and hungry at the same time…

Enough of that, she told herself. She'd be hungry for a lot more than sweets if she wasn't careful. So she cut into a cannoli—were they really going to keep feeding each other?—and lifted the fork to his lips, offering him another taste and leaving a bit of whipped cream at the edge of his mouth.

She reached out and wiped it away with her finger, but as their gazes locked, his hand grasped her wrist and her movements froze. As his face leaned toward hers, time slowed to a crawl and anticipation filled her to the brim.

If she'd thought their last kiss had been breathtaking, she had a feeling that this one would be all that and more.

And she was right.

As their lips met and parted, his tongue swept inside her mouth, sending a heated rush to the most feminine part of her. She reached toward him, her fingers snaking through his golden-brown locks, drawing him closer and deepening the kiss.

Passion flared, rocking her to the core. She couldn't seem to get enough of him or his sweet, creamy taste. And she realized that if he took her hand, drew her to a stand, swept her into his arms and carried her to the bedroom, she wouldn't have stopped him. She wouldn't have even considered it.

How could anything that started out so sweet and innocent burst into all-consuming desire?

When the kiss finally ended—she wasn't even sure who had come up for air first—her mind scrambled to get a grip on both her hormones and her emotions.

What was going on between them?

Was he feeling it, too—the heat, the passion?

"I didn't come over here to take you to bed," he said.

She almost wished that he had. And while she knew she ought to say something, her heart and mind were still spinning out of control.

As she tried to gather her wits, which seemed to be a

real struggle at the moment, a response to his comment failed her.

"You look a little uneasy," he said.

Heavens, no. She was just a little stunned and shaken, that was all. If this was what his kiss did to her, what would making love with him be like?

"I…" She caught herself before she ended up rambling about how deeply that kiss had affected her, how badly she wanted to share another—and anything else he had in mind. "It just took me by surprise."

"I'm sorry if I was out of line."

"Oh, no. Not at all. It's just that…" She struggled for a moment over how to continue, but why beat around the bush and play games? Opting for honesty, she said, "Well, it was a little earthshaking."

Surely, he'd felt it, too.

A grin splashed across his face. "I'd have to agree with you there."

This was probably the time to invite him to stay to dinner, but as the baby cried out, announcing naptime was over and drawing her back to reality, she couldn't bring herself to do it.

"I…uh…better get Anthony," she said. "He's going to want a bottle."

Talk about lousy timing.

But maybe it was for the best. What she'd just shared with Jeremy had been the kind of thing that dreams were made of. And a fussy baby was sure to put a king-size damper on that.

So could a surly brother, who might walk in at any time.

"Is there something I can do to help?" Jeremy asked.

"Not that I can think of." How could she ask him to fix a bottle of formula or to check on Anthony and see if his diaper was wet—or *worse?*

Talk about being jerked out of the dream world and thrust into reality.

"I've got it," she said, as she excused herself to get the baby.

She just hoped that when she returned, Jeremy wouldn't decide that dating her wouldn't be worth the real-life complications she was sure to toss into the mix.

## Chapter Five

Jeremy had never been so turned on by something as simple as a kiss before, especially one in which he and the woman had been fully clothed and seated at a kitchen table.

As Kirsten went into the other room to get the crying baby, he watched the alluring sway of her denim-clad hips, the swish of her honey-brown hair across her shoulders.

She had some kind of a hold on him, although he'd be damned if he knew what it was, and it only seemed to be growing stronger.

He didn't believe in love at first sight, so he knew it wasn't that. Hell, he'd barely had a chance to get to know her, to talk about some of the meatier subjects in life. So whatever he was feeling had to be strictly biological—a mixture of lust, hormones and chemistry.

Or was it more than that?

Either way, there was no getting around the fact that Kirstin would be a dynamite lover. Two kisses had convinced him of that.

So now what? His visit had clearly taken an unexpected turn, and he wasn't sure whether he should stay or go.

He'd clearly surprised her by showing up at her house this afternoon, and while she'd been elbow-deep in some domestic chore and not wearing any makeup to speak of, it hadn't mattered one bit. He still found her beautiful, as well as intriguing. Maybe even more so now.

When she returned to the kitchen with Anthony, he watched as she cuddled the hungry baby while preparing to feed him.

"Need some help?" he asked, even though she seemed to be juggling the infant, a bottle of water and a scoop of powdered formula as if it was all in a day's work.

"Thanks, but I've got it. I have a system that seems to work, even when I'm home alone." She laughed, the lilt of her voice a pleasant sound that played havoc with his senses. "But you should've seen me when Anthony first arrived. I was so inept with this little guy that it was almost funny."

Jeremy found that hard to believe. She certainly looked like a pro as she settled into the kitchen chair and placed the nipple in the baby's mouth.

Anthony quickly latched on and began sucking as though it might be the last bottle he'd ever get.

"Goodness," she said. "Would you look at him go?"

Jeremy was looking all right, but at the whole picture of woman and child. Kirsten was a natural, and he couldn't help picturing her holding *his* baby.

And why would he do that?

He'd never had visions of himself as a father before. Not that he didn't want kids—his life had just been too busy, too complicated, too focused on his medical practice. For as long as he'd been in Sacramento, he hadn't been able to think much beyond the next patient, the next X-ray or the next surgery.

But for some crazy reason, when he was with Kirsten, his entire focus shifted to another level. There was just something about her, about being with her, that made him feel…different.

In some ways, she reminded him of his mom, and he wondered if Kirsten had a playful side, too.

Molly Fortune had adored her five sons, but she hadn't been a pushover. She'd made them each toe the mark. Still, she'd known how to play with them, how to laugh and enjoy their company. And that had made for a happy childhood and a heart filled with memories.

Would Kirsten, like Jeremy's mom, be the playful kind of mother who would help her kids build a tree house in the backyard? Would she lead a Cub Scout troop? And on rainy days, would she help them build a fortress in the living room out of sheets and blankets?

Not all mothers would.

And why should it even matter?

Hell if he knew. Although he suspected that it might be due to the fact that he'd been so studious in school, so driven to get a medical degree, so focused on his career, that he was finally ready to kick back, have some fun and enjoy himself for a change.

Before his mom had died, she'd taken him aside and said, "I'm glad to see you working so hard, honey. But I worry about you. There's so much more to life than work. You really need to take time to play."

Jeremy hadn't taken her seriously at the time, but he wished he had. Her words were just now beginning to sink in.

He watched Kirsten for a moment or two longer, then asked, "Can you get a babysitter on Friday night?" He wouldn't just assume that Max would be around every evening.

"That won't be a problem. Why?"

"I'd like to take you out."

"All right." She smiled, letting him know that the suggestion appealed to her.

"Dress warmly," he said.

Her eyes lit up. "Okay. Where are we going?"

He was just about to tell her, then decided to keep it to himself. "It's a surprise."

A grin splashed across her face. "I love surprises."

Apparently, so did he. Because picking up Kirsten and whisking her off on a fun-filled adventure suddenly sounded like one of the best ideas he'd ever had.

*  *  *

As Max bent over and peered into the refrigerator, looking for a soda, he scrunched his face at all the take-out containers. "What the heck is all this crap doing in here?"

"It's not crap," Kirsten said, as she stood near the sink and poured out the remaining coffee from the carafe. "It's leftover dessert."

He pulled a cola from the fridge and popped the top. "Left over from what?"

"Jeremy had to cut our date short last night, and since we weren't able to stay long enough to eat dessert, he brought all of that by this afternoon."

"You've gotta be kidding." Max slowly shook his head, still standing in front of the open refrigerator. "Don't you think that's a little over-the-top?"

Actually, she thought it was sweet. But it was clear that Max wouldn't agree. So choosing not to argue, she ignored the fact that Jeremy's visit and thoughtfulness had struck a raw nerve in her brother and asked, "Do you want some cheesecake? It's really good."

"I don't want any of that stuff." Max slammed the refrigerator door a little too hard. "I still haven't figured out what that guy's up to."

"He just came by to see me, that's all."

Max chuffed and slowly shook his head.

"Obviously, you don't like him." Kirsten crossed her arms and braced herself for whatever unfounded objections Max might have. "Why is that? He's an orthopedic surgeon. And a darn good one, from what I've learned by doing a Google search. On top of that, his family is not only well-known, but well respected in Red Rock. Have you ever heard of the Fortune Foundation?"

"Who hasn't?" Max leaned against the refrigerator. "Those people think they own the town."

If Kirsten had a violent streak and lacked self-control, she might have punched her brother's lights out. As it was, she disposed of the old coffee grounds and rinsed out the carafe.

"Open your eyes," Max said. "That guy's just trying to snowball you, sis. And, apparently, it's working."

Kirsten shut off the water, set the clean carafe on the counter and turned to face him. "What are you talking about?"

"He's just trying to score, that's all. I heard that he's only visiting in town. He's going to be moving away soon, and then where will that leave you?"

Kirsten might be dating Jeremy, but that didn't mean she would shut down her radar and jump into a relationship that wasn't in her best interest—at least, not knowingly. She also knew that a lot of men weren't looking for something permanent and long-lasting, that some of them only wanted sex. Shoot, she'd met a couple of them and had been disappointed enough times to take things slow and to be careful.

She was also fully aware of the fact that Jeremy would go back to Sacramento one of these days.

But she was a big girl and didn't need her brother telling her what to do.

For Pete's sake, his own radar had certainly been

faulty or nonexistent when he'd first hooked up with Courtney. But rather than let him draw her into another argument that was sure to escalate without solving anything, she decided to calmly end the conversation and put him in his place.

"Jeremy and I are friends," she said. "But even if we were more than that, I'd like to remind you that this is my house and that I'm a responsible adult."

Max's face reddened and he pursed his lips. Kirsten had never seen steam come out of anyone's ears before, unless it had been in a cartoon on television, but she wouldn't have been surprised to see little cloudlike puffs coming out of her brother's head.

What did he have against Jeremy?

The first time they'd met, Max had scowled all the way home from the medical center. And he'd clearly been a grump when she and Jeremy had left the house to go to Bernardo's last night.

Now this. You'd think Max was a jealous boyfriend rather than an overprotective brother. And quite frankly, he was pushing her to her limit. If it weren't for Anthony, she'd ask him to pack up and move out tonight. As it was, she bit her tongue.

But living with Max was *so* not working.

"You were out of line for entertaining him at the house when Anthony was in the next room," he added.

*"Excuse me?"* Her voice rose a couple decibels in spite of her determination to remain cool and in control. "You're overreacting." She blew out an exasperated sigh.

"Anthony is an infant, and he was sleeping for most of the time."

Again, she wanted to remind her brother that she was an adult. And that he was…

Heck, who even knew what he was. For a twenty-six-year-old man, acting mature seemed like a real struggle for him some days.

"Did you kiss him?" Max asked.

Before responding and putting her brother in his place, she took another calming breath, then slowly let it out. "That's none of your business."

He remained silent for a while, as though her words had finally sunk in. Then he said, "I'm sorry, Kirsten. You're right."

His acquiescence surprised her, and she waited for him to interject a "but" to the conversation.

Instead, he said, "I guess I was out of line."

He *guessed?*

"It's just that I don't like to be reminded that you're the responsible one, when I've been trying my best to find a job—*any* job. And to make matters worse, I've got a lot on my mind."

She sighed. "I know you do. Having another human being who is dependent upon you must be stressful, especially while you're out of work."

"It's not just that…" He paused, as if trying to find the words to explain what was really bothering him and why he'd been lashing out at her and Jeremy.

"Then what is it?" she asked. Was her brother missing Courtney? Was he feeling badly that Kirsten might be involved in a budding romance when his own relationship with the mother of his son had fallen apart?

Finally, Max said, "I've got things to deal with that you wouldn't understand."

"Share them with me. Let me help. We're family."

He clammed up, refusing to elaborate any further.

She could have prodded him, she supposed. He was clearly bothered by something and lashing out at her because of it. But spending so much of her energy sympathizing with Max was getting old, and she was just plain tired of dealing with all the problems resulting from his bad decisions.

For as long as she could remember, she'd been both mother and father to him, a role that was slowly wearing her down, especially since Max had such a bad attitude about anything she did or said to help him—unless it was handing him cash in silence.

She would have to resort to tough love again, which had worked well in the past, but now there was the baby to consider.

It was comforting to know that Max had taken on the responsibility of fatherhood, but that didn't stop her from worrying.

As much as she'd tried to convince herself that he was able to handle the baby on his own, she had to admit that she had her doubts.

At a quarter to noon the next day, Jeremy was reviewing an X-ray of an elderly patient. He tried to focus on the scans before him, but in the back of his mind, he couldn't help thinking about Kirsten and wondering if she'd like to have lunch with him.

They had a date tomorrow night, something sure to surprise her, but he wanted to see her sooner than that. So he picked up his cell phone and gave her a call.

She answered on the second ring, and when he told her what he had in mind for today, she said, "Lunch sounds great, but Max is out job hunting again, and I've got Anthony."

"Then why don't I bring the food to you?" he asked.

He could almost hear the smile in her voice. "I'd like that, Jeremy."

"How about turkey sandwiches?"

"That's perfect. I'll have beverages to choose from, some fruit and…" She laughed. "Well, don't bother picking up dessert, either. I've still got leftovers."

Twenty minutes later, Jeremy took a midday break from the clinic and showed up on Kirsten's front stoop with the lunch he'd picked up from the deli.

She'd been expecting him, so it was no wonder that she'd applied a coat of lipstick and had brushed her hair to a glossy shine. But it was her bright-eyed smile that did him in, reaching deep into his chest and turning him inside out.

As she stepped aside to let him into the cozy living room, he spotted the baby in a stroller.

"Going somewhere?" he asked.

"If you're up for a walk." There it went again, that smile and that single dazzling dimple, and he realized he'd be up for just about anything with her.

"There's a community park about a block down the street," she explained. "And the sun's out today. Why don't we take a walk and have a picnic?"

"Sounds like fun."

And Jeremy hadn't had fun in ages.

"I've got some iced tea and goodies packed and ready to go." She reached for a cooler that was on the floor, next to the sofa.

"Here, let me carry that." He took the handle from her. "You'll have your hands full with the stroller."

As they left the house, and she locked the door behind them, he let her direct him to the park. February weather could always be a little iffy, but she'd been right. It was sunny today. And he could see why she'd want to get out of the house.

"What would you have done if I didn't want to picnic?" he asked.

Her blue eyes glistened. "I figured a man who liked surprises wouldn't mind eating in the park."

Once he'd reached adulthood, Jeremy had never really liked surprises, at least not until meeting Kirsten. For some reason, he found himself thinking about things that would be new, fun and exciting. But there was no need to let something like that out the bag. Besides, he didn't care where they had lunch, as long as they were together.

They walked several blocks to a small grassy area that wasn't much more than a playground with a couple picnic tables, but it would do. And since it was a school day, they had the place to themselves.

Kirsten parked the stroller next to one of the tables, in the shade of a tree. Then she set out their meal: the sandwiches, fresh fruit, iced tea and cheesecake. Since Jeremy only had an hour before he had to get back to the clinic, they took their seats and began to eat.

It was easy to talk to Kirsten, who was a good listener. And before he knew it, he was telling her about his morning, about an elderly patient with a broken hip and a boy who'd fractured his arm during morning recess.

She leaned toward him as he talked and listened intently while he shared details that might be boring to someone else.

As the sun shone down on them, as a cool breeze whispered through the leaves in the trees, he realized it would be nice coming home to someone like her every day. But it had only been days since they'd met, so it was way too soon to be thinking about things like commitments and the future. And for that reason, a change in subject was in order.

"How's your brother's job hunt going?" he asked. "Does he have any interviews scheduled?"

"I'm afraid he hasn't had much luck at all." She set down her sandwich and reached for an apple slice.

Jeremy couldn't say that he was surprised. A man's attitude had a lot to do with finding a position with a solid company.

"I might be wrong," he said, "but your brother seems to have a big chip on his shoulder."

"You're right about that. He really hasn't been a happy person for a long time."

"Why?"

"I'm sure it has to do with the bad choices he's made, but he won't do anything to correct them. And to make matters worse, he seems to think that I look down on him."

It would be hard not to, Jeremy thought.

"Don't get me wrong," Kirsten said. "I love my brother and want the best for him. But he seems to have a little gray rain cloud following him all the time. And he can't seem to steer clear of it."

"He's old enough to know when to get out of the rain," Jeremy said.

"I know. I just wish he would work as hard as I did to overcome the strikes we had against us while growing up."

"What kind of strikes?" Jeremy asked, sorry to hear that Kirsten's childhood hadn't been as happy as his had been.

"Our dad left home when I was fourteen." She glanced down at her half-eaten sandwich, then back to Jeremy. "It was tough on me, but Max was only twelve at the time, and he took it especially hard. He acted out as an adolescent, getting into more than the usual amount of trouble, and eventually, he dropped out of school."

The teenage years could be tough, Jeremy realized, even under the best circumstances.

"Our mom had to work two jobs to support us, so I looked after Max and helped him pick up the pieces of his life." Kirsten rewrapped the untouched half of her sandwich and put it in the cooler. "Well, at least I tried to."

Jeremy had a feeling she was taking too much personal responsibility for her brother's failures, and he hated to see her do that. Unable to help himself, he reached out and placed his hand on her forearm. "Max is a big boy now, Kirsten. And as much as you'd like to, you can't keep bailing him out."

"You're right. But I also know what he's been through in the past, so it's hard not to be sympathetic." As her gaze met Jeremy's, he could see the very heart of her in those expressive blue eyes.

Did Max have any idea how lucky he was to have Kirsten in his corner? Jeremy wasn't so sure.

"When my mom died in a car accident five years ago, Max was just getting his life back on track. He'd started attending the adult school, planning to get his GED. But after the funeral, he turned to his friends for support."

He read into what she was really saying; Max had turned away from Kirsten.

"My brother didn't always choose the right friends," she added. "And as a result, he just couldn't seem to stay out of trouble. Of course, it was nothing terrible. But he partied too much on weekends and couldn't keep a job."

"So you've been keeping him afloat ever since?" Jeremy asked.

"For the most part. We received a moderate, wrongful-death settlement after the accident, which was enough for me to put a down payment on my house and to stick some money away for a rainy day. But Max blew through his share. Three years ago, he asked me to loan him money for a car."

"Did you?" Jeremy asked, hoping she hadn't.

"I had to. How was he going to keep his job without one?"

"But he didn't keep it," Jeremy said, connecting the dots.

"No, he didn't. So he couldn't pay his rent, either. And since I'd cosigned on his lease… Well, I had to help out with that, too." She tucked a strand of hair behind her ear. "I finally had enough and told him he was on his own."

"How did he take it?"

"All right, I guess. He hooked up with a girl named Courtney—Anthony's mother—and for a while, every-thing seemed to be on the uphill swing."

"So cutting him off actually helped?"

"Apparently so. When he and Courtney split up, I expected him to go off the deep end again, but he didn't."

"He kept his job?"

She nodded. "Like I told you before, he really enjoyed working at the feed store. He has a thing for horses and animals. So the layoff hit him hard, and I know he's hurt-ing because of it." She glanced at the stroller, where the baby napped in the shade. "And now there's Anthony to worry about."

Maybe so, but Jeremy could see the writing on the wall, even if Kirsten couldn't. Max needed to make his own way for a change.

"The weird thing is," Kirsten said, "my brother needs my help, but at the same time, he resents it."

Jeremy wondered if Max had finally turned the corner, if he would settle down once he found the right job. He hoped so. It sounded as if Kirsten could use a break.

"What about you?" he asked. "You mentioned being out of work, too."

"Yes, but that's just temporary. I've never had trouble finding or keeping a job. I'm good at what I do, and I've got a great résumé and letters of recommendation, so it's only a matter of time."

"I'm sure you're right," he said, thinking about the clinic and the Fortune Foundation. "I have plenty of connections in town. Maybe I can talk to someone and put in a good word for you."

"Thanks," she said. "That's nice of you, but I really want to get a job on my own merits. It's important to me."

He had to admire her for that. And he couldn't help studying her from across the table, amazed how the sunshine highlighted the golden strands in her hair, how it picked up flecks of green in her pretty blue eyes, making them almost turquoise in color.

If he had the rest of the day at his disposal, he might have enjoyed more time with her, but as it was, he glanced at his wristwatch instead.

"You know," he said, "I'm going to have to call it a day. I need to get back to the clinic."

Kirsten stood, gathered the leftover food and placed

it back in the cooler. "Do you have a full schedule this afternoon?"

"Not that I know of, but that can change from minute to minute." Jeremy tossed the used napkins into the trash receptacle, then gripped the handle of the cooler. "Thanks for suggesting that we have a picnic. It's been a long time since I've done something like this."

And even longer that he'd enjoyed kicking back and just being with a beautiful woman.

"A change in routine keeps life interesting," she said.

His mother used to say things like that. In fact, that was one reason she'd let her sons go to Texas each summer and spend time on the Double Crown Ranch with Ryan and Lily. She had wanted them to have an opportunity to experience another way of life and to gain a broader perspective.

As Kirsten pushed the stroller toward the sidewalk, Jeremy joined her, and they made their way to the street on which she lived.

It was a short walk to the house, yet Jeremy found himself walking slower than he ought to and talking about a memory he'd had while exploring a swimming hole he and his brothers had found near the ranch.

"One day, we decided to go skinny-dipping," he said. "But a couple girls, who'd come with their mother to visit Lily, found us and ran off with our clothes. We stayed in that water until we turned into prunes and had no choice but to go home naked."

"Were the girls still there?" she asked.

"Yes, but lucky for us, we found one of the ranch hands in the barn, and he got us something to wear into the house."

"Now that kind of ranch life had to have been a real change of routine." Kirsten turned to him and grinned, revealing eyes sparking with mirth and a smile a man could get used to seeing.

"It was also a lot of fun. In fact, there were times when each of us pondered the idea of becoming cowboys when we grew up."

"What made you decide to become a doctor?" Kirsten asked.

"I was probably ten when the idea first hit me," Jeremy said. "My older brothers and I had been playing in a tree house in our backyard. Nick was climbing up the steps and horsing around with J.R. who was right below him. In the process, Nick lost his balance, fell and broke his arm. It was a compound fracture, and I remember seeing the way the bone jutted out of his skin."

"So his injury inspired you?" she asked.

"It was definitely the first time the thought crossed my mind. I felt sorry for Nick, of course. I knew he was in a lot of pain. But I begged my mom to let me go to the E.R. with them, and for some reason, she gave in. I found the whole hospital experience fascinating and quizzed the orthopedic surgeon until he probably wanted to tape my mouth shut." Jeremy chuckled, looking back on it all from the perspective of an adult.

"I wish I could say that I had an epiphany like that

when I decided on my career," Kirsten said. "But I didn't."

"So why did you choose to become an accountant?" he asked, thinking that she was a natural-born caretaker and might have made a good teacher or even a nurse.

"I've always been good at math, so bookkeeping seemed like the field to study. Looking back, I think that I was drawn to a career like that because it provides order and structure in my life."

Something told him that was because her brother provided so much instability to her life, and at least the laws of math and accounting were constant.

Jeremy couldn't help wondering if there was something he could say to her brother, something he could do to help him get back on track. He had a feeling it would make Kirsten's life a lot easier.

When they reached her house, where Jeremy had left his car parked at the curb, Max was arriving at the same time and parked his small white pickup in the driveway—probably the vehicle his sister had helped him buy.

Max appeared to be in a slightly better mood than before, which made Jeremy think that maybe he'd been wrong about the guy after all.

"How did it go today?" Kirsten asked her brother.

Max shrugged, his expression more of a scowl when he turned her way.

If Jeremy had more time, he'd take Max aside and maybe ask him to join him for a beer. A man-to-man talk might go a long way. But then again, maybe he was only barking up the wrong tree.

Either way, he had to get back to the clinic.

"I'll talk to you later," Jeremy told Kirsten. He was tempted to kiss her goodbye but chose not to in front of Max.

"Okay." She smiled, and he wondered if the same thought had crossed her mind, as well as the same decision. "Have a good afternoon."

"You, too."

As Jeremy opened the car door and slid behind the wheel, he overheard Max tell his sister, "Looks like this is becoming a habit."

Jeremy wasn't sure what he meant by that, but there was a lot of truth to it, he supposed.

For some reason, Kirsten Allen had become habit-forming—and one that might prove difficult to break.

*Chapter Six*

"What were you and the doctor doing?" Max asked Kirsten, as he followed her into the living room. "Playing house?"

Her hands tightened on the grip of the stroller's handle, as she shot a look of disbelief at her brother.

Just moments ago, he'd made a comment about them seeing each other becoming a habit, something she was sure Jeremy had overheard. She'd been embarrassed but had to let it go until she could confront Max when they were alone. So she'd bitten her tongue and taken Anthony into the house.

But she wouldn't hold back any longer. "You're *way* out of line, Max."

"On, come on. You've been hearing wedding bells and dreaming of having a baby of your own since you were a little girl. First you pretended to be my mother when we were kids. And now you're pretending to be Anthony's."

Heat blasted her cheeks as she listened to his false accusations and pondered the absurdity of it all. Sure, she'd played with dolls as a girl. And she'd set them aside when her little brother was born, preferring to cuddle and play with the real thing instead.

But so what? Most little girls who'd been given a baby brother would have happily taken on a role like that. And the fact that Max was implying she had some kind of weird psychological need to...

Oh, for crying out loud, she had no idea *what* he was getting at, but she no longer cared.

"That's it." She parked the stroller near the sofa, turned on her heel and slapped her hands on her hips. "I've had it."

His eye twitched, but he didn't back down.

And neither did she. "Let's get one thing straight, Max. I'm sick and tired of mothering you—no matter what you might think."

"Good," he finally said, although his voice lacked its previous bluster.

"And as for Anthony, he's a precious little baby who needs a mother, since the one who left him here obviously doesn't have a maternal bone in her body. So you should be thanking your lucky stars that I'm willing to be his aunt and help you out."

Her brother's shoulders slumped ever so slightly, although he kept his chin up.

Anthony began to fuss, no doubt preparing for a full-on you-woke-me-up wail. But rather than go to him, gently pick him up and shush him, as had become her habit this past week, she let him cry.

"Your son needs you," she said. "He's due for a diaper change and a bottle. And you're on duty now."

"That's fine."

Kristen strode across the room and retrieved her purse, which was on the shelf near the stairs. After slipping the strap over her shoulder, she headed for the door.

"Where are you going?" he asked.

As she reached for the doorknob, she paused long enough to look over her shoulder and say, "I haven't decided. But I can assure you that I plan to enjoy the rest of my day—alone and free of any family responsibilities."

Then she left the house.

The breeze kicked up a strand of her hair and blew it across her face, but she merely brushed it aside. After climbing behind the wheel of her car, she started the engine and headed to town.

She wasn't sure just what she'd do there. Something unexpected and sure to make her feel better, she supposed.

If she were a woman from another generation, she might buy herself a new hat.

Now that was an interesting idea. She rarely indulged in shopping trips, and while she'd made it a point to curtail her spending until she landed another job and started receiving regular paychecks, she wasn't going to worry about the expense right now. She had a credit card she rarely used and always paid off, so it was free from debt.

Besides, she had a date with Jeremy on Friday—and she wanted something new to wear.

"Dress warmly," he'd told her.

She had no idea what he had in mind, but she decided to splurge on a new outfit. After all, if things worked out the way she hoped they would, the two of them would be going out again—maybe even regularly.

Deep down she knew she might be putting more stock in her budding relationship than she ought to. But she needed Jeremy in her life at a time like this, even if she couldn't count on having him around later. He was so levelheaded, so wise, so easy to talk to, that she wanted to enjoy every opportunity she had with him.

As thoughts of Jeremy swept over her, she relived each heated kiss they'd shared, as well as the rush of desire that had swept through her whenever they touched, whenever she caught a hint of his woodsy cologne.

Maybe, while out shopping, she ought to consider getting some new lingerie—the slinky kind one might find at Victoria's Secret.

Talk about looking forward to their next date.

As she turned onto the highway that led to the Red Rock shopping district, a niggle of insecurity burrowed deep within her, setting her on edge.

Jeremy was a nice guy—a doctor who was seeing low-income patients at the clinic out of the goodness of his heart. He'd make a fine catch for any woman, but why her?

Why would their chance meeting in a parking lot lead to romance?

He'd also offered to put in a good word for her around town and help with her job search. Was he trying to "fix" her, just like he would set a broken bone?

She tried to shrug off the momentary lack of confidence, instead choosing to believe that Jeremy truly had feelings for her, that he wanted to help because he was a caring person and being helpful was part of his nature.

*Don't get your hopes up,* she told herself. Their relationship, whatever it was or might become, was only temporary. And they both knew it.

Besides, he came from a nice family—the Fortunes, for goodness' sake. They wouldn't be used to the kind of drama Max always put her through. Would it be enough to chase him off?

She certainly hoped not. She'd told him a lot of stuff already. Maybe it would be best to hold her tongue from here on out. To keep Max and his woes to herself.

That might be wise if she wanted something to develop between them.

But did she?

As tempting as it might be to throw caution to the wind and experience a wild and wonderful romantic relationship with Jeremy for as long as it lasted, she couldn't help worrying that she might be setting herself up for heartbreak.

After all, if she let herself go and fell for him, saying

goodbye and having him leave Red Rock might shake her very foundation.

And then where would she be?

Yet in spite of her apprehension, she couldn't help daydreaming about becoming Dr. Fortune's wife.

And wondering what it would be like to have a baby with him someday.

After Jeremy returned to the clinic, he put in a couple hours at work, first consulting with one of the pediatricians on a suspicious break that was clearly a case of child abuse and then turning in his report to a social worker. Next he talked to a sixty-two-year-old man about the advantages of a knee replacement. Despite the long consultations, his afternoon ended earlier than usual.

On his way back to the Double Crown Ranch, he stopped by the Fortune Foundation, a nonprofit organization that had been founded in Ryan Fortune's memory.

Since Ryan had always believed in paying it forward, it had seemed only fitting to create a charitable organization that helped others in need. And Jeremy was proud of the work they did.

The three-story brick building, which had a day-care center on the ground floor and a playground in back, was located on the highway, just outside of town.

It was after four o'clock when Jeremy entered the lobby and took the elevator to the third floor, hoping to find Nick, his older brother.

At thirty-nine, Nick, the second born of William Fortune's children, was a financial analyst for the foundation. And he'd never been happier.

Jeremy couldn't help thinking about all the changes there'd been in Nick's life these past two years.

Once a confirmed bachelor, he'd become a guardian of triplets. The baby girls eventually wound up in the custody of their aunt and uncle, but not before Nick fell head over heels in love with Charlene London, their nanny.

Now Nick and Charlene had a baby of their own, a cute little boy named Matthew, with red hair, green eyes and a splash of freckles, just like his beautiful mother.

As the elevator doors opened, Jeremy stepped into the lobby, where an attractive young woman with long brown hair sat behind a desk. He didn't remember meeting her before and assumed she was new.

"Hello, there," she said, in a soft, Southern drawl. "You look lost. Can I help you?"

He'd known exactly where he was going, although he'd been deep in thought. But he couldn't see any point in chatting with the woman. He was here to see his brother.

"I'm looking for Nick Fortune," he responded. "Is he available?"

"I'll check and see. He's been in and out all day." Her gaze scanned the length of Jeremy, as though checking him out. Then she slowly got up and walked around her desk.

She was wearing a stylish black top, with a neckline that might be a smidgen low for an office job, a bright turquoise skirt and a pair of high heels that set off shapely legs. She was, Jeremy admitted, a very attractive woman—probably in her early twenties. Not that he was interested.

"I can let Nick know that you're here," she said.

Yet she continued to study him as though he were a chocolate éclair in a bakery window, leaving him feeling a little awkward.

"And your name is…?" she asked.

"Jeremy."

Her smile nearly lit the room as she instigated a hand-shake. "My name's Wendy. I'm an administrative as-sistant with the Fortune Foundation. Is there anything I can do for you?"

"I'm afraid not."

She paused for a beat, her frown a bit pouty, remind-ing him of a Southern belle who'd been used to getting her way over the years.

Then she reached across the desk for the telephone re-ceiver. As she did so, her bend-and-stretch motion caused her skirt to hike up and reveal a shapely length of upper leg.

He couldn't help wondering if her movement had been deliberate, but before he could decide—and before she could page Nick—a door swung open.

Jeremy turned toward the sound and spotted his brother, who was wearing his customary business-casual attire, tortoiseshell glasses and spiky brown hair.

"Hey," Nick said, picking up his pace as he approached the lobby. "It's good to see you, Doc."

Wendy returned the telephone receiver to the cradle, leaned against her desk and crossed her arms.

"I see you two have met," Nick said, glancing first at Jeremy, then at his assistant.

"Not really." A slow smile spread across Wendy's pretty face as she looked at Jeremy.

"Meet Wendy Fortune," Nick said. "She's from the Atlanta branch of the family and new to Red Rock."

"It's nice to be formally introduced," the young woman said.

"Jeremy's my brother," Nick explained. "He's visiting from Sacramento and staying with Lily out on the Double Crown."

Wendy's smile faded, but she quickly recovered and laughed. "Another cousin? It seems as if every handsome man who walks into the Fortune Foundation ends up bein' a relative of mine."

"Not all of them," Nick said, before asking her if he had any messages.

Wendy straightened, reached for a sheet of paper on her desk and handed it to him. "Mr. Landers called. And so did your wife. But she said it wasn't important. She wanted you to pick up somethin' on your way home."

"Thanks." Nick nodded toward his office. "Let's go and talk where it's quiet. It's been a busy day."

Moments later, Jeremy had taken a seat across from his brother's desk.

"What do you think of our new hire?" Nick asked.

Jeremy shrugged. "She's a little flashy, I suppose. But if she can do the job…"

"That's just it. I'm not sure if she can—or how serious she is about being here—not just at the foundation, but in Red Rock. Her father called last month, asking if we could put her to work as a favor to him. She's the youngest of six kids and dropped out of college a couple months ago. Her dad's a little exasperated with her, and he's hoping that a move to Texas and a job with the Fortune Foundation will give her some direction in life."

"How's it working out?"

"I don't know. All right, I suppose. She's got a good heart, but she's clearly more interested in striking up a romance than in looking for productive things to do."

"She *was* a little flirty," Jeremy said.

"A *little?*" Nick laughed. "Didn't you see the way she zeroed in on you?"

"Truthfully?" Jeremy slowly shook his head. "I really wasn't paying that much attention to her."

"You must have a lot on your mind, then."

He did—a beautiful accountant who had him tied up in knots.

"Is there anything I can do to help?" Nick asked.

"I just came by to pick your brain. I'm looking for a program of some kind that would help a high school dropout get his GED."

Jeremy was hoping to encourage Max to continue his education in the evenings. Of course, he was doing it mostly for Kirsten. The less she had to worry about when it came to Max and his welfare, the easier her life was going to be.

Nick reached for his iPhone and searched the files.

Then he made a note for Jeremy on a yellow sticky note. "Here's the name and contact information for the woman who's in charge of the adult education department at the local high school. She'll be able to answer all your questions."

"Thanks." Jeremy studied the number he would call as soon as he got back into the car. "I'm also going to need information about day-care options, especially for an infant."

When Kirsten went back to work, Max would need to find someone to watch Anthony for him.

"We offer day care on the first floor," Nick said. "But I'm not sure of the age requirement. When you go downstairs, stop by the director's office."

"All right, I will."

Nick sat back in his chair. "So who are you trying to help?"

"Just a friend."

Jeremy must have gotten a dreamy look in his eyes while thinking of Kirsten, because Nick straightened, leaned forward and placed his hands on the desk. "Is this a *lady* friend?"

"Why do you ask?"

"Because Wendy's pretty hot. And you didn't give her the time of day. Even before you knew she was our cousin."

Apparently, Nick had seen clear through him. But then again, he always had.

"It's just a woman I'm seeing. I'm not sure where it's going yet."

"Sounds like she could complicate your life—hopefully, in a nice way."

Jeremy merely smiled.

She already had.

When Jeremy got to Kirsten's house on Friday night, he knew he was arriving a little earlier than the time they'd agreed upon. So he had a feeling she might not be ready to go.

But he hadn't expected her to be gone.

"She went to the grocery store to pick up formula and disposable diapers," Max said, stepping aside to let Jeremy into the living room. "She shouldn't be too long."

Jeremy tried to read the younger man's expression, but wasn't having much luck. Still, he didn't seem to be as irritable this evening as he'd been on other occasions.

Deciding to tell him what he'd been up to—and what was on his mind—Jeremy said, "I'm not sure if you found a job yet, but I know of a ranch that's looking for a hand. Is that something you'd be interested in doing?"

Whatever had masked Max's expression earlier slipped away, leaving him wide-open and easy to read now, as surprise and disbelief washed over him and hope flickered in his eyes. "Sure, I'd really like working on a ranch."

"It's out on the Double Crown," Jeremy said, "which is a great place for you to get some training and experience. That is, if you want to learn and are willing to work hard."

"Are you kidding? The Double Crown is hiring?"

Well, they weren't actually looking for ranch hands. But knowing that Max had enjoyed his work at the feed store and that he had experience working with feed and grain, as well as animals and supplies, Jeremy had taken a gamble.

He'd also decided to trust that Kirsten's instincts about her brother had been right. So after first talking it over with Lily and getting her okay, he'd gone to see Ruben Perez, the foreman. They'd both agreed to take a chance on Max—as a favor to Jeremy.

Noticing Jeremy's hesitant expression, Max, who'd brightened at first, stiffened and reeled in his initial excitement. "I don't need a handout."

"I'm sure you don't. But I'd heard you enjoyed working at the feed lot. I just assumed working on a ranch might be something you'd be interested in."

Max paused briefly, clearly stewing over the possibility, then said, "I would like it. But why are you trying to help me?"

"I'm not, I guess. The ranch needs a good hand. And you're looking for a job. I just thought it might be a win-win for both of us. But it's not a big deal."

Max thought about it a moment, then softened. "Actually, it's a really big deal. And I'd like to apply—if they're accepting applications."

"It hasn't even gone that far yet," Jeremy said. "When I heard about the opening, I put in a good word for you. It's yours if you want it."

Max furrowed his brow, then cocked his head to

the side as if stumped at how to react. Finally, he said, "Thanks. I really appreciate that."

Jeremy had called in a favor, but that was as far as it would go. From here on out, Max would need to prove himself. "You won't let me down, will you?"

"Absolutely not." Max, who was still clearly reeling from the news, slowly shook his head in awe.

Just watching the transformation in his attitude had been worth Jeremy's efforts.

"Wow," Max said, as he raked a hand through his light brown hair and blew out a sigh. "This is so cool. It's hard to wrap my mind around it. Things like this just don't happen to me."

"Maybe your luck has turned. And now all you have to do is your part."

"Oh, I will," Max said. "You can count on that."

"There's just one thing," Jeremy added.

"What's that?"

"The position is only part-time and temporary to begin with, but it could work into something permanent."

"That's okay," Max said. "I'll work my ass off to prove to them—and to *you*—that I deserve a full-time position. I'd do *anything* to work on a ranch like that one."

*"Anything?"* Jeremy asked.

"Absolutely."

A slow smile stretched across Jeremy's face. "I'm glad to hear that."

"Why? What's the catch?"

"Because I heard that you don't have a high school diploma, and one of the Double Crown job requirements will be to enroll in an adult education program. There's one in Red Rock that offers a GED program, but they also have classes in animal husbandry. There's a lot to learn when working on a ranch—and the Double Crown is looking for experienced hands and prefers to offer them long-term employment. But they're willing to give a hardworking, dedicated guy a try."

"I don't know about school, though." Max glanced down at the scuffed toes of his shoes and scrunched his face. When he looked up at Jeremy, apprehension peered through his eyes, revealing a frightened little boy who'd been hurt and disappointed time and again. "I mean, I'll *sign up* and all. That's not the problem. It's just that I'm not sure how good I'll do. I've never liked sitting at a desk in a classroom, mostly because I've probably got attention deficit disorder or something that never got diagnosed. But I'll definitely give it my best shot."

"That's all that matters, Max. You just need to do your best."

The younger man seemed to give that some thought, but only for a beat. "Okay. When do I start?"

"I'd like to pick you up tomorrow morning and drive you out to the Double Crown so I can introduce you to Ruben Perez, your boss. And he can give you a job description and let you know when he wants you to work. Then on Monday morning, you can register for classes." He'd also looked into the day care his brother had recommended and found out it had a sliding scale fee structure, but he'd bring that up later.

"Wow," Max said again. "This is too awesome for words. I don't know how to thank you, Dr. Fortune."

"First of all, just do your best—on the ranch and in the classroom. And secondly, don't call me *Doctor*. I'm Jeremy to you."

Max tossed him a crooked grin, clearly humbled and pleased.

"There's one last thing," Jeremy added. "I hope you take this in the spirit in which its given—I want you to be respectful of your sister, even if you think she's wrong or off base."

Max reached out his hand. "You've got yourself a deal."

As they shook on it, something told Jeremy that Max was going to be a whole lot more pleasant to be around from now on, and that Kirsten was in for a big surprise when she saw the metamorphosis.

"You know," Max said, "I've got to tell you something. I love my sister—I really do. And I don't mean to be disrespectful. She's helped me out a lot over the years, but I beat myself up all the time about a lot of the dumb things I've done in the past, and when she starts in on me... Well, it makes me feel like a stupid little kid." He glanced at the portable crib, where Anthony slept. "And now that I'm a father... Damn. It really scares the crap out of me when I think about letting my son down—like my old man did to me."

"Sometimes an honest chat about what's really going on can help a lot," Jeremy said.

"You're probably right." Max pointed to the sofa. "Why don't you sit down. I'm not sure what's keeping Kirsten, but I'm sure she'll be here soon."

As Jeremy settled into his seat, Max said, "I need to apologize to you. I was kind of a jerk when we first met, and I'm sorry about that."

Jeremy could have brushed it off and made it easy on him, but maybe it was best if Max thought twice about the way he treated people in the future. "I figured you didn't want your sister to have a..." What? A boyfriend? A date? "...another guy in her life."

"It's not that. It's just that..." Max took a deep breath, as if needing a shot of oxygen to give him the right words or the strength to admit he'd screwed up. "I was upset that you were a doctor."

Most family members—or at least parents—liked the idea of their kids either becoming or dating professionals, especially doctors. So he asked, "Why would that bother you?"

"Because I was afraid you would make me look even worse in her eyes. And maybe even in my own."

Jeremy tossed the man a smile. "I'm thinking pretty highly of you right now, Max. It's not easy owning up to your mistakes."

"Thanks for not holding that against me. And for the record, it's fine with me if you're dating my sister."

"I appreciate that." It was going to be a whole lot easier for all of them if Max gave them his seal of approval.

Of course, Jeremy wasn't so sure what their relationship was or where it was going.

All he knew was that he was really looking forward to this evening—and that what he had planned for this particular date was going to be one for the record books.

## Chapter Seven

When Kirsten arrived home from the grocery store and spotted Jeremy's car parked in front of her house, she quickly pulled into the driveway and reached for the reusable grocery totes that contained the formula and diapers.

Max had forgotten to pick up the baby necessities earlier, but since Anthony had been fussy and had just dozed off in Max's arms, Kirsten offered to make a quick run to the market.

She'd thought that she could get to the store and back with plenty of time to spare, but there'd been an unexpected detour on Lone Star Parkway that took her a mile out of her way in bumper-to-bumper traffic. And when she'd finally picked up the items she'd needed, as luck would have it, there was only one check-out lane open.

Fortunately, she was ready for their date. Jeremy had told her to dress warmly, so she only needed to grab a sweater.

Trouble was, she didn't like the idea that Max had been the one to greet and chat with Jeremy until she got home, finding it more than a little worrisome.

Max had been a lot mellower after she'd given him a piece of her mind and had gone shopping yesterday. But that didn't necessarily mean anything. He clearly had taken issue with Jeremy, although Kirsten couldn't imagine why.

So who knew what her brother might have said to him while they were alone?

After locking the car, she let herself into the house and found Jeremy and Max seated on the sofa. A lazy grin stretched across Jeremy's face, and one arm was resting along the back of the cushions, as though he was comfortable and at ease.

He was also wearing a pair of jeans and a sweatshirt—had he forgotten they had a date tonight?

She supposed it didn't matter. After all, he was here, wasn't he?

"I'm sorry I'm late," she said. "But everyone in Red Rock seemed to be at the market this evening, and I had to wait in line for a long time."

"Don't worry about it," Jeremy said, as he got to his feet and took the grocery bags from her. "It gave your brother and me a chance to get to know each other a little better."

"That's good." Kirsten's gaze bounced from Jeremy's smiling face to her brother's.

Ever since she'd gotten home from that shopping trip yesterday, Max had been pretty solemn and pensive. But at least he hadn't been disagreeable and snappish, which had become his habit.

She wasn't sure if Jeremy had anything to do with Max's upbeat mood or if putting her foot down and setting some boundaries had done the trick. Either way, she would count herself lucky.

"I'll put this stuff away for you," Jeremy said.

"No, let me get that." Max sprang to his feet and took the bags, then went to the kitchen, leaving Kirsten and Jeremy facing each other.

She couldn't help taking a good, hard look at him and coming to the star-struck conclusion that he was drop-dead gorgeous no matter what he wore—a lab coat, slacks and a sports jacket...

Or jeans and a sweatshirt.

She glanced down at the new black pants and the pink blouse she'd purchased yesterday. Was she overdressed?

When she glanced back up and caught his gaze, she asked "Should I change my clothes?"

"I suppose I should have said 'casual' when I said to wear something warm. You look great, but you might be more comfortable in a pair of jeans—if you have them."

She had no idea where he planned to take her—only that it was a surprise. But what the heck. She was a good sport and looked forward to spending time with him, no matter what he had in mind. "Sure. Will you give me a minute?"

"Take as long as you need."

She started toward her bedroom, then stopped and glanced over her shoulder. "Are you going to tell me where we're going? Or do I have to wait until we get there?"

"I may as well tell you now." Jeremy tossed her a crooked grin. "There's a new ice rink in town, and I thought it might be fun to give it a whirl."

Ice skating?

She wouldn't have thought that he would take her to a place like that in a million years, although, if truth be told, she would have gone with him anywhere, even if it was to the Laundromat to watch other people's clothes go round and round in a dryer.

And it *did* sound like fun.

She tossed him a schoolgirl grin. "I'll be back in a flash."

As she dashed to her room, she planned to throw a sweater on over her blouse, slip into a comfy pair of jeans, grab a thick pair of socks, brush her hair and add a bit of lipstick. But she wouldn't take long.

She was seeing a side to the doctor she hadn't expected to see—an exciting side of the man that turned her heart on end.

And she couldn't wait to get their date under way.

* * *

They arrived at the rink a little past seven that evening, and after renting skates, they started out on the ice.

Kirsten had had a pair of in-line skates as a kid and knew the basics. She'd also gone to the ice rink in San Antonio when she was a teenager, so she wasn't a novice. But she'd forgotten how difficult it was to balance.

After an hour or so, it seemed to be coming back to her. She was moving faster and feeling less apprehensive about falling.

As she zipped around the rink, she found herself smiling and laughing like a kid again.

What surprised her was how good Jeremy was. For the most part, he skated along beside her, but every once in a while, he'd take off and get a little tricky on the ice, going so far as to skate backward.

As he came up beside her again, she asked, "Where did you learn how to do that?"

"When I was in high school, I dated a girl who was a figure skater."

She wasn't sure why that surprised her. There had to be a lot of things about Jeremy that she didn't know. A lot she'd like to know.

"Her parents had wanted her to compete and maybe go to the winter Olympics," he added, "and while she wasn't as enthusiastic about the idea as they were, we used to hang out at the rink a lot."

"What happened?" she asked. "How did you two split up?"

"We went off to different colleges and drifted apart. I heard that she married a guy who later became a deputy district attorney in the Los Angeles area, and I went on to medical school."

Kirsten wondered about his other dates, the other women he'd kissed, the ones he'd made love with. But it wasn't her place to ask. And even if it was, she wasn't sure she wanted to know those kinds of details. She'd rather think that their relationship was a first of its kind for both of them.

It certainly held that kind of magic for her.

The lively music that had been playing in the background came to an end, and one of the rink employees used the speaker system to announce, "Clear the floor. It's time for couples only."

Kirsten slowed and reached for the side rail, planning to leave the ice.

"We don't need to go," Jeremy said, as he spun around to face her and reached out to her. "Come on. Let's show these kids how it's done."

Her heart clamored in her chest, urging her on, as she took hold of his hand. "I'm not sure about this. I'm doing okay as long as I stick close to the railing and go slow and easy."

"Don't be afraid." The timbre of his voice, the confidence in his tone, the way his gaze latched on to hers, reached deep into the heart of her, bolstering her confidence. And in the blink of an eye, she realized that she wouldn't be afraid to face anything, as long as he was by her side.

As the rink slowly cleared of those skating solo, leaving only the ones who'd paired up, the lights lowered. Multicolored bulbs kicked on in the corners, and a love song began to play, casting a romantic aura over the ice.

Kirsten thought they would go hand in hand around the rink, like some of the other skaters, but apparently, Jeremy had other ideas, as he took her in his arms.

"Hold on to me," he said, "And follow my lead."

Right this moment, she couldn't imagine being anywhere else than in his arms, zipping along on the ice and gazing in his eyes.

He made it all sound so easy—the skate dancing, being together. Leaning on each other.

And God only knew how badly she wanted it to be easy. But she wanted more than that, too. She wanted what she'd found in his arms, in his gaze, in his presence, to last.

Was she getting in too deep?

Or was Jeremy feeling the same way?

As he skated around the ice with Kirsten, Jeremy felt like a kid again—happy and carefree.

He hadn't done anything like this since he'd been in high school, and he hadn't realized just what he was missing.

Or was being with Kirsten what had made this evening so special? Was she the part that he'd been missing?

It was beginning to feel that way.

When the couples-only song was over and the lights

went on, Jeremy continued to skate dance with Kirsten until the rink grew too crowded to maneuver easily.

So he took her near the railing, where she felt more comfortable, and brought her to a slow stop. "Do you want to stay longer? Or would you like to get a bite to eat?"

"It's been a lot of fun, but to be honest, my ankles are getting a little wobbly and sore."

"Then let's go." He escorted her off the ice, then took her to a quiet spot where they could remove their skates and put on their street shoes.

"Do you like Mexican food?" he asked.

"Yes, why?"

"Because tacos sound really good to me. So let's stop by Red. They're hands-down the best restaurant in town."

"Then Red it is."

Twenty minutes later, Marcos Mendoza was welcoming them and reaching for menus.

"It's good to see you back," he said, as his gaze traveled from Jeremy to his date.

It was easy to see that Marcos was connecting the dots, but he was discreet enough to keep his thoughts to himself. Still, when he escorted them to a quiet little alcove with a table set for two, it was clear that he'd picked up on the romantic vibes.

Jeremy tossed him a smile, letting the younger man know that he'd read things right.

Moments later, a busboy stopped by and gave them

water, a basket of warm chips and a bowl of fresh salsa.

When they were left alone, Kirsten said, "You know, it was sure nice to come home this evening and find you and Max chatting. It seemed that you two had hit it off, and I'm glad. I haven't seen him so relaxed and happy in a long time."

Jeremy told her why that might be, going on to mention the job at the Double Crown and the plan for him to go back to school.

"No wonder he was in a good mood." Her eyes glimmered with unshed tears. "I can't thank you enough for doing that for him. He hasn't had anyone take him under their wing like that in ages."

"We'll see if he can follow through on the bargain." Jeremy reached for a chip and dipped it into the salsa. "Maybe he'll surprise us both."

Kirsten brightened. "I'm so glad to hear you say that. I've been clinging to the belief that he's a fully capable person on the inside. So it's nice to know that someone else sees it, too."

Jeremy hadn't actually *seen* anything—yet. He just hoped that Max would be able to hold a job on the Double Crown. And that he would register for continuing education classes and complete them. But Jeremy was a realist. And there were no guarantees. The kid had clearly been floundering for some time.

In all honesty, Jeremy had gone to bat for him on pure faith—but not in Max. He was doing it for Kirsten.

And since he liked seeing a smile light her face and basking in her happiness, he decided to let her assumptions and any doubts he might have slip by the wayside, opting to focus on the possibility that Max would turn over a new leaf and make them both proud.

"I don't know how to thank you for what you did," she said.

"There's no need to do that. Maybe all he needed was a lucky break and a little advice."

"I'm sure you're right." She reached for a chip and took a bite. "What kind of advice did you give him?"

"I told him that we're all on paths leading somewhere. Some of us are destined for success, others are going nowhere. Some are even headed for ruin. But there's only one person who can change the direction he's heading. And the longer he waits to do that, the tougher it'll be in the long run."

"What did he say to that?"

"He just thought about it. Hopefully, he'll realize the truth in what I told him and take the new path he's got in front of him."

Jeremy certainly hoped he would. It wasn't very often that he went to bat for someone who wasn't a tight friend or a close family member. And he could end up with egg on his face if Max blew the chance he'd been offered.

But the younger man's gratitude had seemed sincere earlier this evening. And he'd promised to give adult school and the job on the Double Crown his best shot.

Jeremy supposed time would tell.

Jeremy's surprise had turned out to be a fun, special and memorable evening. And Kirsten was sorry to see it end.

As he pulled along the curb and parked in front of her house, she wanted to invite him in for a nightcap or… whatever.

But with Max and the baby inside… Well, she was afraid that too much reality might put a damper on an otherwise dream date.

In spite of Max's earlier mood, she knew that it could all change in a heartbeat, and she didn't want to risk it. So she opted to tell Jeremy good-night at the front door.

"I had a good time," she told him.

"Me, too."

As he lowered his mouth to hers, the anticipation was almost overwhelming. Her heart opened up like a spinning kaleidoscope as she slipped her arms around his neck and lifted her lips to his.

As the kiss deepened, their breaths mingled and their tongues mated. She closed her eyes, lost in a colorful swirl of hormones, pheromones and musk.

Yet there was something else going on inside of her, something that was more than a physical reaction to an arousing kiss. And while her mind insisted it was happening too soon, that she barely knew Jeremy Fortune, it didn't seem to matter.

He was a dedicated physician who donated time to the clinic and to people who were in need. And he'd gone above and beyond for Max, something he didn't have to do.

So what else was there to know about him?

Jeremy Fortune was one in a million, and Kirsten couldn't help what she was feeling. She was falling in love with him. She didn't know if she should thank her lucky stars—or pull back and protect herself from the heartbreak. Because when he left Red Rock and returned to California, it was going to break her heart.

But she couldn't think about that now. Not when she was locked safely in his embrace, yearning for more of his touch, more of his taste.

As the kiss finally came to an end, leaving her wanting so much more than what they'd just shared, Jeremy ran his knuckles along her cheek.

"Sleep tight," he said, his voice husky.

"You, too."

Then she watched him head for his car, wishing she could call him back, that she could invite him inside and ask him to stay the night.

*His stay in Red Rock is only temporary,* she reminded herself. *Hold on to your heart.*

But she feared it was too late for that.

As she let herself into the house, closing the door quietly behind her, she overheard Max talking on the telephone in one of the bedrooms. She didn't usually listen in on his calls, but she couldn't help tuning into this one.

"You've got to be kidding," he said, his voice loud enough to wake the baby. "Is this a joke, Courtney? I knew something wasn't adding up."

Kirsten froze in her tracks, then slowly eased closer to the hallway that led to the bedrooms. She wished she could hear both sides of the conversation, but would settle for hearing only one.

"So I'm not listed as the father on his birth certificate?" Max asked. "Then who is?"

Kirsten hung on to each beat of the lull in conversation.

"Oh, for cripe's sake, Courtney. What do you mean you don't have his birth certificate? The hospital had to have given you one when you checked out after having him."

Kirsten wished she could hear the explanation Courtney was giving.

A surge of uneasiness rushed through her, as she realized that Max might not have legal custody of Anthony. She wondered what rights he actually had.

Could he even take the child to the doctor if he was sick? And what if Courtney wanted the baby back? Should he take a paternity test?

Max swore under his breath, then slammed the receiver down hard. Clearly, whatever Courtney had said upset him.

Kirsten waited in the living room, near the hallway. She was almost afraid to confront him, to ruin the sense of calm she'd been expecting from him when she got home tonight. But how could she not let him know what she'd overheard?

So she eased to the doorway of the bedroom, where Anthony was lying on the center of the bed. Max sat on the edge, near the telephone.

"I couldn't help overhearing a bit of your conversation with Courtney," she said. "What was that all about?"

Max blew out a sigh, then raked a hand through his hair. "Courtney's a flake."

Kirsten had gotten that vibe the first time she'd met her, but Max had been so smitten that he hadn't seen it back then. But rather than blurt out an I-told-you-so or make him feel any worse than he did right now, she tried to be respectful of him and whatever he was going through.

So she took a seat on the side of the bed, next to him. "Do you want to talk about it?"

"Not really, but I probably should." He rolled his eyes, then heaved a sigh. "When Courtney and I split up seven months ago, I didn't even know she was pregnant. Heck, I was completely shocked when she showed up with Anthony last week."

"I can understand your surprise. But I really admire you for stepping up to the plate and being such a good dad."

"That's just it," Max said. "To be honest, I'm not sure if the baby is mine or not."

"Did she just tell you that?"

"Not exactly. I had my doubts before. But how could I turn away a child that *could* be my flesh and blood?"

Kirsten saw the angst in his eyes, and her heart swelled with pride that he'd taken in the baby and was assuming responsibility, even if there was some question as to Anthony's paternity.

"We can have his DNA checked," she said.

But what would they do if the baby didn't belong to Max? Just hand him back to Courtney?

God, Kirsten couldn't do that to the poor little guy. He deserved so much better.

"Where is she?" Kirsten asked.

"I don't know. She wouldn't tell me. Apparently, she's hiding out."

That was really strange. Kirsten glanced at Anthony, who hadn't asked to be born, to be pawned off on a man who might or might not be his father. And her heart went out to him.

What would make a woman walk away from her own child? If Kirsten had a baby, she'd want him to be with her all the time.

Was Courtney really a flake, like Max had said? Or was she in some kind of serious trouble?

Kirsten bit down on her bottom lip. "Do you think we ought to try to find her? Maybe she's in trouble and needs our help."

Max chuffed. "I'd have to say that looking out for Anthony is a big help to her already."

"But you don't have legal custody." Kirsten tucked a strand of hair behind her ear. "And that could be a problem."

"I don't know," Max said. "I need some time to think about what to do."

Kirsten might have pushed or prodded him in the past, but she was learning to respect him, to let him make those calls from here on out.

As Anthony began to cry, Kirsten turned to him and picked him up. "What's the matter, sweetheart?"

"He's hungry," Max said. "I'll get his bottle."

Kirsten held the baby close and kissed his head, her lips skimming his downy soft hair. A maternal feeling fluttered over her, and she wasn't sure if she should be happy or sad.

What if she bonded with Anthony, only to learn that Max wasn't his father? What if she had to hand him back to Courtney?

Her heart crunched at the thought—not so much at losing him, but being forced to hand him over to someone who might not be good to him.

"Everything is going to be okay," she whispered, hoping she could keep her promise. "You can trust me, Anthony. I won't let anything bad happen to you."

When Max returned with the bottle of formula and handed it to her, she placed the nipple into Anthony's mouth, then watched the baby greedily latch on as if he were starving.

"Was he good for you?" she asked her brother.

"Yeah. He and I watched a little TV. The last two nights he didn't wake up until four, so I decided to keep him up tonight. I thought he might sleep until morning."

"That might work. I guess we'll have to see what happens." As Kirsten fed the baby, she studied his sweet little face. He was precious, whether he was Max's baby or not. And he really deserved a better mom than Courtney.

She looked at the phone, wondering if she ought to call Jeremy and ask his advice. He was so wise, so level-headed. He would know just what to do, what steps they ought to take.

But she couldn't dump this on him. He didn't need to deal with all the Courtney drama.

*Is that what you're really worried about?* an inner voice asked, forcing her to face the ugly truth. *You're not trying to protect Jeremy, you're trying to protect yourself and the whisper of a dream that might come true.*

A momentary rush of guilt swept over her as she realized that was just what she was doing.

She might have come to the conclusion that she was falling for him, but ever since meeting him in the parking lot of the clinic, she'd told herself that a relationship with her was just a passing fancy to him. That it wouldn't last, that he'd return to California and not look back. But she wasn't so sure about that anymore.

After all, he'd gone above and beyond to help her brother, getting him a job on the family-owned ranch.

That had to mean something.

He had to be seeing the possibility of a future with her. She'd felt it in the heat of his touch, seen it in the intensity in his gaze.

And if that were the case, she wasn't about to do anything that might mar the beauty of what they were feeling or destroy the dream that had taken root in her heart.

Sure, all the stars would need to align first. And she would have to pray that her luck held out. But she couldn't still the rising hope that one day she would become... Jeremy Fortune's wife.

# Chapter Eight

On Saturday morning, Jeremy drove to Kirsten's house to pick up Max and take him to the Double Crown. He wanted to personally introduce Kirsten's brother to both Lily and Ruben.

He also looked forward to spending some time on the ranch hanging out with the hands, something he hadn't done since he'd been in high school.

After parking his car at the curb, he walked up the steps to the porch. But before he could lift his hand to ring the bell, Max swung open the door, boasting a Texas-size grin.

"I really appreciate you taking me out to the Double Crown," he said.

"No problem."

Max, who was dressed in a black T-shirt, worn jeans

and a pair of scuffed boots, held an old Stetson in his hands. He was clearly ready to go, but Jeremy didn't want to take off without getting a chance to talk to Kirsten.

Before he could ask to see her, she slipped up behind her brother.

"Hey," she said.

"Hey," he repeated.

A buzz of attraction and a temporary lull in conversation left him feeling a little bit like a love-struck teen who'd been approached by the head cheerleader and was struggling to find his voice.

Kirsten was wearing a pair of jeans and a white blouse today. Her hair hung loose on her shoulders, and her eyes seemed especially blue. Just looking at her set his heart on end.

"Does Max need a lunch or anything?" she asked. "I made one just in case, and packed it in a cooler."

"No, he'll be fine. The Double Crown provides meals for their hands."

There was another lull, another awkward moment.

Jeremy really needed to go, to get the show on the road, but with Kirsten standing there, close enough to catch a whiff of her floral-scented shampoo, close enough to touch, his feet seemed to take root on the porch.

There was, he supposed, only one way to remedy that.

"Would you like to take a ride out to the Double Crown with us?" he asked her. "You can meet Lily while you're there."

Her eyes sparked and her smile deepened. "It sounds

like fun." Then her expression began to fade. "But I probably shouldn't barge in on her like that."

"You'd be keeping her company," Jeremy said, realizing there was a second reason to take Kirsten along. "It'll do Lily good to have someone to talk to."

Waiting for word on Jeremy's dad had taken a real toll on her. Hell, it had taken a toll on *all* of them.

"Then that settles it," Kirsten said. "If you wouldn't mind transferring Anthony's car seat from my vehicle to yours, I'll pack his diaper bag."

At that, Max chimed in. "I'll make the switch. I just need both sets of keys."

Moments later, they were all seated in Jeremy's rented sedan and heading out of town.

Max was unusually talkative, which was a pleasant surprise. His attitude had certainly made a complete one-eighty turn, and Jeremy hoped that meant he was going to work hard at proving himself to both Ruben and Lily. If he didn't, they wouldn't keep him around.

When they reached the ranch, both Kirsten and Max scanned the acres upon acres of grazing land that lined the road.

"I can't get over the size of the place," Kirsten said.

Max merely studied the expanse of property in awe.

As they reached the sandstone wall that surrounded the buildings and the living area, Jeremy gave them a little of the history.

"Ryan Fortune's father, Kingston, bought this place nearly fifty years ago. Back then, the original house was a simple adobe structure with a flat roof trimmed with rough-hewn wood and tile. It had the same sand color as the wall around it now. But over time, as Kingston's family and his holdings grew, he added on and made renovations. But he did his best to maintain its original style."

"It's beautiful," Kirsten said.

Jeremy agreed.

Max, on the other hand, seemed taken by the large barn of weathered wood that stabled horses, the corral and fenced-off areas for branding time and the outbuildings. When he noticed the three-bedroom ranch-style home in the distance, he asked, "Who lives there?"

"That's Ruben and Rosita's house." The foreman and his wife had lived on the ranch for as long as Jeremy could remember. In fact, they'd raised their family there.

After parking in the shade of one of the few trees located near the main estate, Jeremy and his passengers got out of the car.

"Lily should be in the house," Jeremy said. "I'll introduce you to her first. That way, Kirsten and the baby can hang out inside while I take Max to meet Ruben."

He led them through the arched entryway and the wrought-iron gate that opened to the courtyard, with its large purple sage plants, twining vines and bare rosebushes that would be lush and colorful again in a few short months.

"You must love staying out here," Kirsten said, clearly taken with the Double Crown.

"I do." And he was glad he could share it with her.

Maybe someday the two of them could go horseback riding. He hadn't done anything like that since he was a teenager.

Jeremy escorted his guests along the curved stone walkway to the adobe steps that led up to the antique wooden door.

He rang the bell to let Lily know they'd arrived, but he didn't wait for her or the housekeeper to answer. Instead, he let Kirsten and Max inside.

"Lily?" he called. "We're here."

"I'll be right there," she said.

Moments later, the lovely older woman swept into the foyer, her dark eyes glimmering as she graciously welcomed both Kirsten and Max to her home.

Once the formalities were over, her gaze quickly drifted to Anthony. "What a beautiful baby."

"Thank you." Kirsten smiled down at the child, yet didn't explain that he belonged to her brother. But that was okay; Jeremy had already filled in Lily on the details.

In fact, upon hearing how Max had assumed responsibility for the baby he hadn't known about and learning that he was trying to better himself by taking the GED, Lily had been impressed and agreed to hire him.

Of course, she might have agreed anyway—strictly as a favor to Jeremy.

"Can I get you some coffee and breakfast?" Lily asked.

"No, thanks," Jeremy said. "I'm sure Max is eager to get outside and meet Ruben."

Max, who held his cowboy hat in his hands, nodded. "That's right, ma'am. Besides, I ate earlier. But thank you for the offer."

"You're welcome." Lily smiled. "Then do what you have to do. I'll take Kirsten into the great room, where we can visit and play with the baby." She reached out to stroke Anthony's cheek with her index finger.

As she did so, Kirsten smiled at the bundle in her arms.

Again, Jeremy was struck with the thought of Kirsten holding his baby, but he quickly shook it off.

*Slow down,* he told himself. He'd hardly gotten to know her himself. Yet he couldn't deny the feelings she'd evoked in him, unfamiliar yet warm and blood-stirring feelings he had to admit that he liked.

"I love babies," Lily said, reminding Jeremy that bringing Kirsten and Anthony along had been a good idea. Having visitors was sure to help her keep her mind off her worries—at least for today. And he couldn't help feeling a rush of pride, knowing that he'd pulled something like that together.

Of course, it was too soon to know for sure if everything would fall into place, but it appeared that his efforts just might end up being a win-win for everyone involved.

He sure hoped so. In a way, he'd stuck his neck out for Max. And he'd hate to think he'd made a mistake by bringing him to the ranch and asking Lily and Ruben to take a chance on hiring a stranger.

So far, so good, though. Max had been polite and

appreciative. He'd also shown signs of having a work ethic, although whether he'd follow through on it was still left to be seen.

Jeremy bumped Max's arm with his and nodded toward the door. "Come on. Let's go find Ruben."

Then he took Max out into the yard, leaving the women alone.

After the men headed outside, Lily turned to Kirsten and smiled. "Would you like to join me in the kitchen for a cup of tea and some blueberry muffins?"

"That sounds nice." Kirsten tightened her grip on the handle of Anthony's carrier and followed Lily through the great room, which was dominated by a large open hearth on one wall.

She slowed her pace and noted the curved, wooden-framed glass doors that opened up to a lovely courtyard. Even in February, the plants out there were lush. She wondered what it would look like during spring and summer, with the flowers blooming.

As she followed her hostess to the kitchen, their shoes clicked upon the tile floors, where hand-woven rugs in Native American and Mexican patterns had been carefully placed.

The farther Kirsten went into the house, with its mixture of both modern and antique furnishings, the more impressed she was with the decor.

When they entered the large functional kitchen with all the modern conveniences, Kirsten noticed that it still reflected the same Southwestern influence as the rest of the house and couldn't help sharing her impressions. "Your home is beautiful, Lily. You must love living here."

"Thank you. I do. In fact, I can't imagine living anywhere else."

Kirsten understood the feeling. At one time, she hadn't been able to imagine living in any other house but the one she'd purchased on her own and decorated to suit her. Yet the longer she knew Jeremy, the more she was thinking about California.

Would she like it there?

Oh, for Pete's sake, she scolded herself. How could she allow a question like that to even form in her mind? At this point, she had no reason to believe Jeremy would even invite her to go with him to California. And even though she sensed their relationship was becoming stronger each day and that they were growing closer, she didn't want to make any unwarranted assumptions until he gave her reason to do so.

As Lily poured water in a teapot and put it on to boil, she asked, "So how long have you and Jeremy been dating?"

"Actually, we've only formally gone out a couple times. But we've been seeing each other a lot."

"I thought that you might be." Lily smiled. "I haven't seen much of him lately."

"I'm sorry." Kirsten knew that Lily was just as worried about Jeremy's father as he was—maybe more so. And that was why he'd been staying with her and offering his support.

"Please don't be sorry about him being away from the ranch," Lily said. "I'm a romantic at heart and can appreciate it when two people are attracted to each other. Besides, it's time for Jeremy to loosen up and have some fun. He's been so focused on his medical practice over the years that I was afraid he would let life pass him by."

"It's been fun for me, too. Meeting Jeremy has been a real blessing." Not only was he a perfect gentleman and one of the nicest guys in the entire world, he'd also taken Max under his wing. And Kirsten would always appreciate that—no matter what direction their relationship took.

"I felt the same way you do when my friendship with William took a romantic turn," Lily said. "We were going to get married on New Year's Day." Her eyes grew wistful and misty, and the tone of her voice softened. "But he didn't make it to the ceremony."

Kirsten's heart went out to the older woman. "I can't imagine how terrible that must have been for you. How terrible it still must be."

"At first, people suspected that he'd gotten cold feet and took off to avoid marrying me, but I knew better than that. He was looking forward to the wedding as much or more than I was." Lily took two teacups and saucers from the cupboard, placing one in front of Kirsten and the other for herself. "Then three days after his disappearance, his wrecked vehicle was found. He'd been involved in an accident. Or rather, his Mercedes was."

Jeremy had mentioned that to Kirsten. And the fact that there hadn't been any sign of William.

"We wondered if he'd been kidnapped, which could be the case," Lily added, as she pulled several choices of tea from the pantry. "But we never received a call or a ransom note."

Kirsten couldn't help thinking that there'd been some other kind of foul play, yet what?

And why?

As the kettle began to whistle, Lily removed it from the stove and poured water into each cup. "I can't explain it, but I have a very strong feeling that William will return. That he'll be all right. And that we'll be able to marry one day."

"I can understand you wanting to hold on to hope," Kirsten said.

"It's more than that." Lily returned the kettle to the stove. "You may not believe this, but I can almost hear a voice whispering to me and telling me to hang in there, that he'll be home soon. That everything will be okay again." Lily gave a little shrug. "I'm sure that sounds odd to you."

"No, it doesn't." Kirsten knew how difficult William's disappearance had been on Jeremy, and she suspected the other brothers felt the same way. But it had to be especially difficult for Lily, who'd lost Ryan to death and then found love again with William.

How sad to be alone once more. She hoped the family would get news soon—one way or the other. Yet in spite of her best wishes for a happy resolution, a realization shuddered through her.

If and when William was found, Jeremy would no longer have a reason to stay in Red Rock.

The hours seemed to fly by as Kirsten and Lily spent the day together. In spite of their age difference, they really hit it off.

Maybe that was because Kirsten had missed having a mother figure in her life. Or maybe that was only part of it, since she truly liked Lily Fortune as a person.

They'd had a light lunch of lentil soup and homemade French bread, which was unbelievably delicious.

When Jeremy and Max came back into the house in the late afternoon, grinning from ear to ear and clearly having enjoyed their time outdoors, Lily insisted that they stay for dinner, as well.

"It's up to Kirsten," Jeremy said. "I'm game if she is."

Feeling as if she'd somehow become a part of the Fortune family and basking in the acceptance, Kirsten had agreed.

So they'd had an early dinner of grilled chicken with a red sauce, Spanish rice and a zucchini and corn dish that Kirsten thought was especially tasty.

To top it off, Lily had brought out a lemon pound cake and servings of mango sherbet.

All in all, it had been a lovely day. And now they were saying their goodbyes.

"It's been nice having company," Lily said, as she

walked them out to Jeremy's car. "I'm afraid that, since William's disappearance... Well, as much as I believe that he'll come back to me, it's not always easy to stay positive. And having company today helped."

"I had a great time," Kirsten told the older woman, as Max took the baby from her to secure him in his car seat.

Jeremy gave Lily a hug. "Thanks for being such a great hostess—as always. I'll be back after I take Kirsten and Max home."

Moments later, they were on their way to Kirsten's house. As the car sped along the highway that would take them to nearby Red Rock, Max couldn't seem to thank Jeremy enough for the day he'd spent on the ranch. Every sentence seemed to start with "Ruben said..."

"I'm glad you're going to like working there," Jeremy said.

"I love that kind of work. I can't wait to start."

They rode along in silence for a while, then Max said, "Thanks for hanging out all day with me. I know you had other things you could have done."

"Actually, it gave me an opportunity to relive all the summers my brothers and I used to stay on the ranch with Lily and Ryan. I probably had a better day than you had."

"I doubt it," Max said.

Kirsten couldn't help smiling at her brother's good fortune. The job was sure to be a godsend for both her and Max, yet she kept quiet, listening to the men talk.

After all, the trip out to the Double Crown had

been for Max's benefit; Kirsten had only gone along for the ride.

But what a ride it had been.

She settled back in her seat, her heart overflowing with warmth and pride. The day had unfolded nicely, leaving her pleased, content and…happy.

Her brother had a job he was excited about. And he was going to register for classes at the adult school on Monday morning, then drive out to the ranch to work for the rest of the day. She'd never seen him so enthusiastic about the future. In fact, he seemed like a whole new person.

And Kirsten had Jeremy to thank for that.

Her life, it seemed, had changed dramatically since meeting him—and in a wonderful way. Just his smile, his woodsy scent and his touch could set a thrill rushing through her.

She wasn't sure what to make of their romance, but she knew that she wanted it to grow into all that it could be.

The trip home was over before she knew it, and she found herself wishing the night would go on and on.

If Max and the baby weren't staying with her, she would have invited Jeremy in for a nightcap…and a whole lot more. But when the two of them made love, she wanted the mood and the atmosphere to be special, to be perfect.

So she'd have to settle for a good-night kiss. Though *settle* was hardly the right word, since Jeremy's kisses weakened her knees and turned her inside out.

After Jeremy parked the car at the curb, Max got out and removed Anthony from the car seat.

"Kirsten," he said, "if you don't mind holding the baby for me, I'll switch his seat back to your car."

"All right." She took Anthony in her arms, glad to help. Yet she hoped Max would take the baby inside when he was finished and give them some alone time. She was eager for an opportunity to kiss Jeremy goodnight. Maybe she'd even get an answer to the where-do-we-go-from-here question she'd been afraid to ask.

Fortunately, she didn't have to wait long. The seat had been transferred in no time at all. Then Max took Anthony into the house, leaving her and Jeremy outside.

As they lingered in the front yard, where the porch light cast a golden glow on them, she was again tempted to ask Jeremy to come inside—and to stay the night. But with Max in the house... Well, it just didn't feel right.

"Thanks for riding out to the ranch with us," Jeremy said.

"I had a wonderful time. Lily is one of the nicest people I've ever met. She's a great decorator, hostess and cook."

"I'm glad you liked her. She's always been special to me."

They stood like that for a moment, caught up in the silence and the buzz of pheromones.

"I'd invite you in," she said. "But…"

"I understand."

"You do?"

"It's a little crowded in your house tonight."

She wondered if he was as disappointed about that as she was.

"So how about dinner tomorrow night?" he asked. "I've got to attend a board meeting for the Fortune Foundation on behalf of the medical center on Monday, which is Valentine's Day. But we can celebrate on Sunday instead."

*Celebrate?* The day set aside for lovers?

That certainly sounded as though their relationship was progressing. And that her instincts had been right.

"It sounds great," she said.

"I'm glad to hear it." He cupped her face and brushed his thumbs across her cheeks.

Their gazes met and locked. Passion simmered in his eyes, and her heart raced. The anticipation alone made her rethink her decision not to invite him in the house, no matter who was inside.

Had that been a mistake? One she ought to remedy?

She wanted so very badly to drag him into her bedroom, lock the door and turn up the radio so that anything they said and did would be their secret to keep. But she wanted so much more than that for their first time.

As his mouth lowered to hers, she closed her eyes and parted her lips. Her arms looped around his neck, and she slipped into his embrace.

He kissed her deeply, thoroughly. And as their tongues mated, as their breaths mingled, she held him tight, wanting him. Wanting more.

His hands slid along the curve of her hips, resting on her derriere and staking an intimate claim. So she leaned forward and rubbed her hips against his, making a claim of her own.

She wasn't sure how long the kiss lasted—long enough to make it difficult to stand without holding on. Long enough to stir an empty ache in the most feminine part of her.

Her only complaint was that it ended before she was ready to let go.

But then again, she wasn't sure if she would ever be ready to pull away from Jeremy.

"Maybe we ought to have dinner at one of the nicer hotels in town," he said. "We'd have the option of getting a room, which might make things a whole lot easier."

A boyish grin implied that he was teasing, yet desire had darkened the blue of his eyes, which made her wonder if he was testing her response.

"I'll wear my favorite dress," she said. "And I'll go wherever you want to take me."

There. She'd said it. And she'd been telling the truth. She wanted to go wherever their kisses took them, because that last one had whispered of forever.

"I'll talk to you tomorrow," he said.

She nodded, even though tomorrow seemed like a very long time from now. Then she stood alone on the porch and watched him turn and stride toward his car. She struggled with the urge to call him back and to ask him about the future. Instead, she bit her tongue. She would just have to bide her time until he brought up the subject.

But that didn't keep the questions from bombarding her like buckshot.

Would Jeremy ask her to leave town and join him in California?

If so, would she go?

As much as she'd like to remain living in her house in Red Rock—with him—she realized that wasn't likely.

Jeremy had a successful medical practice in Sacramento. And being away from his colleagues and his patients had to be tough on him.

Of course he did have family here. And he'd taken a leave of absence and had no immediate plans to return to California—as far as she knew. He'd also started working at the clinic and seemed to like it.

Would he decide to stay in Red Rock?

He might. But *then* what?

Would he and Kirsten remain lovers? Or would they marry and start a family?

The questions were legion. And she both longed for and feared the answers.

## Chapter Nine

After Jeremy drove away, Kirsten went into the house and softly closed the door. She could hear Max talking to someone down the hall, and while she couldn't make out his words, she also felt his upbeat tone.

Had he actually chuckled? She hoped so. He'd been miserable for way too long, and it was good to see him happy for a change.

She walked past his closed door, then entered her own room. After shutting herself inside, she blew out a sigh. What a day this had been.

And *oh,* she sighed, what a man.

A grin splashed across her face as she realized that Max wasn't the only one in the house who was happy.

While undressing in her private bathroom, she relived that amazing kiss she and Jeremy had just shared, a kiss that had been more of a kickoff to foreplay than a way in which to end the day.

As she climbed into the shower and let the warm water sluice over her, thoughts of Jeremy sent her imagination soaring.

Soft music and candlelight.

Heated kisses.

Blood-stirring caresses.

Clothing falling by the wayside, bodies tumbling onto the bed in a fevered rush.

Making love all night long.

By the time she'd finished showering, she was sorry she'd let him go back to the ranch.

But she had, so she was stuck sleeping alone and dreaming of what might have been.

After putting on her most comfortable flannel night-gown, she turned down the covers and climbed into bed. The sheets were freshly laundered, the house was quiet and her heart was strumming with contentment. Still, it took forever to fall asleep. Her mind was too caught up thinking about what tomorrow night might bring.

She couldn't help wishing that he *would* take her to a hotel and that they'd end their date by making love.

Should she pack an overnight bag just in case? Should she tell Max that he'd be handling the baby care duties on his own since she might not come home at all?

Oh, good grief. Jeremy had been smiling when he implied that they could check into a room.

She'd sure be embarrassed if she walked out with her

makeup bag and toothbrush, only to find that Jeremy *had* been joking about the hotel.

Squeezing her eyes tight, she did her best to shut out the thoughts and try to sleep. But each time she started to drift off, she would imagine them in nearby San Antonio, walking hand in hand along the River Walk at midnight. Or slow dancing at a trendy downtown jazz club to the sensual sounds made by a guy playing the sax.

She wasn't sure what time it was when she finally fell asleep, but it was well after midnight. She slept well, but certainly not long enough.

Just before seven, she woke to the hearty aroma of fresh coffee brewing. Deciding she could use a little caffeine, she threw off the covers and wrapped herself in a robe. Then she went into the kitchen, where Max was standing near the toaster, waiting for his bread to pop out.

He was smiling to himself, and she suspected it had something to do with his new job.

"It's nice to see you in a good mood," she said, as she reached for a cup and poured herself some coffee.

"I can't believe it myself. Just last week, I felt like a loser. I didn't think I'd ever climb out of the rut I was in. But with a couple good breaks, it seems like things are finally turning around."

"You mean the new job at the Double Crown?"

"That, too. But I just got a call from Kelly Thompson last night, after I took Anthony into the house and put him to bed. And we talked for hours."

Kirsten hadn't heard the name before. "Who's Kelly?"

"She's a girl I met while I worked at the feed store. You'd really like her. She's a lot like you."

*In what way?* Kirsten wondered.

Instead, she asked, "How long have you two been dating?"

"Well, that's just it. We went out for a couple months, but then I was laid off and couldn't afford to take her out anymore, which really sucked. I was so embarrassed about being unemployed, that I just backed off and quit calling her. Know what I mean?"

Kirsten nodded. That was what Max always did with her, too. He just withdrew.

"But seeing you and Jeremy coming together made me realize how much I missed having someone in my life, too. So I called Kelly on Friday and left a message on her answering machine."

"And she called you back last night?"

"Yeah. Apparently, she wasn't going to at first. But then she gave in. We talked for a long time, and I leveled with her. She seemed to understand, so I asked her out to dinner. But I told her I was waiting on a paycheck, so it wouldn't be a fancy place."

"I'm sure she was okay with that."

"She was better than okay. She told me not to worry about anything. She had a new recipe she wanted to try out, and that I should go to her house for dinner instead."

"That's great."

"I think so, too."

"Did you tell her about Anthony?"

Max's smile drooped. "No, not yet. I… Well, before I do that, I'd like to see how things go tonight."

Kirsten could understand that. She still found herself tiptoeing around Jeremy, too.

"Anthony is precious," she told her brother. "And if Kelly's the kind of woman you think she is, a baby won't scare her off."

"I'm sure you're right. But having Anthony in my life also means that Kelly might end up having to deal with Courtney, too. And I hate to have that dumped on her."

Kirsten had the same apprehension about letting Jeremy in on too much of that kind of drama. "Maybe we'll both luck out, and Courtney will be history."

"I sure hope so. But she's kind of like a bad penny and keeps calling or showing up when I least expect it."

"Just take it slow and easy," Kirsten said.

"That's what I plan to do."

When the toast popped up, her brother turned around and reached for the butter.

Kirsten took a sip of her coffee. She sure hoped Max's romance worked out for him, just as it seemed to be doing for her and Jeremy.

But speaking of romance, she really ought to tell Max that she had plans tonight, that she wouldn't be able to watch Anthony for him, but she couldn't bring herself to do it.

For the longest time, she'd feared her brother would

never be happy again. That he'd do something stupid and get into trouble. That he'd be a failure.

Having a nice girl in his life might make all the difference in the world. So how could Kirsten not look after Anthony for him?

She would just have to sacrifice her plans for his— which was what she usually ended up doing.

But wasn't that what love was all about?

Moments later, the telephone rang. She answered and found Jeremy on the line.

"What are you up to?" he asked.

"Just having coffee. Why?"

"No reason. I just called to say good morning."

How sweet, she thought. The only thing nicer would have been to wake up in his arms and hear him say it to her.

"I also wanted to tell you that I made dinner reservations at the San Antonio Monarch Hotel," he added. "Are you still willing to go anywhere with me?"

Boy, was she. But how did she let him know that their Valentine's Day celebration wasn't going to work out the way they wanted it to?

Come right out and tell him, she supposed. "There's nothing I'd like to do more than go with you tonight, but Max already has plans for this evening. And I've got to watch Anthony."

"Can you get a sitter?" he asked.

"I don't know who I'd ask." She blew out a sigh, realizing that she was even more disappointed than she'd thought she'd be. "But why don't you come over around four? We'll have the house to ourselves. I can fix an early dinner, then we can…"

She didn't continue, but apparently, she didn't have to.

"Sounds like a plan. I'll see you then."

An hour later, while she was holding Anthony and trying to finish making a grocery list for the dinner she had planned, the doorbell rang.

"I'll get it," she called out to Max, who was in the back of the house.

When she swung open the door, she spotted Cassie Rodriguez, the neighbor's daughter, on the porch.

"I was wondering if you'd like to buy some magazines," the teenager asked. "It's for a good cause. My church youth group is going on a mission trip to an orphanage in Mexico, so we're trying to earn money."

Kirsten smiled. "I'd be happy to buy a couple magazines, Cassie. Come on inside."

"Cool." The dark-haired teen grinned, revealing a shiny set of braces, as she entered the house and handed over the catalog. "Want me to hold the baby for you?"

"If you don't mind. Thanks." Kirsten passed the infant to the girl, then took a seat on the sofa and began thumbing through the pages. "I'd like to order *Parents* magazine. And also *Better Homes and Gardens*."

"All right," Cassie said, adding, "Your baby is really cute."

"Isn't he? His name is Anthony, and he's my nephew. If you don't mind holding him a little longer, I'll go get my checkbook."

"I don't mind at all. I love babies. In fact, I watch over my little cousins all the time."

While Kirsten went for her purse, she had a light bulb moment. The Rodriguez family was really nice. And since Cassie was experienced with kids…

As she returned to the living room, she asked, "Would you like to watch Anthony for Max and me tonight?"

"Sure. That would be great."

Wouldn't it be?

Now Kirsten could tell Max that he would have to relieve the sitter when he got home from Kelly's house. And then she would call Jeremy back and tell him that their night in San Antonio was still on.

Jeremy hoped he hadn't made any false assumptions by thinking that Kirsten wanted to spend the night with him in San Antonio, but he'd seen the agreement in her eyes. So he let Lily know that he probably wouldn't be home tonight, that there was no reason for her to worry.

When he rang the bell, Kirsten answered, looking like she'd just stepped out of a beauty ad in *Cosmopolitan* magazine wearing a simple but classic black dress and heels. Her hair had been swept into a chic twist, revealing diamond studs that sparkled in her ears. But the precious stones weren't any more dazzling than her smile.

"You look beautiful," he said.

"So do you." She flushed, then gave a little shrug. "Well, you know what I mean."

With her on his arm, he actually *felt* dashing.

"Are you ready to go?" he asked.

She seemed hesitant, then bit down on her bottom lip.

"Is something wrong?"

"No, it's just that…" She blew out a little sigh, then crossed her arms. "Should I bring anything other than a purse?"

He laughed, glad that he'd called it right, that she wasn't having second thoughts. "A toothbrush might come in handy."

"Good," she said, her eyes brightening. "I packed my makeup bag just in case. I wasn't sure if you were serious about…" She looked up at him, flushed again.

Damn, she was cute when she was off stride.

He smiled. "I guess you could say that I was covering my ass. If you wouldn't have liked the idea, I would have insisted that I'd only been teasing."

"Aren't you tricky," she said, as she went to get her bag.

Before walking out the door, Kirsten gave Cassie, the sitter, some last-minute instructions. "Max said he would be home by eleven. I hope that's not too late."

"Not at all," the girl said.

"Good. I left his cell-phone number on the kitchen counter. He said to tell you to give him a call if you had any problems."

"Okay, cool. But I'm sure everything will be fine."

"I'm sure it will be." Kirsten thanked her again, and then they left.

"I'm glad you found a babysitter," Jeremy said, as they headed for his car.

"So am I. In fact, when I told Max that I'd lined up Cassie to watch Anthony this evening, he was relieved to know we had some child-care options from now on."

An hour later, they'd checked into their suite at the Monarch, a new hotel overlooking the San Antonio River Walk.

Kirsten held her breath when she opened the glass sliding door and stepped out onto the balcony. "Look at this view."

He was looking. But it wasn't the San Antonio sights that were impressing him. It was the stunning beauty who had kicked off her heels at the door and had crossed the room in her bare feet.

She turned, and with her back to the city, faced him and blessed him with a stunning smile. "I've never been in a room like this."

He'd never been *anywhere* with a woman like her. And while he'd planned to take her to eat at the five-star restaurant on the top floor of the hotel, he wouldn't mind having room service and enjoying the privacy of their room.

"Do you want to go to dinner?" he asked. "Or, if you like the view, we can order in."

"Honestly? I don't mind eating in. It might be nice."

"I think so, too."

After looking over the room service menu, Jeremy ordered a bottle of his favorite Napa Valley merlot and the chateaubriand for two. Then he turned on some soft music on the CD player and joined Kirsten on the balcony.

As he slid up behind her, he caught the whiff of her shampoo—something with an appealing fragrance. "I like the scent of whatever you're wearing. What is it?"

She turned to him and smiled. "It's called Lilac Garden."

As her gaze zeroed in on his, he suddenly wanted to take her in his arms, to kiss her senseless. But what was the rush?

It might be best to get dinner out of the way first, although he was no longer hungry.

Not for food, anyway.

In the background, Michael Bublé sang "Baby, you've got what it takes." And Jeremy had to admit, that when it came to Kirsten, the lyrics were spot-on.

He ran the knuckles of one hand along her cheek, amazed at the softness of her skin.

As his hormones rushed and his pulse rate spiked, he had half a notion to scoop her up in his arms and carry her to the bed, but he wasn't going to rush it. They had all night long.

He took hold of her hand. "Dance with me."

Her eyes glimmered as he led her back into the room and took her in his arms. As they swayed to the music, as their hearts beat as one, Jeremy wondered if he'd ever want to make love to a woman more than he did with this one.

When the music ended, he kissed her—slow and seductively. He took his time, exploring her mouth with his tongue, and her body with his hands. As she leaned into him, as her hands ran along his back to his butt and up again, he wanted to feel the length of her against him—skin to skin.

But with dinner coming, he wouldn't risk it. When they made love, he didn't want any interruptions.

Moments later—or maybe it had been an hour, since time seemed to be standing still when he was with her—a knock sounded at the door.

"Room service," he said.

"Are you hungry?" she asked.

"Only for you." The truth of that hung in the pheromone-charged air as he let the bellman in and tipped him for his service.

Minutes later, they were alone again.

A small, linen-draped table, which had been adorned with a single red rose and a sprig of baby's breath, had been set up on the balcony, providing a romantic ambiance, complete with a view of the city.

It was a bit chilly tonight, Jeremy thought, as he lifted the bottle of merlot and filled their glasses. Then, he raised his in a toast. "Happy Valentine's Day, Kirsten."

"Thank you for going out of your way to make it special." She offered him a smile. "It's definitely going to be a memorable one for me."

He hoped so, because he was going to do everything he could to make sure that it was.

He clinked his glass against hers.

They'd barely had a sip of merlot, when he noticed Kirsten stroking the tops of her arms.

He'd been right; it *was* too cold for her.

"Here, take this." He slipped off his black sports jacket and gave it to her.

"What about you?" she asked.

"I'll be fine." In fact, kissing her earlier had shot a blast of heat through his bloodstream, so he wasn't the least bit cold.

He was, however, ready to zip through dinner and get to something a whole lot more memorable than food.

Kirsten didn't know when she'd had a nicer meal—or better company. Everything about this evening—other than the chill in the air—was perfect. But even then, bundled up in Jeremy's jacket and breathing his scent that lingered on the fabric, she had no reason to complain.

When they finished eating, Jeremy pushed the table into the bedroom area and out into the hall. Then he picked up the phone and asked someone to take it away.

Kirsten, who was still barefoot, removed his jacket and hung it in the closet.

"How about another dance?" he said, reaching out his hand to her.

She couldn't think of anything she'd like better.

Scratch that. She could think of *one* other thing, but she had a feeling that would soon follow.

As she slipped back into his embrace, the music playing softly in the background, she placed her hand on his chest, felt the steady beat of his heart.

Wrapped in Jeremy's arms, surrounded by his warmth

and his strength, she felt a security she'd never known before. And a realization she hadn't been ready for.

She was falling mindlessly in love with Jeremy, risking possible heartbreak in the future. And all she could do was hope he was feeling the same way about her.

They continued to sway to the romantic beat, dancing cheek to cheek and heart to heart, until Jeremy slowly drew them to a stop.

When Kirsten looked up and caught the intensity in his gaze, her pulse spiked with desire and an ache settled deep in her feminine core.

She wasn't a virgin, but she wasn't all that experienced in the ways of lovemaking, either. Yet something told her it didn't matter. That either way, she would never feel this way about another man again, never want one so badly.

Empowered by absolute love and pure passion, she placed her hand on Jeremy's cheek and pulled his mouth to hers.

Their lips came together as if their last kiss had never ended, as if they'd merely put it on hold. Yet this time, they kissed with a hungry desperation.

Their tongues mated, his breaths became hers, and Kirsten finally knew what it meant for two to become one.

Unable to get enough of him, she threaded her fingers through his hair and held him tight.

His hands explored her body, running the length of her torso—over, under, around. As he cupped her breast, kneading it slowly, his thumb skimmed across her nipple and she feared that she would collapse in a heated pool at his feet.

Finally, he reached for the zipper at the back of her dress. She stopped kissing him long enough to say, "Good idea," and to help him peel off the fabric.

Before long, they were both undressed, aroused and ready.

She skimmed her fingers down his muscular chest, taking time to flick his nipples to see if they were as sensitive as hers. She had her answer when he flinched, then clamped his hand over hers—holding her captive, it seemed.

"You're making me crazy," he said.

She smiled. "In a good way, I hope."

"In a *very* good way."

After throwing back the covers on the bed, he scooped her into his arms and deposited her on the mattress, where he joined her. Within a heartbeat, they'd both taken up right where they'd left off.

As he tongued the soft spot under her ear, then trailed wet kisses down her throat, her breath caught, which only seemed to urge him on.

He suckled her nipples, first one and then the other, until she feared she would cry out in need.

His kisses were magic, and so was his touch. But she'd had all the foreplay she could handle without coming apart at the seams.

"I want you inside me," she said, her breathing laden with desire. *"Now."*

He seemed only too happy to oblige, as he lifted up

and hovered over her, preparing to complete what they'd started, what they both wanted.

She opened for him, placing her hands over the curve of his buttocks, stroking and caressing while guiding him right where she wanted him, where she needed him to be.

He pushed inside her, and she arched to meet him halfway. Her body responded to his, taking and giving, as he pumped in and out. Their pleasure built, multiplying a hundredfold. And when she reached a peak so high she thought she might touch the moon and the stars, her body began to contract.

She cried out with pleasure, just as he shuddered and released, spilling into her.

For a moment, she realized they hadn't used protection—which really ought to shake her up. But for some reason, she wasn't all that concerned.

She loved Jeremy. And she'd like nothing better than to be his wife and to have his baby.

There was, however, one thing she really ought to be afraid of. And that was his return to California.

*Please,* she prayed silently, *don't let him leave Red Rock.*

*Not unless he plans to take me with him.*

## *Chapter Ten*

Talk about passion and chemistry.

Kirsten and Jeremy had been so caught up in the heat of the moment that they'd neglected to open the box of condoms he'd brought along.

"Damn," he'd uttered, when he'd first realized what had happened. "I can't believe this. I never take risks like that."

At first, she'd been a little uneasy about his reaction, but when he asked her to forgive him for the slip-up, she relaxed, thinking he'd been concerned about her worries as much as his own.

"It's not any more your fault than mine," she'd said, counting the days in her head and trying to convince herself that it had been a safe time of the month.

Of course, that didn't always mean anything.

An unplanned pregnancy certainly would be inconvenient, she decided, but not the end of the world—to her, anyway. She wasn't sure how he'd take it, though.

They'd gone on to make love several more times that night, relishing every delicious moment, but they'd used precaution from then on.

She finally fell asleep around two, wrapped in Jeremy's arms and completely sated from their lovemaking.

Yet sometime before dawn, a baby cried.

Footsteps sounded, heavy and hurried.

Dark shadows swept over the Portacrib, cold and breezy.

Heartbeats thumped, loud enough to shake the room.

More footsteps.

Another cry.

*Anthony.* Someone grabbed him and ran, disappearing with him in the eerie dark shadows.

Kirsten chased after them as hard and as fast as she could, but her feet moved like tree trunks rooted deeply into the ground. She tried to scream for help, but the words only gurgled in her throat.

*Oh, my God. The baby!*

She shot up in bed, eyes wide, heart thumping. Her breathing was ragged, as if she'd truly been running for all she was worth.

But in a desperate attempt to make sense of it all, she scanned the darkened hotel room, listening for a cry. But she heard only the soft sounds of breathing, saw nothing other than the naked man stretched out on the bed beside her, a sheet draped over his waist.

It had only been a dream.

No, she decided. Not a dream, but a nightmare in which someone had snatched Anthony.

A cold chill ran down her spine, striking fear through every cell of her body.

Could it have been a vision from the past?

A premonition of what was to come?

An omen, maybe, that told her Anthony wouldn't be safe unless she was around to protect him?

She combed her fingers through the tangled strands of her hair. As much as she would like to wake Jeremy, to ask him to hold her until the scary thoughts subsided, until her heart stopped racing and her breathing slowed back to normal, she couldn't bring herself to do it.

Not without dragging him into all the Courtney drama. Families like the Fortunes didn't have things like that to deal with.

So she carefully slid out from under the covers, trying not to jostle the mattress and wake Jeremy. Then she climbed from bed and walked softly to the dressing area, where she'd spotted two white bathrobes earlier. Choosing one, she slipped it on, then went into the living room and took a seat on the sofa.

She wasn't sure how long she sat there, twenty minutes or so, when she heard the bedding rustle and the mattress squeak.

Jeremy was stirring.

"Kirsten?" he called out.

"I'm in here."

He got out of bed, crossed the room and joined her in the living area. The sun was just starting to rise, and as it peered through the window, she could make out her lover's naked form.

His hair was tousled, his brow furrowed.

"Are you okay?" he asked.

"I'm fine," she lied.

Something sparked in his eyes, an emotion too difficult for her to read—compassion? Worry?

"Are you having second thoughts about what we did?" he asked.

"No, it's not that."

He took a seat beside her. "Are you worried because we didn't use a condom that first time?"

She placed her hand on his knee, felt his warmth, his strength. "It was careless of us. But no, I'm not stressed about it."

"Are you sure?"

The man had good instincts and had clearly picked up on whatever vibes she was giving out.

"A pregnancy wouldn't be very convenient," she admitted. "But I think we're safe. And if not, then I'll deal with it."

He placed his hand over hers, as it rested on his knee. "But you won't deal with it alone. We're in it together."

His words and their meaning soothed something deep inside her, easing the fear she'd felt earlier.

They were a team now, it seemed. And she relished

the possibility of having someone on her side, in her corner.

And not just anyone. Jeremy Fortune was a man to be admired. And she was lucky to have met him—and to have caught his interest.

"Thanks." She'd been on her own for so long that she'd forgotten how good it felt to have someone's support. "I appreciate that."

"Is there something I can do to help?" he asked.

He clearly knew she was upset about something, and while she didn't want to tell him exactly what it was, she supposed she had to say something.

But what? She wasn't even sure what was really bothering her.

Finally she said, "Do you believe in premonitions?"

He was quiet for a moment. "I don't know. I never have in the past. But a while back, I had a dream that seemed incredibly real. And it…well, it might have been a premonition of some kind. A good one, though. Why?"

"What did you dream about?" she asked. "Do you mind telling me about it?"

He didn't respond right away, and she wondered why. Was he afraid to share it with her? Even after the intimacy they'd shared last night?

Was he holding back to protect himself, just as she was?

"Let's just say it had something to do with the future," he said. "I'm not sure what it meant, if anything, but it seems to be coming true."

Her tummy knotted, and she felt the bile rise

to her throat. So he *did* have reason to believe in premonitions.

"Did you have a dream, too?" he asked.

She nodded. "But it wasn't a good one. I'm worried about Anthony."

"Are you afraid Max won't take care of him?"

"No, it's not that. Max is really good with him."

He stroked the top of her hand. "Then what are you worried about?"

"I don't know. It's just a vibe, I guess. A bad one. And I can't explain it." She turned to him, hopeful, willing to let him convince her that everything would be okay.

Jeremy didn't like seeing Kirsten so upset. And since she'd obviously had a nightmare of some kind, he was sorry that he'd even mentioned his own dream to her, the one about the woman on the porch holding a baby.

The woman who looked a lot like Kirsten.

To be honest, he wasn't even sure if she actually resembled the dream woman or not. Maybe he'd just wanted her to. Maybe it was a matter of attraction at first sight combined with a little self-fulfilling prophecy.

Who knew for sure? But he had to admit that he'd begun to feel something for her, something he imagined love might feel like.

Either way, he wasn't quite sure what it was or what to do about it. All he knew was that he hated to see her upset, and that he would do whatever he could to make her feel better.

"I really don't believe in premonitions," he said, which

was the truth, no matter how much stock he wanted to take in the dream he'd had about her. "I'm sure you just had a run-of-the-mill nightmare. There's nothing to worry about."

She didn't respond, yet she kept her hand on his knee, clinging to him, it seemed. And he was glad he could be there for her, but he wanted her to come back to bed, where he could kiss away the goblins and bogeymen.

"Are you sure you don't want to talk about it?" he asked.

"No. I'd rather not. It's just that...well, that poor little baby is so vulnerable right now. And he doesn't have anyone but me." She combed her fingers through her hair, then realized that wasn't exactly true. "Okay. So he's got Max, too."

"It sounds to me as if you're bonding with him," Jeremy said.

She glanced up and released a wistful grin. "Yes, I guess I am. Maybe it's just some weird maternal instinct I hadn't realized I had."

If things developed between them, if they decided to have kids of their own someday, he liked knowing that she had those instincts, that she'd be a good mother.

She blew out a sigh. "I hate feeling like this. No one told me how stressful parenthood could be."

He smiled and slipped an arm around her, drawing her against him, holding her close. Then he placed a kiss on the side of her head. "I'm sure you're right. My mom used to make it look like a breeze, but raising five kids had to be tough. I know my brothers and I didn't make it easy on her."

She continued to rest against him, making him feel like some kind of a hero when he really hadn't done anything.

"There were five kids in your family?" she asked.

"Yep. All boys."

He could feel the tension ease in her shoulders, which must be proof that he was doing something right. And that was a relief. He'd been in uncharted emotional waters ever since he'd met her.

"I wish I could have been part of a large family," she said. "It was always just me, my brother and our mom."

"A big family is nice if you're willing to take the good with the bad."

"What do you mean?"

"My brothers and I didn't always get along, and we had our share of bloody noses, black eyes and broken bones. But we were—and still are—very close. I wouldn't trade them or my childhood for anything."

They sat like that for a while, caught up in their thoughts, in their memories. In the emotion their love-making had stirred within them.

Then, as the sun began to rise higher in the sky, lighting the room, he realized that they wouldn't be going back to bed anytime soon.

"How about some coffee?" he asked. "I can call room service and ask them to bring up a carafe."

"Actually, that sounds good." She sat up straight,

which allowed him to reach for the telephone on the lamp table.

He ordered the continental breakfast: coffee, orange juice, fresh fruit and an assortment of toast and muffins.

When the line disconnected, he said, "Why don't you take the first shower. It might make you feel better."

"Actually, *you* made me feel better." She tossed him a smile that didn't quite light her eyes. "But I think I'll take you up on that."

Then she stood and walked to the bathroom.

He had a feeling that the nightmare was still eating at her, but he wasn't sure what else to do about it—other than suggest that they face the day head-on. So, while she was in the shower, he opened the blinds and took the time to watch dawn stretch over San Antonio.

A few minutes later, a knock sounded at the door. After slipping on the remaining robe, Jeremy answered.

"Where should I put this?" the bellman asked.

Jeremy nodded toward the coffee table in the living area. "Right over there."

While their meal was set up, Jeremy reached into his wallet and pulled out a couple bills to give the man, even though the gratuity had already been added into the tab.

"Can I get you anything else?" the man asked.

"No, thank you. This will be fine." After Jeremy signed the slip, the man left.

Rather than wait for Kirsten to come out of the shower, he poured a cup of coffee for himself.

Moments later, the bathroom door opened and she stepped out. Even with her wet hair wrapped in a towel turban, she looked like a million bucks.

*His* million bucks. He had a feeling he'd really struck pay dirt when he met her.

"Coffee?" he asked, as she joined him.

"Please." Kirsten took the cup Jeremy offered her, then added a splash of cream and sweetener before sitting next to him on the sofa.

The shower had done wonders.

And so had Jeremy.

Would another lover have been so thoughtful, so caring? So sweet?

She doubted it. So why was she apprehensive about sharing the uglier shades of her life with him?

There was no reason to feel that way. So she leveled with him and told him some of what Max had been going through with Courtney.

Jeremy didn't say anything right away. Finally, he set his cup on the table. "I find the whole story a little weird. Don't you?"

*Weird?*

Another sense of uneasiness washed over her, as she regretted airing her dirty laundry.

"What do you mean?" she asked.

"Your brother hadn't seen the woman in seven months, and she shows up at his door with a baby he didn't know he had. And according to you, he even questions whether he's the father."

Her tummy knotted. "I know he should have a

paternity test to answer that question, but I think it was admirable of him to take the baby."

"Yes, I can see why you might. But it's not clear if he has legal custody. What if there's a medical emergency?"

She supposed it was only natural that a physician would consider that. "I'm not sure what we'd do. I haven't thought that far yet. But little Anthony is a lot better off with Max than he is with Courtney."

"But he might not be Max's child."

She realized that. However, a parent didn't have to be related to a child by blood to offer it love and a happy home. "Maybe Max can become a foster parent or something." Anything that would allow him to keep the baby and not give him up to Courtney.

What kind of mother dropped off her child and never looked back?

"If Max is going to be working at the ranch during the day and going to school at nights, he's going to be hard-pressed to convince social services workers that he'd make a good foster parent."

The truth of Jeremy's statement stung. She wanted to tell him that she'd offer to be the foster parent, then. That she'd take the baby. But she bit back a response.

"And on top of that," Jeremy added, "she claimed that she doesn't have a birth certificate. Why is that?"

Kirsten didn't know why. Maybe she lost it. Or she moved before one could be mailed to her. Courtney had always been impulsive.

"It's anyone's guess," she said, although she couldn't

shake the feeling that her relationship with Jeremy had just turned south—or that it could easily go in that direction.

*I find that a little weird,* he'd said. *Don't you?*

*Whose* story was weird?

Courtney's? Or Kirsten's?

She reached for a muffin and carefully peeled back the paper, focusing on what was going into her mouth and not what was going on inside her heart.

In spite of what she'd thought, Jeremy wasn't a hundred percent supportive, when she'd really wanted him to be. When she'd really needed him to be.

And that put a damper on both the relationship and on the future.

Maybe she'd been wrong to think that she and Jeremy were having more than a brief affair. Instead he might only be looking for something temporary to fill his days before he headed back to California.

Besides, long-distance relationships didn't work very well, even if he was open to one. And if he asked her to relocate, she couldn't leave Anthony.

Not when she was the only one really looking out for him.

Jeremy spent the next night back at the Double Crown Ranch. His biggest reason for doing so was because he hated to leave Lily alone for a second day in a row. But he was also trying to decide how deep he wanted things to go with Kirsten, and he hoped that some time away from her might help him think.

So that was just what he'd done. But hell, she'd been on his mind constantly, and he was beginning to think that he was falling in love with her.

What else could it be?

As much as he'd told himself that he didn't believe in love at first sight, he would have to reconsider that belief because it sure seemed as if he'd started falling the moment he'd spotted her outside the clinic.

And after what they'd shared last night…

He ought to be concerned about the fact that she might have gotten pregnant, but for the life of him, it didn't seem like that big of a deal. Not if she wasn't worried about it.

They'd work through it, he supposed.

He had no idea what the future would bring. He was going to stay in Red Rock until he got word from—or *about*—his dad.

For the time being, he was settling in at the clinic and enjoying it a lot more than he thought he would. He'd even considered getting hospital privileges at the various medical centers in the area, although he hadn't done anything about it yet.

So much still hinged on his dad.

And on Kirsten, too—now that they'd struck up a relationship.

Ever since he'd checked them out of the hotel, he'd found himself wanting to be with her on a daily basis. And the drive back and forth from the Double Crown was a bit tiring.

Maybe he ought to get a place in town, just to be closer to her. But if he did, what about Lily?

Would she be okay without him to keep her company at night?

Dilemmas, he thought.

He glanced out the kitchen window, saw the morning sun peering over the eastern horizon. He was ready for a shot of caffeine to help him face the day, so he poured himself a cup of coffee.

While he pondered the situation with Kirsten and tried to connect all the dots, the housekeeper entered the kitchen.

"Excuse me, Dr. Fortune. But one of the ranch hands is at the front door. He'd like to talk to you."

"He wants to talk to *me?*" Had someone been injured? Jeremy tossed out the coffee in the sink. "Did he say what he wanted to see me about?"

"No, he didn't. But he did say that his name is Max. And that he's a friend of yours."

Uh-oh. What was wrong? Was the baby sick? Was something up with Kirsten?

Jeremy left his mug on the counter and headed for the back door, where he found Max waiting at the steps, holding his weathered hat in his hands.

His expression spelled trouble. "I'm sorry to bother you, but do you have a minute? I got here early, hoping I could talk to you before I have to check in with Ruben."

"Sure, I've got time to talk. Is something wrong?"

"Yeah. No." He lifted his battered Stetson, raked his

hair with his fingers, then returned the hat to his head. "Heck, I'm not sure. I've got a problem, and I didn't want to share it with Kirsten. We've been getting along a lot better lately, and I don't want her to get all weird on me."

"So you came to see me?"

"Yeah. I hope you don't mind."

"No problem." Actually, Jeremy thought it was a good sign that Max was seeking wise counsel—assuming that was what he'd come for.

"That's good, because I really need a man's perspective on this. Kirsten gets way too emotionally involved in this kind of stuff."

"Women tend to be that way," Jeremy said. "But I think it might make for a good balance."

"Maybe."

"Want to take a walk?"

Max nodded. "Yeah, that might help."

Jeremy closed the door, then followed Max down the steps and out into the yard.

"You know," Max said, "if my old man was still around, I'd talk to him. But he bailed out on me a long time ago."

"I'm glad you came to me, then. Sometimes it helps to talk it out."

Max didn't speak right away, but Jeremy kept quiet, biding his time until Max was ready to open up.

Finally, he said, "I'm not sure how much you know about all of this, but my old girlfriend Courtney showed up at the house, telling me that Anthony was mine."

"Kirsten mentioned it."

"She wanted me to take care of him because she couldn't."

"Does she want him back?" Jeremy asked.

"No, that's not the problem."

Jeremy wanted to press for more details, but continued to hold back, waiting for Max to explain in his own time.

"Even when Courtney brought Anthony to me," he finally said, "I had my doubts about whether I was his father or not. But how could I tell her I wouldn't take the poor little guy? I mean, he's just a baby. And I knew he'd be better off with me and Kirsten."

Jeremy assumed he was right about that.

"Courtney and I had a thing going for a while, but we split up for a good reason. She's a real flake."

Jeremy wasn't about to comment on that. Especially when he had no reason to doubt Max.

"I talked to her last night, after Kirsten went to bed. And it seems that I was right. I'm not Anthony's father."

So she was messing around on Max? And then she had the gall to dump her kid on him?

Flakey didn't seem to describe her as well as a few other choice adjectives might. But Jeremy kept that to himself as well, choosing to let Max continue.

"It seems that his father is some guy named Charlie," Max said. "And apparently, he's bad news. Somehow, he found out that Anthony is with me, although he has no idea where to find me."

Maybe not yet. But if he ever did locate Max, Kirsten would be in danger, which sent every one of Jeremy's instincts on high alert.

An almost overwhelming urge to drive into Red Rock and protect her slammed into him.

"What kind of 'bad news' is this guy?" Jeremy asked.

"She wouldn't tell me. She just begged me to keep Anthony safe. And she seemed to think that he would be, as long as we had him."

"We," of course, meant Kirsten and Max.

"Did you tell your sister any of this?"

"Not yet. I thought it would be best if I talked to you about it first. All I need is for Kirsten to come unglued. And she would. She's a real mother hen. And she's gotten pretty attached to Anthony."

Jeremy had noticed that, too. But he didn't want to see Kirsten in any trouble—or in danger—if that Charlie guy came looking for his son.

"So what should I do?" Max asked.

"I think it's time for you to go to the police. Now that you know you're not his father, you have no legal right to keep him. And you could actually end up in trouble for harboring a child who isn't yours."

"Dang." Max bit his lip. "I don't want any problems like that."

Jeremy glanced at his wristwatch. "What time do you need to start work?"

"I can't stick around here. I've got to tell Kirsten what's going on. And then I need to talk to the police."

Ruben would probably understand, but Jeremy thought it would be best if Max stayed on the job and put in an honest day's work, especially since Jeremy could handle the rest.

He could also make sure that Kirsten was safe.

"You stay here. I'll give Kirsten the news and let her know what you've decided."

"You don't mind?"

"Not a bit. Thanks for trusting me."

"How could I not do that? You've always been straight with me. And you've been looking out for my best interests, even though you don't know me all that well."

No, but Jeremy knew his sister. And that had been good enough for him.

He just hoped that Courtney hadn't involved Max and Kirsten in a dangerous situation.

## *Chapter Eleven*

Making love with Jeremy the night before last had been both unimaginable and spellbinding.

Yet Kirsten couldn't help thinking that he was pulling away from her. After all, he'd taken her home after they'd stayed in San Antonio, then had gone to the clinic to work. But instead of stopping by her house when he was done, he'd gone to the ranch.

He'd said that he needed to check on Lily, and that was probably true—and admirable, of course. Still, Kirsten couldn't help thinking that he might be having second thoughts.

So last night, when she'd pulled back the covers and slid into her bed alone, she'd closed her eyes and tried to imagine his smiling face, the way the sun picked up strands of gold in his hair.

The image she liked most, though, was the one of him stretched out on the bed beside her, his hand resting on her hip, his mouth trailing down her neck and pausing to kiss her breasts.

She'd wanted to sleep the night away just so she could remain in a dream world.

The phone rang at eight the next morning, finally jarring her back to reality.

She squinted as she reached for the receiver on the nightstand, then cleared her throat before answering. "Hello?"

"Kirsten Allen?" an unfamiliar voice asked.

"Yes."

"This is Stacy Grabowski, with the Fortune Foundation. We're looking for an accountant, and I was wondering if you'd like to come in for a job interview."

She'd never applied there, although she wouldn't mind working for the organization. Her first thought was that Jeremy must have had something to do with it. Yet instead of shooting a pleasant thrill through her, the idea left her uneasy.

Did that mean taking her to California was out of the question?

Sadly, it seemed to be the only logical explanation, yet she still felt compelled to ask. "How did you get my name?"

"Fred Nettles, who works in human resources for Alliance Plumbing, is one of our board members. He received the job application and résumé you sent to his company a few weeks back. They were in the process of hiring someone else, but he knew we were looking for someone, too. Since he was impressed with your qualifications, he suggested we interview you."

So her name coming up for that particular position had been a coincidence? Something that came about without Jeremy's recommendation?

Stacy went on to give Kirsten more details and provide a job description, all of which would utilize the skills she'd acquired. In fact, it was right up her alley.

To top it off, the benefits were in line with what she'd been hoping to get, and the starting salary was better yet. So it sounded as though the position would be perfect for her.

She wasn't sure how she'd juggle things, though. Max was going to need a lot of help with Anthony. But if they both had jobs, day care would be affordable.

Part of her insisted that she stay home with the baby until he was older, but how could she tell the Fortune Foundation no? She might never get another chance to work for them again.

There was, of course, the hope that her relationship with Jeremy would work out and become much more involved. But there were no guarantees there, either.

So why put her job search on hold indefinitely?

Besides, she might not even land the position.

And to make matters worse, she had to admit that some of the things Jeremy had said while they'd been at the hotel had been true. If Max wasn't Anthony's legal guardian, Courtney could show up at anytime, wanting him back. And unless Kirsten was prepared for a big legal battle, she'd have to give him up.

Again, she worried about letting him go, but even *that* was still up in the air. So she told Stacy, "Sure, I'd like to come in for an interview."

They'd no more than agreed to a date and a time when Anthony woke up—cranky and hungry, no doubt. So she hung up the phone and went to get the baby out of his Portacrib.

"I'm here, honey. Let me get your bottle." With Anthony resting in the crook of her arms, she padded into the kitchen to mix his powdered formula with water. Then she carried him into the living room, where she sat in the recliner and placed the nipple in his mouth.

As he ate, she watched him gulp and swallow. Every once in a while, he'd look at her, release his hold on the nipple and grin, which sent a dribble of milk down his chin. It was so sweet. And it let her know that he recognized her, that they were connected in some special way.

In just over a week, she'd really grown attached to the little guy. She'd love to keep him, to adopt him, to become a mother to him legally. Yet she also knew that she might have to give him up. But as long as she handed him over to parents who were kind and loving, she'd be okay with that.

She just couldn't stand the idea of letting Courtney take him back.

Kirstin had made a promise to herself—and to

the baby. She would do whatever she could to protect Anthony.

No matter what.

Thanks to another long-distance consultation with a colleague in his Sacramento medical group that tied him up for an hour, Jeremy wasn't able to get to Kirsten's house until just after eight. As concerned as he was for her safety, Max had convinced him that it wouldn't be easy for Charlie to find Anthony in Red Rock.

So he parked at the curb, then rang the bell.

When the door swung open, Kirsten was wearing a pale blue bathrobe and holding Anthony in her arms.

"I'm sorry to stop by so early," he said, "but I wanted to talk to you."

"I was just going to make some coffee," she said, stepping aside to let him into her cozy living room. "Can I get you a cup?"

"No, thanks. As much as I'd like to, I can't stay long. I need to get to the clinic, but I have to talk to you about something important."

She looked a little pale, a little uneasy. "What is it?"

"Max talked to me this morning."

Her brow furrowed. "He called *you?* Whatever for?"

"He didn't call. He showed up early at the ranch and asked for my advice about a problem he has."

"Is he feeling okay?" she asked.

He supposed it was only natural that she'd think his

reason to talk to a doctor would be a medical issue. "No, he isn't sick."

"Then what did he want to talk to you about?"

"About the latest call he got from Courtney." Jeremy filled her in on the details, adding, "According to her, she lied about Max being Anthony's father. Instead, it's a guy named Charlie."

"I don't understand," Kirsten said. "Why would she lie about that? And who is Charlie? Was she seeing him before she and my brother broke up?"

"I'm not sure. But from what Courtney told your brother, Charlie isn't a nice guy."

"Oh, God." Kirsten drew the baby closer to her chest, then slowly dropped into an overstuffed chair. "Are you sure about that?"

"No, that's just it. Courtney's stories aren't consistent. And she's repeatedly lied. So Max can't tell what's true and what's fabricated."

Kirsten looked down at the baby she held, the child who was totally dependent on her. It didn't take a mind reader to know what she was thinking. She was worried about little Anthony, and she had good reason to be. His mother was unstable, and his father was of questionable character.

As far as Jeremy was concerned, there was only one thing to do. They had to contact the police.

"According to Courtney," Jeremy added, "Charlie knows the baby is with Max. So it's just a matter of time before he finds him and Anthony."

*And* before he found Kirsten, too. Jeremy's chest

tightened at the thought that she might be in the thick of it all.

What if Charlie proved to be unpredictable? Courtney certainly was.

Kirsten furrowed her brow, apparently trying to sort through the news she'd been given, then looked up. "Maybe Max should stay out on the ranch for a while. Is that possible?"

"If Charlie comes around, he won't be looking for your brother. He'll be looking for his son."

"Then I'll keep Anthony under the radar," she said. "And if Charlie doesn't know to look for him here…"

"Be reasonable, Kirsten. If Charlie comes looking for Max and the baby here, you might not be safe." And for that reason, Jeremy had packed his clothes with the intention of staying with her until things could be sorted out, although he'd left them in the car.

"Then maybe I ought to leave for a while."

"And go where?" he said.

"I don't know. A hotel. Someplace."

Jeremy blew out a sigh. Why couldn't she wrap her mind around the situation?

"You *can't* keep Anthony," he explained. "He's not your baby, and you don't have any legal claim to him."

Her eyes flashed, challenging him. "I don't care about that. I won't give him up to someone who won't take care of him, someone who can't give him the love that he deserves."

"You might not have a choice," Jeremy countered. "Besides, you may not want to believe this, but there are a lot of kids in this world who aren't loved and taken care of. I see them all the time at the clinic with sad eyes, broken arms, bruises—"

"Stop! I'm aware of that. It sickens me to think about kids being neglected and abused. And you're right. I can't save them from the brutal reality they live with day to day. But I *can* protect Anthony. And I will. I'm not going to let anything happen to him. If that means hiding out with him and not telling anyone I've got him, then that's fine."

"You're being foolish, Kirsten. And you're also risking your own safety, not to mention the baby's."

"Not if no one knows where to find him."

"Oh, for Pete's sake. Courtney knows exactly where he is. And she can't be trusted."

The truth of Jeremy's statement slammed into Kirsten, backing her into a corner, it seemed. But what else could she do?

Her heart sank, but not just out of fear for herself. "If Charlie proves to be dangerous, and if you think that I'm not safe, then how can I let Anthony go with him?"

"You're right. That's why we need to go to the police and let them deal with it."

Kirsten cuddled the baby closer yet, unwilling to let law enforcement step in. Weren't they bound by law to hand Anthony over to his biological parents?

"What do you think your brother will have to say about this?" Jeremy asked.

"It really doesn't matter, does it? If Max isn't Anthony's father, then he can just stay out of it."

"But Max is already involved."

"How do you figure?"

"Come on. Open your eyes, Kirsten. Look beyond the child in your arms and face the larger picture. Max doesn't know any of the details surrounding that baby. What if Charlie *isn't* 'bad news'? What if, for some reason, he was granted legal custody, and Courtney took him away? After all, if she's as unstable as she seems to be, then who knows what's really going on?"

He was right, Kirsten realized. But she couldn't shake the feeling that Anthony wasn't safe unless he was with her. "I appreciate your concern, but I can't call the police. Not yet."

Jeremy chuffed, then muttered, "What a convoluted mess. I can't believe I'm even involved in this."

Kirsten had always been afraid that Jeremy would bail out if Max's drama ever got to be too much for him, so his comment crushed her. But how could she turn her back on the baby now?

Silence stretched between them. And as the minutes ticked by, she threw out the only argument she had left. "Apparently, you don't know what it means to love someone, Jeremy. To be committed to them."

His eye twitched, and his mouth tensed. She'd clearly angered him, and while she hated to think that her love for Anthony had driven them apart, she couldn't help it. He was a helpless little baby, for goodness' sake.

"You're wrong," Jeremy finally said. "I *do* know what

it means to love someone, to want them to be safe and happy. And it frustrates the hell out of me to see her refuse to see reason and to dig in her heels about the simplest thing."

Was he talking about his feelings for *her?*

She thought he might be, but she wasn't sure.

Taking a gamble, she said, "I love you, Jeremy. But you can't ask me to choose between my family and you."

He threw up his hands, clearly frustrated with her, with the situation, with the stalemate they'd reached.

"Maybe you'd better go," she said, wishing he'd have a change of heart, that he would soften with time. That he would be as supportive of her as he was when he found her awake and stewing over the nightmare she'd had—the nightmare about Anthony being in danger.

"Maybe I should." He turned and let himself out of the house.

She wanted to stop him, to try to explain. But what more was there to say?

As she stood at the living-room window and watched him climb into his car, she prayed that he was the one who would see reason. That he'd come back to her.

And that he wouldn't go to the authorities himself.

*Apparently, you don't know what it means to love someone.*

When Jeremy left Kirsten's house, the words she'd thrown at him stung something fierce.

The hell he didn't know what it meant to love someone.

He loved *her.* And the thought of something happening to *her* was making him crazy.

In fact, he was fit to be tied. How could she be so irrational about all of this?

If he had any sense at all, he'd go to the clinic to work, then head back to the Double Crown and call it a day, but he couldn't do that. He was too caught up in the situation.

But he wasn't too caught up to realize that there might be legal ramifications for what Kirsten planned to do. And he couldn't let her make a mistake like that.

So after calling the clinic and letting them know he would be coming in late, he drove to San Antonio, where Rafe Mendoza had opened his new law office.

Rafe wasn't just a friend. He was also family, related to Jeremy by marriage—his half-sister, Isabella, had married Jeremy's brother J.R. And if there was anyone Jeremy could trust to provide sound legal counsel, it was the attorney in San Antonio's newest law firm.

Hopefully, Rafe wouldn't be too busy to see him.

After leaving his car in the underground parking structure, Jeremy took the elevator to the lobby, where he talked to the security personnel, identified himself, then waited for permission to proceed to the elevator.

Rafe's office was located on the fifth floor and overlooked the River Walk. In fact, it wasn't too far from the hotel in which Jeremy and Kirsten had spent the night.

Just being in the area was a nice reminder of what they'd shared together, of what the future might hold if things worked out. And that was why it was important for him to make sure that Kirsten didn't get into any trouble.

When Jeremy finally entered the reception area of Rafe's office, he strode to the legal assistant's desk. "Hello, Vonda. Is Rafe available?"

"I believe so. Let me tell him you're here."

While she paged her boss, Jeremy shoved his hands in his pockets and scanned the spacious office, noting the expensive dark wood and the leather furnishings, as well as an expanse of windows that provided a nice view of the river.

At only twenty-nine years of age, Rafe was doing pretty well for himself these days. He already had a successful law practice in Ann Arbor. And he'd just recently returned to Texas to open a second office.

One of the many things Jeremy appreciated about Rafe was his air of confidence, which made him a good attorney.

Moments later, the handsome, dark-haired man entered the waiting area and reached out his hand to greet Jeremy. "It's good to see you. Did you come by to welcome me back to Texas?"

"Actually, I wanted to discuss a legal issue with you."

Rafe's mood grew serious. "Sure, come with me. Let's talk about it in private."

Once they'd each taken a seat, Jeremy couldn't help noting the glass case that held a variety of trophies and team photos from Rafe's years of playing baseball through high school and college.

"You've got a nice office," he told the well-built athlete who dressed in power suits these days.

"Thanks."

Minutes later, Jeremy had told Rafe about Kirsten, Max and Anthony.

"I'd like to help," Rafe said, "but I'm a corporate attorney and this really isn't my field. I can refer you to a specialist, though."

"I'm not ready to discuss this with anyone else. So even though you're not all that up on family law, you should have an opinion that would be helpful."

"I can do that," Rafe said. "But it seems to me that the first thing to do is to request the birth certificate."

"That's the problem. Courtney, the baby's mother, doesn't seem to have it. Or, if she does, she's not making it readily available. And God only knows who fathered Anthony. She first told Max that the baby was his. Now she's saying the father is someone named Charlie."

"It sounds like a real mess."

Jeremy nodded. "You've got that right. In Kirsten's defense, she only has the baby's best interests at heart. But I'm afraid she's setting herself up for trouble if she doesn't call the police and report the situation."

"I agree," Rafe said. "Who knows what the actual details are? It could even be a noncustodial kidnapping. Maybe Courtney considers Charlie 'bad news' because he's furious at her for leaving and wants his son back."

"That thought crossed my mind, too." And if that was the case, Charlie wouldn't pose a threat to anyone other than Courtney. Hoping for the best, yet not convinced,

Jeremy blew out a sigh. "So you would advise her to report it."

"Well, that's the correct legal move," Rafe said. "But you should probably keep in mind that Kirsten's emotions are involved. And under the circumstance, doing the 'right' thing could prove costly to *you*."

Jeremy suspected that Rafe meant he could win the battle and lose the girl, which would hurt. But he couldn't stand by and watch Kirsten make a mistake that would cost them both a whole lot more.

Rafe added, "It sounds to me as though Kirsten is the type who would sacrifice her own comfort—maybe even her freedom—to keep her family safe."

For a moment, Jeremy wondered if Rafe was speaking from experience, although he was probably reading too much into his tone, into his words. Either way, he didn't question him.

"I guess I'll have to really give it some thought," he said instead.

"I would." Rafe sat back in the desk chair. "Just how important is this woman to you?"

Jeremy hated to admit it, but he leveled with his friend. "Kirsten's come to mean a great deal to me."

In fact, Kirsten was proving to be a real mama bear when she thought one of her cubs was in danger—just like Molly Fortune had been. And he had to give her credit for that.

It was, he supposed, the result of thinking with her heart instead of her head. And it reminded him of the words he'd had with Max just a few hours earlier.

When Max complained that Kirsten got way too emotionally involved in things, Jeremy had said getting emotionally involved was a trait many women had. And that it made for a "good balance" in a relationship.

He probably ought to keep that in mind.

After thanking Rafe for his time, he stood to leave. "Have Vonda send me a bill. I'm staying at the Double Crown."

"No," Rafe said. "I won't be charging you anything. This one's on me. Besides, this really isn't my specialty."

"I needed some sound advice, and you gave it to me. So thanks again. I owe you one."

As Jeremy headed for his car, he realized he would have to go along with Kirsten's wishes for now. But that didn't mean he wasn't worried.

Instead of heading to the clinic, he drove back to Kirsten's house, hoping to set things to rights.

But when he arrived, his heart dropped to the ground when he knocked and rang the bell, only to find her gone.

## Chapter Twelve

Jeremy tried to tell himself that Kirsten was probably at the grocery store or running errands, but that didn't quell his worry.

After ringing the bell and knocking on the front door numerous times, he peered through the small window into the garage, only to see that her car was gone. At least, she wasn't sitting inside, refusing to see him.

So now what?

He'd be damned if he'd just head to the clinic, go to work and pretend as if nothing was wrong. Maybe he ought to hang out here for a while and wait to see if she came home.

Or better yet, he should try her on her cell. But before he could dial out, a call came in.

He answered without checking the display. "Hello?"

"Jeremy? It's Ruben. Your buddy Max didn't show up this morning. Do you have any idea why?"

He didn't show up? "What do you mean? He was at the ranch early this morning. I talked to him."

"Then he must have left before I started lining up the hands for the day."

Damn. This whole thing was blowing up in Jeremy's face.

"Listen, Ruben. I don't know what's going on, but I'll get to the bottom of it. And as soon as I do, I'll give you a call."

When the line disconnected, Jeremy swore under his breath. Then he dialed Kirsten's number. He let out another curse when he reached her voice mail, but went ahead and left a message, asking her to call as soon as she got it.

But where the hell was she? And why did Max take off this morning after Jeremy told him to go to work?

He glanced at his wristwatch. It was Anthony's nap time. So why wasn't Kirsten home? And why wasn't she picking up the damn phone?

His first thought was to do what he'd wanted to do originally, and that was to call the police. But out of respect and courtesy to Kirsten, he held back—at least momentarily. However, if she was in trouble, if Charlie had come around, if…

Jeremy raked his hand through his hair, then tried her number again. Finally, when he was about to disconnect, she picked up, her voice distraught.

"Jeremy?" she asked.

"Yes, it's me. Where are you?"

"I'm driving around town, looking for Max. He came home right after you left my house. He told me that he didn't have to work today after all. So I asked him to watch Anthony while I ran to the market. He agreed, but when I got back, he and the baby were gone. He also took the diaper bag, the supply of bottles and formula and the Portacrib. I have no idea where he went or what he plans to do."

"Have you called him?"

"Several times, but his phone must be shut off. Either that or the battery is dead. I'm really getting worried."

"Where are you now?" Jeremy asked.

"I'm sitting in my car. I pulled over by that new burger place when you called."

"Then come home. I'll be waiting for you. And we'll figure this out together."

Ten minutes later, Kirsten arrived at the house. Her eyes were red-rimmed, her cheeks tearstained.

"You were right all along," she said. "We should have gone to the police. But oh, no, I wouldn't listen. And now Max and the baby are gone."

"Did he say anything to you earlier about where he might go and why? Maybe he was afraid that Charlie found out where you lived. Maybe he's trying to protect you and the baby."

"Oh, my God. Do you think that's what happened?"

"I have no idea. Right now, I'm just grabbing at straws. But it doesn't matter. We'll find them, honey. I promise we will. And we don't have to alert the authorities unless you want to."

Kirsten looked at him, confusion etched across her face. "I don't understand. You were gung ho to call them earlier. Why the change of heart?"

He slipped his arms around her. "I haven't changed my mind. I still think we would be better off going the legal route. But I love you enough to trust that you'll do the right thing when you're ready."

"You *love* me?" She seemed awed, touched. Surprised.

"Yes, I do." He kissed her, his lips lingering over hers for the longest time, his heart fully engaged.

Just as they drew apart, Kirsten's cell phone rang.

"It could be Max," she said, flipping open the lid. "I need to take it."

"Kirsten?" Max said.

When Kirsten heard her brother's voice over the line, her breath caught.

"Where are you?" she asked. "And where is the baby?"

"Anthony's with me. And we're both safe."

Relief flooded through her. "Tell me where you are. If you don't want to come home, at least let me keep the baby for you."

"Can I talk to Jeremy first?"

Before answering her question? Before telling her where he was? She wanted to throttle him, but she handed over the cell to Jeremy anyway.

She supposed she ought to be glad that Max respected the man enough to go to him for sage advice, something that had been sorely lacking in his life since their father left. So she swallowed back her hurt feelings and homed in on the one side of the conversation she could hear.

"What's going on?" Jeremy asked, listening intently. Then he said, "You've got to be kidding me."

What? Kirsten wanted to ask, moving closer, hoping to catch a word or a phrase of whatever explanation Max was giving him.

"You're going to have to stop calling her a flake," Jeremy said. "That doesn't even begin to describe her or her character."

The conversation continued, but Jeremy only uttered a grunt now and then. And by the time he ended the call, Kirsten was beside herself.

"What's that crazy woman done now?" she asked.

"You aren't going to believe this. She just told Max that she's not the baby's mother."

Kirsten was stunned. "Then who's his mom?" she asked. "And where did Courtney get him?"

"She insists that she didn't kidnap him. And she still claims that Charlie is the father, that he left him with her."

Kirsten's head was spinning, and her heart was breaking. That precious little child didn't deserve any of this. God only knew who his real parents were.

"Where are Max and Anthony now?" she finally asked.

"Max is taking the baby to the police department. He said the baby was entrusted to him, and that it's his responsibility to do the right thing."

"What does that mean?"

"He's decided to take the advice I gave him earlier and is going to report this to the police."

"Then we need to meet him there." For a moment, Kirsten feared that Jeremy would remind her that he had to go to the clinic this morning, that he was too busy to get involved, especially in this kind of mess.

But he did just as she'd hoped he would. He slipped an arm around her shoulders and said, "Yes, we do. Get Anthony's car seat, and we'll put it in my vehicle. When I told you we were in this together, I meant it."

Kirsten didn't think she could love the man any more than she did right now.

Ten minutes later, Jeremy drove Kirsten and Max to the police precinct.

"What if they take him away from us?" she asked. "I hate the idea of Anthony going with strangers."

It was better than having the mysterious Charlie find him, Jeremy thought. Besides, Anthony was young enough that he'd probably be okay with anyone who kept him warm and fed, anyone who was loving and kind. But he didn't share that thought with Kirsten.

As far as she was concerned, no one could take care of Anthony as well as she could. And Jeremy had to agree with that.

"Don't worry. I'll do whatever it takes to convince the authorities to let us keep him until things get sorted out."

*"Us?"* she asked, her eyes hopeful and bright.

"Yes, *us*. We're in this together, honey. And I plan to call in some favors. The Fortunes and the Mendozas are highly thought of in these parts. So I don't think you have anything to worry about."

At least, not yet.

Once at police headquarters, Max told the officer in charge why they were there. Then they were taken to a small conference room, where Max reported all that he knew about Charlie and Courtney.

The officer in charge leaned back in his chair. "We'll place the baby in protective custody while we track down the parents."

"We'd like to keep him with us," Jeremy said. "We've got a bedroom for him. And we've been taking care of him for weeks."

"I don't mind placing the child with family," the officer said, "but under the circumstances…"

"I'm a physician," Jeremy said, giving Max a look and a silent message to encourage him to follow his lead. "And this is my fiancée and her brother."

Kirsten didn't say a word, although she tensed a bit at his response. So he took her hand in his and gave it a warm, trust-me-honey squeeze.

"The baby will be much better off with us," he added. "We've also got a list of references, beginning with J. R. Fortune and Jose Mendoza. You won't be sorry."

Jeremy watched as Max began to nod in agreement and as a grin spread over his face. It was clear that he understood what Jeremy was trying to make happen.

Getting the authorities to award temporary custody to Max might have been a stretch, but a solid and dependable couple stood a lot better chance.

The officer thought about it a moment, then said, "I'll have to run it by a judge so that we can get a temporary custody order. Hold on while I see if I can find one who's nearby and available."

When the man stepped out of the room, Max said, "Anthony needs a diaper change. And there's one of those family restrooms just down the hall. I'll be right back."

When they were alone, Kirsten nudged Jeremy's arm. "Your *fiancée?*"

"I thought it might help sway the judge to grant you custody."

Kirsten's brow furrowed, and her expression grew serious. "You're probably right, but I…"

He wasn't sure what was bothering her, the fact that he'd stretched the truth about an engagement, he supposed. But this wasn't a discussion he wanted to have at the courthouse. "We can talk more about it later."

She nodded, yet her apprehension remained.

Twenty minutes later, it was official. Kirsten Allen and Dr. Jeremy Fortune had temporary legal custody of Baby Anthony Doe.

With everything in order, they headed for the car to make the short drive back to Kirsten's house.

"Thanks so much for all you've done for me and my

sister," Max said. "This situation has been pretty tough on us, but having you in our corner sure helped."

"I'm glad everything worked out."

"I'd better give Ruben a call," Max added. "I need to apologize for taking off like I did, but when Courtney said she was leaving the area and that she wanted to meet with me before she went, I didn't know what else to do."

"Hopefully Ruben will cut you some slack," Jeremy said. "But next time something like that happens, you're going to have to level with him—or with whoever your supervisor happens to be. You can't just walk off a job site without an explanation."

"I'll remember that."

"So where did Courtney go?" Kirsten asked.

"She wouldn't tell me. But she did give me this." Max reached into his pocket, pulled out a small gold medallion and dropped it in his sister's hand.

"What is it?" Kirsten asked, as she studied the golden coin in her palm.

"Courtney said that Anthony was wearing it when Charlie gave him to her."

Jeremy studied the medallion. "It doesn't look all that expensive. But maybe it holds a clue as to who he is and where he belongs."

He sure hoped so. They could all stand a few answers right now.

* * *

Meanwhile, miles away in a small Texas town, a teen-ager hanging out at a bus stop spotted an old homeless guy wandering the streets. At least, he looked homeless. He also appeared to be disoriented, maybe strung out on something.

When he approached the bench, where the kid sat, he furrowed his silver brow—confused, it seemed.

He had to be in his late sixties or early seventies. Heck, maybe even older.

As he scanned the immediate area, the bench, the grass, the sidewalk—even the sky—it was pretty obvious that he didn't have any idea where he was.

"You okay?" the kid asked him.

"I'm not sure."

"What's your name?" the boy asked.

Confusion washed over his bearded face. "I…I don't know."

The teen wondered if he ought to report the old guy, although he seemed harmless. Just a little messed up, which was really sad for a guy his age. He ought to be sitting in a rocking chair on a porch somewhere, not wandering around and scrounging for a meal.

Feeling especially sympathetic, the kid reached into his pocket and retrieved a granola bar he'd grabbed from the kitchen pantry on his way out of the house today. "You want this?"

The old guy took it, rolled it over. Then he looked up and smiled wistfully. "Thanks."

"You're welcome."

The kid didn't smell stale booze or smoke on him, but who knew for sure. So he asked, "You a wino? Or maybe a druggie?"

The man slowly shook his head. "No, but to tell you the truth, I feel kind of hungover. Maybe I was at a frat party."

At *his* age? And in *his* condition? No way.

The guy was clearly whacked-out. Maybe he was one of those Alzheimer's patients who wandered away from the nursing home every now and then.

"How old are you?" the kid asked.

"Twenty-five," he said. "Or maybe twenty-six. I forget."

Oh, yeah? Then he must have forgotten about fifty whole years of his life.

"Why don't you sit down on that bench," the kid said. "I'll see if I can get you some aspirin or something for your hangover. Or better yet, I'll call someone to come get you and take you to a clinic."

"No," the old man said. "I'll be fine. It's just that I have something to do. Something very important."

"What's that?" the kid asked.

"I… I'm not sure."

The kid looked up and down the street. Where were the cops when you really needed one?

He was just about to call 911, when his cell phone chimed. His buddy D.J. was texting him, so he flipped to the screen to read the message.

A couple of their friends were going to a movie and D.J. asked if he wanted to join them.

He glanced at the old man. Why did he think it was his job to help? There were a lot of other people around—adults who were better able to deal with the poor guy's issues than he was. So he decided to take off and find his friends.

"You take care," he said. "Okay, dude?"

The old man looked up, just as confused as ever.

Back at the Double Crown Ranch, Lily put on a kettle of water to boil. Then she removed a china cup from the cupboard and took a box of chamomile tea from the pantry.

The phone rang, and she answered.

"Lily," Jeremy said. "If all goes according to plan, I'll be staying at Kirsten's tonight, so I won't be coming home. Are you going to be okay?"

"I'm fine," she said.

Jeremy had always been a sweet boy, and she knew that he'd been staying with her to keep her company until William returned. "Thanks for letting me know."

Silence stretched across the line until Jeremy said, "I worry about you when I'm not there. I have a feeling you're just waiting for the telephone to ring with news of my dad."

"The waiting isn't in vain."

Jeremy didn't respond right away. Then he asked, "Have you heard from the police lately? Have they uncovered anything else?"

Not anything of substance. "No, but I'm sure it's just a matter of time. We'll hear something soon."

As the kettle went off, she turned down the fire. "Why don't you bring Kirsten out here for dinner tomorrow night?"

"I'd like that, Lily."

"Good. Dinner will be ready at six, but you can come whenever you like."

"Thanks." He paused again, then added, "Are you sure you'll be okay without me home tonight?"

"Absolutely. I'm not alone." He probably thought that she meant her household staff and the ranch hands were nearby, but she couldn't help thinking that it was more than that.

"Take care," he said. "And sleep tight."

"I will. Kiss Kirsten and that baby for me. I'll see you tomorrow."

When the call ended, she filled her cup with hot water, then dropped a chamomile tea bag into it.

As she waited for it to steep, she sensed a presence—just like she had several times before.

She couldn't explain it—that warm, inner peace. The sense of calm, of love.

Nor could she shake the words that seemed to speak to her mind.

"Don't give up hope," they whispered. "He'll come home to you."

She nodded, as if she could somehow communicate right back.

*I won't give up. I'll wait for him until the day I die.*

* * *

When Jeremy had called Kirsten his fiancée at the courthouse, her heart had sung with hope.

But when she quizzed him about his comment, he'd said, "I thought it might help sway the judge to grant you custody."

At that point, her song had hit a flat note.

Not that she didn't appreciate what Jeremy had done to ensure that she would get custody of Anthony. But his lie had only opened a new can of worms, and she couldn't help worrying that there might be some legal ramifications if the court ever learned that they weren't really engaged.

He'd told her that he loved her, of course. But he'd never mentioned anything about a commitment.

"We can talk more about it later," he'd said.

But as luck would have it, Anthony had been fussy on the short ride back to her house, and Jeremy had been tightlipped.

Then he'd disappeared for a while, saying he was going to pick up groceries so he could fix dinner for her this evening.

Maybe they would finally have a chance to talk about the future while they ate. She sure hoped so. Not knowing what he was thinking or feeling made her more than a little uneasy.

And to top it off, Jeremy had gone into the kitchen more than an hour ago and had refused to let her in while he cooked.

"It's a surprise," he'd said, each time she'd knocked at the door.

She wasn't sure what he was making, but it certainly smelled delicious.

So, after bathing Anthony and putting on his onesie, Kirsten gave him a bottle and put him to bed. Then she waited on the sofa for Jeremy to announce that everything was ready.

Max, who'd taken a shower and splashed on a bit of his favorite aftershave, entered the living room, dressed to the hilt in a new pair of jeans and a plaid flannel shirt.

He'd been invited to Kelly's house again, which meant Jeremy and Kirsten would have a quiet night alone.

"Don't wait up for me," Max said. "And go ahead and lock the door whenever you decide to turn in. I have a key, but I have a feeling I'll be invited to stay over for breakfast, too."

He was grinning from ear to ear, and Kirsten couldn't help being happy for him.

"Drive carefully," she said.

"I always do."

After Max left, she reached for the novel she'd left on the lamp table and opened to the bookmarked page. But she didn't read more than a paragraph before Jeremy stepped through the doorway, his eyes lit up like a child's at Christmas.

"Dinner's ready," he said.

"Good." She returned the book to the table, then got to her feet.

"Before we eat," he said, "I have something I want to ask you."

"What's that?"

He crossed the room and took her by the hand. Then he dropped to one knee.

Her imagination, as well as her heart, began to race, but she feared that she might be jumping to the wrong conclusion.

"What are you doing?"

He reached into his pocket, pulled out a small, Tiffany-blue-colored box and popped open the lid, revealing the biggest, shiniest diamond she'd ever seen.

"Will you marry me, Kirsten?"

Her heart dropped to the pit of her stomach, then began to rumble back into her chest. She opened her mouth to speak, but the words wouldn't form.

"Is this for real?" she finally asked.

He cocked his head slightly to the side, and his smile faded. "What do you mean?"

"An engagement," she said. "Is it real? Or is it just a part of your plan to sway the judge?"

A grin tugged at his lips. "If you say no, then I'll claim it was only part of that particular plan. But the truth is, I love you, Kirsten. And I want to marry you—judge or no judge."

Tears welled in her eyes. She tried to blink them back, but wasn't having any luck. She knew she should respond to his proposal, but the emotion, the happiness, the dreams of a wonderful future all tumbled around in her throat.

"Aren't you going to say anything?" he asked.

"Yes!" she finally said through tears. "I'll marry you. And I'll follow you to California or Timbuktu. It doesn't matter to me, as long as we're together."

Then she pulled him to his feet, threw her arms around his neck and kissed him with all the love in her heart.

The future might be a little uncertain at the moment, Kirsten decided, but it had never looked brighter.

\* \* \* \* \*

# *A sneaky peek at next month...*

# *Cherish*™

**ROMANCE TO MELT THE HEART EVERY TIME**

## *My wish list for next month's titles...*

In stores from 20th April 2012:

❏ The Cop, the Puppy and Me – Cara Colter

❏ Courtney's Baby Plan – Allison Leigh

❏ Daddy on Her Doorstep – Lilian Darcy

❏ Courting His Favourite Nurse – Lynne Marshall

In stores from 4th May 2012:

❏ The Cattle King's Bride – Margaret Way

❏ The Last Real Cowboy – Donna Alward

❏ Taming the Lost Prince – Raye Morgan

❏ Inherited: Expectant Cinderella – Myrna Mackenzie

**Available at WHSmith, Tesco, Asda, Eason, Amazon and Apple**

## *Just can't wait?*

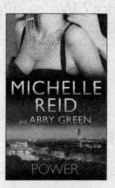

## The World of Mills & Boon®

There's a Mills & Boon® series that's perfect for you. We publish ten series and with new titles every month, you never have to wait long for your favourite to come along.

*Blaze*®
Scorching hot, sexy reads

**By Request**
Relive the romance with the best of the best

*Cherish*™
Romance to melt the heart every time

*Desire*™
Passionate and dramatic love stories

# *Have Your Say*

*You've just finished your book.*
*So what did you think?*

We'd love to hear your thoughts on our
'Have your say' online panel
**www.millsandboon.co.uk/haveyoursay**

- Easy to use
- Short questionnaire
- Chance to win Mills & Boon® goodies